THE
LAUNDRYMAN'S
BOY

THE LAUNDRYMAN'S BOY

A NOVEL

EDWARD Y. C. LEE

HARPERAVENUE

The Laundryman's Boy
Copyright © 2024 by Edward Yee Cheung Lee.
All rights reserved.

Published by Harper Avenue, an imprint of HarperCollins Publishers Ltd

First edition

HarperCollins books may be purchased for educational, business or
sales promotional use through our Special Markets Department.

HarperCollins Publishers Ltd
Bay Adelaide Centre, East Tower
22 Adelaide Street West, 41st Floor
Toronto, Ontario, Canada
M5H 4E3

www.harpercollins.ca

Library and Archives Canada Cataloguing in Publication

Title: The laundryman's boy : a novel / Edward Y.C. Lee. Names: Lee, Edward Y. C., author.
Identifiers: Canadiana (print) 20230578403 | Canadiana (ebook) 20230578446 |
ISBN 9781443470568 (softcover) | ISBN 9781443470575 (ebook) Classification:
LCC PS8623.E43735 L38 2024 | DDC C813/.6—dc23

Printed and bound in the United States of America
24 25 26 27 28 LBC 5 4 3 2 1

For Jinah and Erica, and in memory of
Donald D. C. Lee and Lee Tang Yin

We know that when the Chinaman comes here . . . he is a stranger, a sojourner in a strange land . . . he has no common interest with us. . . . He has no British instincts or British feelings or aspirations. . . . It is not desired that they should come; that we should have a mongrel race . . .

—Sir John A. Macdonald, Prime Minister of Canada
May 4, 1885, Debates in the House of Commons

PROLOGUE

Drink the Waters Deeply Village,
Toisan County,
GuangDong Province,
Southern China.

November 21, 1913

To Hoi Wing, the son of my heart, if not my womb:

This fall, bandits struck at Fung-gong village and stole a woman (I do not know her name). Your third cousin, Jin-Jee, birthed a son with a split lip, but needless to say, I did not preside over that maternity.

The third harvest was poorer than the second, and the villagers of nearby Won-Goong-San are said to be peeling bark from trees. For weeks, we ate only salt-fish flakes on the blackened rice from the bottoms of our pots. Then your first blessed remittance arrived. Now we feast on tender spring chicken and succulent pigskin crackle. Your father paid some arrears on the lots he tills, and he even purchased a new stool so Little Mei-Mei can sit in school. Ten times lucky we are to be a Gold Mountain household!

How do you fare in the New World? Do the lofan ghosts measure seven feet with blood-red faces and hairy paws? Are the women all prostitutes? Wear my amulet! I purchased it from a mad soothsayer on the night of your birth when I succoured your mother through a twenty-two-hour labour. Be well-listening and well-learning with your new employers at the laundry. I know the work is hard and the hours long, but do not despair. Remember the fortune teller's prophecy!

The night watch is banging at my door. Outlaws have been roaming, and the oil in my lamp burns low. I will write again soon. Each night, Little Mei-Mei and I light candles for you and your beautiful mother. Ayah, may the Ancestors grant that this old woman lives to see your return!

Your loving Eldest Great Auntie

P.S. And please don't delay your next remittance. Perhaps you could post it before the new moon passes? The taste of pigskin crackle wets my mouth even now, and a single piece of Gold Mountain silver is worth twenty here. Might the amount you send be augmented?

PART ONE

1

"Chinky-Chinky Chinaman,
Wash my pants.
Put them in a boiler
And make them dance!

"Chinaman, Chinaman,
Belly full of cats.
Next time I catch you
I'll feed you to the rats!"

The first clod of grass and mud stung the back of Hoi Wing's neck. He fell to his knees, unbalanced by the laundry sacks hanging from the pole across his shoulders. Clutching his hat, he turned as another clump of sod exploded against his chest. A half-dozen street children leapt from the barrels outside St. Catharines' largest dry goods emporium ("candies, sundries, gasoline, oils, and more!"), and several more emerged from behind the carriages hitched at the wooden sidewalk. Whooping and whistling, the pack charged, hurling stones and rotting vegetables. Two brandished sticks as they continued their inane chanting. A little boy waved a flag. "Kill him! Kill the Chinky Chink!"

Hoi Wing cursed and tasted blood where a stone had cut his lip. Although there were seven or eight in the gang, none of his grubby assailants looked older than ten years of age, three years younger than he was.

The biggest boy, a bucktoothed hoodlum whose grimy kneecaps peeked out of his torn trousers, pulled his eyes into slits. "*Ching-ching-maka-hye-ying!*" he shouted.

Hoi Wing scanned the storefronts for escape. He would fight any two, three, or even four of the little rascals, but not burdened as he was. All morning, he had been collecting laundry from the uncles' wealthiest customers in town: those who lived in the palatial homes in the environs of Montebello Park, the neighbourhood the men of China called the Golden Li.

A soggy tomato splattered against one of Hoi Wing's sacks. Taunts rang in his ears as he fled past the saddlemaker's. A rock bounced off the small of his back, and a spray of pebbles grazed his cheek. He stumbled, but kept afoot as the laundry swung wildly on his pole.

Anger and humiliation burned in his chest, and the children chased him past a woman pushing a pram and a gentleman in a bowler hat and greatcoat. At a tannery, Hoi Wing paused before a heavy-set man who stepped out into the cloudy autumn afternoon. His apron was splattered, and his forearms were stained brown to the wrists. He had a long, drooping moustache that flicked in consternation as he recognized some of the neighbourhood's scamps running in the street.

"Stop! What are you ragamuffins up to?" The tanner held out his hand. Then he spotted Hoi Wing, and a knowing smirk came to his lips. He waved the little band through. "Get that Chinaman, boys!"

The pursuers leapt forward.

Hoi Wing ran.

Later that evening at the Sam Kee Luk Chinese Hand Laundry, Hoi Wing heaved an enormous sack of soiled clothes over his shoulder and staggered across the floor. He emptied the bag into a vat of boiled water and gripped a long-handled paddle. With both hands, he plunged the splintered blade into the wooden barrel, thrusting, twisting, and agitating the mass of grime-encrusted sheets and shirts.

As Hoi Wing churned the putrid mix, blood, vomit, and bits of fecal matter swirled at the surface. The pork fat he had rubbed on his hands had washed away, and the skin over his knuckles was cracking again. Cramps knotted his forearms, but he sank the paddle deeper into the scalding water. The stench rose, and the paddle slipped from his grip. His stomach roiled as he reached into the soup of excrement to retrieve it.

Gagging, Hoi Wing stumbled from the vat. At the laundry's big window, he breathed deeply, cleaning his hands on a rag and rubbing his bloodshot eyes on his sleeve. He fingered the bandage over his chin where he had been cut during his altercation with the ragamuffin gang earlier that afternoon.

Outside, darkness had fallen, and the gaslights on St. Paul Street spit and flared in a late autumn storm. The roads were slick, and a horse-drawn wagon delivering ice clip-clopped past, its driver huddled beneath an oilcloth cape. As the rain beat against the clapboard walls of the laundry, Hoi Wing wrapped himself in a woollen blanket, shivering despite the heat of the big copper boilers.

How cold it was in this foreign land! Hoi Wing stared out the window into the slanting rain. *Could it only be October?* A week had passed since he had arrived in the town of St. Catharines (called *Seng-cah-doun* by the men of China), and no matter how many garments he pulled over his body, he was never warm.

He remembered the day his father (whom the villagers derided as Ying the Scholar) had told him he would soon be leaving their home in southern China to sojourn in the Gold Mountain.

"I am sending you overseas to work in a washing establishment." Ying the Scholar's eyes had been solemn behind their thick glasses. "Your employers will be two countrymen of ours. The men are brothers. I have not met them, but we have exchanged letters, and they are known to be honest and hard-working. When you arrive, you will address them respectfully as you would any stranger in the village square. You will call them Elder Uncle and Second Uncle."

Hoi Wing's stomach twisted with apprehension. "But I won't know anyone there!"

"You must work and send money from the West. Our second harvest was poor, and the drought continues. Bandits ravage the countryside. War looms on the horizon. Your little sister Mei-Mei and Eldest Great Auntie will be counting the days to the remittance you send each month."

"Will I go to school there?"

His father glanced away. "The work will be hard and the hours long. Your new employers will demand much of you. Education will have to wait."

"But for how long?" Hoi Wing asked, but as was often the case, Ying the Scholar only shrugged his shoulders.

Despite his misgivings, Hoi Wing felt a small spark of excitement at the idea of journeying to the New World. In his home village of Drink the Waters Deeply—nestled in the rolling hillsides of Toisan County in GuangDong Province—Hoi Wing had liked nothing better than to eavesdrop amongst the Gold Mountain veterans whenever they gathered around the town's famous fountain.

In the cool of late summer evenings, he would sit cross-legged on the ground as the men smoked and reminisced. Many of the older adventurers had passed long sojourns in the mysterious West, working to send remittances home each month, returning to the village every four or five years to father a son or daughter before departing after a single year of repose.

Studying their grizzled faces—some scarred, some battered, but all touched in some manner—Hoi Wing was mesmerized by their tales of the high mountain chasms they had scaled, buried to their chests in icy snow (*a frozen white rain, so cold it burned!*), often roped together in a quest for gold and adventure. Others boasted they had laid an iron road across an endless stretch of forest (*trees so tall, they scraped the sky!*), or bored tunnels so long they had not seen the sun for weeks (*I held the dynamite in my fingertips until the fuse was no more than a half inch long!*).

Some lowered their voices—and here Hoi Wing strained his ears—to narrate lascivious encounters on island paradises with foreign women, warm of heart and limb, and epic nights followed by golden dawns over azure seas.

Sometimes Hoi Wing scoffed at the dire tales of ferocious Gold Mountain winters. *Winds so cold as to steal one's fingertips? Frozen birds falling out of the sky?* He had been audacious enough to even sneer (to himself, of course, when no one was looking) at the accounts of Old Kwok, a man so tough, he was rumoured to have hammered railroad spikes with his fists and chiselled mountain tunnels with his teeth.

What was the truth about the foreign lands? Who could tell him? Certainly not his father, Ying the Scholar, who was so ridiculed in Drink the Waters Deeply that the story of how he had travelled as a swollen-headed young man to the provincial capital to write the Imperial Examinations—only to return ignominiously empty-handed—was a joke told so often, its punchline had become superfluous in the Four Counties.

Now, in the laundry, Hoi Wing's thoughts of home were interrupted by the rumbling of his stomach. It was already past six. *When would they be having dinner?* Whatever his father's faults, the man had been absolutely right about the challenges of a Gold Mountain Chinese hand laundry. The work duties consumed every waking minute of every day; the men barely took the time to eat.

On top of that, Hoi Wing had not yet found the courage to speak with Second Uncle about attending school or lessons. Nor had he even met the senior partner of the enterprise. That was Elder Uncle, the older brother, who was away in the big city of Toronto, meeting with other Chinese laundrymen and members of their clan association.

But how would Hoi Wing go to school without first learning the *lofan* tongue, which sounded to his ears like the barking of dogs or squealing of pigs? He knew nothing of the *lofan* people or their customs, and like most Gold Mountain sojourners, he would likely spend the next five years in back-breaking toil. By that time, his window of opportunity for education would have closed.

In Drink the Waters Deeply, the children had teased Hoi Wing mercilessly since his first lonely days in Teacher Lee's schoolroom, and despite everything Eldest Great Auntie had said—the elderly woman, who was also the county's pre-eminent midwife, believed he had been born under a lucky moon—he feared he would never escape the legacy of his father's great failure. Would it be his fate to grow up an illiterate and ignorant laundryman, with no more than a seventh grade education from his own country?

In bitterness, Hoi Wing remembered the *dead-naughty lofan* boys who had chased him through the streets that afternoon. Was this typical of the treatment he would receive here? Would he be fighting every day? He touched the bandage over his chin again. Second Uncle had applied the dressing—along with sticky orange tiger balm—upon his return from deliveries earlier that afternoon.

Hoi Wing's stomach rumbled once more. *When would it be the dinner hour?* He was famished now; he had saved a half-eaten apple in his pocket from his lunch. To help pass the tedium of his work, he had devised a new game: every time he added clean water to the big vats, he allowed himself a tiny bite of apple.

Chewing the fruit, Hoi Wing went to the sorting tables. From the heap of dirty clothes collected from the Golden Li, he plucked a stained ladies' undergarment, the colour of bone, laced and frilled. Holding it before the kerosene lamp, he rolled it in his fingers, luxuriating in its soft, velvety texture. He breathed the faint flowery scent clinging to the cotton. His thirteen-year-old imagination took flight. How was such a garment worn? He toyed with the tiny clasps, picturing the long-limbed *lofan* ladies he had seen on the sidewalks of town, their fair hair bouncing over their shoulders.

The laundry's doorbell jangled. Through the curtain into the reception area, he saw an elderly woman enter, accompanied by a young girl whose head just crested the top of the oaken counter. The woman wore a mushroom-brimmed hat and a gabardine raincoat. She snapped her umbrella open and shut, staining the wooden floor. For an instant, Hoi Wing thought she was Pinched-faced Lady, one of their regulars, but this woman was older, more gaunt, and her lips were withered beneath the rouge.

The two stood in reception, eyeing the packages of laundry crammed into the cubbyholes behind the counter. The woman fitted spectacles over her nose and studied the price list tacked to the wall beside a calendar depicting the recent excavations of the giant locks of the fourth Welland Canal.

On the counter were pads of laundry tickets, spools of thread, and packages of hand-washed clothes. The little girl climbed a stool and rested her forearms on the work surface. Removing her bonnet, she revealed hair the colour of millet. Her cheeks were flushed, and she flicked the beads of Elder Uncle's abacus *click-clackety-clack* up and down. Then she drew a cautious hand over one of the brown paper bundles.

"Oh Nana, it's warm!" she said, not noticing Hoi Wing, who studied her intently through the part in the curtain.

"Child." The woman perused the price list with displeasure. "Don't touch anything!"

Although Hoi Wing could not read the *lofan* words on the sign, the Sam Kee Luk Chinese Hand Laundry—"The best and most economical"—advertised collars for two cents, cuffs for four cents, and shirts for ten cents. It guaranteed "authentic Chinese hand washing without acids, lime, or any other caustic chemicals to destroy the clothes."

Emboldened by her grandmother's inattention, the child traced her fingertip over Second Uncle's smooth-flowing calligraphy painted on the paper-wrapped bundle. "Look! What's it say?"

The woman didn't turn. "Chicken scratch. They're just swiggles."

"But they're beautiful!"

"Nonsense! They're meaningless."

The little girl stretched her body across the counter and peered through the curtain. Her mouth fell open when she spied Hoi Wing at the tubs, clutching his splintered paddle. "Look, Nana, it's a boy!"

"My Lord! Come down from there."

"But who is he? Can he talk?"

"Never you mind." The woman wrestled the girl from the counter. "What are you thinking? Your father would be furious!"

Hoi Wing retreated behind the presser as the woman lifted a bag onto the counter.

"Charlie!" she cried out. "Is anyone home? I have *washee-washee*."

"Second Uncle!" Hoi Wing called to the back of the laundry. "We have customers."

Second Uncle emerged from the drying room, sweat glistening on his naked torso. His muscles were lean and his forearms like braided rope. The crown of his head was as smooth and lustrous as a pearl. A toothpick dangled at the corner of his mouth, and he was the only man Hoi Wing had ever seen who could smoke and clean his teeth at the same time. He towelled his face, pulled a smock over his body, then squeezed Hoi Wing's shoulder as he went to the counter.

"Charlie!" The woman shoved her sack forward as Second Uncle appeared through the curtain. "I need this done *quick-ee quick-ee*. Extra *starch-ee* on the collars."

Second Uncle spilled the bag onto the counter and rummaged through the clothes. "Hmm . . . ten shirt. One *doll-ah*."

"Tsk! One dollar? Come now, let's be reasonable. I can get shirts washed at Foo's Laundry for eight cents apiece. You don't want me to go all the way down to the Foreign Quarter, do you?"

"Mmm, *sol-ly*." Second Uncle shook his head. "Foo Laundry also charge ten cent for shirt. He no washing for eight cent."

The woman opened her purse. "Look, I've the money right here and I've come all this way in this horrid weather! Don't you want my business? I'll give you a deal—eight cents a shirt, and I'll become a regular."

Second Uncle pointed at the price list on the wall. "One shirt, ten cent. Ten shirt, one *doll-ah*."

"Can't we negotiate? You know what I'm *speak-ee*? I've got lots of friends who need a good Chinaman. I'll send them all. Nine cents? Just this once?"

"You send friend. We wash shirt. Ten cent."

"Charlie, you bargain like a damn gypsy! My last offer: ninety-five cents for these shirts. Today only."

"*Ayah!* No eight. No nine. Ten cent!"

The woman snapped her purse and bagged her wash. "Fine. If that's the way you want it. I'll not be *gypped* by a Chinaman!" She straightened her hat and brandished her umbrella like a sword. Pulling the girl away, she left the laundry, slamming the door behind them.

Hoi Wing peered through the curtain. What had the *demon lofan* complained of? He had understood none of the conversation, but her haughty displeasure had been obvious. Until now, most of the customers he had met (Tall-Man, Short-Man, Short-Man-with-Moustache) had been curt but businesslike, dropping off their laundry with few words and reclaiming it days later with even fewer.

A sudden wave of dislocation washed over Hoi Wing, and he gripped the vat for support. The dizziness was akin to the nausea he had experienced on the three-week ocean passage from China. How could he ever hope to understand this savage land? Everything about it—from the bitter rain to this horrid old lady—was alien and hostile!

Yet Hoi Wing found solace in the behaviour of the young *lofan* girl. *What a warm surprise!* Her eyes, gentle and wide, had reminded him so much of his sister's.

What was Little Mei-Mei doing back home right now? Might she be scaling the parapets of the *gong-lau*, the stone watchtowers that guarded the gates to the village? Or was she wading through the pond, netting tadpoles and collecting fireflies as he had taught her?

"Wait for me, Big Brother! Wait for me!" With chagrin, Hoi Wing remembered ducking from Little Mei-Mei in the foothills outside Drink the Waters Deeply. At this hour, she might even be helping Eldest Great Auntie rinse the rice or split snow peas for dinner. The aged midwife had taken to cooking and caring for them since the death of Hoi Wing's mother in childbirth five years before.

The nostalgia and memory of his honourable dead mother brought a sudden dampness to Hoi Wing's eyes, and he rubbed them fiercely with his smock as Second Uncle reappeared through the curtain, muttering and shaking his head.

"I guess you didn't understand any of that discussion I had with that old *demon-lofan* woman." Second Uncle grimaced. "That lady tried to convince me Grandfather Foo was charging only eight cents a shirt at his laundry in the Foreign Quarter. Our prices are low to compete with the *lofan* laundries here, but we Chinese must never undercut each other! Remember, these *lofan* will say anything to cheat us!"

Hoi Wing nodded, grateful for once that the air of the laundry was saturated with the acidic bite of lye and soaps. On the streets, he had seen delivery wagons and even motor trucks operated by the many *lofan* laundries in town. Although there were but two Chinese hand laundries in all of St. Catharines—theirs and the one run by Grandfather Foo, whom Hoi Wing had not yet met—a fierce competition had erupted between the long-standing *lofan* businesses and the Chinese interlopers. Price wars had ensued, and the Cascade Laundry, the largest and oldest of the *lofan* establishments, had recently taken to trumpeting the superiority of its service over that of the "dirty *Chin-ee wash-ee wash-ees*," pasting handbills and adverts on walls and fences about town.

Second Uncle examined the dressing he had applied to Hoi Wing's chin. "Don't worry, this little cut will heal without marring your handsome face. And I'll work on something to help you avoid those *deadnaughty lofan* brats."

"Is it always like this here?" Hoi Wing asked.

The toothpick at the corner of Second Uncle's mouth sagged. "I won't lie to you. This land has never welcomed us. We've had to scrap and fight for every crumb we've ever earned. My older brother will return from Toronto shortly. I'm sure he'll also have some advice on dealing with those little demons."

"I'm not afraid of them."

The man nodded solemnly. "I don't doubt your courage or the size of your heart, but I think your biceps might benefit from some exercise. Commencing tomorrow, I'll give you some instruction in *gung fu* to build your constitution and your *'chi*. My brother is a more skilled practitioner of the fighting arts, and he will train you as well. Remember, with you adding to our number, the odds are canting in our favour. Now we are four men of China in this town."

"What is Grandfather Foo like?"

A smile lit up Second Uncle's usually pensive face. "He is an older gentleman of great wisdom and scholarship, with more sojourns to this foreign land than even my older brother. We call him the Tiger-mouse."

"Tiger-mouse? Why?"

Second Uncle laughed as he returned to the drying room. "I'll let you ask him yourself. When you meet him."

Hoi Wing felt he could learn to like working with Second Uncle, although the man had the annoying habit of neglecting to complete the stories he started. Second Uncle had also failed to mention dinner. The boy's stomach rumbled once more. Would it be unforgivably rude to ask when they would be sitting down to supper?

Hoi Wing wrestled the tub to a cement trough and emptied the waste water down the copper drain. Now, only four baskets of soiled clothes remained, although the sacks were still piled high on the table. Outside, the rain drummed against the window, and lightning illuminated the livery stables across the street. Hoi Wing shivered and stretched the muscles at the base of his neck. Then he drew out his half-eaten apple, sliced it with his pocket knife, and took a bite.

2

In his dream, Hoi Wing tended his father's fields. Boulders heaved in the meandering furrows, and *bak-toy* lay wilted beneath the sun. He clutched a watering can filled with his own urine—but all the crops were burned and brown! The mocking voices of the villagers drifted over an arid wind: "Ying the Scholar, the only farmer who would sooner compose songs than compost sod!"

As Hoi Wing watered the withered *gai-lan*, beautiful Fourth Youngest Auntie appeared, calling him to lunch. She had steamed *haw-gow*, his favourite shrimp dumplings. She slid a porcelain plate before him and a pair of ivory chopsticks. On a side dish were sprigs of fresh coriander and red peppercorn sauce. As he lifted a steaming morsel to his mouth, Fourth Auntie moistened her lips. She released the gold pins from her braid. Then she shook her hair and unfastened the buttons of her blouse. "Fourth Auntie," he choked.

"Get out of bed, you *dead-lazy* worm!" A man shook Hoi Wing's shoulder and rolled him over his pillow. "Wake up! Morning's half-over.

I promised your father I would turn a little farm boy into a laundryman!"

Hoi Wing woke with a start, his dream dissipating like smoke. His bed was made of tongue-and-groove planking, balanced on four washtubs in the laundry's main room. Triple-folded towels composed his mattress. A man stood over him. He was half a head taller than Second Uncle, and his chest was as wide as a fully grown hog's.

"Elder Uncle, is that you?" Hoi Wing shaded his eyes with his hand, still caught in the netherworld between dream and reality.

"Boy, get out of bed!" Elder Uncle thrust the curtain from the window. "It's a new dawn! There are sheets to wash, shirts to starch! You think these damn *lofan* are going to wait for you?"

Outside, a rooster crowed, and golden light flooded the laundry, glinting over the wringers and copper boilers. Hoi Wing shivered, wanting to pull the blanket back over his head. Part of him wished to return to his dream—never had beautiful and vivacious Fourth Youngest Auntie appeared in such a manner—but another part of him was mortified by the images conjured from his subconscious.

How could he have dreamt of Fourth Auntie like that? She had tucked him into bed from his earliest days—although, since he had reached the age of thirteen, such images (even during his waking hours, he had to admit) had been insinuating themselves more and more into his consciousness.

"Boy!" Elder Uncle knelt before the pot-bellied stove. "You'd better be on your feet before I have this fire lit!"

The warning from the big man made Hoi Wing forget his dream. All thoughts of Fourth Youngest Auntie were banished as his bare feet touched the frozen floor. Performing a little dance against the cold, Hoi Wing searched beneath the bed. When his feet were safely ensconced in a pair of woollen socks, he studied the man crouching at the stove.

Elder Uncle's back was broad, and he was impressively muscled under a thin cotton shirt, seemingly impervious to the frigid temperature of the air. His hair was like the pelt of a wild animal, and the sinews of his forearm stood out in relief as he fed kindling to the tiny flame. All the stories of Gold Mountain adventurers came to Hoi Wing's mind: fearless, unflinching men who traversed icy crevasses, hundred-pound packs slung over their shoulders. Men who lit bonfires in the frozen wilderness with but a twig.

Hoi Wing peered closer. Despite the obvious physicality, there was an odd imbalance in the manner Elder Uncle crouched, unlike Second Uncle, who was slighter but more graceful in his movement. Still, the fraternal resemblance was obvious, although the placid features of the younger brother were warped with age and impatience on the face of the senior. Was the man always this ill-tempered, or had he just had a bad night? Hoi Wing hoped fervently this wasn't his everyday disposition.

"Elder Uncle, I'm very pleased to meet you." Hoi Wing gave a little bow, remembering his father's admonition to be respectful. And Elder Great Auntie had told him it was always important to make a good first impression. "I thought you wouldn't be returning from Toronto for another few days."

"Disappointed that the big boss is finally here?" The man's lip twisted unpleasantly, his attention still fixed on the flame in the stove box. "No more slacking off for you, Farmboy. Now that I'm here, you're going to learn what laundry work is all about!"

"I've been working hard," said Hoi Wing, taken aback by the accusation. "I'm no slacker."

Elder Uncle turned and rose to his full height. His eyes were fierce, and his brow was deeply furrowed. "Oh no? It's your job to light this stove and fill those boilers every morning. Did you forget, or are you just lazy? We're never going to best the Cascade and the other *lofan* laundries if you sleep the day away!"

Hoi Wing winced at the scorn in Elder Uncle's voice. "I was just about to get up."

"Farmboy, you were snoring like a babe! From now on, you'd better be working when I come down from that attic or you'll regret the day your father apprenticed you to me."

Hoi Wing felt a surge of hot blood. "I'm—!" He swallowed his retort mid-sentence. The man standing before him seemed as wide as the cement trough, but the left sleeve of his shirt hung limp and empty. It was then Hoi Wing realized he had been angling his body so his right side was always forward-facing. "Elder Uncle, you've got only one arm!"

The statement caught the older man off guard. His lips moved soundlessly, and his features, so stiff and chiselled, seemed suddenly young and vulnerable. For an instant, Hoi Wing saw how handsome he had once been.

"Elder Uncle, I apologize for my words." Hoi Wing lowered his gaze, knowing he had spoken like a child. Why had he blurted out the man's obvious disability? It had been rude and thoughtless.

Elder Uncle threw back his head and filled the laundry with booming laughter. "Go to the head of the class, Farmboy! *I am a one-armed man!* At least there's nothing wrong with your eyesight. Too bad I can't say the same for your work ethic."

"But I didn't mean any insult."

"Farmboy, I don't give two shits about your insults! And I can do more work with one good arm than you can with your entire body. Now stop your idiotic gawking and get those damn boilers lit."

"I wasn't gawking!" Hoi Wing shouted back. "And stop calling me Farm—"

"I'll call you whatever I want!" Elder Uncle shook his fist. "You'll do what I say."

"Ho! What's all this shouting about?" Second Uncle appeared at the top of the basement staircase. His face was raccooned with dust, and a bucket of coal hung from each hand. "You two are going to wake the neighbourhood."

"Second Uncle!" Hoi Wing leapt forward to take the pails from the man's hands. "Good morning!"

"Good morning, Young Man." Second Uncle grinned. "I see you've already met my big brother and our senior boss. Try not to be overly dismayed. The dragon's bite is only half as bad as its breath."

"He-aah!" Elder Uncle shook his head. "Why are you fetching coke from the basement? That's Hoi Wing's job. His father boasted that he worked the farm, but I think he sent us a lazy schoolboy with twigs for arms!"

"Take it easy on Hoi Wing, Big Brother." Second Uncle wiped the coal dust from his face. "He's been working hard while you've been in Toronto. I can attest he's not lazy. And if you keep yelling at him, you'll have to explain to his father why he went deaf after only two weeks in the Gold Mountain."

"He's a *dead-lazy* worm! He's been sleeping instead of lighting those boilers!"

Second Uncle yawned. "Hoi Wing and I worked extra hours yesterday evening. Then we had a late dinner and conversation. You weren't expected to arrive last night at all."

"But I'm up this morning before him," Elder Uncle growled. "He'd better shape up if he's going to make it as a laundryman. Keep coddling him, and the *lofan* will chew him up and spit him out into the street!"

"I'll make it just fine," Hoi Wing spoke out, not wanting to shelter behind Second Uncle's words.

Second Uncle ran his hand over the crown of his head. "Big Brother, you're starting to sound like an old woman again. Why don't you stop your nagging and go make some breakfast for us all? Our new apprentice and I will take care of the boilers."

The older man opened his mouth to speak but thought better of it. Still glaring at the other two, he disappeared into the little kitchen.

Hoi Wing let out his breath as he emptied the buckets of coal into a wooden crate. His hands were trembling, and his face was flushed. The air in the laundry seemed ten degrees hotter. "I'm sorry. I didn't mean to shout, but Elder Uncle was wrong. I've been working hard since I got here."

Second Uncle flicked his toothpick from one side of his mouth to the other. He leaned against the wall where packages of unclaimed laundry were crammed into shelves. Some of the abandoned garments had been held for their owners for years.

"Young Man, I don't blame you for shouting. Your father said you loved your studies, but I can tell you are more than a mere schoolboy. My big brother intimidates far bigger and older men than you. Every day here the *lofan* try to beat us down with their lies and insults and even their fists. They hate and curse us and do all they can to chase us back to our homeland. If you had been cowed by my brother's onslaught, or broken into tears, I would not have bet five cents on your survival in this hard land. But you stood up to him and spoke out for yourself. You have passed your first test."

Passed a test? Would every day be like this from now on? Hoi Wing breathed deeply, still feeling the tension in his neck and shoulders. He had always been hot-tempered. When he was a child, his honourable mother had chided him constantly, shaking her head whenever he returned from school with bruised knuckles and skinned knees. "The son of Ying the Scholar leads with his pen, not his fists!" she'd say, and she didn't care that he was fighting for her.

But Eldest Great Auntie could scarcely suppress a smile. She always hated how the villagers disdained her nephew, Ying, and she deemed it ten times unfair when schoolyard bullies meted out the same treatment to her grandnephew. "Don't ever forget"—she had shaken her arthritic finger—"Hoi Wing's fiery temperament is due to the intensity of his *yang* energy. After all, he was born in dragon mist, under the largest, reddest blood moon I have ever seen!"

In the laundry, Hoi Wing went to the hand pump and filled a pair of five-gallon buckets with water. Then he lifted the buckets and lurched past the tubs, clothes racks, wringers, and ironing boards. Back and forth he went, filling and emptying, filling and emptying, until the copper boilers were full to the brim.

Second Uncle watched from his seat at the dining table. "You have backbone. With the *gung fu* I'm going to teach you, you will grow stronger, but one has to be born with a spine. You'll find my older brother is the type of boss who blows off steam without meaning his threats."

Hoi Wing stared at the kitchen where Elder Uncle had gone. From within came a clash of pans and the sudden *swish-swish-swish* sharpening of a cleaver. In the aftermath of his outburst, Hoi Wing wondered again whether Ying the Scholar had committed yet another calamitous error by hiring him out to these two men.

"I was viewing our basement while fetching coal," Second Uncle continued. "It'll need some sweeping, but if you move the workbench aside, there'd be plenty of room for you to create your own quarters. It'd be far more comfortable than sleeping up here. You can set up a bed, desk, and chair. There's an old chest of drawers. We'll seal the door to the coal bin. There are even a few windows for fresh air."

"I would like that." Hoi Wing stretched the muscles of his shoulders. The two brothers slept in an attic space accessed by a narrow ladder. As far as he was concerned, the farther away he was from them, the better.

Second Uncle pounded the boy's back. "That's the spirit! Now let's go through this exercise routine together. It's getting chillier every morning. The Gold Mountain winter will soon be upon us, but the cold can be good for your constitution."

For the next twenty minutes, the two practised *gung fu*. Second Uncle led Hoi Wing through an increasingly demanding series of stances and movements, instructing him on his positioning, breathing, and the centring of his *'chi* within the core of his abdomen.

For his part, Hoi Wing soon forgot the morning's conflict. Instead, he concentrated on his horse stance, steadying the muscles of his thighs as he lowered his buttocks toward the floor, all the while keeping his back straight and imagining he was riding one of the giant stallions he had seen pulling wagons from the fruit farms outside the city. Slowly, he extended his palm from his waist, imagining he was thrusting against the great locks the *lofan* engineers were building at the canal that wove through the city.

"*Ayah*, what are you doing with Hoi Wing now?" Elder Brother entered from the kitchen bearing a wide tray on the crook of his one arm, balancing a teapot, cups, a plate of fried eggs, bowls of soda crackers soaked in evaporated milk, and *jook*, a fragrant rice gruel simmered with dark turkey meat. "I told you the boy had to light those boilers!"

"Relax, Big Brother," answered Second Uncle. "We're just practising *gung fu* to toughen up Hoi Wing for the day's labours. We can't all be natural-born musclemen like you."

Elder Uncle laid the tray on the alterations table. "Little Brother, can you forget our new assistant for half a minute and spare a few thoughts for the lifeblood of our business? Our wives and children back home will thank you for it. Did you notice our coal stock while you were down in the basement?"

Breathing deeply, Second Uncle towelled his face and slid into a chair at the table. He poured three cups of tea. "We'll need another delivery soon. Grandfather Foo says the *demon* coal companies charge the *lofan* laundries only two-thirds what they charge us. He says our laundrymen's associations must band together to demand better prices from the *lofan* collieries."

Elder Uncle thumped the table with his one fist. "Does Tiger-mouse imagine he's Sun Yat-sen himself? He can talk about Chinese unity until his tongue falls out of his mouth, but the damn *lofan* will still try to cheat us out of our profits!"

"President Sun Yat-sen says diplomacy and democracy are the keys to our nation's success!" The toothpick at Second Uncle's lips fluttered like a hummingbird's wings. "United we stand! Only then will we cast the foreign invaders from our land."

Still exercising, Hoi Wing eavesdropped as the uncles debated the attributes of Sun Yat-sen, the leader of the revolution and the new Chinese republic. Back home, such discussions had been never ceasing, but he had not thought the Gold Mountaineers would be so intensely attuned to the internecine struggles roiling their native land at this very moment.

"Do you think General Yuan Shikai can replace Dr. Sun Yat-sen as the new president?" Hoi Wing spoke suddenly.

"Young Man, we are starved for news of back home!" Second Uncle said excitedly. "Are you knowledgeable about current events? Your father wrote that you had an analytical mind."

In spite of himself, Hoi Wing felt a flush of pleasure that Ying the Scholar had described him in that way. In the village, no one denied his father's intelligence, but the derision as to how he had squandered his great gift was deafening.

"The revolution is already endangered." Hoi Wing parroted statements he had heard his father make. "Yuan Shikai will never inspire our people as Dr. Sun Yat-sen has inspired them. He is more thug than diplomat. Can we trust him to subdue the warlords, placate the dissident factions, and expel the Western invaders?"

"My thoughts exactly." Second Uncle nodded. Even Elder Uncle murmured his assent before spooning another mouthful of rice gruel to his lips.

Hoi Wing rose from his horse stance. His *gung fu* complete, he went to the boilers and tore strips of newsprint from a stack of old newspapers in a wicker basket. The paper sheets had a dual purpose: the men used them to prime their fires, but also whenever they attended the wooden privy in the laundry's backyard.

At the boilers, Hoi Wing lit the kindling. Then he examined the leftover newsprint in his hand. It was a faded broadsheet with a proud masthead in the handsome but incomprehensible *lofan* script he remembered seeing in his father's books back home. Ying the Scholar had taught him that the entire *lofan* tongue could be learned through the acquisition of only twenty-six characters, but how was that possible? In Hoi Wing's homeland, any schoolboy graduating from junior school could read close to five thousand ideograms.

"Do you read *lofan*?" asked Second Uncle, who watched Hoi Wing study the newspaper.

"No, but I intend to learn," he answered.

"Learn?" Elder Uncle snickered. "You won't have time for that nonsense. I hired you to wash sheets, not read ABCs."

"I'll find a way to do both!" Hoi Wing glared at Elder Uncle.

"Farmboy, in case you haven't noticed, we have a schedule here. Monday wash, Tuesday dry, Wednesday iron, Thursday pick up and deliver, Friday and Saturday—repeat the previous. If lighting those boilers is any indication of how fast you work, you'll be hard pressed to wipe your ass with that newspaper, let alone read it!"

Hoi Wing felt his blood heat up again. "I will learn to read, and I will go to school!"

Second Uncle waved his hand. "You're arguing for no reason. There's simply no school for you to attend here. Now come have some breakfast."

"I'm not done with my exercises!" Hoi Wing retreated to the window, biting back his anger. Deep down, he knew Elder Uncle's comments were as true as they were infuriating. His father had contracted him to wash clothes, not attend school. For the next five or so years his duty was to work and send money home each month.

How could he even think of shirking his duty? Ying the Scholar's word had bound him to the laundry. And Second Uncle was probably right. There was not a single Chinese student enrolled in a St. Catharines school.

"I thought of something in Toronto," Elder Uncle said excitedly. "We've been washing these *lofan*'s sheets and scrubbing their stained undershorts for years now, but we'll never get rich that way. We've got to think big! Expand our services to the hotels, hospitals, and spas!"

"But the hotels and spas deal with the Cascade and the *lofan* laundries," said Second Uncle. "How will we convince them to hire us?"

"We'll beat them at their own tactics. We'll undercut their prices, shorten our turnaround times, provide same-day pickup and delivery! Maybe we could even launder for ships' crews as they pass through the locks in the canals. If we poach just one major client, we'll break the Cascade's monopoly and have those *lofan* laundries shaking in their boots!"

"How will we accomplish that? And if we did, could we even handle that volume of work?"

"Little Brother!" Elder Uncle waved his one arm. "We're no strangers to hard labour. And we brought in our new apprentice, didn't we? He's got two good arms and claims he works twice as fast as I do! In between washdays, he'll finish middle school and graduate from university! Isn't that right, Farmboy?"

Hoi Wing gritted his teeth and stared at the window as Elder Uncle's raucous laughter erupted again. Outside, the storefronts were lit by the dawn, and horse-drawn wagons delivered milk and bread. A boy slumped past, dressed in baggy pants and long argyle socks. His back was bent beneath a sack of rolled newspapers.

Second Uncle nodded. "Big Brother, it seems you did more in Toronto than just play mah-jong and fan-tan. If we picked up some big hospital clients, we could work longer. Sleep less—five, maybe six hours a night? And we have Hoi Wing now. I told you, he's a hard worker. Look, his horse stance is already much improved. Even his voice sounds deeper. The Gold Mountain air is making a man out of him."

"Little Brother, air doesn't make a man." Elder Uncle ladled more *jook* into his bowl. "Work does."

But Hoi Wing wasn't interested in Elder Uncle's grandiose plans. As a hired hand, he had no share in the laundry's profits. And he had his own worries. How could his father have condemned him to such a wretched situation! Was there any hope he might find a way to learn *lofan* and attend school?

In the afternoon, Hoi Wing was assigned pickup and delivery duty again. Today, Second Uncle gave him a map he had drawn, detailing some of the St. Catharines streets, the city's winding canal and topography.

Despite the map, Hoi Wing soon became lost on the meandering roads, and he stumbled laboriously about, the sacks of laundry swinging on the pole across his shoulders. Unable to ask directions, he wandered, seeking the homes where he was to exchange packages of clean clothes for sacks of unwashed garments.

On the dirt roads, he passed many *lofan* townspeople—white men, women, and children—most of whom looked through him as though he were invisible. For his part, Hoi Wing tried not to stare, but it was difficult to mind his manners. How odd were the *lofan's* pale, washed-out faces and their strange, glasslike eyes! Many of the men had bristling beards and broad, pink-veined noses.

There was one peculiar fellow Hoi Wing spotted in an alleyway. He was a large, unkempt man who was thrusting a hooked pole into a heap of trash. Dressed in bedraggled clothes, he had a raggedy beard and a greasy sack hung over his shoulder. As Hoi Wing stared, the man sang out in a funereal voice, *Rag and bone! Rag and bone! Raagg-gaan-boone!*

Later in the day, Hoi Wing somehow managed to complete his circuit of deliveries. Weary, he paused near St. Catharines' downtown. As he stood on the wooden walkway, a horse-drawn dray, loaded with tin canisters of milk, merged into a chaos of human, animal, and vehicular traffic. Horses, carts, and motor cars (*of all the Gold Mountain marvels, this truly was the most impressive!*) clogged the brick roadway as cyclists, delivery boys, pedestrians, and dogs darted willy-nilly.

A cacophony of horns and clanging streetcars assaulted his ears. The ammoniac stench of the manure piles brought tears to his eyes. A tram shook the ground as it rumbled over iron tracks.

It was dizzying to take it all in! Hoi Wing dropped his sacks to the ground. In his hometown of Drink the Waters Deeply, there had been but a single dirt road wide enough to accommodate a bullock cart. The town's inhabitants, most of whom were tenant farmers, comprised some eighty households, and the better part of them shared his family name, Woo.

As he rested at the St. Catharines street corner, Hoi Wing heard the ebullient laughter of children. Without noticing, he had stopped near a sprawling three-storey brick building. In the yard were a dozen or so boys and girls, playing tag or tossing a ball. One yellow-haired girl skipped rope.

It was a school! Hoi Wing's interest was piqued. Back home, he had already completed seven years of junior studies in Teacher Lee's class at the ancestral hall. These *lofan* children were somewhat younger than he was, but might he one day become a student here? Was there a principal or headmaster to whom he might make inquiry? He hurried forward and called out.

At the sound of his voice, a boy looked up from where he had been shooting marbles in the dirt. Suddenly, he pulled his eyes into slits and stuck out his front teeth. Other children began to laugh and point. A few reached for stones.

Hoi Wing realized he had made a mistake. As he rushed back to his sacks, the boys launched their first barrage of rocks. One ricocheted from the trunk of a tree and struck his ankle. A second salvo followed. Screaming and hollering, the pack charged.

Hoi Wing cursed aloud. Once again, he found himself fleeing from a gang of rock-hurling schoolchildren, but not before he recognized the little girl who had been skipping rope in the yard. Tears streamed down her cheeks, and she waved frantically, trying to stop the other children. It was his little friend who had visited the laundry yesterday evening.

3

Every day was colder than the previous. In the mornings, Hoi Wing awoke to the rude jangle of an alarm clock (borrowed from Second Uncle) and rolled out of his cot into the frigid air of the basement like a silkworm torn from its cocoon. His new subterranean quarters provided the space and privacy he sought, but the small windows leaked like a sieve, and the fieldstone foundation smelled of loam.

Groggy with sleep—Fourth Youngest Auntie had not reappeared since that memorable night, and his dreams were utterly forgettable once more—he dunked his face in a basin of icy water and washed his body with a rough towel. He cleaned his teeth with a toothbrush of bamboo, applying a grey powder that tasted of salt and sand.

Ablutions complete, he dashed up the stairs to the laundry's main floor, where—shivering and wishing the padded cotton sweater Eldest Great Auntie had given him was thicker—he hastened to fill the boilers and light the burners before Elder Uncle (huffing, coughing, and snorting) descended the attic ladder from his bedroom, lurching from side to side like some great one-armed ape.

He ate breakfast at the circular dining table, squeezed into the corner the men called the Wall of Family. In the little nook, the uncles had hung framed photographs of family and friends. Elder Uncle, as senior proprietor, always sat beneath the photos of his wife and three daughters, and Second Uncle sat adjacent to his wife and two sons. In that manner, the brothers dined in the company of their families every day.

As the junior member of the household, Hoi Wing sat farthest from the photos and next to the kitchen, where he could easily replenish the teapot (a duty reserved to the youngest person at the table) or refill a bowl of rice. He had yet to add any of his own pictures to the wall, although Second Uncle had expressly invited him to do so.

To shake off his early morning drowsiness, Hoi Wing often studied the gallery. His eye was always drawn to a sepia-toned photograph of two Chinese miners who posed on the bank of a fast-flowing river before a scree of mountain rubble. Wooden sluice boxes and pickaxes lay at their feet, and the men stood, each resting his arm over the shoulder of the man beside him.

The grinning man in the photo was the taller and more handsome of the two. Bearded, he was much slimmer than he was now, but his broad chest and powerful shoulders were unmistakable. Hoi Wing had stared long and hard, trying to reconcile the impossibly young and good-looking Elder Uncle with the grim man he had come to know.

When had Elder Uncle hunted gold in the great Far North? Who was his brave companion? Hoi Wing had already questioned Second Uncle about Elder Uncle's adventures, but he had declined to speak, saying the story was not his to tell.

Beside the photo of the gold prospectors was a portrait of Elder Uncle's wife. The woman's eyes were dark and mysterious; her lashes were long and the bridge of her nose was proud. Her cheekbones were regal, although there was a hint of sadness in the press of her lips.

Elder Uncle had recently returned from a joyous fourteen-month visit back home, and it would be at least four or five more years before he could save enough money for his next reunion in China. What was it like to be separated from a woman so desirable your mouth went dry just looking at her? Lately, while working, Hoi Wing had devised a new game: every time he finished a tub of wash, he allowed himself a moment to gaze into the eyes of Elder Uncle's beautiful wife.

Second Uncle's contributions to the Wall of Family revealed a wife who was not a beauty like Elder Uncle's, but Hoi Wing imagined her a kindly, good-natured woman who would rise early to brew tea or warm a bowl of rice gruel for her husband. Hoi Wing liked her photo and was glad that Second Uncle had found such an agreeable wife.

When would Second Uncle next return home? His time must be nearing, as business partners such as the uncles often took turns, one sojourning home while the other minded their affairs in the Gold Mountain. But that meant Hoi Wing could be left alone with Elder Uncle as early as next year. He thrust that thought from his mind.

The rain fell in slanting sheets that flooded the horse troughs outside. Autumn storms buffeted the laundry's storefront window, and the wind howled like a dog that had seen its master's ghost. In October, an early frost sugar-coated the surface of St. Paul Street. Hoi Wing raced upstairs and watched a motor truck leave a white furrow like a skunk's back down the middle of the road. *Was that snow—the mythical frozen rain?*

"The true Gold Mountain winter has arrived!" he announced as the men descended from the attic, but Elder Uncle only guffawed.

Work swallowed everything. Aided by the practice of *gung fu*, Hoi

Wing's body slowly acclimated to the demands of the laundryman's labour. Sort, wash, dry, iron, package, and deliver. Day in, day out. The sixteen-hour workdays, six days a week, were becoming routine. Each night, he collapsed into bed, falling instantly into a deep slumber, only to be awoken far too soon by his wind-up alarm clock. Life melded into an endless cycle of toil, and he startled himself on occasion, waking to discover he had been dozing on his feet, his paddle clutched in his hands as he swayed precariously in front of a vat of boiled laundry.

Second Uncle told him he was beginning to learn the "Way of the Wash," but Hoi Wing thought he would sooner die than accept this fate. It was tedium he feared, not work. The uncles escaped the monotony by staring blankly into space as they folded mountains of shirts or plied irons across acres of sheets. Hoi Wing vowed never to let his mind succumb to the stupefying effects of mundane, repetitive labour. But how to keep his brain sharp?

All his life, Hoi Wing had been surrounded by books. He grew up cloistered in the little house on Beggars' Row by the swamp (only the distance of a sneeze from the village's community outhouses), which Ying the Scholar had rented after *his* father had disowned him. Within those four walls, Hoi Wing's beautiful mother, Fong-Fong, lit fragrant joss sticks to cleanse the air and hung scrolls bearing his father's poetry. Later she added parchment sheets bearing Hoi Wing's first brush pen scribbles. Hoi Wing learned to sit, crawl, and toddle over the porcelain tiles of the floor, navigating between the stacks of his father's texts, tomes, and teachings.

Ying the Scholar believed the skills of any métier could be assimilated through diligent study, and he had hammered shelves to accommodate his scholar's library, comprising not only the Four Classics, the Five Books, and the Four Great Novels but also treatises of agriculture and the chemistry and composition of soils, as well as collections of local folklore, herbalism, acupuncture, geomancy, and geographies, and (*astonishingly!*) even a few choice, hitherto indecipherable works penned in English, their leather spines cracked and the gilded pages faded.

Like a waterfall, the books spilled from the crooked shelves, but they drew the tottering and newly peripatetic Hoi Wing like a magnet into their musty redolence of ink, paper, and leather, no matter where Fong-Fong set him down. "He is his father's son," she declared proudly.

In this fashion, Hoi Wing passed a bucolic infancy blissfully unaware of the scandal surrounding his parents, and never knowing that his father, Ying, had at the tender age of twenty years been widely touted as a candidate for the Imperial Civil Service.

But in the laundry, Hoi Wing grew ever more despondent. For him, the experience with the rock throwers at the schoolhouse was an evil portent that foreshadowed his permanent exclusion from schooling of any kind in the New World.

Furthermore, he had little or no time for formal study, just as Elder Uncle had said. The Sam Kee Luk Chinese Hand Laundry was officially closed on Sundays, and the men profited from the break by greasing the rollers on the wringers, mending wicker baskets, and performing the thousand and one necessary and mundane tasks required to operate their business.

Hoi Wing longed to explore the city and its surrounding woods, but the weather remained inclement, and he retreated to the copper boilers, rubbing his arms, stamping his feet, and blowing into his hands. Late one evening, he was surprised to observe Elder Uncle immersing himself in a meaty novel procured from some secret stash in the attic. As Hoi Wing sidled close to discern its title, the man gripped the book to his chest and growled a warning for the boy to back off.

On another occasion, Elder Uncle descended from the attic bearing a small bundle wrapped in blue silk. Going to the dining table, the man unfolded the cloth to reveal as venerable a set of the Four Treasures of the Study as Hoi Wing had ever seen: brush pen, ink, inkstone, and paper. Hoi Wing's eyes went wide as the one-handed man ground the inkstone and dipped his pen to compose a long missive on a sheet of translucent onion skin paper using a calligraphy as crisp and forceful as that employed by Ying the Scholar.

Where had Elder Uncle learned such a beautiful hand? And to whom was he writing with such solicitude? Surely it had to be the woman whose portrait graced the Wall of Family. Even more astonishingly, the man often hummed as he wrote, and Hoi Wing was doubly disconcerted at how the melodies transported him back to his own childhood on Beggars' Row when his beautiful mother would sing to him in her haunting soprano. He even recognized tunes that Fong-Fong had once favoured.

Hoi Wing had to reset his opinion of Elder Uncle once more. The world was just as his father had taught him. Nothing was ever what it first seemed, and understanding was only gleaned through quiet observation, contemplation, and study.

Second Uncle had a wholly different pastime. He liked nothing better than to sink into the moth-eaten armchair by the drying room and roll his toothpick between his lips as he sketched in a thick pad of ivory-coloured sheets positioned on his lap. Pencils, watercolours, ink and brush, oily crayons: he had them all. Sometimes he drew from memory, staring at the wall of unclaimed laundry with the same far-off expression Hoi Wing had spied in his father's eyes when he came upon Ying unbidden in the fields, the man's hoe tossed to the ground and the crops seemingly forgotten, his lips moving soundlessly as he composed some verse in his mind.

Other times, Second Uncle placed a bowl of apples or a clump of withered grapes onto a plate and drew from life. Once, he arranged a flatiron, the tin atomizer, and a booklet of laundry tickets in a composition that tickled the eye. When Hoi Wing peeked over the man's shoulder to see the progression of the drawing, he could not help but appreciate the transformation of the everyday tools of their trade into *objets d'art*.

Where had the man gained his skill? At work, Hoi Wing caught Second Uncle staring at him as if to etch his features into his brain, and sure enough, Second Uncle's sketchbook began to fill with depictions of Hoi Wing churning wash before the big tub, ironing at the storefront window, or balancing the laundry pole across his narrow shoulders. At first, Hoi Wing feigned consternation at seeing himself so immortalized, but secretly, he could not have been more pleased.

In the month before his journey to the West, Hoi Wing, his father, Little Mei-Mei, Eldest Great Auntie, and Fourth Youngest Auntie had all travelled in Old Soong's bullock cart to the market town of Nam-toun to stand before a painted backdrop of Hong Kong harbour in a photographer's studio for a family portrait. The resulting image, framed in mahogany, still lay beside the picture of Hoi Wing's mother in his valise. Ying had also commissioned a solo photograph of his son, and that now hung in Beggars' Row on the wall opposite the family shrine.

Hoi Wing had been shocked at the way his father expended their precious savings, but Little Mei-Mei giggled delightedly when she saw the portrait. Fourth Youngest Auntie declared him the handsomest thirteen-year-old in all the Four Counties, which caused him to stare hard at his cloth shoes, his cheeks suddenly afire.

Nevertheless, having now viewed Second Uncle's art, Hoi Wing wished his father had not dispensed his hard-earned coins in the little studio in Nam-toun. It was not that the photographic print had failed to capture his face; the sombre likeness generated by the alchemy of silver nitrate was a faithful reflection of what he saw in mirrors and the small pond in which he often bathed. But Second Uncle's drawings exceeded mere two-dimensional renderings. Despite their economy of stroke, the man had caught something else with his deft line and subtle shadows.

In the basement under lamplight, Hoi Wing scrutinized the sketches Second Uncle had so magnanimously given him, and discerned a new-found maturity in his chin and the line of his jaw. There was a certain defiant expectation in his eyes. He peered closer. *Were his biceps rounder?* Whatever magic Second Uncle had wrought, it was as if the man had distilled Hoi Wing's essence and brought forth a bolder and better version of him: one who would not be daunted by mere weather or ragamuffin gangs. One who would dare a fate other than the laundry.

Inspired by the uncles, Hoi Wing hovered at the curtain behind the reception area to eavesdrop on their conversations with their customers. He strained to hear every word and studied the *lofan's* lips. How were they creating the sounds they emitted? Afterward, he repeated the meaningless syllables until he could say them in his sleep. Soon he discovered he could parrot the pronunciation and syntax used by their clients more accurately than either of his employers. He began to make notes on a pad of paper, and he recited a lexicon to himself each morning as he washed his face, and during the few minutes he managed to remain awake every night.

Hoi Wing entreated the laundrymen to speak *lofan* with him whenever possible and to name every object within their four walls and whatever else they could see from the big window. What do the *lofan* call this cup of drink? *"Wah-tah."* What is that four-legged beast pulling the wagon?

"Hoss-see." What was the *lofan* name of this town again? *"Seng-cah-doun."*

With their help, Hoi Wing managed to identify the letters printed on the newspapers in the wicker basket. One night, he took a few sheets into the basement, and he held the newsprint to his face as if proximity could confer literacy.

The words swam before his eyes, but the photograph beneath the headlines depicted a tall *lofan* with a heavy beard. The man stood before a podium, gripping a wooden cane as an audience applauded. His fine worsted suit and tie denoted his importance to Hoi Wing, who was becoming an expert on the subtleties of Western attire. Was it an artifice of the photographer's medium, or was there a predatory gleam in the man's eyes? When Hoi Wing could no longer keep his own eyelids open, he folded up the broadsheet, extinguished his lamp, and fell into an uneasy sleep.

One fateful evening, Hoi Wing conducted a ceremony of his own. He opened his valise and placed his family portraits on the chest of drawers. Fourth Auntie's adventure novels followed. Then he added two dried peonies Little Mei-Mei had flattened in one of their father's books, and three polished river stones, the favourites culled from her collection.

He took out Eldest Great Auntie's amulet. She had told him to wear it on the shores of the Gold Mountain. It was a disc of jade with a dragon carved along the outside edge. His name was etched in the centre. He fastened the delicate gold chain and breathed deeply as the disc fell to the hollow at the base of his neck.

His throat was already thick when he drew out his father's massive Chinese-English–English-Chinese dictionary for the first time. The tome's binding was blue and faded from use. The spine was ungluing. He flipped the threadbare cover to discover an inscription inside:

For Hoi Wing the Scholar, who will find a way,

Your father

Hoi Wing gasped. For a while, he stared at his father's words. No one had ever called him that. All his life he had just been "the son of Ying the Scholar," with all the attendant embarrassment, resentment, frustration, and suppressed rage. Friendless throughout childhood, he had learned to keep his eyes forward when he heard the whispered jeers and jibes. To pretend he was no different from any other farmer's son in Drink the Waters Deeply.

He remembered turning from his father when the man offered to help with his homework, and how, at the age of nine, he had vowed to memorize the multiplication tables (up to fifteen times fifteen), analyze sonnets, and complete every one of Teacher Lee's assignments without going to his father. He remembered that sometimes when they walked through the village, he had run ten paces ahead.

He had not even thanked his father when the man pulled the dictionary from a sack and handed it to him on the quay in Heung San village where he boarded the sampan that was to carry him to Hong Kong and then the New World.

In the basement, Hoi Wing's breath shuddered, and he clamped his hand over his mouth to stifle a sob. Suddenly, all the pent-up emotion endured over a lifetime as the son of Ying the Scholar flooded his chest. A moan escaped his lips, and hot tears spilled from his eyes. *What kind of son was he? He had not even turned to wave goodbye as the boatman sculled the little craft from the wharf!*

For long minutes, Hoi Wing wept reproaching himself, regretting so much of his young life, and lamenting his father's lost years in the fields. He sobbed and blew his nose. Slowly, the spell subsided, and he took deep, cleansing breaths, grateful that the uncles could not hear him in his underground hideaway.

When he felt himself once more, he splashed cold water over his face. Despite the hour, his resolve was keen and his soul purged. He set the dictionary on the workbench and pulled up the stool. Then he began the Herculean task of translating the front page of the *St. Catharines Herald*. Without knowledge of grammar, syntax, or even the use of verb tenses, he found the effort slow and difficult. Nevertheless, as time passed, letters, patterns, and even words became recognizable: A-B-C.

It was a start.

A week passed. One afternoon, Elder Uncle returned from the dry goods store, where he had purchased galvanized wire, brown paper, clothespins, string, bluing powder, starch, and soap. On the way back, he had also stopped at the post office.

"Letters from home!" he called out. "We have mail!"

There was a whoop of excitement from the drying room, and Second Uncle burst through the curtains hung to contain the heat of the braziers. "Give me my letters!"

Elder Uncle laughed and set his bag of purchases down. Then he pulled a bundle of envelopes from within his jacket. "Ho! There's even a couple for Farmboy! I thought everyone back home had forgotten him!"

All thought of work was banished as the brothers commenced a mock battle for their missives from the village. Once the mail was distributed, Elder Uncle clutched his letters to his heart. Second Uncle settled into his armchair. Hoi Wing retreated into the basement.

There, he sat on his cot and carefully slit the first onion skin envelope with his pocket knife. He drew out a letter from Fourth Youngest Auntie.

To my favourite nephew,

Last week, I rounded with Eldest Great Auntie for the first time, and we travelled to Bak-Sieuk to visit a young woman, early in her seventh month. So tiny was the young mother-to-be, but already swollen like an overripe melon, with veins in her legs like long, dark worms. The poor girl's worry was palpable, but Eldest Auntie bade her lie down and placed sure hands over her distended belly. "Twins, you are carrying!" Eldest Auntie proclaimed. "A birthing without complication portends!" How relieved the young woman was! Oh, that I could learn Eldest Auntie's bedside manner!

When I returned home, I found your letter. Thank you for sending the sketches! In your maturing face, I see the man you will become. That is why I will strive to answer your questions now, although I can only tell you what I know.

As a young girl, I remembered your father's achievements in Teacher Lee's class and how all believed he would bring honour to our village. Some imagined he might even gain a position as eminent as the one held by the legendary and venerable Woo Gon Wen, our town's most illustrious ancestor.

Thus, when your father travelled to the provincial capital, I had no doubt he would pass the Imperial Examinations. Yet weeks later, when he returned with neither fanfare nor diploma, I wondered how Ying the Scholar had failed at the examination chamber. What happened? In shame, our father grew incensed and expelled him from our house. For years, I watched our townsfolk ridicule your father, so that one day I ventured into the fields and questioned him.

I have never forgotten the answer he gave me. Ying the Scholar said, "I left for the capital seeking my heart's desire, and I returned, having found it."

And then I remembered, your father came home that night with your mother, Fong-Fong.

With love as always, Fourth Youngest Auntie

P.S. And thank you for your last remittance. We look forward so much to the next!

4

In the sorting area, the laundry sacks were piled higher than Hoi Wing's head. He heaved a bag over his shoulder and spilled the damp sheets, towels, nurses' caps, masks, and gowns onto a table.

It was almost noon, a week since their last mail call, and Elder Uncle's grand scheme of expanding their clientele was bearing fruit. Not only had they poached a few customers from the Cascade, but this morning he'd picked up laundry from the St. Catharines Sanatorium for the Treatment of Tuberculosis and Coughing Maladies. The new contract included a standing rush order and a turnaround of no more than four days, including weekends.

Hoi Wing stared at the mountainous heap of burlap bags, imprinted with white letters spelling the sanatorium's name. He could now ascribe meaning to most of those words, but the acquisition of even this glint of knowledge had been excruciatingly slow.

It turned out that reading was much harder than he thought, and mastery of the *lofan*'s twenty-six characters did little to enhance one's comprehension of their endless combinations and permutations. Moreover, his attempt at translating the *lofan* newspaper had sputtered and stalled, much like the trajectories of some of the motor cars he watched from the laundry's windows. Exasperated, he had relegated most of the purloined pages of the *St. Catharines Herald* to their more primordial function in the laundry's backyard outhouse.

His plan to become conversant in *lofan* hadn't achieved much success either. He still eavesdropped on the uncles' conversations, but the handful of words they exchanged with their clientele rarely amounted to more than a quick haggling over a price (*"five cen, ten cen, twen-dee cen"*) or the scheduling of a return date for pickup (*"to-mo-low, no, Fli-day you come"*).

Furthermore, his ear—well schooled by his mother's music lessons—told him the uncles' accents bore little resemblance to the speech employed by their customers, and the last thing he wanted was to speak *lofan* the way they did. He was fast realizing he would never learn proper *lofan* without formal instruction.

Hoi Wing fingered Eldest Great Auntie's amulet around his neck. He dragged another sack of hospital laundry across the floor. Until now, he had considered the wash from the Springbank Hotel the most stomach-turning, but nothing could compare with the rotting-flesh stink of the hospital sacks, oozing with body fluids. To mask the odour, he had tied a handkerchief sprinkled with lavender around his neck, causing Elder Uncle to mock his dainty sense of smell, but Second Uncle told him he would soon grow inured to even this.

Needing a rest, Hoi Wing opened the small window and drank in the crisp November air. This afternoon he would be outside, making pickups and deliveries in the Golden Li. It would be his third time performing this important task in the stately neighbourhood surrounding Montebello Park (*"Mong-tah-beah-loh-pak"*), but this was the first occasion Second Uncle had entrusted him with performing all three circuits.

It felt good to know Second Uncle had faith in him, although more and more he realized what he missed most was someone with whom he could talk and share his innermost thoughts. Back home, he had never had a real friend. His status as "the son of Ying the Scholar" had ostracized him since his earliest days. This week, he had set himself another challenge: he wanted to meet and speak with three new *lofan*, but how likely was that to happen?

He stared out the window as a pair of young women hurried by in grey raincoats, laughing and chatting. One had curly brown hair and wore high heels with dark hose. The other's hair was loose, and her coat was open to the wind. They were likely shopgirls, heading downtown to one of the many "Women and Girls" stores or a fine haberdashery. Second Uncle had told him the laundry owed much of its success to this wave of young women who would no longer submit to the drudgery of domestic service in the wealthy homes of *"high class-ee lofan."*

"Hey, Farmboy!" Elder Uncle poked his head through the doorway. "How's that new hospital contract? Got enough lavender? I can hear the cash register sing!"

As Elder Uncle headed out the front door, Hoi Wing returned to the sorting tables. He watched the big man march confidently down St. Paul Street in search of more business.

Hoi Wing stifled a yawn and spilled another bag of soggy sheets onto the table. Then he dabbed more lavender onto his handkerchief. To pass the hours, he had created a new game: every time he sorted a sack of wash, he allowed himself a mouthful of rice and sausage from the bowl he had saved from breakfast.

∞

"There be the sacks, boy!" The *lofan* maid stood in a doorway and waved at a pile of laundry bags. "Now be off with yah!"

Hoi Wing bowed low. *"Teng-kou—"* But the woman shut the door before he could complete his much-practised response. For a moment, he stood alone at the back of the house, staring at the mud room door and the sign tacked beside it. Then he pulled out a pencil stub and copied the *lofan* script onto a scrap of paper: *SERVANTS AND HIRED MEN.*

It was mid-afternoon in the Golden Li. Hoi Wing knelt to add the new bags of laundry to those already secured to his pole. Although he had completed two full circuits in the neighbourhood, he had yet to exchange more than a handful of words with any of the women who had opened the door to him.

Nevertheless, Hoi Wing couldn't muster any umbrage at their refusal to engage him in conversation. It was obvious the maids, whether young or old, bedraggled or sauce-splattered, hands gripping mops or dustpans, had been too inundated with their own duties to waste time with him. Astonishing as it seemed, could *lofan* maids work as hard and thanklessly as he did?

When Hoi Wing finished knotting the sacks to his pole, he consulted Second Uncle's map once more. All afternoon he had trudged past the tall brick turrets, wrought iron fences, and wraparound porches of the Golden Li homes, but he had not glimpsed a single *high class-see lofan*, despite encountering dozens of domestics and labourers. Where were the rich folk who inhabited these mansions?

Hoi Wing lifted his laundry across his shoulders and staggered to his feet. He trudged toward the front of the great house. As he stepped onto the road, he saw a horse and wagon waiting several houses down. The cart was brightly painted in blue and gold. An older teen lifted a heavy sack to a younger boy in the wagon box.

Hoi Wing paused. The two boys were doing exactly what he had been doing all afternoon. Then he noted the sign on the back panel of the wagon. The words were too familiar: CASCADE LAUNDRY—DRYERS AND CLEANERS.

It was their chief competitor! Hoi Wing felt an impulse to spin around and retreat, but swallowing his trepidation, he stepped briskly forward. As he approached, the older boy heaved another sack to the smaller boy. The small boy looked up from his work and spotted Hoi Wing. For an instant, he just stared; then he snickered.

"Stop goofing about, Jimmy!" his older brother said. "We gotta get these bags—"

Then he too spied Hoi Wing. A smile came to his face, and he dropped the sack to the ground. He wiped his nose with the back of his sleeve. Then he stepped into Hoi Wing's path.

Hoi Wing halted not two paces away. The older teen was tall and lanky. His hair was close-cropped, and his ears jutted from the sides of his head. A shadow of a moustache darkened his upper lip, but his chin was weak. He had the look of a rat.

Ratface sneered, exposing large, uneven teeth. "Well, well, *look-ee* what we got here."

"Give the Chink hell, Billy!" the boy on the wagon exclaimed with a laugh.

Ratface stepped so close, Hoi Wing could smell the sweat of his body. "You Chinamen trying to muscle in on our business? Think you're gonna steal our customers?"

Hoi Wing took a half step backwards. His mouth was suddenly dry, and his stomach clenched with nerves. The last thing he wanted was to fight this bigger, older teen.

Ratface shoved Hoi Wing, who stumbled back, just managing to keep the laundry across his shoulders. The teen shoved him again.

Hoi Wing staggered another three or four steps backwards. Then a sudden rush of blood and adrenalin surged through his body. Gritting his teeth, he shouted in Chinese as loudly as he could, "You go die, you damn ugly bucktoothed *dead-ghost-bastard-boy*!"

"What?" Ratface said, startled. "What was that Chinky talk?"

"Get 'im!" The younger boy swung his fist in the air. "Give it to 'im!"

Ratface raised his fists and charged. At the last instant, Hoi Wing twisted his body. Ratface slammed into the laundry sacks, almost impaling himself on the pole.

"Oh-oof!" The breath whooshed from Ratface. The two boys fell heavily to the ground. Impeded by the laundry bags, Hoi Wing and Ratface wrestled in the dirt, clawing at each other's faces. For a moment, Hoi Wing was on top, hammering Ratface's nose and cheeks. Then Ratface rolled him over and pressed down. As the boy on the wagon screamed encouragement, the older boy threw a flurry of punches.

Struggling for breath, Hoi Wing covered his face. Black spots swam before his eyes. He felt himself weakening.

"Now you're dead!" Ratface cocked his fist.

"Hey! What's that ruckus?" A grey-haired manservant in a dark suit emerged from the hedgerow at the side of the big house. "You, boy! I'm not waiting another minute! Get these bags now—or I shut the door!"

"Huh?" Ratface looked up. Hoi Wing kicked the other boy in the belly. The two sprang to their feet, but it was Ratface who retreated to the side of the wagon.

"I'm closing up at the count of three!" shouted the man.

"Yes, sir!" Ratface called out. "Right away, sir!" He turned to his brother. "C'mon, Jimmy, we got to get the rest of the laundry!"

"But what about the Chi—"

"Forget him! Pa will kill us if we don't get the wash!" He helped his brother from the wagon box before turning back to Hoi Wing.

"We're not finished, Chinaman!" Ratface growled as he rubbed his eye. Then he and the younger boy raced down the hedgerow toward the back of the house, following the manservant.

The blinkered horse neighed and stamped its hooves. As his adversaries ran into the laneway, Hoi Wing sagged against the wagon. Ratface had caught him with a glancing blow to the chin, but Hoi Wing remembered with a grim satisfaction that he had managed to thrust his thumb into Ratface's left eye. Still, he knew he had been saved only by luck and the chance intervention of a *lofan* servant. He touched Eldest Great Auntie's jade charm to his lips.

As Hoi Wing bent to recover his laundry, he noticed a small figure standing before a majestic house across the road. It was a young girl in a black maid's uniform with a white apron and ruffled cap. Her face was pale and delicate, and her hair, where it peeked out from her cap, was that audacious *lofan* shade of copper. In each hand, she gripped a leash tethering an enormous mastiff. The two beasts stood silently at her command, sniffing at the air and the ground.

She stared at Hoi Wing with dark eyes. Were they full of concern? Sympathy? Something told him she had witnessed his battle with the bigger, older boy. Hoi Wing wanted to say hello. He wanted to tell her he had not been afraid. He had to communicate in some manner, but nothing came to mind. The moment passed. Without a word, the girl turned and led the massive dogs through a gate in the hedge surrounding the house.

Across the road, Hoi Wing shifted the laundry onto his shoulders, feeling a disappointment surpassing any in his entire Gold Mountain experience. Why hadn't he called out to her? If only he had thought of something to say! Then he shook himself. His luck could not last forever. Hoi Wing left the neighbourhood as quickly as he could.

Later that afternoon, he was in St. Catharines' downtown, returning from his final circuit of the Golden Li. All his pickups and deliveries were complete. The last round had been the shortest, but he slumped under a full load of dirty laundry. His thighs twitched, and the laundry pole bit into his shoulders like a steel trap. At least he had not encountered Rat-face or the Cascade's wagon again.

As Hoi Wing turned onto St. Paul Street, he passed a pair of swarthy street cleaners, their moustaches as bristly as their brooms, shovelling a mountain of manure. Overhead, the sullen skies had cleared, and the air, so often dusty from the excavations at the Welland Canal, tasted fresh and clean. He turned sideways to bypass a young woman, and a carriage driver cracked his whip. "Ware away, yah bloody idiot!"

After what seemed like weeks of endless rain, the late November sunshine had drawn St. Catharines' citizenry outdoors, and shoppers ducked under colourful awnings as they entered and exited shops selling millinery, haberdashery, dry goods, and hardware.

Hoi Wing drew energy from the hustle and bustle. He spied a green-jacketed constable patrolling on his bicycle. Men doffed their hats, and women and girls curtsied as the "green-jacket" passed. He saw delivery boys pulling heavily loaded carts and couldn't help thinking how much easier a cart would make his job.

The tip of his pole snagged an awning, and Hoi Wing peered into a piano store. Inside, a woman sat at a piano bench, instructing a little girl beside her. He remembered his beautiful mother positioning and repositioning his fingers over the neck of her *er-hu* as she struggled to share her love of music. He had chafed at the lessons, but now he recalled the warmth of her body against his—and, toward the end, the sensation of his unborn sister kicking within the hard bubble of her belly—and the pitch of her voice as she sang over the notes he tried to find. She had taught him at a frenzied pace, as if she knew her time was short, and indeed it had been.

On St. Paul Street, the piano teacher commenced a short sonata, surprising and delighting Hoi Wing. The sprightly melody danced up and down, trickled like rainfall, and cascaded to a glorious climax. Exhilaration filled his chest, tinged with sorrow. He had heard this; his mother had not. He was alive; she was dead.

Hoi Wing wiped his cheeks, now wet with tears. Once more, he was glad that he was invisible to most *lofan*. Gathering his thoughts, he resumed his way through the crowd, ignoring several children who grimaced like monkeys and pulled their eyes into slits.

Outside a three-storey building of red brick, Hoi Wing saw the familiar red-and-blue flag of the British Empire. At the curbside was another of the new horseless carriages he loved to watch motoring through the narrow streets of St. Catharines. Their drivers, clad in leather caps, goggles, and gloves, seemed to him magicians, commanding locomotion without visible means of propulsion.

He let his laundry slide from his shoulders and approached the vision of gleaming metal and glass. Leaning over the door, he studied what resembled a row of miniature timepieces and knobs set in a dashboard of burnished maple. The steering wheel was ebony, and the seat was ample and inviting. He wanted very much to climb aboard. What were the secrets of this mechanized marvel?

"What are you doing, boy?" A heavy hand clamped down on Hoi Wing's shoulder. "Get away from there!"

The man thrust Hoi Wing down to the sidewalk. Pain jolted his ankle, his buttocks, and his elbow. When he looked up, he saw a heavy-set figure in a bowler hat and greatcoat. The man was bearded from cheek to jowl, with fierce overgrown eyebrows. He raised his cane.

"Stop, Mr. Braddock! Stop!" A young woman raced from the brick building. "What are you doing to that lad?"

The man froze. His eyes shone like an animal's. "This is not your affair, Miss Primmons. This little thief was tampering with my motor car!"

"He most certainly was not!" The woman stepped between Hoi Wing and the man. "I watched his every move from my window. He was merely admiring your vehicle, although why he would do so, I have no idea!"

"His kind are like monkeys—they see something shiny and they want it. We cannot allow their thievery to go unpunished, or they will steal our very livelihoods from under our noses!"

"Oh, is that it now?" answered the young woman. "You are afraid of their competition?"

The man sneered. "Don't be foolish! Even our esteemed prime minister has said they are a blight on our British nation! Let us send them all home—they must not establish themselves here, or we will be awash in a veritable yellow peril!"

"Leave our prime minister out of this—he is as thick-headed as any man. And these Chinese laundrymen have every right to compete with your businesses! Is that not your laissez-faire motto? Fair competition and a chance for all working men?"

For a moment, the large man seemed flummoxed. Then he ran his hand through his beard and brandished his cane once more. "Step aside! He deserves a good caning!"

"Don't you dare harm him!"

Hoi Wing sat up, studying his attacker. He was a very poor judge of *lofan* faces (they all looked the same), but this man seemed vaguely familiar. Much of his face was hidden by his beard, and his cheeks were florid. His incisors were long and predatory. Where had Hoi Wing seen him before?

For a moment, the stalemate continued. Several pedestrians stepped forward. The man glanced about. Slowly, he lowered his cane. He straightened his tie and the tilt of his hat. There was a glint of cufflinks as he tucked his cuffs into his coat sleeves.

"Very well, Miss Primmons. Take the young miscreant's side. No good will come of it!"

Touching his hat stiffly, he stepped to the front of the car. He bent before its hood, cranked the engine, and the motor snarled. The man climbed into the seat and fitted a cap and goggles over his face. The automobile backfired before lurching from the curb. Then it merged into the chaos of horses, carriages, and bicycles clogging St. Paul.

Hoi Wing watched the motor car disappear into the traffic. Was Elder Uncle right? Were all *lofan* mad? His hip throbbed, and the nerves of his elbow jangled as though they were on fire. He rose to one knee as the woman turned to face him.

"Are you all right?" She held out her hand. "Do you need help?"

Hoi Wing was happy to turn his attention to his rescuer. The young woman could not have been much older than Fourth Auntie, and she had earnest, caring eyes that tilted downward in that strange *lofan* manner. Her hair was rusty-brown, and her neck was long and patrician. There was a tiny cleft at the tip of her nose.

He took her hand, and she drew him upright with surprising strength. *"Theng-kou."* He bowed as he tested his weight on his left foot. *"Theng-kou vel-lay much-ee."*

His first foray into *lofan* brought a delighted smile to her lips. "Why, you're very welcome," she answered. Then she launched into a stream of gibberish.

Hoi Wing shook his head sadly. *The touch of her fingers had been exhilarating!* He shrugged to emphasize his utter lack of comprehension.

She spoke slowly, gesturing at him, herself, and the laundry sacks on the ground. "Adele. Adele Primmons," she said, touching her breast. "Adele Primmons. Adele."

Ah-Del? thought Hoi Wing. Was she telling him her name? *"Ah-Del?"* he spoke aloud. *"Ah-Del?"*

"Yes, yes, my name is Adele!" She laughed and spoke again, pointing at him repeatedly. The inflection of her voice rose.

He answered in his own tongue. "I am Hoi Wing. Woo Hoi Wing."

"Your name is Hoi Wing!" she repeated. "Hoi Wing, am I right? Hoi Wing?"

Now he had to laugh. Her accent was as mangled as his own, but he nodded vigorously in response.

The lovely stranger spoke again, pointing at the building from which she had emerged, and pantomimed reading a book and writing on a sheet of paper. Then she waved her hand at the spire of a *lofan* worship hall, rising in the distance several blocks away.

Frustrated, Hoi Wing shook his head. What was she telling him? Did it have to do with reading or writing?

"Wait. Your necklace has come loose." The young woman reached out and touched his amulet. "Oh dear, has it snapped?"

Hoi Wing's fingers went to Eldest Great Auntie's charm, and he grimaced in dismay. He lifted it from his neck and studied the twisted clasp.

"I'm sure it can be repaired," the woman commiserated. "That jade is a lovely shade of aquamarine. What does the engraving say?"

Hoi Wing tucked the amulet into his pocket for safekeeping. It must have broken in his altercation with the crazy *lofan*! Turning, he looked in the direction where the man's automobile had disappeared. He pointed down the street and mimed holding a steering wheel.

She nodded. "Yes, it likely happened when Mr. Braddock threw you to the ground. I would avoid him at all costs. Do you understand? Stay away from him! Jonathan Braddock." She pointed down the street. "Braddock."

Blah-dok. Blah-dok? Was that the mad *lofan*'s name? She had spoken the syllables with such vehemence. He remembered the intense gaze of the man's eyes. Where had he seen him before?

His rescuer was speaking again. She pointed down the street and rubbed her hands. Once more he shook his head. If only he could tell her how grateful he was for her kindness! The woman sighed and a look of resignation came to her face. Then she plucked a slip of paper from her pocket and drew out a pencil. She printed something and handed it to him.

"*Teng-kou vel-lay much-ee*," he said again, adding another bow for emphasis.

"It was a pleasure meeting you, Woo Hoi Wing." She reached out and squeezed his arm. "I know we're going to be friends." With a little wave, she turned and headed back to her building.

Hoi Wing watched her pass through a pair of oaken doors. Her hair gleamed in the afternoon sun, and her ankles were very slim. *Ah-Del* was her name. *Ah-Del Plee-mon*.

When the doors shut behind her, Hoi Wing glanced at the little scrap of paper she had given him. He took out his own pencil and copied the words of the sign adorning the building she had entered: *PUBLIC LIBRARY AND READING ROOM*.

On the street, the shadows were lengthening, and the wind rose suddenly from the canal, chasing the warmth from the November day. Hoi Wing decided it was time to get home. His back now chilled with sweat, he lifted his pole across his shoulders and recommenced his journey.

As he continued eastward, the storefronts and edifices grew less imposing. The banks, doctors' offices, and jewellers were gradually replaced by hotels and cafés, theatres, pool halls, and the odd tavern. Farther east were the rooming houses, junk dealers, the tin peddler's home, and the home of the blind woman who sewed gloves.

Now he wondered what the uncles would cook for dinner. Chicken and potato rice? Fried rice with fish? As Hoi Wing's shadow stretched before him, a drunkard lurched from an alley and stumbled against his bags. The man cursed, but Hoi Wing continued on without missing a step. It occurred to him that he had fulfilled the little challenge he had set for himself that week: he had met and spoken with three new *lofan* in a single day.

Dinner that evening was curry chicken and potatoes, and Hoi Wing, famished from his labours, partook of three heaping helpings, shovelling the food into his mouth with his chopsticks non-stop and mumbling monosyllables in answer to the uncles' questions about his day.

"Farmboy's eating us right out of house and home," said Elder Uncle. "Our food budget's gone through the ceiling."

"He earned every bite today, making those deliveries in the Golden Li," said Second Uncle. "And he did it in pretty good time too. Did you have any troubles at all with those circuits?"

Hoi Wing kept his head down. He was tempted to tell the men about his encounters, but something inside wanted to keep it all private, especially his meeting with *Ah-Del*. Later that night, after work was done, Hoi Wing turned down a challenge from Second Uncle to play Chinese chess. Elder Uncle took up the gauntlet and immediately suggested they bet on the result: the loser would have to perform the washing duties of the winner.

As the laundrymen set up the board and discs, Hoi Wing descended to his bedroom, wanting to repair the broken clasp of his amulet (another debt he promised he would repay to Ratface—or had *Blah-dok* been the one who snapped the chain?). He also needed to make new notations to the map Second Uncle had given him.

Most of all, he wanted to consult his father's dictionary and decipher the beautiful *lofan*'s note: *Cordially yours, Miss Adele Primmons, Town Librarian*. From her pantomime, he was sure she had wanted to talk to him about reading and writing.

Hoi Wing found his mind wandering back to the young maid with the monstrous dogs, who had watched him fight Ratface. He hoped she had found him brave and unafraid of the bigger boy. She looked about his own age, and he wondered what circumstances had thrust her into the menial role of a domestic servant. What was her name? Again he wished he might have communicated with her.

On the map Second Uncle had given him, Hoi Wing extended the roads and back alleys he had explored. He placed an X at his encounter with *Blah-dok* and *Ah-Del* on St. Paul Street. With a tiny skull, he marked where he had battled Ratface. But then he printed the address of the fabulous mansion where he had seen the young maid. Last, he took his one coloured pencil and added a big red star to her home.

5

At dawn the next morning, Hoi Wing was lighting the copper boilers when Elder Uncle interrupted him.

"Leave that for now," he said. "Go and clean the backyard."

"Why? What happened?"

Elder Uncle plucked the box of matches from Hoi Wing's hand. "Just go and help your Second Uncle, will you?"

Puzzled, Hoi Wing passed through the kitchen and stepped out the back door. The morning air was bracing, and his breath fogged at his lips. He stood in the small yard where the men dried their wash in the summer, enclosed by a tall cedar fence of faded boards and rotted rails.

Second Uncle stood with a wheelbarrow and shovels near the wooden outhouse. The usually neat yard was littered with horse manure, putrid vegetables, and soggy newspapers.

"What happened here?" Hoi Wing wished he had grabbed his coat before coming outside.

Second Uncle chewed his toothpick grimly. "It's been months since the last time, but every once in a while someone dumps a load of garbage during the night. We put a padlock on our gate, but they always find a way to get in, or they throw it over the fence."

The man's voice was flat, and he spoke with casual indifference, but Hoi Wing could discern the tension of the muscles at his jaw. "But why?" he asked. "Who's doing this?"

"Very good question." Second Uncle shrugged. "Why do the *lofan* do anything? As for whom, we can only surmise it was the little gang of *dead-naughty* ghost children who live down the street. The ones who ring our doorbell in the evenings and run away. Or perhaps it was the group of little *demons* that seem to inhabit the laneway itself. The ones who throw pebbles at our windows or dirt on our laundry when we hang it out back. What do you think?"

Hoi Wing said nothing. He thought of the Cascade, with its delivery wagon and horse. Could Ratface be the culprit? Or might *Blah-dok* have had a hand in the hooliganism? Hoi Wing kept his suspicions to himself.

Second Uncle began to shovel the garbage from the beds of vegetables he tended every summer. "Take that shovel and work some of that manure into those flower beds next to the woodpile. We can turn the tables on these idiot *lofan*—what they think will repulse us will beautify our home next spring."

Hoi Wing took the other spade. The ground was not yet frozen, and he was able to mix the manure into the dark earth. "I never knew these were flower beds. What did you plant here? Roses?"

"Not roses. Your Elder Uncle planted peonies several years ago, and each summer the yard blooms with them. I've painted some of the blossoms. I'd be happy to show you later."

Elder Uncle had planted peonies? Hoi Wing shook his head at the incongruity of the idea. He remembered his mother loving flowers, and his father often delaying his dinner after a long day in the fields to tend the stalks of peonies outside their home in the swamp.

In the laundry's backyard, Hoi Wing shovelled manure into the wheelbarrow. Second Uncle dumped a load of refuse into the compost heap. The two worked steadily, and soon half the yard was cleared.

"I saw a green-uniformed constable in the street yesterday," Hoi Wing said. "Why can't we get the green-jackets to stop these hooligans from vandalizing our yard?"

Second Uncle lifted his eyebrows. "Young Man, did you not know those same green-jackets patrol the streets of Shanghai, Peking, Nanking, and even Hong Kong? Of course, they patrol on behalf of the accursed British, French, Russian, and Japanese occupiers who have built their 'Foreign Concessions' in our nation. Those areas where their laws are paramount and we find signs in what were once our own parks that read No Dogs or Chinamen Allowed."

"But I thought the green-jackets enforced the law and protected the people!"

Second Uncle laughed unpleasantly. "Whose laws do they enforce? Whose people do they protect? In China today, no *lofan* foreigner may be convicted by a Chinese court regardless of the crime he has committed against a Chinese citizen. A *lofan* may assault, rob, rape, kidnap, or even murder a Chinese man or woman on Chinese soil and fear no repercussion from the courts of our people."

Hoi Wing lifted another shovelful of debris from the ground, revealing a broken broomstick, melon rinds, rotting cabbage, and the decaying body of a small rodent. "But can't we get someone to help us here?"

Second Uncle wrinkled his nose at the stench. "Who's going to help us?"

∞

Long after the garbage had been cleared, Hoi Wing seethed. The injustice! The unfairness! It rankled that *lofan* police officers, sanctioned by the colonial invaders, permitted the abuse and assault of Chinese citizens in their own land.

In class, Hoi Wing remembered Teacher Lee railing against the British occupiers who had flooded China with opium for decades, condemning generations of Chinese to slow, wasting deaths. The Chinese defeats in the two Opium Wars and in the more recent rebellion led by the Boxers of the Righteous Society of Harmonious Fists had resulted in millions of Chinese deaths and the imposition of crippling financial penalties exacted by the colonial powers. "Imagine the audacity!" Ying the Scholar had shaken his head. "Being charged a fine because you fought to liberate your own country from foreign invaders!"

As the day progressed, Hoi Wing caught himself staring into the laundry's backyard, imagining booby traps he might set for future intruders. That vandals could so defile their yard with impunity was maddening. What could be done? He looked to the uncles, but both had returned to their work, seemingly nonplussed and not displaying outward signs of perturbation, although every once in a while Hoi Wing spied a nerve jump in Elder Uncle's jaw and a clenching of the man's heavy right fist.

The inequities tore at Hoi Wing's belly. Somehow, ten thousand *li* away from Drink the Waters Deeply, the magnitude of the transgressions occasioned upon his homeland and its people seemed more real and immediate. Close to twenty foreign nations had banded together to defeat the Chinese Boxers in the rebellion where they had charged machine guns with nothing more than their fists. "The poor, brave, misguided sods!" Ying the Scholar had commiserated, but he did not lay all the blame for China's woes at the feet of Western imperialists.

Hoi Wing's father had taught him that empires ebbed and flowed, and power was a wave that washed from one end of the earth to the other. The Middle Kingdom had grown complacent and arrogant, overly assured of its own superiority and culture. A succession of narcissistic emperors had turned their backs on the "barbarian" nations, too myopic to understand that Western nations had superseded China in many fields, not the least of which included the industrial and military sciences. "What one could see," Ying the Scholar had been fond of saying, "if one only opened one's eyes."

The revelation almost made Hoi Wing drop his paddle into his vat of laundry. Was this why his father had sent him to the West? Could this be what Ying had meant by "finding his way"? More and more his father's words, long relegated to the dustbin of his brain, were ringing in his mind. It was as if Eldest Great Auntie were shaking her bony finger at him once again as she curled her lip against the townsfolk in the village square: "One day you will understand who are the fools and who is the Scholar!"

The next day, Hoi Wing manned the drying chamber. The small room at the back of the laundry was criss-crossed with clotheslines, and wood fire braziers were set over the floor, burning haphazardly among the sheets and drying shirts.

As the day progressed, Hoi Wing fanned sheets and listened to the murmur of Second Uncle's conversations with customers at the front counter. Suddenly, he strained to make out the dulcet tones of a feminine voice. To whom was Second Uncle talking? Was Hoi Wing imagining it, or did she sound familiar?

The boy raced from the drying room, rushing to the front counter. He breached the curtain just as the front door swung shut. He glimpsed a tall, brown-haired woman striding down the street, and a tantalizing fragrance hung in the vestibule.

"Who was that?" he asked. "Who was she?"

"Well, well." Second Uncle gave Hoi Wing a sly smile. "That was a young woman from one of the *lofan* worship halls in town. You've made quite the impression, Young Man."

"What did she say?" Hoi Wing said, absolutely sure it had been *Ah-Del Plee-mon*, his rescuer from the street.

"She asked about you. She wanted to know your age, your relationship to us, and what you do here. Naturally, I told her as little as possible. These nosy *lofan*! But most of all she wanted—"

"What did she want?"

Second Uncle held up his hand. "Why don't we wait until your Elder Uncle gets home for dinner? I'll have to muddle over this myself."

"But—"

"Later. There's no need to talk at the moment. Now, don't you have more sheets to dry?"

At dinner, Hoi Wing could hardly remain seated. He picked at the main course (a bass stir-fried in ginger, garlic, and onions) as the men discussed the recent progress of their business plan.

Elder Uncle waved his chopsticks in frustration. "All of a sudden, I'm running into a wall. Since our initial success, it's as if someone's rallied the townsfolk against us. Even some of the contracts we've won with the hotels have been reneged."

Second Uncle plucked another morsel of bass from the serving plate.

"Maybe our old friend *Blah-dok* is up to his tricks again?"

"Did you say *Blah-dok*?" Hoi Wing asked, thinking of his encounter on the street. "I think I met him. A big *lofan* with a thick beard and a cane?"

"The same!" said Second Uncle. "But how did you cross paths with him so soon?"

"I only peeked at his motor car—but he took offence."

"Farmboy, you're sticking your big nose where it doesn't belong!" Elder Uncle thumped the table. "You need to concentrate on work, not sightseeing."

"Calm down, Big Brother. You can't blame the boy for simple curiosity. And *Blah-dok* has been our enemy since long before Hoi Wing joined us."

"But who is he, and what is his quarrel with us?" asked Hoi Wing.

Second Uncle sipped tea before speaking. "*Blah-dok* is a wealthy businessman who owns a popular brewery, hotels, spas—how the *lofan* love their healing waters!—and more recently even a chain of laundries, which of course compete directly with our own. But his enmity extends far beyond the bounds of simple commerce.

"His family originally immigrated to British Columbia, where his father spearheaded those first campaigns against our countrymen who had settled there after building the most murderous stretches of the railway that spans this country.

"*Blah-dok*'s father lobbied for the passage of the exclusion laws that prohibit us from bringing our wives and families here even today, as well as requiring all Chinese to pay a five-hundred-dollar head tax on entry. His son, whom we have come to know in St. Catharines, carries that grudge against us even now.

"The younger *Blah-dok* heads the Asiatic Exclusion League here and conveniently forgets that he himself is an immigrant. They hate all new-comers but have a special distaste for us. Despite his wealth, he somehow fancies himself a champion of the common man, denouncing us as cheap labour and strikebreakers."

"Now you understand why you shouldn't antagonize him," Elder Uncle growled.

An image flashed in Hoi Wing's memory, and before the startled men could say another word, he darted down to the basement, where he rummaged through his shelf of books. Tucked within the pages of his father's dictionary was the slip of newspaper he had saved from the outhouse.

Hoi Wing hurried back upstairs and unfolded the faded newsprint sheet beside the plate of bass on the table. The men studied the photograph accompanying the article on the front page of the *Herald*'s August 16, 1913, edition. There was no mistaking the large-bodied man with a ruff of dark beard and a cane, oozing self-importance.

"*Blah-dok*, the devil himself!" Second Uncle mumbled under his breath. "But what does the article say about him?"

WELL-KNOWN ST. CATHARINES ENTREPRENEUR
ADDRESSES CITY COUNCIL

The President of the city's Chamber of Commerce, Jonathan Braddock of 99 Cherry Street, spoke at length to business leaders and members of St. Catharines town council yesterday, advocating the creation of a new blueprint for the growth and cultivation of our fair city.

"St. Catharines is growing in leaps and bounds. We are at a crossroads in our development as an international hub of business, industry, agriculture, and enterprise," Braddock said. "We are uniquely situated to service markets both east and west, north and south. To take full advantage of our situation, we must ensure that our citizenry are well-served as well, and to do that, we must take more of a hand in the planning of the direction and growth of our municipality.

"For far too long, we have let the city expand in willy-nilly fashion. The continued lack of direction has allowed certain neighbourhoods to be invaded by miscreants, hoboes, and degenerates. Even worse, we have also seen a recent influx of foreigners, immigrants, ne'er-do-wells, and other undesirables. To create a prosperous future for all, well-run businesses are not only desired, but necessary. We need an action plan to make the city more welcome to the right kind of enterprise. I propose that we create a secondary council specializing in the growth and expansion of our business core to ensure the prosperity of our citizens

(continued on page 9)

For a time, the three laundrymen gnawed at the words, and it was Hoi Wing, having gone through much of the piece with the aid of his dictionary, who deciphered the article for the other two.

"This surpasses even my worst imaginings," said Elder Uncle. "Our enemy seeks to impose his will on what businesses may operate within the city itself!"

"Thank the Ancestors he's not on the city's council," Second Uncle pointed out.

"At least, not yet," Elder Uncle muttered.

Hoi Wing remembered the fierce animal gleam in the man's eyes. "He was going to strike me with his cane, but I was helped by a *lofan* woman."

"Ah, that reminds me," said Second Uncle. "That same woman came in today to ask about our young apprentice. She was a church lady."

Hoi Wing sat up. This was what he had been waiting for!

"Another of their elder grannies?" Elder Uncle gave a wry smile. "Did she want to shovel their *Jesus-ghost* down his heathen throat?"

"No elder granny this one," Second Uncle answered. "She was young and spry and pretty. She runs an English for Foreigners class, and wants to give Hoi Wing *lofan* lessons every Thursday night at the worship hall. Seven to nine o'clock sharp."

A lofan class! Hoi Wing's mouth fell open. He could hardly believe his good fortune. *So that's what she was trying to tell him!*

Elder Uncle waved his soup spoon dismissively. "Come on, Little Brother. That's just a ploy to convert him to their inane beliefs. Don't you remember the missionaries back home? The ones that dressed up in our clothes and wore their hair in queues? 'A bowl of rice if you can memorize this Bible verse!'"

"Of course I remember, but I think this woman genuinely wants to help Hoi Wing."

"And what would he do with all that learning? They aren't letting any of our children into their schools. Do you think they'd ever let him work in their offices and businesses? He'd be like the dancing bear in one of their summer fairs. Or the dog that walks on its hind legs. It's a waste of time for him to learn the barbarian tongue."

"Wait!" Hoi Wing broke in. "What are you saying?"

Elder Uncle shook his head. "Farmboy, with our new clients and *Blah-dok* attacking us again, I need you working in the laundry—every minute, every hour, every day."

"You're not making sense." Hoi Wing stood up. "You can't just refuse—"

"Sit down!" Elder Uncle answered. "I've just refused your request. That's my final word."

"Final word? No, I want . . . I need those classes!" Hoi Wing struck the table with his fist, knocking over Second Uncle's teacup.

For an instant, the uncles sat stunned. Then Second Uncle grabbed his teacup as a dark stain spread over the tablecloth. Elder Uncle stabbed his finger at Hoi Wing. "See what comes of your impudence? Now you'll have to wash that tablecloth."

Hoi Wing sputtered and looked at Second Uncle. "Say something! I thought you were on my side."

Second Uncle dabbed at his pants with a napkin. "Young Man, you're shouting at your employer. He's the senior partner here, and you must abide by his decision."

Flabbergasted, Hoi Wing stared at the two men. A thousand angry words bubbled up in his mind, but he sank into his chair, clenching his teeth. He wanted to scream or tear out his hair or throw his rice bowl against the wall.

"The subject is closed." Elder Uncle reached for the plate of fish, and the men continued their dinner. For a time, there was no sound in the laundry but the click of chopsticks.

"Big Brother, this fish is really exceptional—" said Second Uncle.

Hoi Wing stood. "I've had enough of dinner! And the two of you. I'm getting those lessons no matter what you say!" He crossed the room to the basement door and slammed it as he went down the stairs.

6

Hoi Wing spoke to neither man the next day, nor the day after that, although on Saturday evening he noticed that Elder Uncle had cooked soy sauce chicken and potatoes, one of Hoi Wing's favourite dishes. Second Uncle made sure he got two drumsticks and a wing.

On Sunday morning, Hoi Wing woke early and came upstairs as Second Uncle was boiling water in the kitchen.

"Tea?" Second Uncle said.

Hoi Wing shook his head and took a flask from a shelf. He grabbed a tin of condensed milk and a pair of green apples from a crate. With a spoon, he scraped yesterday's hard rice out of a dish into a tin and fastened the lid. He threw everything into a sack he tied to his bamboo pole.

"Why are you up so early?" Second Uncle poured water into the teapot.

"It's Sunday, isn't it?"

Second Uncle nodded.

"I'm free today, aren't I?"

"Yes, of course."

Hoi Wing went into the main room. The early morning sky was leaden, and the street was empty. Usually he slept in on his day off, but he had woken early, filled with resolve because of Elder Uncle's decision about the *lofan* classes.

He was putting on his coat when Elder Uncle came down the attic ladder, yawning and scratching his belly. Second Uncle entered the room. "Stop a minute. Where are you going?"

Hoi Wing was tempted to ignore the question. Despite everything his father had taught him, it seemed a man could be rude or unpleasant whenever he wished, so long as he was ready to accept the consequences. Hoi Wing was certainly working like a man, and now he would be rude whenever it pleased him. "I'm going out for the day."

"With a sack of provisions over your shoulder?" Second Uncle asked.

"You said it was my day off. I'm going to explore the town and the forests."

Elder Uncle cocked his eyebrow and gestured at the window. "Anyone going into the forests today had better be prepared. I see a lot of grey clouds scudding fast, and my hip has been groaning at me for two days. It's still early December, but this is the Gold Mountain. There'll be snow before nightfall—do you hear me?—a heavy accumulation on the ground before the day is done."

Snow? Hoi Wing placed his hand on the doorknob. "I'm going out now, and you're not stopping me."

"No one's stopping you, Farmboy," answered Elder Uncle. "You're a grown man, and Sunday's your day off. You can do as you please. Go out into the streets. Visit Rosie and her girlies in the Foreign Quarter. You can even hike into the deep woods and freeze to death in a blizzard if you insist. But I don't like to lose my hired help, especially when I've invested so much time and money in training."

"Are you sure you know what you're doing?" Second Uncle looked concerned.

Hoi Wing felt a twinge of trepidation. Was a Gold Mountain blizzard really on its way, or was Elder Uncle just trying to intimidate him again? And who was Rosie in the Foreign Quarter? He glanced outside, where the sky was just lightening. All the stories Hoi Wing had heard about frozen birds dropping from the sky and piss freezing on its way out of one's body returned to him.

"I'm not afraid, no matter what you say," said Hoi Wing.

"Wait. Don't go yet." Second Uncle climbed up to the attic. In a few minutes he returned with a battered canvas rucksack on a wood frame. "Take this pack and gear with you. It belonged to your Elder Uncle when he hunted gold in the great high north."

Hoi Wing looked at Elder Uncle.

"Go ahead." The man shrugged and lit a cigarette. "I'm not using it any time soon."

Hoi Wing ran his hands over the rucksack, with its pockets and flaps mended, patched, and stained (*with blood?*) in many places. The beaten straps were of thick leather, and the buckles, tabs, and rings were rusted and well-worn.

"I carried that pack in the harshest terrain I have ever known," said Elder Uncle. "Minus fifty degrees in blinding snow squalls. Across chasms whose bottoms I could not see. Fully loaded, the pack weighed ninety-five pounds, but I could still break trail up a mountain path faster than most—"

"Through snowdrifts up to your chest and roped to the next man?" Hoi Wing interrupted.

"Huh?" Elder Uncle looked surprised, and Second Uncle threw back his head in laughter. The older man scowled at his brother.

"Just check inside the bag, Farmboy. Your life may depend on it. You should have a woollen blanket, sweater, hat, gloves, and socks to go with your boots. Tinderbox, hatchet, compass, tin cup, pot, and spoon. I assume you have the brains to pack your own knife. Stay on the road. Mark the path behind you. Without a compass, a fool who strays into the woods will turn around twice and never come out. And a man will perish, wet or unsheltered, in a single night at this time of year. Most importantly, return before dark. If in doubt, stack your fists between the sun and the horizon. You have one hour of daylight for every fist."

Hoi Wing felt his pants for the pocket knife he always carried. Then he rummaged through the bag for the gear Elder Uncle had described. Finally, he transferred everything from his own bag into the rucksack, and lifted it over his shoulders. The weight was good, and he imagined himself ploughing through glacial snowfields, breathing the clear, rarefied air of the high mountains of the great north. "Thank you."

"Take this." Second Uncle thrust a jar of peanut oil, spiced with hot peppers and garlic, into his hands along with a package wrapped in brown waxed paper. It was the leftovers from last night's chicken, rice, and potatoes.

"Did you hear me?" added Elder Uncle. "Winter is coming. Be back before dark!"

Hoi Wing nodded and left the laundry. For the first time in two days, he did not slam the door. Somehow he had thought there might be more objection to his departure this morning.

Outside, the street was coated in frost, and ice crusted the water in a horse trough on the walkway. His nostrils clenched against the bite of the wind. By the time he had walked twenty-five yards, his hands were chilled, and he knew the day, although bright, was colder than any he had yet encountered in the New World. He searched Elder Uncle's pack for the hat and gloves. As he pulled on the woollen garments, he felt a moment of doubt, but it was too late to turn back. He was surprised and grateful the uncles had lent him the equipment. Still, he knew if he returned now, Elder Uncle would never let him live it down.

With no destination in mind, Hoi Wing turned up his collar and increased the length of his stride. For a while, he followed his feet, heading westward on St. Paul Street. As he hiked through the sleeping city, he saw no one, although he surprised a raccoon nosing through a pile of refuse outside the wheelwright's. On a whim, he turned south down a narrow laneway, which soon degenerated into a long, twisting path, overgrown with weeds, thistles, brittle bushes, and bent saplings.

The ground was frozen and the ever-increasing slope a hazard, but he descended cautiously toward the canal that cut through the city. He emerged from the underbrush and approached the embankment. At the edge of the dark water, he halted and scoured the shore for flat stones. The chill of the air was a slap against his lungs, but he smelled fish, and gulls wheeled in the early morning sky.

As he cocked his arm to skip a stone, he saw an animal nosing amongst a mass of bulrushes at the water's edge. It was bigger than a cat but smaller than a dog. Its tail was a feather duster of reddish-brown fur, and its ears were cocked and high. The animal raised its tawny head and spotted Hoi Wing.

A fox! Hoi Wing held himself like a statue. A dozen bedtime tales Fourth Auntie had recounted returned to his mind. In the legends he loved best, Fox was a shape-shifter who assumed the form of a beautiful damsel to seduce unwary farmers and woodcutters. Did they have such tales in the West?

Second Uncle had told him the *lofan* considered foxes vermin as they often devastated backyard chicken coops or laid waste to rabbit hutches. Farmers trapped and shot them on sight. Rich *lofan* rode them down on horseback with packs of hounds.

Hoi Wing studied the little beast. Her lithe lines—she was so beautiful, she had to be female—and feline grace seemed incompatible with that rapacious reputation. Her head was delicate, and her jaws curved gently in a semblance of a grin. How could such a creature be so maligned? For a magical moment, boy and beast locked gazes, each seeking to intuit the other's intention.

Suddenly, the fox pounced. She arced through the air, landed, and snapped at something between her paws. Hoi Wing glimpsed a small rodent body thrashing in her jaws, and then, with a flick of her head, the fox broke her prey's neck.

So graceful was the strike that Hoi Wing's mind had registered only a golden blur. Then he blinked as the creature, bearing its prize in its muzzle, dashed up the bank and vanished into the underbrush.

Hoi Wing rubbed his eyes, feeling a strange kinship with the little hunter. She too was a loner, braving the very edge of a hostile world, filled with cruel dogs and crueller men who would hunt and skin her on sight. That such a beast could live and even thrive in this environment gave him a much-needed lift. With a last look at the water, he turned from the canal, stepping more lightly than he had in days.

Back on St. Paul Street, Hoi Wing walked quickly through the downtown core until he paused before the wide stone bridge at the western edge of town. Below him in the canal were moored ships and boats, some awaiting tarring and refitting. He adjusted the weight of his pack and crossed the bridge to the opposite bank.

On the other side of the canal, houses became fewer. Rough undergrowth and low trees filled the ever-widening spaces between them. Hoi

Wing passed farms, vineyards, and fallow fields. Canneries and ware-houses. A foundry and an ironworks. All was quiet; no one worked on Sunday morning.

As Hoi Wing hiked on, the cloying sweetness of fermenting hops wafted to him on the breeze. He paused before a cluster of brick buildings, two and three storeys high, topped with orange slate tiles and tall chimneys. Motor trucks and wagons were parked in a neat row. A large sign read BRADDOCK'S BREWERIES—HOME OF BRADDY'S BEST BEERS.

So this was the heart of their enemy's empire! Hoi Wing scanned the grounds as his hand went to his hip where he had been thrown to the sidewalk. What an opportunity for revenge! He lifted a palm-sized rock from the road and threw it as hard as he could. The missile sailed through the air and struck the brick wall with a solid thump. Wiping his hands with satisfaction, Hoi Wing resumed his journey.

He trekked onward, and by mid-morning the ever-narrowing road grew marred by pits and rutted with the tracks of horse and wagon. Trees lifted their skeletal arms on either side, and vast fallow tracts, interspersed with long stretches of mature oak, birch, and ash, stretched ahead. All thoughts of Braddock faded, replaced by the simple pleasure of being outdoors and the thrill of exploration.

As Hoi Wing came upon a wide field, a man's voice drifted over the air. Through the trees, he spotted a troop of young men and boys drilling as a duo of mounted officers cantered amongst them. Hoi Wing bent low and crawled to a sprawling oak. Unseen behind the tree, he shrugged off his rucksack. The chill of the morning had dissipated, and his neck and back were drenched with sweat.

He edged closer as a sergeant-at-arms barked commands in a brisk cadence. This man was almost apoplectic as he berated his charges. Few of the recruits had uniforms, and no more than a half-dozen carried rifles.

Even to Hoi Wing's eyes, many of the weapons were ancient. The rest of the men wore overalls and drilled with shovels, rakes, or brooms. Some looked no more than two or three years his senior, and they stumbled about in a comical attempt at marching in unison, turning to their right, to their left, about-facing, forward-facing, and then reversing again, all to the staccato commands of the exasperated drill sergeant.

One of the left-footed recruits lurching back and forth looked familiar. His ears were large and jutting. Hoi Wing blinked in the sunlight. *It was Ratface!* But what was he doing with this group? And could that be his younger brother, tripping over his feet behind the older boy?

Why were they drilling? Were they mobilizing, or was this merely some form of pageantry? Hoi Wing remembered his father talking about the ebb and flow of power and the rapacious hunger of the Western imperialists. Was an army being raised? If so, this regiment was a sorry excuse.

"Ho! You there!" the sergeant-at-arms called out.

Hoi Wing started. Some in the little brigade had spotted him and were pointing in his direction. One of the mounted officers brandished his baton, and the other wheeled his animal toward him. Hoi Wing ducked back and threw his pack over his shoulders. He broke into a dash, stooping under low branches and leaping rotted logs. Running blindly, he crashed through the undergrowth.

The voices of the men and the hoofbeats of their horses faded. A stabbing pain erupted in Hoi Wing's side, and he clutched his ribs as he slowed to a half-walking, half-jogging step. Back on the road, he checked over his shoulder. He heard nothing, but only when he could limp no farther did he allow himself to collapse against the bole of a tree.

Winded, he bent over his knees. Despite having done nothing wrong, he had panicked at the thought of being trampled by horsemen. Tugging his canteen from his pack, he drank deeply. When the stitch in his side subsided, he took his bearings with Elder Uncle's compass. Still wary, he set out once more, marching at his best speed.

An hour later, the sun had reached its zenith. Hoi Wing saw no more soldiers. He found himself passing wide swaths of land that had been husbanded with long rows of fruit trees. At a fork in the road, he skirted an orchard and entered a field where the crop had been ploughed back into the earth. A line of trees had been planted as a windbreak, and there he stopped for lunch.

Hoi Wing knelt beneath a tree and opened Elder Uncle's pack. He spread the woollen blanket over the ground and drank from his flask. The noonday sky was clear (*so much for Elder Uncle's know-it-all weather prognostications*), and he rummaged for his tin of rice, leftover chicken, and apples.

At the bottom of the rucksack, he discovered an old pair of binoculars with one lens cracked, and he lifted them to his eyes, panning across the field. The magnification of the glass rendered the distant hedgerow in sharp detail. Hoi Wing wondered what vistas Elder Uncle had viewed with this instrument on his quest for gold in the Far North.

Then he slipped the binoculars into the pack and turned his full attention to his lunch. He ate ravenously, scraping every grain of hard rice with his chopsticks, wolfing down the chicken, and chewing his apples until there was nothing left but dark seeds and stems. With the tinderbox and kindling he gathered from the windbreak, he lit a small fire and poured a can of condensed milk into his pot. When the milk had boiled, he sat against the tree and sipped from his cup. Then he drew out a pen, ink, and a sheet of paper. He commenced his letter to his father.

He had been composing the missive in his mind for two nights, but now he struggled to put words to paper. What should he say? He was sick of the laundry and the mind-numbing toil. He hated the long hours, the isolation, and everything Elder Uncle had thrown at him, but that was not wholly surprising. It was growing up ignorant and illiterate that was unacceptable. He could not live a life where he would learn no more than how to darn socks or starch shirts.

Dear Father,

How do you and Little Mei-Mei fare at home? Has the harvest been good? I hope your rice bowl is deep and full.

Here in the new land, I have found a wondrous opportunity I did not expect. A kindly lofan woman I met has offered to teach me lofan, for two hours every week. I have promised my employer that I will make up the lost time on my free day, but he is refusing me this chance to study. I know this will cost you much face, but I cannot accept this answer. It will doom me to grow up illiterate and stupid. I know you would not wish me this fate, and you will understand why I must leave this place and find other work.

Father, please don't worry. I will find other employment here and will continue to send my remittance each month. You and Eldest Auntie can still count on the money coming regularly. I will not rest until . . .

For a time, Hoi Wing laboured at his composition, employing his best calligraphy and seeking the appropriate tone of contrition, resolve, and determination. He wrote steadily, telling his father about the uncles' defeatist and casual acceptance of the vandalism and venom they faced daily. For all Elder Uncle's bombastic threats, his actions marked him as a coward, and Hoi Wing took great pleasure in denouncing him as such.

When Hoi Wing's little campfire burned down, the cold began to permeate his body. He had laid his pen down when he heard the distant baying of hounds. The sound emanated from the east, and he could

discern the pounding of hooves and a cacophony of horns. *The soldiers!*
Were they coming for him? Panic gripped Hoi Wing, and he tossed his
belongings into the rucksack. He ducked into the trees as a troop of ten
horsemen and almost twice as many dogs burst out of the underbrush at
the distant end of the field.

They were not the militia he had spied that morning, but riders in
tailored red-and-brown jackets, pith helmets, and tall leather boots.
Their mounts were as impressive as the ones he had seen earlier, and the
hounds were all jaws, teeth, and slobber. For a while, the men milled
about on their animals as the long-eared canines barked and growled.
One black-and-white dog lifted its leg against a tree stump. There was
something familiar about the tall, bearded rider who seemed to be leading the group.

Were they hunting? Or was it just exercise? None of the men carried
weapons, but the apparent seriousness of the endeavour told Hoi Wing
this was no simple Sunday morning pleasure ride. He pulled the binoculars from his bag and scanned the mélange of man, horse, and dog.
As he adjusted the focus, the image of the leader fused into clarity. The
craggy face, fierce eyebrows, and beard were unmistakable. It was *Blah-
dok* himself!

Then a large, deep-chested hound caught scent of the prey. Baying
and calling, it sprang from the others. Its packmates followed as *Blah-
dok* brought his crop down on his mount. For an instant, chaos ensued.
A horse stumbled against another, and a man lost his helmet. Then two
riders lifted horns to their lips, and the horsemen fell into a clumsy formation. Even from such a distance, he could hear the pounding of hooves
as the hunters galloped after the hounds.

Not twenty yards from where Hoi Wing sheltered, a tiny beast burst
from hiding, revealing a flash of red-brown coat and a delicate, catlike

head. He gasped as the fox passed him in a blur and darted through the windbreak into the adjacent field. *Go! Go! Go!* Silently, Hoi Wing urged his little friend to greater speed (of course, he could not be sure she was the same creature he had seen earlier that morning, but he was convinced she had to be, as they shared fates, or at the least a common path). Then he hurled himself into the trees as the dogs plunged after the fox.

Hoi Wing buried himself in the dead leaves as the horsemen neared. For a terrifying moment, it seemed they might trample him beneath their hooves, but they halted at the windbreak. "Go around! Go around!" *Blah-dok*'s voice was almost preternaturally loud as the man brandished his crop.

The fox hunters spurred their mounts and galloped to an opening through the trees. The horns sounded again and again. Hoi Wing rose from hiding as the riders raced after the dogs. He watched them vanish into the next windbreak. Silence fell over the day once more.

Hoi Wing returned to what was left of his little fire. Despite the fox's courage, he doubted she had much chance of escape. The sobering thought brought him back to his task, and he gathered more wood and heated a pot of tea. Once it was properly steeped, he filled his tin cup and drank.

Hoi Wing fished his writing implements from his rucksack. Seated on his blanket, he continued his message. The wind rose, and the temperature sank. When his letter was finally completed, his fingers were numb as twigs, but he felt great relief. The deed done, he folded his missive into his pocket. He would post it tomorrow and let the uncles know he would be leaving as soon as possible.

He had repacked the rucksack when he heard the cry of the hounds once more. He jerked the binoculars from the pack and lifted the worn barrels to his eyes. Sure enough, the canines were heading across the field again. The huntsmen were not in sight, and neither was the fox, but the little beast must have doubled back to elude her pursuers. Jumping up and down, he began to shout, "This way! Hurry! Hurry!"

The hounds were strung out in a ragged line, but they seemed to be closing. Now he could make out the fox in the eyepieces of the binoculars. Eyes and tongue protruding, she raced before a cyclone of canine fury. The animal was clearly spent and headed straight toward him. He had to help her!

Hoi Wing grabbed the jar of peanut oil from his pack and splashed it over the blanket of dead leaves in the windbreak. He kicked in the burning coals of his fire. The wind fanned the hot ashes like a billows, and there was a whoosh of heat as the spiced oil ignited. Fire climbed the saplings like monkeys on vines. Pungent smoke rose in a greasy smudge. A gust of wind whipped the brush fire higher, and branches began to crackle and snap.

Hoi Wing retreated, his eyes tearing and his cheeks feeling sunburned. The fox raced past, not ten feet away. He grabbed his pack and ran, just as the riders broke into sight at the far end of the field. When the hounds neared the burning windbreak, their pace faltered, and their rough claws skidded in the dry topsoil. One dog almost went head over paws into the flames. Barking, yelping, and whining, the pack came to a confused halt. None would pass the fire, and the scent of the fox was camouflaged in the miasma of acrid smoke.

Hoi Wing reached the shelter of the trees at the side of the road and threw himself to the ground. *Blah-dok* was the first huntsman at the windbreak, jerking back the reins of his horse and dismounting. Others pulled up behind, including the Master of the Hounds. He was an older rider with a lined face and a grey-peppery beard, but he leapt from his horse with the ease of a man half his age. "Come, Alfie! Daisy, to me now! You too, Bella!" He began to leash his animals.

Last to arrive was a young man whose facial hair was trimmed to a goat's tuft. Swaying precariously in his saddle, he gripped the reins with tight fists. Curly dark hair spilled from the edges of his helmet, and he almost toppled from his horse as he dismounted. Rushing to the windbreak, he stamped at the flames with his boots.

From his hiding place, Hoi Wing lifted the binoculars and studied *Blah-dok*. A wormlike vein pulsed at the man's temple, and flecks of spittle clung to his beard. *Blah-dok* dug through the ashes of Hoi Wing's campfire with his boot, kicking the charred rocks over the ground. Then he looked up and scanned the woods as though he could burn the forest with his gaze.

Hoi Wing held his breath. Even beneath the trees, he felt like a rabbit hunted by an eagle. A sudden mad exhilaration gripped him. He wanted to leap from hiding and taunt his nemesis. *It was me, you demon-bastard! It's me, Hoi Wing! I spoiled your hunt! I saved my friend the fox!*

Without thinking, Hoi Wing half rose from his crouch. Through the binoculars, he realized *Blah-dok* was looking right at him! For the second time that day, Hoi Wing locked eyes with another mind (this one far more malevolent than the first), and then he dived to the forest floor as *Blah-dok* shouted.

When Hoi Wing peeked through the bushes, *Blah-dok* was pulling the Master of the Hounds in Hoi Wing's direction. A half-dozen dogs strained at the leashes in the older man's hands. Four more animals sniffed at his legs. *Blah-dok* pointed at Hoi Wing's position, but the other man shook his head. They were joined by the young man with the unruly hair. For a time, the three seemed to argue. Frustrated, *Blah-dok* tried to uncollar one of the dogs, but the Master of the Hounds tugged the animal away.

The Master of the Hounds beckoned to the third man, and the two of them turned toward their horses. *Blah-dok* shook his head. He gestured repeatedly at Hoi Wing's position, but many of the riders were already in their saddles, their intention evident in their posture.

As the huntsmen began to move off, *Blah-dok* scattered the ashes of the campfire with another kick. Hoi Wing smiled as he watched the other's frustration, but then *Blah-dok* bent and plucked something shiny and green from the blackened stones. Hoi Wing gasped as his hand went to his throat. It was his jade amulet!

Now it was *Blah-dok*'s turn to gloat. Grinning broadly, he held the gold chain before him like a prize, as if daring its owner to retrieve it. Hoi Wing gritted his teeth and forced himself to remain hidden. How could he have been so stupid? He was sure he had repaired the clasp! Now he had lost Eldest Great Auntie's charm to his arch-enemy.

The Master of the Hounds called from his horse, and *Blah-dok* tucked the amulet into his jacket. The man with the goatee clambered awkwardly onto his mount. Without waiting for either man, *Blah-dok* leapt onto his horse and spurred away. For an instant, the two remaining men looked at each other, and then the Master of the Hounds galloped off as though he had been born to the saddle. The third man straightened his helmet and took a last look in Hoi Wing's direction before following the others as best he could.

The troop rode off, and the horns sounded a long, mournful note. When the riders and their dogs had cleared the field, Hoi Wing rose from his hiding place. Dead leaves and thistles clung to his clothes, and he brushed them off with his hands. He slaked his thirst from his canteen.

The wind swept through the trees, and Hoi Wing shivered, his back soaked with sweat. He lifted his pack onto his shoulders. The temperature was falling, and the euphoria of disrupting *Blah-dok*'s hunt had evaporated, replaced with the despondency of losing his lucky amulet to the man. How would he ever get it back?

Stacking his fists beneath the sun, Hoi Wing estimated he had less than two hours of daylight. Weary and bruised, he had a long way to go on blistered feet, but if he walked steadily, he would be within city limits before nightfall. For a moment, he wondered if saving the little fox had been worth the sacrifice. Then he commenced the long hike back.

An hour later, on the road, something white and downy began to tumble through the treetops. Startled, Hoi Wing lifted his head. All around him feathers drifted downward against a slate-grey sky. He gasped. *Snow! This was snow!* A snowflake planted an icy kiss on his cheek. Another anointed his forehead. He licked his lips and caught a third on his tongue. *The Gold Mountain winter had finally arrived!* Then he spun on his heels, laughing and shouting like a madman. How did Elder Uncle do it? He'd been right again.

7

The next morning, Hoi Wing woke to find tendrils of ice on his basement window. Ice crystals had formed in a glass of water left on his dresser. When he came upstairs, he pressed his face against the big window and stared into a curtain of wind-whipped snow. The street was buried. A horse trough was an unrecognizable mound. Across the road, the contours of roofs, dormers, and chimneys were melded into a single glacial sheet.

"This is it." Second Uncle stood beside him. "That real Gold Mountain winter you've been waiting for."

"It's beautiful," Hoi Wing whispered.

Second Uncle grimaced. "You'll say different when you're lugging fifty pounds of sheets out there."

A horse and dray appeared, hauling a heavy load of milk churns from the countryside. Grey hairs lightened the blinkered beast's muzzle, and its bony back and withers were coated with wet snow. Steam plumed from its nostrils as it struggled to find purchase on the roadway. The farmer had wrapped himself in a woollen blanket, and a hat and scarf hid all but his eyes and nose. He disembarked to throw his weight against the back wheel. His feet flew from beneath him, and he disappeared into the powder.

"Good thing you kept your little hike short yesterday." Second Uncle headed toward the kitchen. "We wouldn't have found your bones until next spring."

Good thing indeed. Hoi Wing thought of the letter he had penned the day before. He had not posted it. Instead, he had slipped it into the rusty tool box in the basement. He would write his father a different letter. And he wouldn't mention leaving. Not yet, at least. Where would he go? When he set out yesterday morning, he had a vague notion that he might just keep placing one foot ahead of the other until he came to the next village. Now he realized how foolish that idea had been.

He wondered how his little friend of the woods was faring. What did wild beasts do in a storm of such magnitude? He hoped his fox was sheltering in a dry den, safe from threats, meteorological or human. In any case, the memory of spoiling his enemy's hunt warmed Hoi Wing's heart. If only he had not lost his amulet.

Outside, the farmer emerged from the snow like some beast-man of northern legend. He gripped the tackle and floundered to the horse's harness. No matter how the man tugged, the animal would not budge. Hoi Wing went to help Second Uncle with breakfast.

As the storm raged, Hoi Wing was assigned ironing duty. For the first time, he was tasked with handling delicates and preferred customers. Cuffs, nurses' caps, bankers' and barristers' wingtip collars. Items that would singe at the barest touch. As Second Uncle hovered nervously, Hoi Wing studied the two-, five-, and ten-pound irons in their metal sleeves, baking over the pot-bellied stove.

"Check the temperature, check the temperature." Second Uncle fingered an atomizer.

"I'm checking, I'm checking!" Hoi Wing reached for the first of the five-pound irons.

"Remember what I said."

"I remember, Uncle!"

Hoi Wing could smell the heat radiating from the iron. Temperature was everything. Red-hot would sear even the roughest fabric. An easy-to-grip handle was too cool. And the in-between was oh so difficult to judge. The iron had to be uncomfortable to hold, and it could never rest, not even for an instant. The trick was to spit on the polished surface. If the spittle vanished in an angry hiss, the cotton would blacken and burn. But if it leapt and danced before disappearing, several passes of the iron's obdurate weight would render a wrinkled garment as smooth as a pan of ice.

Hoi Wing spread the shirt over the ironing plank. It belonged to Thick-Moustache Man, one of the laundry's most loyal customers. Although the shirt was well-worn, Hoi Wing had washed it himself, and he felt a surprising stab of pride that his labour had rendered it as white and luminous as anything in the town's finest haberdasheries.

Elder Uncle came in. He had said little when Hoi Wing returned the rucksack earlier, and for his part Hoi Wing had told the uncles nothing about his latest encounter with *Blah-dok*. Instead, he acted as though his whole adventure in the forest had been little more than a walk through nearby Montebello Park.

Now Elder Uncle held a half-dozen shirts and pants folded over his forearm. "Here are some alterations jobs for Hoi Wing—"

Second Uncle shushed him. "He's about to iron this shirt."

Hoi Wing lifted a five-pounder and scrutinized its flat underbelly.

It possessed a comforting heft, and through the padded grip he could feel the heat. This was the perfect temperature. Holding the iron, he closed the distance until it was a hair's breadth from the waiting shirt. Second Uncle leaned over his shoulder. Elder Uncle swallowed. Hoi Wing pressed down.

"Ayah!" shouted Second Uncle as a wisp of smoke rose from the fabric.

"You've burned it!" Elder Uncle clutched Hoi Wing's shoulder.

"Oh no!" Hoi Wing jerked the iron away. Frantic, he grabbed the atomizer and dowsed the scorch mark. Aghast, he stared at the triangular imprint seared over the lapel. Hoi Wing slapped his forehead. How could he have been so careless! Would Thick-Moustache Man's patronage be lost?

"Second Uncle, Elder Uncle, I'm sorry. I didn't mean it. I was sure the iron was cool enough."

Hoi Wing looked up shamefacedly and saw a smile tugging at the corners of Second Uncle's mouth. Elder Uncle had turned away, but his big shoulders were shaking.

"What's so funny?" Hoi Wing asked.

The brothers could restrain themselves no longer. Elder Uncle threw back his head and laughed uncontrollably. Second Uncle guffawed until his eyes teared. "It's no customer's shirt." His toothpick fell from his lips. "It's just one of my old ones. I was going to use it for a rag."

Elder Uncle pounded Second Uncle's back. "Do you see the boy's face? Whiter than a *lofan*'s!"

"What's the lesson you learned?" Second Uncle brandished the atomizer. "Always moisten the fabric first!"

"You two *dead-crazy no-brains*! I thought I burned a customer's garment!" Hoi Wing thrust the iron into its sleeve and blew on his fingers. The uncles retreated into the backrooms, still laughing and chuckling.

Muttering, Hoi Wing went to the icebox and soothed his hand with some ice chips. He rummaged in the first aid box for the tiger balm and smeared the ochre gel over his palm and fingers. The amused voices of the older men were audible from the next room. The burned shirt lay on the ironing board, the blackened triangle a glaring indictment of his negligence. He tossed it into the rag bin. "Not funny! Not funny!" he called out.

Only after a cup of tea did he allow himself a wry smile. It was then he realized he had been made the butt of the very first joke played upon him by the uncles. And it had been pretty funny.

Another day passed. As the blizzard continued to batter St. Catharines, Hoi Wing huddled by the stoves, dancing, stamping his feet, and rubbing his hands. He asked again if he might borrow from the racks of unclaimed winter wear, but the uncles were adamant that the laundryman's code required them to safeguard customers' garments untouched until their return, whenever that might be.

Nevertheless, as the snowdrifts grew ever higher, Second Uncle relented and found him an old duffle coat, but Elder Uncle said he would charge Hoi Wing for its rental: one penny per week.

On Wednesday, Hoi Wing awoke to a strange silence. It took him a moment to realize the wind had died. The basement was dark, and the windows were sheathed in snow. He went upstairs to stoke the boilers. The laundry was quiet, but when he peered out of the big window, he saw the uncles buried to their waists in snow, shovelling a path before the front door. At the livery stables, three men worked to clear the gates. Even the blind woman who sewed gloves was sweeping a broom over her porch. Hoi Wing went to light the boilers, more than grateful he wasn't scheduled to be outside today. He'd let St. Catharines dig itself out first.

After breakfast, Hoi Wing cut little squares of linen and stitched them onto socks. Then he marked each little square with indelible ink for identification. He struggled with the needle, poking his fingers again and again. They were nearing the lunch hour, and Hoi Wing's stomach was already growling.

Second Uncle entered the room. "We have an urgent request for a special delivery. You need to go right now."

"Urgent delivery? It's almost lunchtime!"

"Doesn't matter. Go now."

"Look at it out there!" Hoi Wing motioned to the window. Outside, a draft horse the size of an elephant was pulling an enormous plough down St. Paul. Crews of men with shovels trailed in its wake.

"I'm sick of your whining! Now go deliver these clothes to the address on the package."

The uncharacteristic gruffness from Second Uncle was surprising, and Hoi Wing put on his winter boots and duffle coat. When he was dressed, he glanced at the address on the package: "Miss Martha MacIntosh, 74 Maple Street." It was a new customer, but he recognized the street name. The home was in a neighbourhood (neither *"high class-ee"* nor *"low class-ee"*) south of the Golden Li, near the ridge that transected the city, where the houses were modest and had neither carriage houses nor servants' quarters.

Hoi Wing tucked the package under his arm and stepped out the door. Outside, the sun was blinding as it reflected off the snow. Drifts topped the height of his chest, and the wind scythed through his duffle coat.

This was the true Gold Mountain winter! Everywhere Hoi Wing looked, townspeople were digging and shovelling snow. Shivering, he marched resolutely onward, sinking to his thigh with each step. Finally, he came to 74 Maple Street. Exhausted, he banged on the brass knocker. The door swung inward, and *Ah-Del Plee-mon* appeared in the doorway.

"Hoi Wing! How good to see you!"

Hoi Wing almost swooned. She was the last person he thought he would see. "Very *please-sed* to meet you!" he answered, using the *lofan* he had gleaned from manning the counter at the laundry.

"Welcome to our home." Adele stepped aside to let him in. He was so surprised that he entered without thinking. As she shut the door behind him, a sudden blanket of heat engulfed him, and the air was permeated with the smell of burning hickory from a fireplace. Adele motioned for him to remove his boots and he did, keeping his damp socks on. What was *Ah-Del* doing here? Where was Miss MacIntosh, whose name was on the package he carried? He held the bundle out to *Ah-Del*.

"Where— Who— Miss-*ee* MacIntosh-*ee*?" he asked.

"That's my Auntie Martha. This is her house, and it's her laundry you've got. Come, I've told her all about you."

Hoi Wing understood little of what *Ah-Del* said, but he followed her down a narrow hallway to a pair of doors that were made with bevelled glass panes. The two entered what he recognized was a small salon. Here the walls were papered in a bright floral design. A large fireplace dominated the room. There was a settee and a sofa, both well-padded. Three cats lounged on the furniture: one had a bandit's face (tan with black ears), another was a tortoiseshell tabby, and the third looked like a ball of white fur. Hoi Wing stepped forward.

"Off, Snowball! Come on, Kai! You too, Marcus! Let's give our guest a place to sit." Adele clapped her hands, and two of the three cats leapt from the couches. The Siamese remained obstinately in place. "Hoi Wing, please have a seat. I'll get my aunt. She's been itching to meet you!"

Hoi Wing understood he was to sit, and he brushed the cat hairs from the sofa, his hands still tingling from the cold. He didn't wish to appear rude, but his delivery was now complete, and he was hungry for lunch. As glad as he was to see *Ah-Del*, he wondered how much longer he should linger.

"Hoi Wing, this is my Aunt Martha." Adele stepped into the room, accompanied by another woman. "This is her home."

An older woman entered the parlour. Her hair was loose and flowing, but tinged with grey. She looked about the same age as Elder Uncle, and it was obvious she was related to *Ah-Del*. She was a little shorter, but her posture was just as straight and upright. Her nose had the same tiny cleft at its tip. A pair of glasses hung from a black cord around her neck.

"Auntie," Adele continued, "here he is, the boy I've been telling you so much about!"

Hoi Wing stood immediately and bowed. "*Please-sed* to meet you too," he repeated, happy to practise his stock phrase once more.

The woman smiled broadly. Then she cleared her throat and spoke in a firm but gentle voice. "*Welcome to our home, Young Man. Have you had your rice today?*"

Ayah! Hoi Wing almost fell into his seat. Had his ears heard right? She was speaking in *his* own tongue! "*You speak my language!*" he said in Chinese. "How is that possible? Where did you learn it?"

"Oh, bother it all!" said Aunt Martha. "Now he's speaking too quickly for me. I'm not catching all that he's saying!"

"But Auntie!" said Adele. "You said you spoke Chinese!"

"My dear, I said I spoke *some* Chinese, but mostly the Honanese dialect where I was stationed for years with our Inland Mission. He's speaking a rural Cantonese dialect, of which I know only a little."

"But surely the Chinamen know their own tongue. Otherwise, how would they communicate amongst themselves?"

"It's a country of four hundred million people! We haven't even numbered their dialects yet. When I was there, we called their language the Devil's Tongue, but that was just our Western arrogance. We never accounted for the size of the country, its population, and how many languages they spoke."

Hoi Wing waved his hands, too excited to remain silent. "Kind Auntie!" He interrupted their discussion. "How do you know my tongue, and where did you learn it?"

"Please call me Miss Martha," the woman answered in Chinese. "And I learned your language, or as much as I can speak, when I lived in your homeland many years ago."

"Auntie," said Adele. "Tell him we want to teach him English!"

"Hush, dear, this is difficult enough without you shouting in my ear."

"But tell him we can give him a short lesson every week at this time. I've already gained the approval of the other Chinaman."

"My dear, if you learn anything at all about the Chinese from me, then learn just this one thing: 'Chinaman,' as you so quaintly put it, is the word we use to degrade and denigrate them. They call themselves 'men of the Middle Kingdom, *Chong Gok*,' or sometimes they speak of themselves as the People of the Tang, one of their greatest dynasties."

"But is it any different from calling one of us an Englishman or a Frenchman?"

"Unless you wish to insult them, I would not use that term," said Miss Martha. "Now, why don't you bring him some of that lunch we prepared. The lad looks famished. I'll see what I can remember of my Cantonese and try to let him know what his uncle has agreed to. I hope I can make myself understood!"

Hoi Wing watched the two *lofan* women conversing. He had so many questions for the older woman! When Miss *Ah-Del* left the room, Miss Martha lifted the third cat from the settee and sat down. She seemed to be composing herself for some difficult task. Then she placed her eyeglasses over her nose and turned to him with a smile. Clearing her throat, she began to speak in broken Chinese.

What a difference a day made! Late that night, after work, Hoi Wing sat in bed and marked Miss Martha's house on his map. Then he took out the sheet of vocabulary words Miss *Ah-Del* had given him. His eyelids were heavy, but nonetheless he had resolved to review them in his father's dictionary before going to sleep.

With the help of Miss Martha, he had learned more *lofan* in thirty short minutes than he had in the previous two months on his own. And he could look forward to going to their home every Wednesday for a "special delivery" so long as they kept it secret from Elder Uncle. Hoi Wing had whispered a thank you to Second Uncle, who had made the arrangements.

Perhaps his luck had not failed him after all, even with the loss of his amulet. It wasn't the weekly two-hour class he had hoped for, but it was better than nothing.

"Laun-*dree*," he said aloud, trying to roll the tricky *r* sound. He stifled a yawn and tried to mimic Miss *Ah-Del*'s tone and inflection. "Laun-*dree*."

The next afternoon, Hoi Wing was back on deliveries in the Golden Li. Many roads remained snowbound, and Hoi Wing had suggested they postpone deliveries, but Elder Uncle wanted him out "waging enterprise," so all St. Catharines could see how hard the men of China worked.

Hoi Wing grumbled to himself. Despite Elder Uncle's grandiose expectations, no one seemed impressed by his labours. On his third and last circuit, he heard the joyous cries of children at Montebello Park. He stumbled through a copse of evergreens and saw a line of tobogganers jostling along the crest of a snow-covered ridge. As he watched, a boy plunged down the slope on a contraption of wooden planks. Others followed. Some of the snowcraft were store-bought, with polished runners, but many children sailed downward on no more than sheets of cast-off tin.

This was sledding! How Hoi Wing wanted to ride a toboggan! For a time, he watched, imagining himself sailing down the hill with the wind in his ears. Was he the only young person in St. Catharines not tobogganing today? As the afternoon light began to wane, he gave one last glance to the ridge and turned away.

Resuming his deliveries, he continued into the Golden Li until he came to a road where the blizzard had split a towering maple. A massive branch had toppled into his path. With no detour possible, Hoi Wing heaved his bags over the tree limb and was clambering over when he heard the jingle of tack and the quick *chuff-chuff-chuff* of horses.

Astride the broken branch, Hoi Wing saw the Cascade's horse-drawn sledge coming down the street. The *lofan* laundry was similarly showcasing its diligence to their customers! The driver was a grey-bearded old man whom Hoi Wing had never seen.

The big sled slid to a stop before him, and Ratface rose suddenly from the wagon box, a large bucket in his hands. With a cry, the teen emptied the pail at Hoi Wing. Hoi Wing tumbled from the branch, ducking a spray of fetid liquid. Ratface laughed, and the driver cackled. The horses churned snow as the sledge pulled away.

Horse piss! Hoi Wing grimaced with pain. Most of the bucket's contents had missed him, but he had fallen on the ankle he had turned when *Blah-dok* attacked him in the street. Gingerly, Hoi Wing probed his foot and cleansed his coat with snow.

Limping, he completed his last three deliveries, including the stop at 88 Cherry Street, near the house where he had fought Ratface in November. On a whim, he crossed the street to have a closer look at 99 Cherry Street, where he had seen the young maid.

This was a palatial home surrounded by an imposing hedge. Hoi Wing had no doubt a person of great wealth and influence lived here, but there was no sign of the girl. He was about to leave when a small figure emerged from the laneway beside the main house. Was it the maid?

Forgetting his ankle, Hoi Wing chased after her. Before he knew it, he was in the alley behind 99 Cherry Street. Here he found himself amongst stables, an enormous backyard garden, and carriage buildings. A warren of paths had been dug in the snow and a row of trash bins was placed by a mud room beside the house. From within came the faint barking of dogs.

Hoi Wing did not see the young maid, although he saw tracks leading into the ravine behind the grounds. He was about to follow when he noticed an overturned trash bin with its contents spilled to the ground. Half-buried in the snow was a cast-off sled. Its runner was bent, and the chassis was caved in, but he felt a pulse of excitement as he lifted it from the ground.

This was something he could use! With some work, he could repair it with the tools and scrap lumber in the basement. What a lucky find!

"You there, boy! What're you doing?"

Hoi Wing dropped the sled as though it were one of the laundry's hot irons. The speaker was the little maid! She stood in the doorway of the mud room under a globe of electric light.

The girl stepped into the snow. She was about his own age and wore a rough grey dress with a much-splattered apron. Her cap was frilled and of bleached cotton. Two five-gallon buckets brimming with food slops hung from her hands.

"Who are you? What do you want?" She hunched her birdlike shoulders against the weather.

Hoi Wing dragged his bags out of the shadows. "Uh . . . hel-lo . . ." he began. "How you?"

"You're the laundryman's boy!" The girl looked at him as if he were something she had found in a chamber pot.

Despite her haughty tone, she was no taller than the tip of his nose, and her face was all angles. Her hair, where it escaped her cap, was lank and uncombed, but it was that astonishing shade of polished copper.

Hoi Wing rose to his full height, wincing as he shifted his ankle. Tired as he was, he could not let this kitchen waif speak to him so. "I . . . I am . . ."

The girl's mouth twisted. "Go away! You *speakee*? Go away!" She elbowed past him toward an enormous composter by the carriage house. The maid placed her buckets on the ground and threw open the heavy lid. With a grunt, she heaved in the contents of the first pail. The stink of kitchen effluent carried to him: putrefied fish and rancid meats, greying fruit rinds, and eggs gone bad.

Hoi Wing felt a grudging respect for the young scullery maid. Without hat or coat, she had to be cold. And for all her airs, she was no stranger to hard work. But when she lifted the second pail, it caught the edge of the bin and slipped from her hands. The bucket struck her as she fell into the snow, spilling the kitchen slop over her legs. "Jesus, Joseph, and Mary!" she cursed.

Hoi Wing was tempted to laugh. Served *Haughty Girl* right! But he hid his amusement before she could see it. Why take pleasure in her misfortune? Like him, she was just a simple labourer, likely with an employer no less a slave driver than Elder Uncle.

Hoi Wing went to her side. "You . . . good?"

"For bloody sakes! Look at me!" The girl sat in thigh-deep powder, a slurry of kitchen waste staining the snow around her.

Hoi Wing held out his handkerchief. For an instant, she looked at him as if he might be mad, but then she took it and wiped her legs and apron as best she could. Hoi Wing picked up the bucket and emptied the remaining contents into the compost, partly, of course, to demonstrate he was stronger than she was, but also because he liked her feistiness. Then he grabbed a spade from the wall and shovelled the spilled garbage into the bin. When he turned around, she was on her feet, brushing her uniform with her maid's cap.

In the late afternoon light, her hair tumbled over her shoulders, as audaciously red as the pelt of the fox he had seen in the fields. The angles of her face were softened, and her eyelashes were long and golden. She might have sprung from the were-legends of his homeland, but he glanced at her hands and knew she had known work all her life.

Haughty Girl looked up. Her eyes were green or grey. He couldn't read the expression on her face, but her earlier hostility was gone. She seemed about to speak. Or was she daring him to make some sign? He opened his mouth, feeling utterly tongue-tied. When he said nothing, she held out his now-stained handkerchief.

Before he could take it, the mud room door opened. A large-bodied woman appeared. Her calves and ankles were thick, and she gripped a broom. When she spotted the two at the garbage bins, she loosed a torrent of vitriol and thrust her broom like a spear.

The scullery maid cursed beneath her breath and grabbed the buckets. Slipping in the snow, she hurried back to the house. As she dashed inside, the big woman took a swipe at her head.

As Hoi Wing approached, the woman's lips curled in disapproval. She too wore a simple grey dress and cap, but her apron was spotless and ironed. And her bosom was enormous. *Big Bosom Woman* spat some words at him, but he gave her a low bow.

"*Thank you*, ma'am." He remembered a salutation learned at *Ah-Del's* house. "Good day for you."

His formality disarmed her. She spoke again, less stridently this time, but he still didn't understand. Turning, she shut the door. The light winked out.

Left in the darkness, Hoi Wing returned to the broken sled. It had clearly been thrown away, and he felt no qualms about scavenging it. But how was he to get it home, burdened with his laundry? As best he could, he lifted it in one hand and rebalanced his pole across his shoulders.

Now the winter night had fallen. Despite his fatigue and his aching ankle, he felt a sense of accomplishment. He was already imagining how he would repair his new treasure when the mud room door swung open. The electric light flicked on. Haughty Girl reappeared in the threshold. Caught red-handed, he froze, the sled clamped under his arm.

Backlit, the girl studied him intently. Seconds passed, and neither said a word. Ever so slightly, she lifted her hand. Then the door closed, and the light was extinguished once more.

Late that evening, while the uncles played cards on the main floor, Hoi Wing retired to the basement. He placed his sled on the workbench and used a hammer to remove the damaged runner and broken slats. Somehow he had to replace the metal blade and build a seat and cargo area. The rebuilt sled would be multi-purpose. He had a vision of what he wanted: something wide and stable, able to carry a big load, but fast and manoeuvrable.

He worked until his eyes fogged over. Putting his tools away, he reviewed Miss *Ah-Del*'s vocabulary words. The last thing he did before sleeping was update his map.

He added another X where Ratface had ambushed him with a bucket of horse piss, and pencilled in the ravine behind 99 Cherry Street. Then he used his red pencil and sketched a fox's head at Haughty Girl's house. It was only then he realized the little fox-girl still had his handkerchief.

8

The wind sifted snow like desert sand. Wan shadows painted the noonday streets. Hoi Wing paused before the wall of windows at McGregor's, the city's largest retailer and only department store. He stared at the winter scene mounted within: a life-sized mannequin of a bearded old man stood beside a wooden sled, an enormous bag of gift-wrapped boxes resting inside. Trees rose in the background, painted and frosted to appear snow-caked.

It was mid-December. Second Uncle had told Hoi Wing the birthday of the *lofan Jesus-ghost* was fast approaching: a holy day more important than even the New Year, which loomed shortly after.

Hoi Wing moved aside as a pack of excited schoolchildren charged the display window. Two jostled him, and a third kicked the ankle he had injured previously. Hoi Wing gasped in pain. A boy pressed his face to the window and beckoned to his mother. "Mummy! I want those!"

∞

At noon the next day, Hoi Wing sat at the dining table in Miss Martha's home. The woman was seated beside him. To celebrate the season, the ladies had affixed holly boughs to the plate rail, and they had a Christmas tree lit by tiny electric lights in their living room. Today, the study of grammar had been paused to work on conversation and vocabulary. Miss Martha lifted the tortoiseshell cat from the table and turned a page in a tattered photo album. It contained images from her missionary days in China.

Hoi Wing looked away from the Christmas tree—there was a gift-wrapped present with his name underneath—and peered at a photo in the album. In the picture, hundreds of *lofan* men and women paraded through a crowded street. Bystanders, six and seven deep, lined the sidewalks. Many waved the British flag. Some lifted torches and candles.

"How I remember that night in 1888!" Miss Martha's breath caught in her throat. "This is Toronto in late September. I was so young back then, barely into my twenties, when I joined Canada's first large-scale Mission to China. Oh, to feel such fervour and dedication—how caught up I was! Chinese were dying! We had to save their heathen souls!"

"Chinese dying?" Hoi Wing asked. To his surprise, he had come to prefer Miss Martha's teaching over that of Miss *Ah-Del*, whose endless vocabulary lists and exhausting verb tenses often left him with a headache. With Miss Martha, his tongue seemed unglued, and he understood far more. "Why Chinese dying?"

"Well, that was what our superiors told us." Miss Martha sighed. "Thousands and thousands of people were perishing each and every day. We had to salvage their souls before it was too late. There was not a moment to lose. We had to fulfill our Great Commission. On that day in September 1888, we marched all day from one church to another, praying and singing. *Onward Christian Soldiers! Marching as to War! With the cross of Jesus, Going on before!*

"Can you imagine? Singing at the top of our voices, we paraded from Harbord Street down to Union Station. Our favourite hymn was 'Bringing in Chinese,' sung to the tune of 'Bringing in the Sheaves.' *Bringing in Chinese, bringing in Chinese, we shall come rejoicing, bringing in Chinese!*"

"Then you go China?" Hoi Wing flipped to another page in the album.

"Yes." Miss Martha nodded sadly. "Off we went. From Union Station we took a train across Canada on the very railroad the Chinese had so recently completed. Do you know there were Chinese men on that same train, being sent back to British Columbia for deportation, but they weren't permitted to ride with us? On the very railroad they had built!"

Hoi Wing studied another set of photos. In one photograph, Miss Martha stood on a crowded dock surrounded by dozens of bare-chested coolies, some bearing loads that seemed equal to or even greater than their own body weight.

"That was me journeying inland in China," the woman explained. "Waiting to board a British steamer that would take us hundreds of miles up the Yangtze River. In some places, the water levels were so low, our boat was drawn upstream by ropes—pulled by dozens of barefooted men, women, and children who lined the banks of the mountain passes. Some of those poor waifs looked no more than five or six years old."

Hoi Wing flipped more pages. In one picture, Miss Martha was seated in a heavy wheelbarrow with a wood-slat wheel, pushed by a Chinese peasant. In another, she stood amongst a group of elderly Chinese, who waited, mouths open, to be examined by a *lofan* dentist. In a third photograph, Miss Martha posed with a *lofan* doctor behind a trio of crippled Chinese. The invalids were seated, and each gripped a set of crude wooden crutches. Their chests peeked out from open smocks, emaciated and sunken. Two of the men had a leg amputated at the thigh, and the third had no legs at all.

Hoi Wing grimaced and turned the pages. In later photographs, Miss Martha was seen at the Inland Mission in Honan, standing with young Chinese students and a tall Chinese in scholar's robes. His head was smooth-shaven and well-shaped. His eyes were kind, and he appeared regularly in the photos, always with Miss Martha.

"Who this?" asked Hoi Wing, his interest piqued.

Miss Martha coloured slightly. "Well, that is . . . was Han. He was my . . . friend. In fact, he was our very first convert. He started as a translator and became one of our regular teachers. He was of great help."

"He in many pictures." Hoi Wing pointed to other photos on the page.

Miss Martha's cheeks deepened to an ever redder shade. "Yes, well, he . . . and I . . . We were very proud of him. I had never seen a Chinese pick up English so quickly and with such fluency. Had it not been for him, my years in China would have been very different."

"Would they have, Auntie?" said Adele, coming into the dining room. She bore a tray of soup and sandwiches for lunch. "Is Hoi Wing getting you to open up about your time at the Mission? That's more than you've ever told me about your mysterious Han. From what you say, one would almost think you and Han were more than—"

"Oh, thank you for bringing us lunch. I think Hoi Wing was getting quite hungry, and he'll have to be back at the laundry soon."

"Where Han now?" asked Hoi Wing. He liked the scholar's face and wanted to know more.

"He died." Miss Martha looked down. "In the Boxer rebellion."

Adele sucked in her breath. "You never told me that."

"Well, dear, you never asked."

"Then he was murdered by the Boxers, like so many of our poor, innocent missionaries?"

"No, not at all." Miss Martha's lip curled. "Like so many of the Chinese, Han was slaughtered by British regulars, shot in the back by the very army that was to 'save' us from those same Boxers."

For a moment, neither woman said anything, and Hoi Wing eyed them both before setting the photo album aside. More and more he understood their conversation, even when they spoke as though he were not in the room at all. Miss Martha's friend was obviously a mystery, but why had the mention of his name engendered such a heavy silence? Whatever the secret, Miss Martha was not about to reveal it now.

In the silence, he took a bowl from Miss *Ah-Del*'s tray and peered at the red-orange soup she had prepared. Carrots? Tomatoes? *Lofan* food, like everything else about them, was often full of surprises. He took a first cautious mouthful. Too much salt, he thought.

Later that night, Hoi Wing stood at his workbench in the basement. His sled was finally complete. Or as complete as it could be at this time. It still didn't have the steering and braking mechanisms he'd envisioned, but he was proud of what he had contrived from cast-off materials scavenged from the trash of a saddler, a cabinetmaker, and the smith. His new vehicle had leather traces, straps, and a harness to distribute the weight across his chest and shoulders.

Hoi Wing yawned and ran his fingers over the greased runners. It was well past the eleventh hour. There had not been a peep from upstairs since the uncles went to bed. With sandpaper, he smoothed the rough edges of his sled.

Everything was ready. All that remained was a test drive. Outside his basement window, the night was still. No one would be at the toboggan run. What was stopping him from going right now?

A three-quarter moon lit the streets of the Golden Li. Subtle greys and whites tinted the snow. The polished runners of Hoi Wing's sled ran smooth and true. All the way from the laundry, his blood sang. As he pulled, the wind was a song and his chest like a billows. His ankle barely bothered him. *His sled ran fast!*

When he reached Montebello Park, he abandoned the road and plunged through the trees. The new-fallen snow threatened to swallow his boots, but he raced onward, pulling his sled past the bandstand and the long-buried rose gardens. He commenced a slow, steady climb. As he neared the top of the ridge, he threw everything into a final sprint, churning his thighs against the stubborn ice and snow. At the summit, he jerked to a stop and unhooked his harness. He opened his jacket, and the night air plumed with the heat of his body.

Beneath the moonlight, he stood where he had seen children positioning toboggans into their favourite lanes. A dog barked in the distance. On a nearby tree, an owl swivelled its head to fix him in its golden gaze. Below him, the field was unmarked by track, rut, or footfall. The gazebo was a white mushroom, and he turned a slow 360 degrees, imagining himself the last living person in a glacial world.

To the southeast were the laundry and the city. To the west was the road he had followed the day he confronted *Blah-dok* in the woods. And across the park was a wall of trees sheltering the wealthy neighbourhood where Haughty Girl lived.

Hoi Wing wiped the sweat from his face. Kneeling, he caressed the flanks of his snow craft. She was beautiful and swift. Fierce and powerful as a dragon. A conqueror of this wintry land. That was it! He would call her . . . the *Dragon of the Snows*. He laughed. It was the perfect name.

This was the moment he had been waiting for. He positioned Dragon of the Snows at the edge of the precipice. He climbed onto the padding he had attached to the flatbed. "Come now, Dragon of the Snows." He nudged it forward. "Let us ride."

He gave one solid push, tilting the sled past its equilibrium. Slowly, it began its descent. At first, Dragon of the Snows seemed to crawl, but within seconds it was gliding faster than he could run. The trees slipped past in a blur, and he imagined himself a bird, soaring on the currents. Faster he flew. He hit a first bump and almost lost hold. The only thing that kept him astride was the leather loop around his wrist. A second mound loomed just ahead.

He cried out loudly as Dragon of the Snows went airborne. Despite his two-handed grip on the harness, his stomach catapulted into his throat. But then he slammed into the third, the emperor of all bumps. Dragon of the Snows sailed twenty feet through the air and came down hard, the impact a lightning strike through his buttocks, up his spine, whipping his head backwards.

Hoi Wing laughed like a madman as he plunged on, accelerating with every second. It was wonderful! Marvellous! He steered with his harness, willing his mount into a wide, swooping curve as the slope levelled into the basin of the park. He shot past the pond where he had watched ducks gather in the fall and stick-wielding boys chase each other in bladed boots. He flashed by a merry-go-round and a set of swings (the seats stashed away for the season), startling a pair of lovers huddled by the benches for a clandestine winter rendezvous. "It's me! It's me!" he shouted to the shadows. "I am Hoi Wing!" The park echoed with his voice. "*I am Hoi Wiinnng!*"

9

"Second Uncle, how did you meet your wife?"

Second Uncle lifted another sheet onto a clothesline. His toothpick disappeared into his mouth and re-emerged, wet and splintered. "How does anyone meet their wife? She was a distant cousin, thrice removed, living in a far-off village. My father found her."

It was late afternoon, the day following Dragon of the Snows' maiden ride. Clad in only their shorts, Hoi Wing and Second Uncle were hanging wash in the desert-like heat of the drying room.

"But what if your father doesn't choose well?" said Hoi Wing, remembering Ying the Scholar's fields of *bak-toy*, withered under the blistering sun. "What if you were to find a girl on your own? One your father couldn't meet?"

"That's a novel idea." Second Uncle gazed intently at Hoi Wing's face. "You aren't talking about someone in particular, are you?"

Hoi Wing wrung a shirt in his hands. "No! How could . . . I don't know. There may be . . . No, I haven't quite spoken to her yet."

Second Uncle gave a low whistle. "Well, well. Young Man, you are full of surprises! Who is she? Where did you find her?"

Hoi Wing squirmed under the questions. Now he was sorry he had ever brought the subject up, but at that moment the front door was flung open with a bang.

"Ho!" Elder Uncle called out. "I'm back with good news!"

Second Uncle rushed from the drying room to help his brother. Hoi Wing followed, towelling his face and body. What had he been thinking, quizzing Second Uncle about marriage and women? The man was no fool!

Elder Uncle shoved through the curtain, a sack of laundry the size of a small pony over his shoulders. Snow clung to his red plaid jacket and wool trousers, and he shook a spray of snowflakes from his thick hair. "Great news! I've won us a contract with another spa!"

"Well done, Big Brother!" Second Uncle slapped the other man's back. "Let's knock off early and feast tonight!"

Hoi Wing watched the brothers dance an awkward jig of celebration. Elder Uncle's cheeks were flushed, but his breathing seemed laboured and his shoulders sagged. Was he shorter than he used to be? Hoi Wing returned to the drying room. He didn't remember as much grey in the man's hair a few short months ago.

"Keep eating, everyone!" Elder Uncle lifted his chopsticks. "This new contract from the Sparkling Waters Spa and Resort will bring us more work than ever!"

It was late evening. The men had closed shop early and lingered at the dinner table. The chessboard and pieces were already set on a crate. Outside, the snow swirled in the street lamps like swarms of moths.

Second Uncle thumped the table. "Ah, Big Brother, your business acumen still impresses me! How did you snatch this latest work from the *lofan* laundries?"

"Who knows?" Elder Uncle lit a cigar. "Perhaps some of those cheap *lofan* noticed our apprentice here, delivering laundry in the midst of the worst blizzard we've seen in years." He turned to Hoi Wing. "Fill my cup, Young Man. Why the sombre face?"

"Our young apprentice has been pensive lately," said Second Uncle. "All afternoon, Hoi Wing quizzed me about matters of the heart. He asked me what he might do if he found a secret love his father could never meet."

Hoi Wing was mortified. "Don't tell him—"

Elder Uncle laughed. "Farmboy is full of surprises! I suspected he was doing more in his spare hours than just hammering nails into that sled of his. By the way, I expect you to pay for that lumber of mine you used."

"But I built that sled to make deliveries!"

"Haven't you been tobogganing at the ridge?"

Hoi Wing sputtered. "Of course I'll pay, you cheap old—"

"Big Brother, let's forget Hoi Wing's sled for the moment. Share some of your wisdom with us. How can Hoi Wing win the girl of his dreams? What should he know of women and their hearts?"

Elder Uncle stared at the Wall of Family, his eyes full of longing. "Women," he lamented. "They are half the sky. All the sea. And the very ground underfoot. Without them, we would still be savages, grunting and stumbling about on our knuckles as we chewed raw meat or foraged the nests of birds."

Hoi Wing's mouth fell open. At best he had expected the man to tell a ribald joke or scoff at his questions. But this was different. Elder Uncle was being . . . *funny*. Yet poignant and true, all at once.

"But how do you get a girl to speak to you?" Hoi Wing said. "How do you make her want to spend time with you?"

"Ah, the two most intelligent questions Farmboy's asked since his arrival," Elder Uncle answered. "Tell me, Young Man, can you serenade this mystery woman in a fine tenor? Compose sonnets worthy of Lao-tzu?"

"No. No."

"Are you exceedingly tall or handsome? Have you gold enough for two? Are you a merchant or landowner?"

"No." Hoi Wing hung his head. "No. I'm none of those things."

"Well then, congratulations. You have as much chance of capturing your heart's desire as the next man."

"I do?"

Elder Uncle gripped Hoi Wing's shoulder. "Yes, you do. In truth, it is the women who choose us, at their discretion. Despite our warts, bad teeth, and the stench of our breath. In our arrogance, we men think we are the pursuers, but all we can really do is stand on our heads, shout at the tops of our lungs, and hope they notice us, waving up at them.

"Trust your instincts. Great risk accompanies great reward. When the moment comes, grasp it in both hands! Take the tiger's leap forward!"

Hoi Wing stared at the man's face. Once again, he could see how handsome Elder Uncle had been in his youth. Had his been an arranged marriage, or had Elder Uncle won his beautiful wife in some heroic fashion?

"Young Man, always be kind and true," Elder Uncle added. "Never play them false. Thus you may yet win the woman of your heart."

"I don't even speak her tongue," Hoi Wing whispered.

"*Ayah!* My teacup is empty." Elder Uncle pounded the table. "Little Brother, am I wrong or did we not procure sweet loaves for dessert tonight?"

Second Uncle went to the kitchen and returned with a tray of buns and preserved fruit. "Come and get it, fellow grunting savages! I couldn't forage any nests of birds or raw meat, but perhaps sugared breads and canned lychee will suffice.

"Nephew!" Second Uncle waved at Hoi Wing. "Cease stumbling about on your knuckles and come partake of dessert!"

The next day, Hoi Wing made sure Elder Uncle saw him load Dragon of the Snows with laundry for delivery in the Golden Li that afternoon. What the man had said rankled, although he knew, in his heart of hearts, he had not built the sled for mere tobogganing.

By late afternoon, he had already completed his first two circuits in the Golden Li, and he was overjoyed at how the sled facilitated his labour. On his third circuit, he cut through Montebello Park. Once again, the ridge was packed with sledders and snow craft of all shapes and sizes. For a moment, Hoi Wing stood there, itching to take Dragon of the Snows for a ride, but Elder Uncle's admonition echoed in his ears. Reluctantly, he turned from the ridge.

At the northern perimeter of the park, he was struggling through the snow when a pair of giant dogs burst from behind the bandstand. Barking madly, they raced toward him with enormous, bounding strides.

Hoi Wing froze. For an instant, he had a vision of the pack chasing his little fox friend, but these dogs seemed more akin to lions or bears than bloodhounds. As they neared, he held up his hands in a last, futile gesture of self-defence.

"Antony! Cleo! Stop! Stop!"

Hoi Wing blinked his eyes. The speaker was a tiny figure who waved a pair of leashes.

"Get away from him!" she shouted.

Impossibly, the two mastiffs checked their charge at the last instant. Still paralyzed, Hoi Wing watched the animals circle in opposite directions, moving fearlessly around him, thrusting their big snouts into his hands and forearms, sniffing deeply at his legs, backside, and crotch.

As the beasts continued their exploration, Hoi Wing relaxed. Their dark eyes were filled with intelligence and curiosity, especially the slightly smaller female, and feeling surprisingly confident, he removed his mitten to let her lick at his fingers. Slowly, his heart rate returned to normal. He had never been in danger at all.

"It's the laundryman's boy!" The small figure who stood before him was none other than Haughty Girl, the little red-haired maid. "Don't be afraid. They'll not harm you."

"I not afraid." Hoi Wing hoped he had masked his terror of a few moments before, even as the larger male poked him in the small of his back with an ursine snout.

"Antony! Down, boy!" The girl stepped forward and swatted the animal good-naturedly over its muzzle. The animal cowered instantly at her feet. Cleo, the female, continued to lick Hoi Wing's hand. "What are you doing here, boy?"

Hoi Wing couldn't help but notice she addressed him in the same easy manner she used with the beasts. "Working." He gestured at Dragon of the Snows. "I delivering *laund-dlee.*"

The girl, who was dressed in a dark-green overcoat and a woollen beret, glanced at the sled. "You've not been idle, I see. Have you apprenticed as a carpenter? Woodworking or such, no doubt?"

This last sentence was incomprehensible to Hoi Wing, but he nodded because he intuited it was the right way to respond. He fondled the ears of the animal that had curled up at his feet. "They very . . . beautiful."

At this, the little maid laughed. "Aye, beautiful they are, although that's not what most would call them! And they've taken to you. They don't like many of the people I meet on our walks."

Now he had made her laugh, and he felt bolder and more confident than ever. Inspired, he reached out to tug her sleeve for an instant. "You come. *To-bog-gan* with me."

"What did you say?"

Hoi Wing searched his mind for the right words. "Come. Tonight. Here. *To-bog-gan* with me." He pointed at Dragon of the Snows.

"You're asking me to toboggan with you?" She sounded incredulous.

"Yes! You come ten o'clock tonight! We ride sled hill!"

"Well, I might still be at my duties."

"Please, you come, no?" Was she turning him down? Hoi Wing felt panic course through his body. Now was the moment for the great tiger's leap Elder Uncle had spoken of. He racked his brain for something to say. "Uh, what you name?"

"You want my name now, do you?"

Hoi Wing wished he had thought of something more engaging. "Yes, what you name?"

She crossed her arms. Her eyes were green in this light. "Well, I'm . . . Heather."

"*Heah-tha?*"

"*Hea-ther.*" She stretched the word into its syllables.

"Heather." He rolled the *lofan r* the way *Ah-Del* did. "Heather."

"Not bad . . . for a Chinaman. What's yours?"

"Me?"

"What's your name? I can't keep calling you the laundryman's boy, can I?"

"Me Hoi Wing." He stood to his full height. "I am Hoi Wing."

"Hoi—what?"

"I am Hoi—"

"I think I'll call you Harry."

"But I am Hoi Wing."

Heather tugged the larger animal to its feet. She whistled at the second dog, which had run into the nearby bushes. "Harry, I've my work to do, and Cook will have my head if I don't finish. I can't promise I'll be here tonight."

"You come, please!" Hoi Wing adjusted his harness over his shoulders and tightened his straps. "Heather. Pleasing to meet you, tonight at ten!"

She laughed again. "Goodbye, Harry. Pleasing to meet you too."

Hoi Wing watched as Heather led the dogs toward the bandstand. She seemed absurdly small to be in command of such monsters, but they trailed her like a pair of lambs, before the three of them disappeared into the trees.

His heart was buoyant, and he felt he could pull Dragon of the Snows through another half-dozen circuits. Could Elder Uncle have been right yet again? Hoi Wing knew he was no more a poet than he was a virtuoso tenor, but somehow he had found the words to invite this *lofan* girl to a nighttime rendezvous at the toboggan run.

That night, Hoi Wing was at the ridge well before ten. The sky was cloudless and the moon bright. The park was empty, and he saw neither owls nor clandestine lovers. He stood at the summit, blowing in his hands. Then he knelt and unloaded Dragon of the Snows.

For a time he worked steadily, spreading out his woollen blanket and lighting his candles. He had heated a pot of tea into which he added milk and sugar (from *Ah-Del* he knew the *lofan* liked it that way). He set plates and cutlery. Then he used his pocket knife to open a can of sweet lychee, spooning the syrupy fruit into his bowls.

When all was ready, Hoi Wing sat and waited. And waited. Even without a pocket watch, he knew it was soon past the appointed time.

He strained his eyes at the trees and shadows. Nothing moved; there was no sound.

As minutes ticked by, his feet grew numb, and he paced the ridge, stomping up and down. What had happened to her? Was she not coming? He continued watching, hoping against hope, unable to admit that what he most feared might be happening.

His candles burned lower, and he drank cup after cup of tea. Motionless, he stared at the trees. An eternity passed. And then another. The first candle winked out. The second followed. When the last expired, the night gripped him like a glove. Heather had not come.

10

Bells rang throughout the city. It was Christmas Day, the *lofan*'s most anticipated celebration. Hoi Wing spent the morning at the ironing boards, staring out the window. St. Paul Street was empty. No trams ran, and there was neither four-legged nor four-wheeled traffic.

In the afternoon, children emerged from their homes, many pulling new sleds or carrying skates they had found beneath Christmas trees that morning. Some slid about on long planks strapped to their feet. A snowball battle commenced, one army of boys claiming the north side of the road, the other the south.

Five days had passed since Hoi Wing invited Heather to the ridge. In that time, he had not once ventured out on Dragon of the Snows after work. Instead, he moped about the laundry, refusing to play chess, cards, three-handed mah-jong, or even to sit for Second Uncle's sketches. Unfinished letters to his father and Eldest Great Auntie lay on his night table, and he had neglected his study of *lofan,* as well as the homework assigned by Miss Martha and *Ah-Del,* both of whom intuited something had occurred to bring about his ill humour.

As he watched the children on the street, he thought again of Heather. Why had she not come to the ridge? Could it be that she had been working, as she mentioned? He wondered what she was doing this Christmas Day. Had she been given gifts? Was she enjoying a free day?

When the winter light began to fade, Second Uncle told him to take the rest of the day off. Hoi Wing needed no further encouragement. *Ah-Del* had invited him over to collect his Christmas present, although he could muster little enthusiasm for the event. With half a fist of daylight left, he grabbed his coat and headed out to partake of the *lofan* Christmas.

Outside, the snowball warriors had disappeared. As he walked, a group of carollers went door to door. Stars winked into sight as he entered the Golden Li. Here the celebrations were more muted, but carriages and motor cars were everywhere, chauffeuring families to visitations. Every hearth seemed ablaze; every window shone with welcome.

His feet led him inexorably to the big park, where the ridge was busier than ever. Every boy or girl in town seemed to be tobogganing. As he watched intently, he failed to notice a pack of teenagers circling through the trees. Like wolves, they kept to the shadows.

As Hoi Wing emerged from the pines, a snowball shot out of the darkness and exploded against his face. Snow blinded his eyes and filled his mouth. Sparks exploded in Hoi Wing's head. A fusillade of snowballs followed.

Howling like beasts, the teenaged boys leapt from the trees. It was Ratface and his gang! Discombobulated, Hoi Wing slipped and fell to his knees. He tried to count his assailants, but in the darkness he couldn't be sure.

"Run, Chinaman! Run!"

"We gonna kill you!"

Hoi Wing ran. Impeded by snow, he slipped and slid across the ridge toward the tobogganers. Children scattered before him. Hoi Wing fell and got up again. Ratface was ten yards behind. Two boys sprang before him, arms wide, grinning like demons. "Grab 'im! Circle him!"

As the pincer closed, Hoi Wing hurled himself onto the slope. Sliding on the ice, he plunged downhill. Momentum took over, and he somersaulted out of control. As tobogganers hurtled by, he rolled head over heels, accelerating into a hapless, dizzying descent. At the bottom of the hill, he sprawled to a halt.

Stunned, Hoi Wing lay like a broken doll. His shoulder pulsed with pain and the old wound in his ankle throbbed. Snow covered his face and hair. It filled his coat, pants, and boots. The park spun as he sat up.

At the top of the ridge, Ratface and his gang shook their fists. Nausea engulfed Hoi Wing as he staggered to his feet. His vision was blurred, but he counted six of them. "You *dead-bastard demons*!" he shouted in Chinese.

The gang began to descend the slope. Hoi Wing rose and lurched into a skipping, hopping gait, heading toward the bandstand. Ratface and his boys chased him from the park into the Golden Li. Twice he thought he lost them (once by crawling under a veranda and a second time by ducking behind a snowbank), but each time they sniffed him out. On the second occasion, Ratface actually grabbed his foot, but Hoi Wing scored a vicious kick to the boy's face.

Hoi Wing's breath grew ragged; his ankle protested with every step. He dodged and doubled back, turning into an alley behind the Golden Li homes. In the laneways, the snow was deep, and he forced himself past carriage houses and sheds. Fleeing into a narrow ravine, he plunged through dense saplings and brittle underbrush. With a burst of effort, Hoi Wing increased his lead. Where was he now? Far behind, he heard their threats.

"We gonna kill you!"

"Whoo-hoo, you're dead!"

The moon sheltered behind clouds as Hoi Wing ducked through the trees. A branch whipped across his cheek as he passed a ramshackle chicken coop and fence. He slammed face first into a tree. Stunned, he fell into the snow.

"You're dead! You're dead!" He heard their cries.

"We got you now, Chinaboy!"

Their voices were growing stronger. Ratface was not yet in sight, but they would be on him in seconds. Hoi Wing rose and stumbled again. His lungs felt like sacks of sand. He would have to fight, six against one. Panic gripped him as he searched for escape.

The pounding of his heart filled his ears, and Hoi Wing forced himself upright. Through the trees, he thought he could see his pursuers. He clenched his fists and braced for the charge. Suddenly, a door opened up in the underbrush beside him. It swung outward from the slope, striking his shin. "Get in!" a voice rose up. "Now, you idiot!"

Hoi Wing dived into the hole just as Ratface rounded into sight. He tumbled down some wooden rungs and struck his face. The door slammed shut, trapping him in the darkness. Someone rolled on his chest, and a hand was clamped over his mouth. He choked on soil and the detritus of the forest floor.

"Shh!"

Pinned to the ground, Hoi Wing held his breath. From above, he heard Ratface's gang cursing and shouting as they rampaged through the ravine. Gradually, the noise faded, and their voices drifted away. Finally, there was only silence.

In the darkness, Hoi Wing couldn't even see his own fingers before his eyes. He struggled beneath his captor's weight. "Who—?"

"Shhh!"

Whoever was holding him ascended the ladder. The trap door was raised, and a sliver of shadow sliced the blackness. Too quickly, the hatch fell shut. Blind once more, Hoi Wing rose and rammed his head against something hard and unforgiving. He slid back down. What was this place? A match was struck, and a blue-orange flare hissed into flame. A candle was lit. Hoi Wing stared into the face of his rescuer.

"*Heather!*" he gasped.

Her eyes were green in the candlelight. "Harry, you're bleeding."

Exhausted, Hoi Wing fell into a corner. It was almost too much. He thought he might weep. One minute ago, he had been running for his life. He had thought he was about to die.

"You poor thing, let me look at you." Heather studied his face ("turn a little bit to the side—now look the other way") before filling a little bowl from a canteen. Then she dampened a handkerchief and touched the bridge of his nose.

"Ahhhh!" He winced as she dabbed at his cheeks and mouth. The hanky came away scarlet, and she rinsed the blood in a bowl, touching him again and again until the cloth was only tinted with pink.

"Hold this over your cheek." She positioned the handkerchief against his face. Hoi Wing ran his tongue over his teeth and lips, and probed his forehead where he had rammed the tree. Nothing was broken, although everything was puffy and tender. The handkerchief was cold and the press of her hand warm.

In the candlelight, he saw their little shelter was a hole in the ground, perhaps six feet by six feet. Beneath his buttocks was hard-beaten earth. Pine shelves lined the walls. Neither he nor Heather could have stood without stooping, and the only access was the little door above.

"You have a hard skull, but you'll have a goose egg for sure." Heather pressed a flask into his hands. "Drink some of this grog."

Hoi Wing took an obedient gulp and choked on a mouthful of liquid heat.

She chuckled. "Take another."

This time he sipped, and the warmth coalesced in his belly, sinking to his toes. His eyes were suddenly watery and his nose clear. Heather's grog was thick and fruity, leaving a raw and deeply satisfying burn over his throat. The little hidey-hole was becoming cozy. "Heather, where—what this place?"

She curled her legs under her hips like one of Miss Martha's cats. Her skin was pale as ever, although her eyes were dark and shadowed. In the flickering of the candle, her fox hair was lustrous. On her face was a look of mischief.

"It's an old root cellar but not used anymore. I found it last summer. I built up the bushes around the door and rolled some rocks all around. I come here when I need to get away from the house. Nobody knows of it, except you now. I come here as often as I can."

He shook uncontrollably, still feeling the adrenalin rush of his wild flight.

Heather wrapped a striped blanket around Hoi Wing's body and tucked it under his chin. "I've seen you, running through the neighbour-hood with your sacks of wash. Pulling that sled you found in the trash." Heather edged closer until their legs touched. "You poor thing, I know you've been harassed by Billy and his boys before."

"Who?"

"Billy Hugh Williams and his brother. And their gang, I think. Their father owned the Cascade Laundry before Mr. Braddock bought it out from under them. They've been chasing you, haven't they?"

Hoi Wing eased his head from under a shelf and massaged his neck.

The root cellar seemed almost hot now, and the sensation of her hands on his body had been like fire. Her hands, her voice, and her smile seemed so very alive!

"I never did like bullies," Heather said.

"The park." His hurt and disappointment welled up inside. "Why you not coming?"

"What do you mean?"

"To park! I ask you tobogganing!"

Heather looked down. "Harry, your invitation was kindly, but I can't come and go as I please. My duties in the house hold me late most nights."

What were her work hours? Was it possible this *lofan* girl had a job as arduous as his own? Hoi Wing stared into her eyes. She had meant it when she had told him that she might be unable to leave.

Heather took the handkerchief from his hand and studied it. Seemingly satisfied, she rinsed the cloth in her little bowl. From behind her back she brought forth a small pot swathed in a coarse towel. She cradled it between her knees and lifted the lid. A tantalizing odour permeated the root cellar, and he was suddenly ravenous.

She tilted the pot for his inspection. Inside were slices of dark poultry, chunks of potato, peas, niblets of corn, and a mash of carrots and radishes, mixed with cuts of giblet, sausage, mushrooms, and green onions—all smothered in a thick, creamy sauce. She lifted a forkful toward his lips. "Try this. Cook'll never miss it."

He took a mouthful and almost swooned. He had not realized how hungry he was. The food was so rich and buttery, he emitted a soft moan.

"You'll choke if you swallow too fast." She held out another forkful. This time he chewed slowly, savouring the unfamiliar tastes and textures.

Heather sipped her grog and pressed the bottle to his lips. He leaned back, stretching his legs against hers, and settled into the unexpected feast. With each gulp of grog, his shyness diminished, and for a time there was no sound as they shared fork and pot.

When the pot was empty—he would have licked it clean if she had offered—Heather brought out a small casserole dish. With a flourish, she revealed a palm-sized square of golden pastry, decorated with whipped cream and a brown sauce. She scooped a mouthful onto her fork and held it to his lips. "Try this. I took it from the master's own table."

The flavour exploded over his taste buds. He shut his eyes and tasted sheer bliss. Now he was sure he had died and reached the heavens.

"That's chocolate." She licked the tines of the fork.

Hoi Wing lay back, enjoying the weight of Heather's legs over his own. His head felt light, and his face tingled. Contentment crept over him. He was sleepy as a bear, ready for hibernation.

Heather giggled at the sight of him. "Happy Christmas, Harry."

11

In the days that followed, Hoi Wing would seek refuge in the little root cellar, arriving late after work with bated breath, always hoping when he lifted the hidden trap door that he might find Heather seated on her striped blanket with a stub of candle burning on a saucer.

Sometimes she would be there, waiting with a casserole or a plate of leftovers purloined from the master's kitchen, but other times he would sit alone, content in the knowledge that she would join him once her work was done for the day.

Heather called her little hideaway the Sanctuary. Hoi Wing scribbled the word as best he could onto a slip of paper when he thought she wasn't looking and spent twenty minutes with his father's dictionary before he located "Sank-choo-wer-*ee*." The name was perfect: a secret oasis where they could be safe from bullies or the persecution of their bosses. A refuge where they could speak and act as they pleased, far from criticism, censure, or correction.

Even more perfect was its location. Disoriented as Hoi Wing had been on the night of his rescue, he would never have guessed the Sanctuary was in the ravine just behind the great house where she toiled as a base-ment scullery maid. Nor would he have found it; her camouflage had rendered it invisible to all but the most discerning eye.

After a time, Hoi Wing and Heather devised a series of drop points—an abandoned mailbox hammered into the top of a wood post, a tin can in a bole of a tree, and an old bird's nest on a low branch—wherein they could deposit notes to signal that they had entrenched or planned to entrench themselves in their little hidey-hole.

"Come meet me at the Sanctuary at 10:30," she would write in the cursive script he soon came to recognize. Her handwriting was always neat and the letters perfectly formed.

In that first week, Hoi Wing marvelled at how Heather welcomed him into this most intimate of spaces. Sometimes he wondered what Ratface and his gang might have done to him had she not come to his rescue. Had their places been exchanged, he might have wanted the hide-away kept secret, although if faced with the choice, he told himself he would have leapt out to save her even if Ratface had been accompanied by a gang of a hundred.

In any case, she seemed gladdened by his recurring visits, and when she noted him jotting words down, she began to add to his vocabu-lary purposefully. "Write this next one," she would say. "*Perseverance*. Or how 'bout this? *Diligence*. *Intrusion*?" She was a trove of words, and she quickly made it a point to enunciate everything, moving her hands (like little birds, he thought) to elucidate her speech.

For his part, Hoi Wing could not be happier. In Drink the Waters Deeply, he had passed a friendless childhood, and Heather, with her chatty and ingenuous nature, was the perfect foil for his shy and intro-verted manner. Best of all, he spoke to her with neither intimidation nor hesitation in a way he could not with Miss Martha or *Ah-Del*. Ideas, thoughts, and pent-up emotions spilled from his lips, sometimes before he had the words to express them.

"I hating Elder Uncle!" he spat out.

"I hate Cook!" she responded.

"I hate *laund-dlee!*"

"I hate scullery work!" she replied with a laugh.

"Miss *Mac-Intosh-ee* teaching me English-*ee*."

"You have a half-hour English class every week?" Her voice rose when he told her he was meeting regularly with the two women in secret. "You lucky devil—they're giving you an education!"

Hoi Wing noted the envy in her voice. It seemed bizarre that anyone might consider his situation enviable, but he soon discovered she loved books and learning as much as, or even more than, he did. To his delight, she began to bring volumes "borrowed" from the library in the great house ("Oh, nobody ever goes into there anyway, especially the master!") to the Sanctuary.

In the late evenings, she read excerpts of her favourite books in a clear, steady voice as he hovered over her shoulder. In the dim light of the candle, his lips traced her words and the movement of her finger with its chewed nail over the pages.

The novels Heather picked were invariably beyond his reading level, but she augmented the experience by providing a running commentary on the narrative, filling all gaps created by language, culture, or experience. She had a flair for the dramatic and adopted the appropriate voice and accent for the protagonists, channelling what she believed were their personalities and idiosyncrasies. After testing several opening chapters, she settled on a novel she herself had not yet read. It was a recent publication and so well-received that everyone in St. Catharines seemed to be talking about it: *Anne of Green Gables*.

Hoi Wing was initially less than enthusiastic about her choice—could she not have chosen something with sword-fighting warriors?—but he soon found himself enthralled by the story of the little orphan who had been taken in by an elderly matron and her timorous brother. Anne's predicament was not unlike his own—was Elder Uncle an analogue of Marilla, and Second Uncle, Matthew?—but what was especially striking was the universal desire to seek betterment in education, as embodied in Anne's struggles to attend school, win a scholarship, and gain access to university studies.

Astonished, Hoi Wing recognized the story of his father, Ying the Scholar, as well as his own humble tale. How could a novel set half a world away on a tiny *lofan* island be so like his own life? Within the Sanctuary's confines, Hoi Wing squirmed with impatience as Heather voiced Lucy Maud Montgomery's words. "Keep reading book," he said when Heather yawned at the end of a chapter. The developing romance between Anne and Gilbert Blythe had captured his imagination. "Turn page. Faster!"

It was New Year's Eve 1913. Hoi Wing arrived at the Sanctuary late that night, bearing a large cushion. Respecting the directives of the uncles, he had forgone any of the abandoned linens amongst the unclaimed laundry and purchased the pillow from a downtown store.

He had also bought gifts for Heather: a gilded picture frame, a small mirror, and a necklace of shiny glass beads, all wrapped in brown paper. He had not given her a Christmas gift, but he was determined to make up for the omission on the occasion of the New Year, in his homeland the most pre-eminent of all holidays, often meriting a two-week celebration.

When Heather finally arrived, her face was flushed, but he noticed immediately that her maid's uniform had been laundered, its tiny pleats sharp and well pressed.

"The master's throwing a party!" She clambered down the ladder. In one hand she carried a large soup bowl covered with an embroidered napkin. "We've been preparing all week, and I can't stay long. Everyone in town is here tonight!"

"Everyone?" He took the bowl from her hands as the aroma of roast beef filled the little space. "Who everyone?"

Heather sat down before him. "Every bigwig you can think of—the mayor, the town aldermen, and anyone else with a fat pocketbook and sweaty hands! They've been eating and drinking and dancing all evening!"

"Dancing? How?"

"If only you could see the decadence! The women twirl like butterflies in their gowns, and the young men are so dashing in black tie. They swirl and spin to the music, as if they were floating on air!"

"Why you hating them so?"

"They dance grandly to all hours and feast on the food we dish up in the swelter of the kitchen. If you could see us—the sweat dribbling down our cheeks, up to our elbows in dirty dishes, and the hot oil splattering our forearms like pinpricks of fire! How they stuff themselves! There's never enough for these soft-palmed dandies with their silken hankies, though they've more money than you or me and every other commoner in St. Catharines!"

He remembered how he had seen dozens of maids and workmen during his deliveries in the Golden Li, but few *high-class-ee lofan*. Now he knew what they did on New Year's Eve.

"Oh, I've got to be getting back!" she said. "Cook'll have my head if she catches me gone!"

"But Heather, wait! I have present for you!"

"Presents for me?" Her face coloured even more as she noticed the gifts he had behind his back.

Hoi Wing handed her the gifts and had the pleasure of watching her tear the wrapping paper from each one.

"Oh, how lovely!" She fastened the necklace around her neck and held up the mirror. She set the picture frame on one of the shelves. "Harry, I can't thank you enough, but it's nearing midnight and the entire staff is on all fours tonight. There'll be hell to pay if I don't get back to the master's ball."

Now he was confused. "What ball?"

"A ball. It's another word for a grand party. It's Master Braddock's annual New Year's Eve ball."

"Blah-dok?" He blinked in surprise. "You working in *Blah-dok*'s house?"

"I thought you knew." Heather placed her foot on the lowest rung of the ladder. "I work in the house of Mr. Jonathan Braddock."

What did it mean that she worked in the house of their great enemy? It was three nights later before Hoi Wing had the opportunity to return to the Sanctuary. This time, they put *Anne of Green Gables* away, and he told her how *Blah-dok* had been a thorn in the side of the uncles for years. He recounted the periodic strewing of garbage in the backyard, as well as Hoi Wing's own misadventure with the man's motor car on the street. Last of all, he described the events at the fox hunt and how *Blah-dok* had scavenged his lucky amulet from the campfire to taunt him in the forest.

Heather wore the string of glass beads Hoi Wing had given her around her neck under her maid's dress. She had hung the mirror on the wall of the little closet where she slept in the great house, and the gilded picture frame remained on the shelf in the Sanctuary, still empty.

"A jade charm?" She looped her index finger in and out of her new necklace absent-mindedly. "I've not seen your amulet, but it's got to be in the master's drawing room. That's where he hatches all his plans. I've never been inside, but they say the walls are covered with the heads of the beasts he's slaughtered. He fancies himself quite the world traveller too. He subscribes to the *National Geographic*, and he's got maps of every continent on the walls.

"A right intrepid explorer our Mr. Braddock is, or so he'd have you believe. There's framed photographs of him everywhere, and a wall of relics where he exhibits his bizarre knick-knacks, like the finger bones of a saint or a piece of the True Cross.

"But the pride of his collection is this whole section devoted to China. It's far more than just masks and spears and shields. Visitors come from far and wide just to view it. No one's to touch any of that stuff, the artifacts are so dear to him."

Hoi Wing nodded. Second Uncle had already pointed out the most head-scratching paradox in all the Gold Mountain: the *lofan* hatred for the Chinese people was matched only by their love of Chinese art and culture. Since before the Opium Wars, wealthy *lofan* collectors had looted China's treasures, and Hoi Wing had even seen examples of chinoiserie—cheap imitation wares of Chinese sculpture, dishes, furniture, and paintings—on sale in some of St. Catharines' shops.

Heather continued. "If Master Braddock has your amulet, it'll be in that drawing room."

"I must be getting it back," Hoi Wing vowed.

"Don't be a fool. Your lucky charm is lost for good."

"But *Blah-dok* stealing from me!"

"You'd not be the first. Many a man's borrowed from Mr. Braddock at a cheap rate but lost their shirt when the loan came due. There's more to him than just his brewery. He has friends in high places, and he throws an annual picnic each summer. Everyone in town is invited. His Braddy's Beer is free on tap for all, and everyone is given a twenty-five-cent piece on arrival. Imagine!"

"He hate our laundry."

"He owns the Cascade laundries, and now you're the competition. He'd hate you for that alone, even if you weren't Chinese."

"How to getting my jade charm back?"

"Your charm is lost forever." Heather reached for the book behind her head. She settled herself on Hoi Wing's new pillow. "I'm sick of talking about the master. Let's see how Anne is faring in Avonlea."

Several days passed. At work, Hoi Wing racked his brain over how he might recover his amulet as he churned sheets, folded napkins, pressed shirts, and scrubbed collars. On his next visit to the Sanctuary, he surprised Heather with leftover rice and ginger-tomato beef from the laundry's dinner table earlier that evening.

"What's this?" she asked. "Chinese food?"

"For you." Hoi Wing enjoyed watching her eat, but she seemed to him thin and birdlike—so much so he wondered how much they fed her in the great house.

Heather sniffed the offering suspiciously. "What is it?"

"Try it." Hoi Wing took out bowls and two tiny teacups from his bag. Then he presented her with a pair of wooden chopsticks.

"You eat with those little sticks?" Despite Heather's incredulity, her fingers were deft, and she quickly grasped the fundamentals of chopstick usage.

Hoi Wing laughed delightedly as he watched her consume mouthful after mouthful of Elder Uncle's cooking. She also loved the Chinese tea, which he poured from his thermos (liberally dosed with cream and sugar), and of course she adored sweet canned lychee, to which he finally had the occasion to treat her.

The festive spirit of the *lofan* holiday season faded as the townsfolk burned their Christmas trees in their hearths. The early weeks of January 1914 were achingly cold and dark. The atmosphere in the laundry grew ever more dreary, and even Elder Uncle seemed to lose his enthusiasm for new contracts. Any fascination Hoi Wing had initially felt for snow had vanished, and pulling Dragon of the Snows lost its allure. He settled himself in for what a glum-faced Second Uncle warned were more months of harsh Gold Mountain winter.

Hoi Wing continued to visit Miss Martha's home for clandestine tutoring during the weekly noontime "special delivery," although he was always worried Elder Uncle might discover the truth. Both Miss Martha and Adele were disappointed that he had not visited them at Christmas, but they presented him with his gifts soon afterward: a leather satchel with shoulder strap, a notebook, and (most intriguing of all) an orange card from the St. Catharines Public Library and Reading Room with his name printed across the top.

"You can use this to borrow any book you wish to read." Martha stood at a slate board by the window. "It'll advance your learning, although I've never seen a Chinese student pick up English so quickly. It's almost as if you were getting supplemental instruction elsewhere."

Hoi Wing avoided her eye. "I studying hard now. All the time." He lifted a cat from his lap and let it drop to the ground. Which one was it? Kai? Or was that the orange-haired one? Although he tried to ignore them, the felines rarely let him be when he visited.

"You seem to have adopted a touch of Irish in your voice," Adele noted. Then she handed him a text from a pile of books on the buffet. "Will you look at chapters six and seven?"

Another reader? Hoi Wing hid a yawn behind his hand. He had hoped to spend today's session conversing with Miss Martha, questioning her about Han and the Boxer War of Independence. Nevertheless, he studied the cover of the textbook, which featured numbers, formulae, and a figure of a circumscribed triangle. The chapters inside were filled with geometric shapes and mathematics problems. "What this?" he asked. "Arithmetic now?"

Miss Martha let her eyeglasses dangle from their cord. "Adele, are we expanding our subject matter beyond reading and speaking? Isn't that a secondary school maths book?"

The young woman winked at her aunt. "I've a mind to test his general knowledge in every subject. I think if Hoi Wing attended our two-hour class on Thursday nights, we could teach him enough to place him into grade eight this fall."

Hoi Wing felt his head spin. Was Miss *Ah-Del* serious? But Elder Uncle had already expressly forbidden him from attending the Thursday night class.

"My dear, how do you expect to place him into grade eight?" asked Miss Martha. "Aren't you just raising the boy's expectations for no reason?"

Adele grinned. "Hush now, Auntie. I've already said more than I should have. You can't be the only one with secrets!"

∞

The Chinese Lunar New Year was fast approaching. The laundrymen set aside an extra hour each evening to scrub out the wooden tubs, oil the mangle, polish the irons, and ply the mops endlessly over the floors. Everything had to be cleaned, shined, and repaired for the celebration of the pre-eminent holiday in the Chinese calendar. An invitation was extended to Grandfather Foo to celebrate the occasion. All omens were favourable, and the men's moods grew buoyant as the big date, January 29 on the *lofan* calendar, drew near.

Hoi Wing emerged from his winter doldrums. He was galvanized by *Ah-Del*'s plan to ready him for grade eight, although when he reviewed the conversation in his mind, he realized she had explicitly reminded him that all might still come to naught.

Several nights later, he visited the Sanctuary again. This time, he brought his maths text and problem sheets. "Look," he said. "We study together."

Heather flipped the pages of the textbook indifferently. "I'm afraid arithmetic's always been my Achilles heel. I've no brain for numbers and ciphering."

He could not keep his good news to himself. "But this easy! Miss *Ah-Del* say I go to grade eight in September!"

"Oh." Heather's face was flushed, and she blinked her eyes rapidly. "If it's true, then I'm glad for you."

He looked at her with sudden understanding. "You want go to school too?"

"Yes, of course! I don't plan to be a scullery maid forever."

"But you are girl!"

"And you're Chinese!"

Hoi Wing sat back against the wall. He stared at her callused hands. Of course she wanted better for herself! And if their places had been reversed, could he have been glad for her? He liked to think so. "I know. We prepare together! You teach me English. I teach you mathematics."

From then on, they spent part of each meeting reviewing Hoi Wing's homework. Heather had never been coached in the basic operations of arithmetic, and Hoi Wing took to rectifying this situation. "What is five times seven? Eight times nine?"

She was far more adept than she professed, and her numeracy progressed much faster than he expected. To his surprise, she had an intuitive grasp of mathematics, and soon she was working out problems on her own and poking holes in the solutions he had devised. Somewhat flummoxed by the acuity of her brain—and yet another reversal of their positions—Hoi Wing asked her again about her duties in the master's house.

"I'm the scullery maid—up at five o'clock every morning to clean the flues. All seven chimneys. I light the fires to warm the house. Then I polish the hearth, the stove head, the fender, and the grill until they shine. After that, I'm at the doorknobs, knockers, and mailbox with the Brasso, or dusting the crystal in the chandeliers, and scrubbing the stone steps and walkways. I work the boothole. That's a closet where I polish shoes—blacks, browns, oxbloods, and tans. I even iron the laces. Then it's pots and pans in the kitchen sink. Knives are worst—fruit knives, carving knives, pallet knives, bent knives, paring knives, every last one. And the spoons, forks, sieves, and sifters. Every day! And all before noon or I catch it from Cook."

"What you catch?"

Heather rolled up her sleeve, and Hoi Wing saw purple bruises running over her forearm.

He sucked in his breath. "Cook hit you?"

"Squeezed me, more like."

How dare anyone harm her! Hoi Wing's heart ached at the nonchalance of her words. The uncles were fierce taskmasters, but they had never struck him. What were Heather's origins? Where was her family? Although he had told her of how he had come to the Gold Mountain, she had kept silent about her own story.

In this way, she reminded him of his own honourable dead mother, Fong-Fong. She had died birthing Little Mei-Mei when he was eight, but he had never even learned his mother's family name, nor met any of her relatives. He knew nothing of her history. The mystery became no clearer after her death. His father had remained tight-lipped as well.

Two days before the Chinese Lunar New Year, Hoi Wing stood before the doors of the St. Catharines Public Library and Reading Room. It was his noon-hour break. Slung across his shoulder was his leather satchel, and in his hand was his new library card. Elder Uncle had asked him where he had obtained the satchel, but Hoi Wing retorted that he was free to spend his hard-earned salary any way he wished.

Hoi Wing and Heather had now almost completed their reading of *Anne of Green Gables*, and he found himself blinking back tears when Heather read the penultimate chapter relating the death of Matthew Cuthbert. Ashamed of having been so moved by a book, he turned his face, but Heather noticed immediately. "Harry, you're crying!"

With the end of *Anne of Green Gables* in sight, Hoi Wing decided he would explore the library and choose their next book. Leave it to the *lofan* to come up with such an institution! A place where you could read any book you wanted, for free!

Now, at the library, Hoi Wing pushed through the heavy doors. The noise of the street was stifled immediately. In the silence, he faced a wide, rectangular room. Miss *Ah-Del* was nowhere in sight, but bookshelves lined the walls, and stuffed birds in glass cases perched here and there, keeping watch with unblinking eyes. The odour of musty paper, book-binding glue, and mothballs tickled his nostrils.

In the middle of the room were wooden tables where several patrons sat, each reading silently beneath a brass-hooded lamp. In a corner was a leather armchair on which an elderly woman was seated, perusing a newspaper. She lifted her head from her newsprint and eyed Hoi Wing suspiciously, up and down.

For a moment, Hoi Wing did nothing but relish the sight of so much knowledge. What would Ying the Scholar have said about this? If he could read but a hundredth of these books, how smart would he be?

For ten minutes, he wandered the stacks. There were thin picture books, medium-sized texts, and door-stopping tomes with gold-embossed titles. He ran his fingertips across their spines. How to tell a good book from its cover? It was a conundrum he had not expected. With so much choice, what should he borrow?

Unsure of what to do, he slid into a seat at one of the tables. Someone had left a small pile of books on the corner. Unconsciously, he flipped the first open. It was a science text, filled with formulae, letters, and symbols he didn't recognize. The second was somewhat better: a wide-format hardcover, replete with colour plates of waterfowl. The birds were rendered in exquisite detail, but Hoi Wing wanted a novel.

He picked up the third book. Its cover page featured the head of a dog on a field of rock and snow. His mind went immediately to Heather and her beasts. *What was this about?* He flipped through the chapters, and an illustration leapt before his eyes: the same dog—now snarling, its fangs white and gleaming—was jumping at a man who gripped a club in one hand. *Now this was something he might like!*

Hoi Wing turned to the first chapter. The reading level was well beyond his abilities, but the first sentence hooked him like a fish. For a time, he read quickly, skipping words, phrases, and whole sentences he didn't understand. Caught up in the narrative, he read ten or so pages before he sensed someone approaching his table.

"Hoi Wing!" said Adele. "I was wondering when you would visit us."

For the next fifteen minutes, she gave Hoi Wing a tour of the library, taking him through the fiction and non-fiction sections, texts of general knowledge and information, and even the map room. She made recommendations from the young readers' section, but Hoi Wing eschewed all her choices, having made his own.

Adele felt the book he had chosen was too far above his reading level but nonetheless stamped his card as he waited. Hoi Wing secured the new-found treasure in his satchel and exited the library in triumph, eliciting one last disapproving look from the elderly matron reading the newspaper. He was not sure, but he thought he recognized her as the woman who had come into the laundry months before to barter a lower price from Second Uncle.

Ten minutes later, he trudged through the streets of the Golden Li, inspired by his successful navigation of the library. Nothing could stop his march to an education. Moving through the snow-covered roads, he descended into the ravine behind the grand mansion where Heather worked. It was his intention to leave the new novel in the Sanctuary. He imagined the delight that would come to her face upon discovering it.

As he arrived at the Sanctuary, he waited to ensure there were no observers. Only when satisfied he was alone did he step forward to lift the hidden trap door. Inside, it took only a few moments to place the library book prominently on Heather's cushion. Everything was ready for his little surprise. He was about to leave when he noticed a note on a shelf. Her missive made him forget his new book.

Urgent! Master Braddock hatching new plan to close laundry!

Hoi Wing raced back to the laundry. When he arrived there, the uncles were outside, arguing with the big policeman he had seen patrolling in town. The officer was barrel-shaped and had a neck like bread dough rising. As Hoi Wing watched, the constable looped a chain and snapped a padlock across the front door. A yellow cotton sheet, soaked in carbolic acid, had been hung over the storefront window, obscuring the name of the Sam Kee Luk Chinese Hand Laundry.

The officer turned a key in the padlock and tacked a paper to the door. "You're shut down, do you hear me, Chinaman? Your laundry is *close-ee*! *Close-ee*!"

"What shut down?" said Elder Uncle. "Why you closing?"

The constable stabbed his finger at the notice. "By order of the Department of Municipal Health. We've received a complaint about your *wash-ee wash-ee*. You have vermin, and your premises are in a filthy, unsanitary condition."

"What filthy? We no vermin here!"

"That's not what the complainant said. The inspector will be here in two days to finalize this order."

"What inspector? When two days?" asked Second Uncle.

"I don't have time to explain this to you! Read the notice! In two days the City Health Inspector will shut you down for good."

Hoi Wing ran up just as the officer departed. "What's happened here?"

"Farmboy, make yourself useful. What does this notice say?" Elder Uncle asked.

The three laundrymen put their heads together to decipher the words of the edict. Hoi Wing entered the laundry through the back door and brought out Ying the Scholar's dictionary.

Notice of Violation Under By-law 19-13(b): By Order of the St. Catharines Municipal Health and Sanitation Department, this washing-drying establishment, the Sam Kee Luk Chinese Hand Laundry, is hereby closed pending inspection, due to unsanitary conditions, unclean vectors, contagions, lack of hygienic practices, and the presence of vermin.

City Health Inspector: Mark Joseph Smythe

"But how can they do this?" said Hoi Wing. "We've been cleaning for days in anticipation of the New Year. We have no vermin or unsanitary conditions!"

Elder Uncle shook his head. "I sense the invisible hand of our great enemy, *Blah-dok*, using the city's corrupt officials to shut us down."

"Yes, without a doubt, this is *Blah-dok*'s doing." Hoi Wing remembered Heather's warning.

Second Uncle looked at him. "We'll have to clean the entire laundry again. It must be spotless for the inspection."

Hoi Wing noted pedestrians making a wide detour past the yellow sheet covering the window. Some grimaced and spat as they hurried by. "We are losing clientele as we speak," said Hoi Wing. "And if the inspector is corrupt, how will we convince him to pass our laundry, no matter how clean it is?"

"We can beat these damn *lofan* at their own game," answered Second Uncle.

"How will we do that?" asked Hoi Wing.

"Simple." Elder Uncle grinned. "We will bribe the inspector."

With the laundry closed, the men spent the rest of the day cleaning. Everything they had done over the past weeks was repeated. Hoi Wing scrubbed the floors, Second Uncle sanitized the kitchen, and Elder Uncle tackled the main work area. In the late evening, the men ate a hasty supper and retired to bed. Exhausted, Hoi Wing went downstairs with the intention of sneaking out again to visit Heather, but the efforts of the day had been too much. He fell asleep sitting up and woke the next morning in his winter coat.

The laundrymen spent a second day cleaning. Hoi Wing concentrated on the basement, and the older men put their efforts into the attic. None of them knew the extent of the inspection to come. It was late evening when the men paused in their labour, but the laundry sparkled and shone. Not a speck of dirt was to be found anywhere. Even the big store-front window, hidden under its sheet of yellow cotton, was spit-shined to a high gloss.

"It is enough." Elder Uncle wiped his brow. "The laundry is immaculate."

Hoi Wing felt a surprising sense of pride. "It's pristine."

Each man looked into the others' faces, knowing he had given his all. The inspection would take place on New Year's Day, the most portentous date in the Chinese calendar.

"Our doors will be closed forever," said Second Uncle, "if the *lofan* inspector does not accept our bribe."

"He will take the bribe," said Elder Uncle. "I know these *lofan*. We will outsmart *Blah-dok* and his greedy officials."

Hoi Wing yawned. He was exhausted and did not feel any of Elder Uncle's confidence. Without another word, he went downstairs to bed.

12

It was January 29, 1914, Chinese New Year's Day. The morning dawned bright and cold. The men were up early and wished each other Happy New Year in the stark light of the dawn.

At breakfast, the uncles surprised Hoi Wing by handing him a *houng bao*, a small red envelope that held one silver dollar of "lucky money," the traditional New Year's gift given to children in every Chinese family. Elder Uncle had another red envelope in his back pocket for the *lofan* inspector. He would bide his time for the opportune moment and surprise him with the bribe.

For the rest of the morning, the men waited. None of them could remember if the policeman had mentioned the time of the inspection, and there was some debate as to whether they had misunderstood the date of the inspection itself. Just when they began to think there might be no inspection at all, there was a knock at the door. The men heard the metallic click of the padlock and the rattle of the chain as it was pulled aside. Elder Uncle opened the door.

"Mr. Chan?" A grey-haired *lofan* carrying a heavy leather valise stood in the doorway. "My name is Smythe. I'm here to inspect your premises for suspected violations to the city's health codes."

Hoi Wing gave a tiny gasp. There was no mistaking the *lofan*'s grey-tinged beard and wind-burned face. He remembered how the man had sat upon his saddle as though he had been born to it. The inspector was none other than the Master of the Hounds from the fox hunt!

Second Uncle joined the men at the door. Within a minute, the uncles moved aside and the inspector entered the vestibule, removing his coat and rolling up his sleeves. As he placed his valise on the counter, he caught Hoi Wing's gaze, and there was the slightest flash of something—recognition?—in his eye. It disappeared instantly, and the man nodded nonchalantly. "Hello, lad."

The inspector laid out a white sheet on which he placed tweezers, brushes and combs, a whisk broom, a tin dustpan, cotton swabs, several bottles of blue and green liquid, glass jars and tubes, and a pile of folded towels. Then he pulled on a pair of white cotton gloves and fitted wire-framed spectacles on his face. He tied a mask over his mouth and nose.

For the next three hours, the man conducted a meticulous inspection of the laundry, kneeling before and wiping the undersides of the counters, running his linens over the walls and floorboards, peering and sweeping behind and beneath the machinery, sniffing, swabbing, and scraping the bottoms of the tubs and baskets. Moving methodically and purposefully from room to room, he opened closets, cupboards, and boxes. He examined the sinks, pump, and drains, and used a knife to scrape and pick at the lead pipes.

During the assessment, the laundrymen did nothing. Hoi Wing scrutinized the inspector's every move. He remembered that the man had not wanted to proceed with a search through the woods on the day of the fox hunt.

Not a square inch of the laundry was overlooked by the man's inspection. At one point, he uncorked a small bottle near the rack of irons and waved his hand over the opening. Then he added several drops of blue liquid from another bottle and shook the first in his hand. The resulting solution became pink, and he examined the tint in the light of the small window before comparing it to a coloured sheet he brought out of his briefcase.

Finally, the inspection seemed finished. The inspector returned to the counter and checked his timepiece. He took out a pen and ink. Then he flipped open a large ledger and made copious notations. When he finished, he began to put the tools of his trade back into his valise.

Elder Uncle shot Second Uncle a glance. Now was the time to offer the bribe. His hand in his back pocket, he approached the *lofan*. He drew out the envelope. "*Ah*-Inspector, it Chinese New Year today. We have gift for you."

The inspector shrank back. "What are you talking about, Mr. Chan?"

Elder Uncle waved the red envelope in the other's face. "This is gift. For you, Inspector. Happy New Year!"

"I don't want any gift!"

"You no want? This money for you. For very good luck today!"

The inspector fended off Elder Uncle. "Put away your thirty pieces of silver, man, and I'll pretend you did not attempt to bribe an officer of the city! I've completed my inspection, and I've discovered no trace of contagions, bad vectors, unsanitary conditions, or vermin. You have passed the inspection!"

"Passed?" Elder Uncle's hand dropped, and his mouth fell open.

"Aye. You've passed. Had I found otherwise, all the gold in the world would not have availed you, but I'll not fault you greatly for your maladroit attempt at bribery. I dare say you've come up against crooked examiners before."

"You mean we not *clos-ed*?" asked Second Uncle.

The inspector put on his coat. He picked up his valise. At the door, he crumpled the notice of violation in his hand. Then he went to the big window and tore away the yellow sheet. The noonday light flooded the laundry, lending an oaken glow to the floorboards and glinting off the irons.

"Your premises are as clean as any, and that will be my report to the Municipal Health Department. You're free to go about your business. Now I have other work to attend to. Good day."

As he turned to go, he gave Hoi Wing a tiny smile. "And you, lad, stay out of the forests. It's no place to be trampling about in the winter."

The laundrymen watched him stride down the street, his back straight and his head held high. Elder Uncle shook his head with a mixture of admiration and disbelief. "He didn't want our bribe."

"Did you offer him thirty pieces of silver?" asked Second Uncle.

Hoi Wing blinked in the sunlight. "I knew he was a good man."

Elder Uncle turned to Hoi Wing. "What was he saying to you about trampling through the woods?"

That night, Hoi Wing sat at the dining table, his chin resting on his hands. He rubbed his tired eyes. Dinner was over, and the men had cleared the dishes in anticipation of the arrival of Grandfather Foo. Hoi Wing stifled a yawn. With the recent happenings, he had almost forgotten that they had invited the man the uncles called Tiger-mouse for a New Year celebration.

"Ho, Young Man!" Second Uncle pounded the tabletop. "Stay awake or you'll miss tonight's party!"

"When is our guest arriving?" Hoi Wing mumbled. "I'm exhausted."

"How's Farmboy ever going to find time to learn *lofan* if he can't even stay awake to have a drink with his friends?" asked Elder Uncle.

"I'm awake!" Hoi Wing sat up to Second Uncle's laughter.

The doorbell jangled. Hoi Wing hurried through the vestibule and opened the front door. On the threshold stood a small man, facing the gaslights on the street poles. He turned.

"Grandfather Foo!" Hoi Wing bowed low.

"So you are the new apprentice." The elderly man nodded approvingly. He was not much taller than Hoi Wing, but his beard was frost-white and as tangled as the tentacles of a jellyfish. With a flourish, he handed Hoi Wing a small package. "These are for you." He winked. "I hope these slave drivers are not treating you too harshly."

Before Hoi Wing could respond, Elder Uncle appeared through the curtain. "Tiger-mouse, you old goat! You're late again!"

"How can you tell, One-Arm? You haven't a watch on your wrist. Oh, I forgot, you haven't a wrist!" The two men laughed. Grandfather gave Elder Uncle the visitor's customary gift (a bag of six small oranges, somewhat withered and hard, albeit the first Hoi Wing had seen in the new land), and he removed his navy-blue peacoat. He doffed his cap to reveal a scalp as bare as Second Uncle's. The garments were passed to Hoi Wing, and the small man followed Elder Uncle inside with spry, birdlike steps.

Second Uncle emerged from the kitchen, bearing a wide tray of sweet loaves and cakes. The breads had been purchased fresh from the bakery.

"Grandfather Tiger-mouse, have you had your rice today?" Second Uncle employed the ritual greeting of the southern Chinese.

"Ah-Chung ah, I have already eaten well!" Grandfather responded in the accepted manner, addressing Second Uncle by his given name, which Hoi Wing had not heard before that moment.

"Come now, Tiger-mouse," said Elder Uncle. "Our table is humble, but surely you have room to sample a little of our fare."

"Well, I might have a bite, but only if you insist." Grandfather splayed his hands as if forced to concede his appetite.

Hoi Wing grinned at the charade. Back home, a starving man would not touch another's rice unless invited. Second Uncle and Grandfather clasped hands as Elder Uncle laughed and thumped the older man's back. The camaraderie was infectious, and Hoi Wing could feel his exhaustion evaporate. He hung up the man's coat and hat. Then he sliced the oranges and arrayed them on a plate.

This was it, Hoi Wing thought as he bore the fruit to the table: every man of China in St. Catharines was in this very room. Second Uncle had told him that there were perhaps a thousand Chinese men in the capital city of Toronto, and maybe another five hundred in all the rest of Ontario. Even worse, the heartless Canadian exclusion laws had allowed no more than perhaps fifty Chinese women to enter the entire province. "That's their way to keep us from settling here—as if we'd want to!" Elder Uncle always said.

In the laundry, Second Uncle steered Grandfather Tiger-mouse to the most comfortable seat at the table. Hoi Wing unwrapped his gift. For an instant, he couldn't believe his eyes. *Preserved plums and dried red-hot ginger in waxed paper!* They had been his favourite treats back home. Similar to the oranges, he had seen nothing like them since his arrival. "Grandfather, thank you so much!"

The old man looked up. "You're welcome. I never had sweet plums and spicy ginger as a boy, but I love them now! By the way, when I first became a laundryman, I could hardly breathe from the stink of the wash. Stick a big chunk of ginger in your cheek whenever you're working. Everything will smell a little better, and you won't feel like emptying the contents of your belly."

"Hoi Wing doesn't need ginger and sweet plums," said Elder Uncle, coming back from the kitchen with tea and a tray of dim sum. "He's a real man—he uses a lavender-scented hanky!"

"That's because he's too smart to breathe the stench of *lofan* sheets, Big Brother!" said Second Uncle. "Now stop riding him, and let's get on with the celebration!"

Everyone gathered at the table and Hoi Wing poured tea, commencing with Grandfather. Second Uncle served the sweet loaves and dumplings, but Hoi Wing left his untouched as he stuffed candied plums and red-hot ginger into his mouth.

"Tiger-mouse, I don't think much of your last letter to the editor." Elder Uncle slapped the most recent edition of the *Dahan gongbao*, a Chinese newspaper published in Vancouver (called the City of Salt Water by the men of China), onto the table. "You really think those petty skirmishes in a few tiny *lofan* countries will blow up into a shooting war?"

"One-Arm, have you not been following the happenings of the world?" Grandfather swallowed a dumpling before he polished his wire-framed spectacles with a handkerchief. "Yes, those 'tiny' European countries are but vassals to the great powers, but the treaties binding them to their masters form a web of alliances and backdoor allegiances that span the globe."

"What do you foresee, Grandfather?" Hoi Wing glanced at the man's article and was reminded of Ying the Scholar's intellect.

Grandfather stroked his wispy beard. "I am no fortune teller, but every good prognosticator knows the gong that clangs in one's own courtyard resounds far and wide. Make no mistake—the revolution in our home-land is but the harbinger of many to come. Our learned Dr. Sun Yat-sen speaks true. We must throw off the yoke of the foreign invaders and return China to the Chinese, but our struggle is mirrored in many lands. Common people all over the world are rising. No longer will they be slaves to the rich and privileged."

"But what can they do, Tiger-mouse?" Second Uncle sipped tea. "Kings, tsars, and emperors hold the leashes to the dogs of war. At their command, armies march and cavalries ride."

Grandfather grinned widely, revealing a golden eye tooth at his upper left lip. "You forget, I was stolen as an infant and sold into slavery. Long ago, I won my freedom. Others can do the same."

"You won your freedom?" asked Hoi Wing. "How did that happen?"

"It was so long ago." The old man shook his head.

"Tell the tale, Tiger-mouse," said Second Uncle. "We haven't heard a good story in a long time. But before you start, let me fetch a drink to match the intensity of your account."

Second Uncle went to the attic, and Elder Uncle entered the kitchen before returning with shot glasses and a bowl of ice from the wooden cold box. When all four were seated again, Second Uncle placed a tall bottle of golden liquid on the table. It was adorned with the image of a striding man wearing a top hat and a scarlet coat with tails, and bearing a cane.

"What is this drink?" Hoi Wing asked.

"Scotch whisky." Second Uncle chewed his toothpick. "Will you do the honours, Big Brother?"

Elder Uncle filled four shot glasses with ice. Then he poured Scotch for Second Uncle, Grandfather, and himself. Finally, he added water to the fourth glass and splashed in some liquor. This diluted glass was placed before Hoi Wing.

The men raised their glasses. "To tigers and mice," said Elder Uncle.

Hoi Wing lifted his glass and sniffed its aromatic, medicinal sweetness. The men downed their drinks in a single gulp. For an instant, Hoi Wing hesitated. Then he threw back his head and did likewise. *Ayah!* He gasped. *The golden liquid was searing his throat!*

"Are you all right?" Second Uncle pounded his back.

Grandfather leaned across the table. "Breathe deeply, young apprentice!"

"Farmboy," said Elder Uncle, "a man may sip his whisky if he is so inclined."

Hoi Wing coughed repeatedly. His nose had cleared, and a fire raged in the pit of his belly. But the *lofan* drink was akin to Heather's grog, although more mellow and less sweet. It was also something he thought he might get to like. "Can I have another?"

"Ho!" shouted Second Uncle. "I told you he was a man!"

Elder Uncle laughed as well, nodding at Grandfather. "Perhaps this would be a good segue into your story."

Second Uncle filled the shot glasses again, this time only dribbling a few gulps for Hoi Wing. Elder Uncle lit a pipe.

Grandfather sipped his Scotch and commenced his tale. "I was stolen by bandits from my family as a child. It happened when I was so young, I don't even recall my honourable mother's name. I was sold to a Grand House where the aged Matriarch engaged in the great game of *soy mah*, or horse racing. The House owned dozens of horses, and their bloodlines were renowned throughout the Middle Kingdom.

"From the youngest age, I lived in the stables, shovelling manure, cleaning stalls, feeding, watering, currying, and caring for the great beasts. I ate, drank, lived, and slept with the animals, until I came to know them better than I knew myself.

"They called me Mouse, and no animal, no matter how timid, shied from me. So I slaved in the compound until I reached my sixteenth year. By that time, Fiery Hooves, Desert Rider, Wings of the Storm, and all the other beasts were my friends. I grew to be one of the finest riders the House had ever known, second only to the Horsemaster, who ruled the stables with a golden lasso.

"Each year, it was customary for the Great Matriarch to view all the slaves she owned on her birthday. She was ancient, and in the compound it was rumoured she had three eyes, the third in the middle of her forehead. On that momentous day, I was led into the grand mansion with a hundred others and brought before the Great Mother in her antechamber.

"On either side of the old woman was a retinue of nobles, resplendent in their silks, golden threads, and brocades, but I, as a young man, saw only the beautiful face of the young girl who sat at her right. Her name was Ling, and all in the compound knew her as the ward of the Matriarch, already betrothed to a man many years her senior, to cement the riches of two noble families.

"When I was led before the Matriarch, the Horsemaster announced me. 'Step forward, Mouse!'

"I had always hated my slave-name, and as I approached, something caught in my throat. Madness overtook me. I looked at the beautiful young girl and shouted, 'My name is Tiger!'

"Bedlam ensued. A half-dozen guardsmen leapt forward. My life was forfeit, but as a guard raised his blade, the Great Mother broke out in a rasping, breathless cackle. 'Tiger, he calls himself!' She laughed. "Let him be known as Tiger-mouse from now on!'

"I was led away to be beaten, but not before I noted a tiny smile play on the lips of the beautiful young girl."

Grandfather wet his lips with Scotch and continued speaking.

"Later that year, the House acquired a stallion they believed would sire the greatest bloodline in the Middle Kingdom. They named this wondrous beast Emperor, but so fierce and powerful was he that none could ride him, not even the Horsemaster. I, myself, could barely keep a seat on his back, and only for short periods at a time.

"So Emperor was put to stud. Breeding horses is a testy affair at any time, and doubly so with such an immense and temperamental animal. In the stalls, the mare had to be secured in a paddock scarcely as wide as her girth. The stallion would be tethered from behind so as not to injure the other horse, but not so much as to despoil the mood. So secretive was the process that only Horsemaster and I would attend those sessions. No others were permitted in the mating stalls.

"When the time came, Emperor proved more than equal to the task. With each mare he serviced, he stamped his hooves impatiently. Were there no more? he seemed to say. As I led another mare into the paddock, I heard a sound from behind some bales of hay. I peered behind them.

"I gasped. Kneeling before me, behind the hay, was none other than Ling, the beautiful ward of the Great Matriarch. Imagine the audacity of her actions! Stealing into a breeding barn to witness the mating of a great horse. Whoever would dare such a deed? And a mere girl, at that!

"As the young woman motioned me frantically to silence, I leaned forward and stole a kiss from her vermilion lips! So surprised was she that she could find no words. My audacity had matched her own! Shushing her with my finger, I positioned the mare in the paddock. Horsemaster, who had his hands full with Emperor, had not noticed Ling.

"So began my assignations with Ling, the beautiful ward of the Great Matriarch. We met in secret, coming together in hiding, all over the compound and outside. I learned she hated the thought of being married off to an old man (much like a brood mare herself) but could see no escape from the fate set for her by the Matriarch.

"Thus I plotted to gain my freedom to save Ling from this cruel destiny. Sometimes she rejoiced at the idea of running away with me, but other times she lamented about our future. How would we live, penniless and afraid? The days counted down to when she would be sent to her betrothed.

"For weeks, I exercised Emperor, riding him farther and farther afield. Each day, he carried me a little longer without throwing me. I knew, if I could but keep my seat, no other horse in the Middle Kingdom would ever catch me.

"Finally, the day arrived for our great escape. I had arranged to meet Ling at the birthing stalls on a moonless night. She had delivered a flagon of wine to the night watch, drugged with a sleeping draft. I waited at the stables for Ling. All night I watched. And waited. Then I realized she was not coming. She had chosen the gilded cage over a fugitive's life of freedom.

"But then I faced my own choice, I paced in indecision, pondering what to do. With but one hour before the dawn, I placed a saddle over Emperor's back. The mighty beast galloped through the compound's gate, and never did I look back. Together we rode all day and the next to our freedom. Nor do I now begrudge Ling and her decision. Without her prompting, I would never have dared escape.

"That is why, today, you see before you a free man called Tiger-mouse."

Hoi Wing sank back in his seat, his mind still lost in Grandfather's story. He wondered if he himself might one day escape his situation at the uncles' laundry, or if he might somehow help Heather improve her predicament at *Blah-dok*'s.

Another bottle of whisky appeared as if by magic. Second Uncle left the table and returned with a battered case from which he drew out an *er-hu*. As he tuned the instrument, the men toasted Grandfather's story, the New Year, and the honest health inspector. Then Second Uncle drew a first melancholic note with his bow.

Soon, Second Uncle warmed to his song, and Grandfather thumped his boot to the beat. Elder Uncle hummed an accompaniment. Hoi Wing threw back his head and tilted another glass over his lips. The men drank another round, and the temperature in the laundry seemed to rise. Hoi Wing's cheeks felt swollen, and the conversation grew uproarious.

"To stealing more clients from under their *lofan* noses!" Elder Uncle bellowed. The men cheered and raised their glasses again. Hoi Wing had lost count of the bottles, and the festivities approached a fever pitch.

"Grandfather Tiger-mouse!" he shouted, feeling the sudden urge to get something off his chest. "You have the most asinine nickname in all the Gold Mountain!"

Second Uncle laughed so hard his toothpick fell from his lips. "See what I mean? Our young apprentice has teeth!"

"Second Uncle." Hoi Wing turned to the man. "You play the *er-hu* like a child!"

Now Grandfather laughed until he almost fell off his chair, but Hoi Wing had saved the best for last. Leaning across the table, he shook his finger at Elder Uncle. "You heartless, one-armed bastard! How dare you try to keep me from learning *lofan*? I am the unstoppable son of Ying the Scholar!"

Everyone laughed at that one, including Hoi Wing. Tobacco fumes choked the air, and the men downed more of the golden elixir. Elder Uncle began to sing. It was a ballad of love, a beautiful woman, and a reunion that never takes place. Hoi Wing's mouth fell open. Even inebriated, he could appreciate the man's virtuoso talent.

Grandfather got up to dance. He lurched about like a sailor on the high seas, slapping rhythmically at his knees, shins, and heavy leather boots, gesticulating wildly, almost burning the others with his cigar. Second Uncle's *er-hu* screeched. Elder Uncle's voice rose in pitch and volume.

Hoi Wing shoved his glass aside. His stomach had become a cauldron of churning Scotch and the undigested spicy chicken and *gai-lan* consumed hours before. He rested his head on his forearms as Second Uncle's bow stroke grew ever more frenzied. As Hoi Wing's eyelids fell shut, the last thing he remembered was Elder Uncle's magnificent tenor, reverberating within the walls of the laundry, and the smouldering gaze of the man's beautiful wife, looking down from the Wall of Family.

Two nights later, Heather was at the Sanctuary when Hoi Wing arrived after dark. He had thought she might be worried, but she had already learned in the house that the laundry had passed its inspection. After all, Braddock had manufactured the complaint himself. What she had not heard about was the attempt at bribery.

"Surprised your *lofan* inspector turned out to be honest, Harry?" she asked with a smile.

"Yes," Hoi Wing answered. "He is honest *lofan*."

"Oh, ye of little faith." She giggled delightedly at his look of incomprehension.

The threat of closure lifted, Heather held up the book Hoi Wing had left in the root cellar several days earlier. She had been reading in his absence and was already several chapters into the novel. "This is a fine choice. Shall I read?"

"Yes, please." He sat back on his cushion and made himself comfortable as Heather flipped to page one of *The Call of the Wild.*

∞

Soon they were halfway into *The Call of the Wild*. Hoi Wing was engrossed by the adventures of Buck and barely breathed as he sat at shoulder, following the movement of her finger over the page. He loved the story and was thrilled to learn of the Yukon gold hunt.

One night, he entered the Sanctuary with his forearms cramping after a day's work at the irons. He found that Heather had finally placed a picture in the wooden frame he had given her at New Year.

"My family," she said. "My only picture."

Her family! Hoi Wing squinted at the sepia tones of the photo. It depicted a young but recognizable Heather, seated and flanked by two younger children, both of whom leaned across her thighs. Heather's arms were draped over their shoulders, and all three wore the same dark clothes and sombre expressions. "My brother, Aemon, and sister, Sheelagh. Back home, before we came to the colonies."

He studied their solemn faces. She had a Wall of Family too, but it was housed entirely within a single picture frame. "Where are brother and sister now?"

Her voice dropped to a whisper. "It's just me and Aemon now."

"What?"

"Ma died back home. Pa barely came round, except when Ma was flush. Then he would pester her for money until she gave in. He would have drunk it all if he could have. The landlord would pound on our door, hollering for the rent. When Ma couldn't get washing or needlework, we'd share our space with another family. With no money coming in, we'd go begging for bones from the butcher. Otherwise, we'd have starved. Then Ma died. It was the almshouse for us—Aemon, Sheelagh, and me. That or the hayloft, the asylum, or even the reformatories."

"But where your brother and sister now?"

"Sheelagh got the cough on the crossing and didn't survive. Aemon came ashore like me in Quebec. Those Bible women said we'd find new lives in the Dominion across the sea. Fresh air with room to grow. Home children, they called us. Like we were ever going to have a home! More like waifs, paupers, or waywards! I went to Miss Frost's Western Home in Niagara. Boys got placements on the farms, but we girls got the service.

"They sent Aemon to some farmer up north. He writes me every few months, but he was never much for words. This is the last letter I received." She held out a crumpled envelope. "He's being worked to the bone!"

The candle on the shelf burned low. Hoi Wing held the letter in his fingertips and edged closer to Heather. She leaned into his chest. They talked no more. When the candle burned out, he lit another. And then another.

13

In mid-February, there came a thaw, and the roadways slickened with slush. Pedestrians sank mid-calf into potholes of icy water. The sun poked its face from behind the clouds, but then it paled and hid once more. Hoi Wing stood at the big table, wrapping shirts in brown paper. He grimaced when he looked out the window, but Second Uncle said spring was not far around the corner.

Hoi Wing continued his late night visits to the Sanctuary. Several riveting chapters remained in *The Call of the Wild*, and he looked forward to the denouement of Buck's saga in the Far North. Never again would Hoi Wing stroll past a library without wanting to peer inside. He had discovered a new novel he wanted them to undertake, Jules Verne's *From the Earth to the Moon*, but Heather insisted their next choice should be hers: *Little Women*.

When Hoi Wing next attended a "special delivery" at Miss Martha's house, Adele surprised him by setting aside his textbooks and sitting him down before a chessboard and pieces. *Lofan* chess! Hoi Wing had always wanted to learn the Western version of the game.

"This is a pawn," said Adele as she picked up a wooden piece.

Hoi Wing studied a black piece shaped like a horse's head. The goal of the game was no different than in Chinese chess, but it featured knights, bishops, and rooks rather than chariots, elephants, and leaping cannons. Hoi Wing quickly grasped how each piece moved, and the two were into the mid-game when Martha entered the dining room with lunch.

"Are we not continuing our regular lessons?" asked Martha, putting down her tray.

"We've been pushing Hoi Wing so hard, I felt we needed to do something just for fun. Chess is wonderful for the brain and relaxing as well."

"But what about your plan to get Hoi Wing into school next September?"

Adele sighed. "A half-hour each week is just not enough. I'm never going to cover the curriculum. We need Hoi Wing in our two-hour class on Thursday nights."

Hoi Wing looked up from the chessboard. He was beginning to see some of the stratagems of Western chess. "I no can do Thursday night. Elder Uncle say no."

Adele moved her queen to an open file. "Then I will just have to take matters into my own hands."

That night, Hoi Wing lay in bed, unable to sleep. He rose and lit a candle at his workbench. Then he completed his latest letter to Eldest Great Auntie, telling her of the clandestine *lofan* classes he was attending and *Ah-Del's* plan to enrol him in the public school system. He questioned Eldest Great Auntie about his mother's origins and the stories about his father's great failure at the examination tables. When he put down his pen, he went back to bed, feeling a sense of accomplishment. Perhaps now someone would finally give him the answers to the questions that had haunted him all his life.

Two days later, he returned to the laundry in the early evening from deliveries to find Elder Uncle fuming.

"You've been taking secret classes with those busybody *lofan* women!" he shouted.

Hoi Wing glanced at Second Uncle. He didn't need either man to say that Adele and Miss Martha had come by to speak with them.

"Why is that so bad?" Second Uncle threw up his hands. "Those ladies are only teaching him to read and write. If Hoi Wing's *lofan* improves, it helps the laundry too. And that's a special order every week. Those ladies are paying for it."

"Farmboy, you will stop attending those classes immediately!"

"Why?" asked Hoi Wing.

"Don't you see?" Elder Uncle said. "Those nosy church ladies are just raising your hopes without reason. No school will accept you here. You'll never be given a chance—no matter how much *lofan* you speak!"

"What if I finished my deliveries by six o'clock? Why couldn't I take the Thursday night class? With my sled, I can complete those circuits in less than four hours."

"Farmboy, your mouth runs faster than your feet. No one finishes the deliveries by six o'clock. And you still haven't paid me for that lumber you used to build your little toy!"

"Dragon of the Snows is no toy! I use it for my work in *your* business." Hoi Wing took a deep breath. "I propose a wager. If I complete the Golden Li circuits in five hours or less, Dragon of the Snows is mine, free of charge, and you will release me every Thursday evening to attend *lofan* classes at the worship hall."

Elder Uncle laughed. "Do you take me for an idiot? I'm not taking that bet. You already owe me for the lumber."

Hoi Wing had expected this answer. "Then let's raise the stakes. If I fail to complete the deliveries in five hours or less, I will forfeit three hours every Sunday afternoon to do additional work for you. But if I succeed, you will allow me to attend those *lofan* classes and regular school in the fall!"

"Young Man, don't be silly!" said Second Uncle. "No one can make those deliveries that fast!"

Elder Uncle looked Hoi Wing in the eye. "Farmboy, your terms are ridiculous, but I'll allow you to attend school here, because that will never happen. How about this wager? I bet you *can't* complete the Golden Li circuits in less than three and a half hours, and when you fail, you will pay me triple the price of the wood, and you will work six extra hours every Sunday afternoon for me."

"That's outrageous!" said Second Uncle. "Hoi Wing, don't take that bet. You're risking far too much."

"Farmboy, that's my last offer. We do this next Thursday or never."

Hoi Wing hesitated. In the past few months, the laundry's delivery list had grown, with clients spread across the city. Elder Uncle's challenge was monstrously difficult and the odds usuriously unfair. Still, a quiet confidence had been building within him.

"I accept your wager! If I win, I get the lumber free, the *lofan* classes, and the right to go to school in the fall."

He and Elder Uncle shook hands to cement the agreement, but Second Uncle slapped his forehead in dismay. "What are you thinking? The recent thaw has turned the streets into sheets of ice!"

Elder Uncle laughed. "My knees are already forecasting a blizzard of slush and sleet!"

Heather gave a low whistle of appreciation when he told her about the bet. "Do you think you can do it?"

Hoi Wing sighed. "No choice for me. I must make deliveries in less than three and half hours or lose six free hours for all Sundays."

The two were at Montebello Park late at night, three days after he had made his wager with Elder Uncle. Antony and Cleo frolicked in the hard-crusted snow. The air was crisp, and the moonlight transformed the parkland into a field of diamonds.

"How long does it take you to make the deliveries now?" Heather threw a stick over the heads of the dogs.

Hoi Wing had never actually timed himself, although he knew it took much longer than three and a half hours. "Four and half hours? Maybe five? All afternoon and early evening I am making the deliveries."

"So you have to better your usual time by one or even one and a half hours to win this gamble of yours?"

Hoi Wing nodded glumly. The immensity of the task weighed heavily on his mind. He had been so caught up with winning the *lofan* classes that he had completely failed to contemplate the consequences of failure. If only he had thought more carefully before accepting the wager!

"Has your Miss Adele said anything more about your entering school this September?"

He shook his head. Unconsciously, he reached within his jacket for the lucky amulet that was no longer there. Was he now to lose half his precious Sundays due to the groundless promise of a *lofan* woman he scarcely knew?

"Can you change the bet at this time?" Heather wrested the branch from the jaws of Antony.

"Too late to change now." Hoi Wing watched the dogs race across the field as Heather threw the stick again. If life were a book, he would harness Antony and Cleo to Dragon of the Snows and have them pull him through the Golden Li. "I will lose six hours on Sunday and pay three times price of wood."

"Harry, don't say that. If you don't try, how will you ever succeed?"

"But three and half hours is too short!"

"Too short for the way you run the circuits now, but what if you ran them differently?"

"How differently?"

"What if you pulled Dragon of the Snows through the back alleys and ravines instead of the streets? Cut through the parks and backyards? Wouldn't you avoid all traffic and pedestrians? Wouldn't you be faster than any motor car, horse, or wagon?"

A scintilla of hope sparked in Hoi Wing's chest. "But how, Heather? How?"

Ever practical, Heather picked up a twig and traced a map in the snow. "You've already charted most of the city's laneways. You must prepare a route that will save you as much time as possible. See here? This is Montebello Park and the adjacent streets. Where are your deliveries? Let's mark them out now."

Her enthusiasm was infectious. Hoi Wing plucked the twig from her hand and placed an X at every stop. Heather was right. He couldn't give up, no matter what the odds. He had to plan it perfectly. He had to run a little faster. He had to win.

∞

The days before the big race passed quickly. Monday, Tuesday, and Wednesday he sorted, washed, dried, and ironed. In the evenings, he prepared. First, he inspected every inch of Dragon of the Snows, sanding, gluing, and repairing her wooden chassis. He greased her runners, oiled her harness, and replaced the ropes used to fasten laundry to her bed.

Each night, he reviewed his map. After much consideration, he and Heather had broken the race into two components. There was a first, longer trajectory where he would take the alley behind St. Paul Street and head west until he took a shortcut through a ravine to the park. Once in the Golden Li, he would make most of his deliveries from the back lanes. Why hadn't he thought of that before? The workmen's entrance was always at the back of the house.

The second loop was shorter, and although it included two outlier homes at the very edges of the city, he would return to the laundry via the alley behind St. Paul.

Every night, he studied the weather. The temperature remained below freezing, which might provide better footing, but a few degrees higher and everything would turn to mush. What would happen then? There were just too many variables to know whether his plan would work.

14

On the morning of the race, Hoi Wing sprang to the window. The early dawn was bright, and there was no new snow. He whooped with joy. *So much for Elder Uncle's weather prognostications!*

After breakfast, he folded and wrapped laundry. He shuffled and reshuffled his packages, planning for optimal efficiency. Every so often, Elder Uncle would comment on his work. "That collar is uneven," he'd say. Or "Farmboy, perhaps you should trim that twine." Once he sang out: "I'm already planning all the extra duties you'll be doing for me on Sunday afternoons!"

Hoi Wing watched the sky, which seethed with pewter clouds. Would snow come? Elder Uncle's blizzard had not materialized, but snow, sleet, and even rain remained a possibility.

In the end, his preparations were complete at two o'clock. Finally, he stood in the backyard, tightening a strap over a fully loaded Dragon of the Snows.

Second Uncle stepped into the yard. "Young Man, are you ready?"

"Never so ready for anything in my life."

"The odds are against you. And if you lose, you will rue this day. There's still time to come to a compromise to save face and your freedom on Sunday afternoons."

"No. I plan to win and nothing else."

Second Uncle gripped his shoulders. "Very well. You have made a man-sized wager, and there is a price to be paid should you lose. Grandfather Foo will be joining us later to cheer you on."

Hoi Wing bent to adjust another binding, but when he raised his eyes, the sky had turned to lead. Snowflakes were drifting downward.

Second Uncle handed Hoi Wing a hip flask. "Drink from this only when you feel great fatigue or fear your courage has deserted you."

Hoi Wing slipped it into his pocket. The snow crunched underfoot as he jogged in place. It was ten minutes past two. The sky swirled like laundry swill, and the snow blew in from the canal.

"Run hard and fast. Heed the route you mapped," Second Uncle said.

Shutting his eyes, Hoi Wing reviewed the trajectories he had plotted. He saw every corner, alley, and secret laneway where he could steal a second. The trails and ravines would be his best friends. Feet would pass when hooves and tires could not.

"This is your chance to win those *lofan* classes you want so badly," said Second Uncle.

"And to go to school." Hoi Wing gripped Second Uncle's hand, wanting to thank him for everything and more.

"Ho! Does Farmboy still think he can run the circuits in under three and a half hours?" Elder Uncle stepped into the backyard. "The blizzard's starting! And it's cold enough to freeze your balls off."

"A little snow's nothing to a Gold Mountaineer like Hoi Wing," said Second Uncle.

Elder Uncle tugged Hoi Wing's cap over the boy's eyes. "What do you say? Still want to go through with this?"

Hoi Wing shoved the man's hand away. "I'm going to win this race!"

Second Uncle fixed the other man with an odd look. "Big Brother, he is the image of another confident young lad I remember. Full of spit and fire. Courageous to the sky. Undaunted by any challenge."

"Let's just get this race started." Elder Uncle coughed. "With the extra work he'll be doing on Sundays, I'm already counting the coins!"

Second Uncle dangled a pocket watch from his fingers. "Young Man, the race begins in thirty seconds. Are you ready?"

Snowflakes swirled, tossed by an invisible hand. Beyond the backyard fence, the sky was fading to white. Hoi Wing tightened the strap against his chest. All he had fought for was in play. The *lofan* classes he wanted. A chance to attend school. Nothing mattered but the next three and a half hours. He visualized himself flying across the city.

"Nephew, on your mark!" Second Uncle raised a handkerchief. "We are ten seconds to start. Eight! Five seconds! Ready, set . . . GO!"

Hoi Wing leapt forward, throwing his body against the harness. His boots churned snow and ice. Dragon of the Snows fishtailed as he charged past Second Uncle. Within seconds, he had crossed the yard and was through the gate. He swerved hard to the right.

Beyond the fence, the wind rasped, and snow blinded his eyes. Visibility was fading quickly. Then he found purchase over the hardpack and accelerated into the lane. Fifty yards down the alley, he realized Second Uncle had given a great shout and kicked Dragon of the Snows forward as Hoi Wing passed him. And he didn't have to look back to know the man was cheering madly behind him.

∞

In his mind, Hoi Wing was a racehorse. His breath was a cloud, and the wind squeezed tears from his eyes. The harness bit across his chest. By the second pickup, he was already overheating, and he tossed his hat and gloves onto the sled.

The snowfall intensified. On his fourth stop, he collected two sacks of linens, oozing brown fluid. Precious time was squandered rearranging bundles to keep his packages untainted. On the ninth stop, a maid he had never encountered before ignored his frantic knocking until he tossed pebbles at a window. Then she opened the door and berated him for a full five minutes before allowing him to pick up the new load. His fingers fumbled as he worked the icy buckles. Who could have foretold a change in domestic staff? What was the time? Faster, he had to go faster!

The afternoon light was waning when he made his final pickup of the first circuit. Now he could barely see fifty feet ahead. As he left the Golden Li, a massive shape towered out of the snowstorm. Heavy hooves pounded, and a giant horse veered past him, pulling a sledge with its burden of two men and a mountain of ice.

"Be wary, lad!" the man sang out. He was perched high atop the ice blocks harvested from Martindale Pond, an axe riding casually over his shoulder.

When Hoi Wing reached downtown, the streets were choked with horses, carriage drivers, and stalled motor cars. The apothecary and the confectioner had closed their shops. At the junction of Ontario and St. Paul Streets, Hoi Wing caught his boot in a streetcar rut. He turned his ankle and went down hard. *Now he had done it!* Rising, he probed his old injury. Later there would be hell to pay, but for the moment his ankle was still loose and flexible. *It only hurt when he moved.*

Near the printer's shop, Hoi Wing veered into a back alley. Empty and open, it bypassed the clogged thoroughfares. He ran into the laneway between the sheds and maples. The path was strewn with garbage and discarded furniture. He drove Dragon of the Snows past a rabbit hutch and a chicken coop. And despite a recent city ordinance, he heard the squeal of a pig from behind a rickety fence.

A teenaged boy leaned from a backyard window and shouted as Hoi Wing ran by. He looked familiar; was he part of the gang who had chased him at Montebello Park? Did one of his enemies live so close to home? Hoi Wing didn't have time to worry about that. The light was fading from the sky. And he still had to run the second circuit!

Finally, Hoi Wing passed a familiar oak, and the laundry's backyard loomed ahead. He swept through the weathered gate as Second Uncle and Grandfather Foo cheered.

"What is the time?" Hoi Wing gasped.

"You're twenty minutes ahead of schedule!" Second Uncle lifted a pair of bags from Dragon of the Snows.

"You're favouring your ankle," Grandfather said. "Let me look."

He pressed Grandfather's hand away. "Stop jabbering and help me with these bags!"

When Dragon of the Snows was fully loaded again, Second Uncle spoke. "You bought yourself time with the first circuit. The second loop is shorter and easier. Just maintain your pace."

Then the snowfall turned to sleet.

Hoi Wing fell to the ground. Dragon of the Snows' runners were mired in slush. He cursed and pulled himself upright. Within his boot, his ankle was throbbing.

For the last hour, he had run without pause. The precipitation had become rain, sleet, and snow again. Water pooled over the streets. Ice sheathed horse troughs, hitching posts, and the branches of trees. Had it not been so treacherous, it would have been beautiful.

Despite everything, he was making fair time, but he had only covered half the final circuit. His clothes were soaked, and he prayed the laundry was dry under his canvas sheet. As he shivered uncontrollably, his legs felt weighted with cement. For the first time, he felt his dream was in jeopardy.

He reached for Second Uncle's hip flask, still untouched against his leg. In one swift motion, he downed a heavy gulp. Tears came to his eyes, but he choked down another nostril-clearing swig. The cement dropped from his legs, and he slipped Second Uncle's flask back into his pocket. Then he began to run again. The golden liquor had come to the rescue.

At last he stood at the back entrance to 121 Elm Street, his very last stop. He danced to keep warm and pounded at the door.

The light flicked on, and a maid appeared. Her face was stern, and she clutched the shawl at the base of her neck. "Hurry, boy! I'll not be standing in this foul weather all day!"

Hoi Wing unloaded his bundles from the sled and carried the packages inside. When he was ready to load the household's wash, he saw there was nothing for him. "Where is laundry for me?"

"We'll no be using your service anymore," the maid answered. "We've engaged the Cascade instead."

"Why?"

The woman grimaced. "Your laundry's diseased with contagions and bad humours. We don't want your kind touching our wash. Now be off with yahs! You're not welcome here."

The door slammed in his face. Hoi Wing stood in the dark. For the first time, he realized that for many customers *Blah-dok's* complaint would have been enough to change their minds.

Rain fell as he refastened his canvas tarp. His jacket and pants were soaked through. But the second circuit was complete; all that remained was to take the laundry home. And his burden was reduced. He did not have the usual four or five bags from his last stop. Hoi Wing lifted Second Uncle's hip flask to his lips. Not a drop remained.

With no time to lose, Hoi Wing pulled Dragon of the Snows down the middle of the street. As he neared an intersection, a motor car swerved into his path. The car's horn trumpeted like an elephant, and its headlights were like exploding suns. Hoi Wing screamed as he wrenched Dragon of the Snows aside. The car skidded past, and Hoi Wing plunged off the road.

Hoi Wing lay in a ditch, tangled in his traces. He rose and ran his hands over his legs and body. The crotch of his pants was hot and wet. Feeling faint, he tried to still the beating of his heart. What had that driver been thinking?

The straps holding his laundry had torn loose, and his bags had spilled onto the wet snow. Fighting nausea, he righted the sled. Then he wrestled the sacks onto the flatbed and refastened their bindings. He gasped in pain when he placed his weight on his left foot.

Hoi Wing crawled out of the ditch. The motor vehicle was long gone. Shaking, he dragged Dragon of the Snows back onto the road. The automobile had passed so close, he could have plucked the driver's goggles from his face. And the more Hoi Wing thought, the more certain he became. The driver had been *Blah-dok*.

∞

The storm was spent by the time he reached the narrow alley behind St. Paul Street. He had never been so cold or exhausted, and he moved with a limping, lurching gait. Dragon of the Snows dragged behind him as if he were hauling an elephant.

Every step he took made him wince. What was the time? Had he lost the wager already? Biting his lip, he willed himself to greater speed. The stink of backyard chicken coops and rabbit hutches came to his nostrils.

In the darkness of the laneway, a barrier loomed twenty yards ahead. As he neared, he discerned a haphazard mess thrown across the alley. It was composed of tree limbs as thick as a man's thigh, loose planks pierced by rusted nails, barrel staves, and a torn couch, its upholstery like spilled viscera.

What was this? Hoi Wing came to a halt, almost glad for the chance to rest his aching ankle. Confused, he turned full circle, searching for clues in the shadows. He stared at the nearby sheds and fences, but nothing moved. A chill descended upon him, and the back of his neck prickled with unease. Something was wrong!

"What you want?" he shouted. When there was no answer, he attacked the barricade, ripping out a plank and hurling it into a snowbank. Then he braced his hand against the couch and drew out a chair with three legs.

He was wrestling with a length of stovepipe when a chorus of whoops shredded the silence. A pack of boys emerged from the shadows. Hoi Wing's mouth went dry. The six of them formed a semicircle before him.

"Well, well," Ratface snickered. "Look-*ee* what we got here. Our old friend, the Chinaman."

Hoi Wing felt like vomiting. How had they known he would be here? They must have seen him on the first circuit. He locked eyes with each of the boys in turn: Ratface, Buck Teeth, Mean Handsome, Crooked Nose, Cross Eyed, and Little Brother.

Standing before the barricade, Hoi Wing scanned right and left. He clenched his fists, but his legs felt lead-weighted. And his ankle was badly sprained. There was no escape. No place to run. No root cellar to open magically underfoot.

The boys charged. Hoi Wing swung the stovepipe, and the metal clanged against Buck Teeth's forehead. The boy toppled into Mean Handsome and Cross Eyed, but the others ploughed into Hoi Wing.

A flurry of blows ensued. The scrum went to the ground, rolling, grappling, kicking, and cursing. Hoi Wing gouged someone's eye and kneed another's crotch. Twisting and squirming, he locked his arm around Crooked Nose's neck and bit him through his sweater. He lashed out with his arm and rose to one knee, but Ratface flattened him with a punch. Blows rained down as he tried to cover his face with his hands.

"Kill him! Kill him!" someone was shouting.

On the ground, Hoi Wing writhed and curled his body, trying to protect his head and belly. Stars exploded as a boot slammed into his ear and another into his ribs. It was as if they were stamping out a fire.

Dimly, he sensed a boy swinging a plank against Dragon of the Snows. Hoi Wing surged upright and head-butted Mean Handsome. He managed to kick Ratface between the legs before he was tackled again. Within a circle of pain, his body crumpled beneath the beating. He heard Dragon of the Snows splintering and his laundry bags ripped from their ropes. Someone was howling. The wooden club came down again and again. This was the end. Sparks flashed, and he saw no more.

∞

"Is he awake?"

Hoi Wing groaned and tried to lift his head.

"Stay down," said Grandfather Foo.

"Lie back." Second Uncle pressed him to the pillow. "Don't move. You must rest now."

Pain spiked Hoi Wing's skull. It was as if his head had been thrust through the big wringer. His ribs ached, and his ankle throbbed. "Where am I?"

"You're back in the laundry," said Elder Uncle.

Hoi Wing opened his eyes again. This time, the lamplight was less searing. He was in the attic. On the sloped roof, clothes hung from nails and hooks. It was hard to breathe. His fingers fumbled on a thick bandage over his nose. "What happened?"

"Don't touch that." Second Uncle lifted a bowl of ice. His forehead was furrowed with worry as he dabbed at Hoi Wing's face with a washcloth.

"Drink this." Grandfather Foo supported Hoi Wing's shoulders and held a cup of dark liquid to his lips.

Hoi Wing gagged and spat out the bitter draft.

"Drink it down," said Elder Uncle. "Tiger-mouse has spent hours brewing it for you."

Hoi Wing tried to sit up, but his head was too heavy for his neck. Bile filled his mouth, and the room spun. Suddenly, he remembered. "Did I win the race? What was the time?"

"Rest now, young man," said Second Uncle.

"Where is Dragon of the Snows?" Hoi Wing gripped Grandfather Foo's wrist, but the man's face dissolved before his eyes.

"Let him sleep," said Elder Uncle. "We can tell him later."

∞

He awoke to the sparkle of dust motes in the air. As before, he lay on one of the uncles' beds, but the clouds had cleared, and the ringing in his ears was gone. He could breathe, albeit with some difficulty through one nostril. His ribs still ached, but the throbbing in his ankle was much lessened. His tongue felt like shoe leather.

"Nephew!" Second Uncle sprang from his chair in the corner where he had been dozing. A sheet of paper and pencils spilled from his lap. He stared into Hoi Wing's eyes and laid his hand against his cheek. "You're awake. How do you feel?"

Hoi Wing threw his legs over the side of the bed. "I need the outhouse."

"You haven't opened your gift." Elder Uncle came down the basement stairs, a sack of laundry over his shoulder.

"I don't want it." At the workbench, Hoi Wing sat before a small box wrapped in red paper.

Elder Uncle let the bag of laundry fall to the floor with a heavy thud. "Your Second Uncle will be greatly disappointed. After what he's spent, he'll be squeezing pennies for months."

Six days had passed since the sled race. Two days before, Hoi Wing had returned to his own bedroom in the basement. His left arm still hung in a sling, and his rib cage and ankle were bandaged, but as Grandfather Foo had predicted, everything was healing clean and straight.

"The bruises on your face have faded." Elder Uncle pulled up a chair and sat down. "No one will ever know where their blows landed."

Hoi Wing's headaches were gone too, although coughing still caused a little pain. That afternoon, he had sorted and ironed. But what did it matter? He felt nothing: no relief over his health returned, no excitement about getting back on his feet. On the floor were the pieces of Dragon of the Snows, salvaged from the alley. He nudged the shattered planks with his toe.

"Come, Farmboy. Did the fight rob you of your curiosity as well? Don't you want to open Second Uncle's gift?"

The bruising and puffiness were gone, but when he looked into the mirror, the boy who stared back was a stranger. Why had that boy worked so hard to build a sled? What had been so important about learning to speak *lofan*?

Elder Uncle nudged the package within a hand's span. "Tiger-mouse says you don't need that sling anymore. Take it off and open your gift."

Hoi Wing felt empty and weightless. When he walked, he feared the wind might blow him away. Why had his father sent him to this accursed place? What had he hoped to accomplish?

"Open it!" Elder Uncle pressed the box into his fingers.

Hoi Wing stared coldly at him. With his right hand, he shredded the red tissue paper, revealing a cigar box of balsa wood. He raised the lid and found a half-dozen pencils with hard and soft leads, an eraser like a wad of gum, a bottle of indigo ink, and a pair of silver fountain pens. Beneath them lay a sheath of thick paper, bound in a leather cover.

"You will need these," Elder Uncle said, "when you attend the *lofan* class at the worship hall."

"I am not attending any *lofan* class."

"Why not? The church women are still conducting them every Thursday evening. You can start as soon as you can walk easily. It's the thing you've wanted most since you arrived."

Hoi Wing tossed a pencil onto the workbench. "What's the point of learning my ABCs? Even if I spoke perfectly, they'd still treat me like a dog."

"If you don't want those classes anymore, you are truly defeated!"

"I lost the wager. I didn't earn those classes. Those *lofan* bastards stopped me."

Elder Uncle sighed. "You were very close when you were ambushed. Only two hundred yards from home when we found you. You would have bested our wager by over twenty minutes. A boy pulling a sled. Twice as many stops. In the ugliest weather of the year. Don't you see? Sometimes it is in how we try that we succeed. The effort itself is the victory."

"That's nonsense!" Hoi Wing answered.

Elder Uncle knotted a rope through a ceiling joist and hoisted the heavy burlap bag into the air. "I haven't forgotten our wager. From now on, you will attend class with me as well."

"Are you insane?" Hoi Wing shook his head. "What are you going to teach me?"

Elder Uncle stepped back from the heavy bag and danced lightly. With his chin tucked, he snapped his right hand forward, and the bag jumped at the impact of his strike. Ducking and weaving, he threw a sudden flurry of punches and spinning kicks, the bag crumpling and sagging with each blow.

A sheen moistened the man's forehead as he paused. His eyes gleamed savagely. "When we found you, your attackers were still in the laneway. Six against one! Theirs the advantage of surprise. And five of them older and heavier. Of your assailants, you left one with a mask of blood. Another had to be helped away by his friends. And a third was crawling on the ground, weeping and clutching the fork of his legs!"

Hoi Wing remembered the surge of heat he had felt during the fight. "One was weeping and crawling?"

Elder Uncle steadied the bag with his hand. "Stand up, Farmboy! Are you a Gold Mountaineer or not?"

Hoi Wing rose slowly and slipped the sling from his arm.

"Step back." Elder Uncle positioned him before the heavy bag. "Keep your weight on the balls of your feet. That's it. Now raise your hands. Higher. Clench your fists, thumbs in. Now move, dance! Jab with your left! Roll your fist on impact! Again!"

Hoi Wing threw a few tentative punches, but the bag barely swayed.

"Come on, Farmboy! Faster! Keep your wrist straight! Imagine your jab as the strike of a dragon. Twist your hip. Power flows from our core and legs. Without our *chi*, we are nothing. Now strike! Again!"

Hoi Wing threw punches, trying to imitate Elder Uncle's dancing and weaving. The bag remained as solid as a mountain, and his injured arm began to ache. Soon his breath grew laboured, and the basement became stiflingly hot. But then he snapped a punch, and the heavy bag jerked on impact. He punched again and felt the exhilaration of the power flowing through his core, shoulder, and fist.

"That's it!" Elder Uncle cried out. "Now strike again! And this time exhale as you throw your punch. Loudly. Once more! Again! I want to hear it."

PART TWO

15

To Hoi Wing, the son of my heart, if not my womb:

Last month, the Red-spot fever ravaged two nearby villages, although only Old Wan the Tinker succumbed in our town. A young woman from Bak-Sieuk birthed healthy twins earlier this winter, and your Fourth Auntie continues her training. One day she will surpass me as the finest midwife in the Four Counties.

So many questions you posed in your last missives. In your words, I sense self-doubt and uncertainty. You wonder if you will ever be permitted to go to school in your new home. You ask yourself how you will attend your new lofan classes and complete the tasks your employers demand of you. You fear the taint of your father's Great Failure at the examination chambers.

Do not be dismayed by these challenges! How do I know you will not fail? Let me tell you the full tale of the prophecy foretold at your birth.

How well I remember that night! I had spent the day at the mah-jong tables in the ancestral hall, riding my hottest streak of luck since the last Opium War. There I was, seated east in the high rollers' game, coins and paper bills piled like buffalo dung before us.

The raucous click-clackety-clack of mah-jong tiles filled the air, and ciga-rette smoke curled to the ceiling. As the game neared its climax, the players' breathing grew quick and shallow. Tiles were drawn and tossed at breakneck speed. I rubbed the lucky charm at my neck and drew the one tile I needed to complete my four poongs and a pair. "I'm eating it!" I cried in triumph.

Then I spied your father's wan face in the doorway, and my heart fell. I knew your mother's time had arrived. I shovelled my winnings into a purse and followed your father to your home. There I found your poor mother on the bed, her hands pressed over her distended belly. All day and well into the night, I tended at her labour, trying to ease her pain as you stubbornly refused to enter this life.

Unbeknownst to me, during those long hours, an itinerant fortune teller had wandered into our village. Alone and unheralded, he had passed through the western guard tower, unimpeded by the night watch, who had noted his scraggly beard, his tattered once-red robes, and the bend of his back over his staff. In the darkness, the soothsayer found his way to Drink the Waters Deeply's renowned fountain, where he slaked his thirst. Then he went from door to door, declaring in a loud voice that he had momentous portents to share.

Once again, warlords had been pillaging nearby, and no villager would allow him ingress. The homes were dark, and the moon was shrouded under thick clouds. He cursed bitterly, wondering if he might have to throw himself upon the open ground for the night. Then, from one of the meanest houses, he heard a woman's anguished wail that crescendoed into a screech. He threw himself forward and burst through a doorway, stumbling into your moth-er's bedroom where I was crouched between her knees, whispering words of encouragement.

I shrieked as the aged fortune teller crashed through the door. For an instant, I was convinced the ghost of my useless dead husband had appeared to claim Ying's first-born (should you ever arrive), but then I saw the intruder had feet, and despite his withered skin and ghastly pallor, he was a man like any other, although uglier and perhaps smellier than most.

In that moment, your mother gave a last, desperate cry, and you slid from her body in a slurry of blood and purple. I screamed in triumph and caught you in my sure hands.

"Such a propitious day! All omens are good!" The magician knelt by the bed and fingered the talismans of yellow paper hanging at his belt. He rummaged in his sack, pulling out a bag of tiny bones. Eagerly, he cast the I Ching.

"Give me my baby," your mother whispered. I cleansed you with a towel, and placed you at your mother's breast. The fortune teller studied his casting and consulted the Book of Changes. He began to intone: "I have seen his future. He will travel far—farther than an eagle flies in its lifetime. His fortune will be vast. One day, he will have gold enough for ten!"

I looked up from where I had been knotting the cord. My fingers were slick with bodily fluids, and my knees groaned as I climbed to my feet. I glared at the old man, whose hand was held out for payment. "Out, you old charlatan! This poor girl needs her rest!" I shooed the fortune teller with my hand and sank my foot into his rucksack.

"Ayah! Woman, are you mad?" The soothsayer scrambled for his bag and staff. As I raised my hand again, he fled from the house, almost colliding with your father, whom I had banished to a neighbour's home.

I left you with your parents and rinsed my hands in a basin, chuckling to myself that I had somehow mistaken the old beggar for the ghost of your worthless dead great-uncle (was that an omen of sorts?). I laughed at the generic "fortune" he had told. It could have applied to half the men in the village—so many had ventured to the New World!

But as I stepped outside, I gasped in wonder. An enormous full moon hung low over the hills, brighter and more blood-red than any I had ever seen. The *night was bathed in a dragon's beard of mist. My mind swirling, I fell to my knees. Did the old man know more than I had thought?*

I scanned the dark laneways but saw no sign of the fortune teller. Then I went to the village square and found him drinking from our fountain. There he told me of his journey from the distant hills of Gong An, and I purchased the good luck charm you wear today.

So that is how I know you will succeed with your lofan classes. That is how I know you will not disappoint your employers. And that is how I know I can count on your monthly remittance without fail.

Your Eldest Great Auntie

P.S. Perhaps you could send more? We need the Gold Mountain silver more than ever.

Hoi Wing sat on a tree stump in the forests outside St. Catharines. He read Eldest Great Auntie's letter a second time, digesting all she had said and trying to discern what she had not. Her words had meant to be a comfort, but she had pointedly ignored his questions about his mother's death and his father's great calamity. Even her story about the prophecy at his birth (amusing as it was) had not dispelled the doubts in his mind.

It was Sunday in early May. In the warmth of the noonday sun, Hoi Wing drank from his canteen. Almost three months had passed since the sled race. True to his word, Elder Uncle had permitted Hoi Wing to attend a noon-hour class every Monday whenever he performed a "special delivery" at Miss Martha's, as well as a two-hour session at English for Foreigners (where he was the only student) every Thursday evening at the church.

Nevertheless, Elder Uncle had also been steadily increasing Hoi Wing's workload at the laundry (out of spite?), and he constantly threatened to rescind his agreement if he thought Hoi Wing was slacking at his duties. As a result, Hoi Wing was busier than ever, often working late into the night and then studying at his workbench before falling exhausted into bed.

During the last months of the winter, it had seemed the snow would linger forever, and the laundry had become a silent, dreary place, broken only by the odd word or gesture by the laundrymen. Finally, the temperature had risen, but weeks of rain ensued, and Hoi Wing had felt he might go mad if he spent another day inside with the uncles. When he woke that morning, he had quickly slung on his rucksack and was out the door, telling the uncles only that he would spend the day hiking and exploring.

Now Hoi Wing lay back on the ancient tree trunk, listening to the trickle of ice melt and the faint hammering of a woodpecker. The first crocuses had pierced the forest floor. Sitting up, he stretched his arms. The warmth of the day was lulling him to sleep, but he had come into the forests to renew his spirit. He rose, shouldered his pack, and continued through the woods.

For a time, he followed a game trail that merged into an old logging road. Winding through the trees, it was deeply rutted by fresh tire tracks, wagon wheels, and hoofprints. Where did it lead? The road was unfamiliar and headed neither toward nor away from St. Catharines, but northward into a section of the forest where he had never ventured.

On a whim, he continued on the old road for another half-hour until he came to a wide expanse of bog and drowned trees. Beyond the swamp, he spied something that hinted of human hand: a fence and a sprawling encampment of sorts. Hoi Wing drew the binoculars from his rucksack. Through the eyepieces, he could make out wooden buildings and what might have been a guard tower. *A road to nowhere and now a secret base? This was too good to miss!*

Twenty minutes later, he drew his boot from the mud of the bog and knelt in the shelter of trees. Before him was a razor wire fence and tall cedar posts. Through the wire, he saw barracks, sheds, and stables. Rows of trucks, motor cars, and carts. A battery of artillery pieces. In one corner, ranks of men performed jumping jacks, squats, and push-ups. Others thrust bayonets into straw dummies. On the open field, troops leapt from concealed positions and charged. Battle cries rent the air, and master sergeants blew whistles.

Hoi Wing remained in the trees. The controlled chaos was a far cry from the amateur boot camp he had witnessed last fall, and these soldiers looked far more professional. But what was happening? Everything Grandfather had told him about the simmering internecine feuds in Europe came to mind. But there was no war as of yet. He wiped the sweat from his brow. Whatever this was, it was not play-acting.

"Put your hands on your head," someone said from behind him. "Now turn around. Real slow."

Hoi Wing felt his blood go cold. *He had been discovered!* Lifting his hands, he turned.

Two soldiers emerged from the trees. Their faces and khaki uniforms were camouflaged with mud, branches, and leaves.

"Well, well, *look-ee* here. A Chinaman!" hissed the first soldier.

"What are you doing here, son?" asked the second.

Hoi Wing groaned inside. How could he have been so careless? The two infantrymen stood less than eight feet away, their heavy rifles levelled at his chest.

"Down on your knees!" The first soldier motioned with his gun. "Keep your hands up!"

Hoi Wing knelt, his hands on his head. They had him dead in their sights. Dimly, he sensed the cold earth through his knees, but the air was stiflingly hot, and his mouth had gone dry.

"How long have you been here?" The second soldier was the older of the two, and his voice was low and calm.

"Five minutes only," Hoi Wing answered.

"He's a spy!" said the first. The barrel of his rifle jerked alarmingly as he spoke. "Just like they told us!"

"No! I am not a spy."

"Shut your goddamn mouth." The first soldier stepped forward, aiming his gun at Hoi Wing's head.

"What have you seen?" the second soldier asked.

"Nothing." Hoi Wing choked out the words. "Men. Soldiers. Horses."

"What's your name?"

"Harry Woo. I live at—"

"He's a spy!" The first soldier's breathing was shallow and quick. There was a click as he slid the bolt of his rifle forward. "We can shoot him on sight."

"No! Do not shoot!" Hoi Wing stared into the enormous black muzzle. He had a vision of Eldest Great Auntie and Little Mei-Mei weeping when they learned of his death. He wondered if he would feel the impact of the bullet crashing through his forehead and shattering his skull into a thousand pieces.

"Hold your fire, Billy!" said the second soldier.

"But he's a spy!"

"I said lower your weapon, soldier!"

"Aw, for Chrissakes." The first soldier dropped the barrel of his rifle.

There was something familiar about the first soldier's voice. He removed his helmet and wiped the mud from his face with his sleeve. Hoi Wing let out his breath in recognition. It had been only months since he had last seen him, but the young soldier's chin had widened with maturity, and his eyes seemed less beady than before. With a little satisfaction, Hoi Wing noted the boy was no longer as tall as he had once seemed.

Ratface spat in disgust. "Why do I have to lower my gun? He's a damn spy!"

The second soldier studied Hoi Wing with an even gaze. "He's no spy. I've seen him in town. He's just the laundryman's boy."

Hoi Wing did not get off scot-free. Ratface and the other soldier marched him through the stockade, past the ranks of men, and into one of the main buildings. There, Hoi Wing was brought before a tall, mustachioed officer and interrogated as to why he had been lurking at the fence. For two hours, the questions continued, and Hoi Wing found himself describing virtually all his activities since his arrival in Canada approximately eight months before. The officer seemed particularly interested in the clothes-washing process they employed. How many days did the laundrymen take to do the wash? What was the nature of the bleach they used?

Did they really think him a spy? Or was the officer merely trying to impress upon him the severity of his trespass? In the end, Hoi Wing was released with a strict warning not to speak of what he had seen and to never be found in the vicinity of the camp again. Ratface and the second, older soldier were eventually tasked with escorting Hoi Wing from the camp (this time with their rifles slung over their shoulders) and marching him a thousand paces down the logging road.

There, Hoi Wing looked the older soldier in the eye. "Thank you," he said. The man gave a slight nod before heading back to the encampment.

As Hoi Wing hiked back, his thoughts kept returning to the secret base. Today he had ventured far and seen something he should not have. Clearly, changes were afoot in St. Catharines and the wide world, and he would have to consult Grandfather about these developments.

In the late afternoon, Hoi Wing re-entered the city. Motor cars and horse-drawn carriages clogged the roadways. The downtown streets were filled with pedestrians enjoying the sunshine, although the shops were closed, as were the parks, where the swings were wound up and the teeter-totter padlocked because it was Sunday.

Hoi Wing wondered who amongst the townsfolk knew of the military encampment scarcely an hour from their city limits, and he strode proudly in their midst, self-satisfied with the information he possessed that they did not. Were the green-uniformed police officers riding on bicycle patrol in the know? He felt a smug confidence and a new-found sense of awareness.

At the corner of St. Paul and Ontario Streets, a small crowd had gathered, jostling to read some handbills that had been pasted prominently on lampposts. He sidled up beside them and perused the announcements.

The first was an advertisement for Lakeside Park, a popular beach destination at nearby Port Dalhousie. The poster featured illustrations of children in swimming wear, and promoted boating, fireworks displays, a carousel, amusements, and dancing.

But it was the second handbill that drew his attention:

COME ONE, COME ALL
MEN, WOMEN, AND CHILDREN

TO JONATHAN BRADDOCK'S
ANNUAL SUMMER PICNIC

An Open-Air Entertainment to Be Held This Year at Montebello Park!
SUNDAY, JUNE 21, 1914, 2:00 PM–6:00 PM

Refreshments and Meals Will Be Served!

Brass Band to Play!

Prizes, Contests for Men and Women, Games for Children

SPEECH TO BE MADE BY MR. JONATHAN BRADDOCK, ESQ., CHAIRMAN OF THE ST. CATHARINES BUSINESSMEN'S ASSOC.

GOD SAVE THE KING!

It was close to six o'clock when Hoi Wing returned to the laundry. He stepped inside and saw a stack of freshly laundered shirts awaiting pickup on the counter. Someone had left a sack of clothing by the wall. Hoi Wing lifted the door in the counter and passed through the curtain into the backrooms.

There, he found Elder Uncle seated in an armchair, a cup of tea at hand. His hair was now sprinkled with white, and he was immersed in a book. Second Uncle stood before him at an easel, his brush and a palette of watercolours in his hands. The man cocked an eyebrow as Hoi Wing peered at his latest work.

On the sheet of paper was an image of Elder Uncle, and Hoi Wing was once again impressed at how Second Uncle had rendered the older man's craggy but handsome features. Somehow, in the eyes and the line of the jaw, he had captured a hint of Elder Uncle's indomitable spirit.

"What do you think, Young Man?" Second Uncle mouthed his toothpick.

"It's a fine likeness."

"Did you have a good time this afternoon, tramping about in the woods?" Second Uncle asked.

Hoi Wing nodded and dropped his rucksack to the floor.

"Don't get too relaxed, Farmboy." Elder Uncle looked up from his book. "In a few weeks, I'll be lending you out to Grandfather Foo so he can teach you alterations work."

Another duty? thought Hoi Wing. "But I hate sewing!"

"I don't care. Every good laundryman knows how to hem pants or darn socks. It's part of the trade, and it'll be far more worthwhile for your future than all those damn *lofan* classes you've been wasting your time with."

Hoi Wing hung up his jacket, wondering how he would fit these new tasks into his already busy schedule. At least he would get to spend time with Grandfather Foo, whom he had not seen lately. He went to the kitchen for a cup of tea. Then he headed down to the basement. He had some homework to finish before tomorrow's special delivery at Miss Martha's.

16

The next morning, Hoi Wing worked steadily and without a break at the sorting tables until noon. Then he rushed out the door, waving a hasty goodbye to Second Uncle, who was rolling up his sleeves at the ironing boards.

On the way to Martha's, Hoi Wing ran past a city ballpark. He didn't want to be late for the special delivery. Often they spent their sessions in free-flowing conversation; sometimes he and Adele played chess. It was always a welcome change from the strict curriculum they followed on Thursday evenings.

At the home of the *lofan* ladies, Adele rushed him to the dining room, which was set up with the usual slate board and textbooks. Martha waited there, but today another person stood beside her, leaning against the buffet.

The visitor was a slim, dapper man, dressed in a fine tweed jacket and pleated trousers. A bright-blue tie was knotted about his neck, and he wore a neat goatee, although his sandy hair was in need of a trim.

"Hoi Wing," said Martha, "this is Professor Stephan Marsden, an old family friend. He just came back from Columbia University last fall. And he's our new superintendent of schools."

Hoi Wing's mouth fell open in surprise. Although the *lofan* gave no sign of recognition, there was no mistaking him: he was the third, awkward rider who could barely hold his seat at the fox hunt last fall!

"*Pleas-sed* to meet you, sir," said Hoi Wing, trying to find his composure. He held out his hand.

Professor Marsden nodded stiffly, although he shook Hoi Wing's hand with a firm grip. The man turned to Adele, who had re-entered the room bearing a platter of tea and sandwiches. "This is your little diamond in the rough? You never mentioned he was an Asiatic."

"Does that matter, Stephan?" answered Adele. "If he qualifies for school, it should make no difference."

Professor Marsden took a cup of tea. "Unfortunately, it may present a difficulty I had not anticipated. We have no students of his kind in our schools here, and studies indicate that Orientals will never succeed when mixed with our students."

"Aren't you prejudging Hoi Wing without any knowledge of his capabilities?" Martha said.

"I know of what I speak. Although my dissertation was on societal impacts and academic achievement, I am familiar with most of the scientific literature on intelligence gradients amongst the different races. My colleagues would say Hoi Wing's people are not overly intelligent, although they possess a form of devious cleverness that can lead an innocent to believe they know more than they do."

"That's absurd!" Adele said. "Hoi Wing's command of English and mathematics is remarkable!"

"I don't mean to be insulting, but I can't ignore the data." Professor Marsden glanced at Hoi Wing and sipped his tea. "Why don't we do this? Perhaps we should just engage in some simple conversation to see whether Hoi Wing can understand us at all."

Hoi Wing had not understood all the discussion, but clearly, he had to convince Professor Marsden that he belonged in school. For the next fifteen minutes, the foursome chatted over lunch. The ladies plied Hoi Wing with questions about his work, and Hoi Wing, flush from his interrogation at the mystery camp, spoke at length about the laundry.

"Well, Stephan," said Martha. "What do you think of our little 'diamond in the rough' now?"

Professor Marsden tugged at his goatee. "It's clear he can certainly make small talk about topics with which he's obviously familiar. Nonetheless, I am a scientist, and I wonder if any true language acquisition has occurred here."

Adele raised her eyebrows. "But you can't be saying no learning has occurred. He spoke not a word of English when he arrived last fall."

"And in terms of language skills alone, he's clearly qualified to enter into our school system as a newcomer, is he not?" Martha added.

"Let's not jump to conclusions." Professor Marsden frowned. "He has a rudimentary grasp of our tongue, but I once saw a parrot with a vocabulary of some two hundred words. In the same way, a circus horse can count bales of hay by stamping its hooves, but that doesn't convince me it knows mathematics. Hoi Wing may be a good mimic, but could he keep up in a classroom of our own students?"

Hoi Wing opened his mouth to speak, but Martha motioned him to silence. "Surely he could learn with the other children."

"Martha, in today's ever-evolving schoolroom, the students are taught to apply rational thought and analysis. The literature would suggest this boy's kind might be competent at repetition and memorization, but that is not true learning or comprehension."

"But I—" Hoi Wing began.

Adele interrupted him. "Stephan, you've already made up your mind without letting him demonstrate any of those attributes you've described."

Professor Marsden spread his hands. "I've no magic wand to transform him into a capable scholar. No one sews a silk purse from a sow's ear. And how would I convince any principal to take him? He looks old enough for the eighth grade. The newspapers are filled with stories of the yellow peril. Will our schools be swamped with hordes of Asiatics?"

Adele put her teacup down. "I don't believe what I'm hearing. He's one student! And you've branded him ill-fitted without giving him a chance. You haven't any basis to your statements whatsoever!"

"Please, I've upset you again, but there's no refuting the evidence. Science may serve up some unpalatable truths, but it rarely lies. In addition, the Orientals would have a bad effect on our students."

"What 'effect' do you mean?" asked Adele.

"Disease and contagions. But there would also be the problem of moral turpitude, degeneracy, and deplorable habits. Martha, you must have seen this during your missionary days in China."

"I saw desperate poverty and sickness—much of which had been caused by the actions of our own 'civilized' peoples in a 'backward' land. Do you not know the vast and unmitigated harm that has been caused by our flooding of their country with opium? Do you have any idea of the suffering we brought to generations of their people?"

"You have me at a disadvantage. I've never been to China. I only point out that the Almighty has always smiled on our people and given us dominion over the good earth, its beasts, and the lesser peoples."

"You're misquoting Scripture now! It doesn't say anything like that at all," said Martha.

"But our own prime ministers say this is a white man's nation. It has even been upheld in our courts that white women must not work for the Asiatics. Should we allow them in our classrooms?"

"Now you're confounding religion and politics. Render unto Caesar that which is Caesar's and unto God that which is His."

Professor Marsden shook his head good-naturedly. "I concede that I can never match Scripture with you, but look at the practicalities of what you are asking. I know you both mean well with your little pet project, but he's done nothing to prove he can compete with our students."

Hoi Wing had been squirming in his chair, squeezing his fists, and clenching his teeth as he listened to the back and forth (rapid-fire as it was). Now he rose out of his seat. "Then let me be proving it to you, Professor Marsden!"

The man turned to Hoi Wing in surprise. "What did you say?"

"I can compete with students!" Hoi Wing answered. "Give me test. Any test. I will write."

"Hoi Wing is right." Adele nodded. "If it's science you're seeking, why don't you test him?"

"Surely you have a ready diagnostic you could easily apply," added Martha.

The man smiled. "Very well. You have cornered me nicely. I could certainly conduct such a diagnostic, but before we go to all that trouble, why don't we simply examine his abilities in English?"

Professor Marsden addressed Hoi Wing directly for the first time. "Hoi Wing, I see, at the very least, you have won the respect and confidence of two very capable champions, both of whom I hold in high regard. This is highly irregular, but at their request I will ask you to write me an essay of some three hundred words on a topic I will choose. This must be written on your own, of course. If you present me with a passable essay, on the grade eight standard, I will test you in a comprehensive manner to see if you qualify for a place in one of our schools this fall."

Adele leapt to her feet. "That's a capital idea!"

"Bravo!" Martha clapped her hands. "Thank you, Stephan, that's as much as we'd hoped for."

Hoi Wing sat down as Adele squeezed his shoulder excitedly. He still wanted to rebut the professor's statements, but had he heard right? All the man wanted was an essay of three hundred words? Given a fair chance, he was sure he could do that. And he would make Marsden eat his words! Only what, exactly, was an essay?

"I don't know if I like your Professor Marsden," said Heather.

"I have to write a essay for him," Hoi Wing answered.

"An essay."

"*An* essay," Hoi Wing repeated.

It was late at night. Hoi Wing and Heather were seated in the Sanctuary. They had recently started reading *David Copperfield*, but today the book lay untouched between them. Hoi Wing bit into a biscuit she had looted from the kitchens.

"Professor Marsden seems highly suspicious of you and your countrymen."

"He is very polite and speaks correctly."

Heather took a sip of hot tea from Hoi Wing's flask. "Polite speech means nothing. You'll have to prove yourself by writing the best essay you possibly can, although the topic he's chosen is certainly going to be a challenge: 'Why I Am Glad to Be a British Subject.' Harry, are you a British subject?"

"No, but I have two weeks for writing three hundred words."

"Two weeks!" Heather waved her hands in exasperation. "What do you even know of the British Empire?"

"The British Empire is not good for we Chinese."

"Nor is it good for we Irish. How will you ever complete this assignment?"

Hoi Wing stretched out his legs, enjoying Heather's indignation. In the cramped space of the Sanctuary, he saw she had hit a recent growth spurt, and a gentler contour had come to her form. Her face was less angular. There was a pleasing curve to her forearm, and a weight to her thighs and hips he had never noticed.

It was weeks since Heather had been so fired up about anything. Now their relationship seemed tilted back to what it had been: the two of them against the world. He edged a little closer. "I saw poster in town for Mr. Braddock's picnic."

She shifted away, maintaining a space between their bodies. "Master Braddock's picnic is to be the biggest and grandest yet. They've been talking about it in the house for weeks."

"I can go?"

Heather paused. "I'll be working there. But the whole town is invited. If we're careful, you could attend. Who would notice you in a crowd unless you made a spectacle of yourself?"

Hoi Wing was not sure what a spectacle was, but he was fairly confident he would not be one. "I want to go."

"That's next month. You need to think of your essay first. You need to decide what you'll write."

Hoi Wing sat up and stifled a yawn. "Don't worry." He spoke with an assurance he didn't quite feel. "I find three hundred words for Professor Marsden."

∞

For the next week, Hoi Wing kept a pencil and notebook at hand as he sorted, washed, ironed, and packaged the laundry. Whenever a thought came to mind, he jotted it down. One lunch break, he found time to visit the library, where Adele helped him research books relating to the history of the Dominion of Canada and its place within the British Empire. Then she gave him a short lesson on composition, opinion, and expository writing. "You need to begin with a topic sentence," she said.

That night, after work, Hoi Wing spread his books, his notes, and his father's dictionary on the workbench. His eyes itched with fatigue as he tried to conjure a topic sentence. What did he want to say? Much of what he had read at the library bore little relation to his own life in China. Nor was he entitled to most of the benefits that had accrued by birth to the *lofan* around him.

On Friday night, Hoi Wing met Heather in the Sanctuary. He plied her with questions about her past. Was life better here or in England? What did she miss most about the mother country?

Heather closed her eyes and flicked her tongue over her lips. "Ice cream! Back home, there was a little Italian man who pulled a rickety cart up and down the street, calling out, *Ice-ee cream! Ice-ee cream!* A moustache covered half his face, and his eyebrows were just as overgrown. Aemon and Sheelagh and I, we'd spend our days searching the gutters for coins or bottles we could sell, just to have some ice cream."

Several days later, Hoi Wing was on the street returning from an errand when he spied Elder Uncle on the road in front of him. The man was perhaps thirty paces ahead, carrying a sack of laundry over his right shoulder.

Hoi Wing was about to hail him when he noticed a pack of five or six boys trailing in Elder Uncle's wake. *They were the little monsters of the ragamuffin gang!* Giggling and pointing their fingers, they followed Elder Uncle, chanting a refrain that was all too familiar. *"Chinky-Chinky Chinaman!"*

As Hoi Wing watched, a boy pulled a straw from his back pocket. He blew a mouthful of soggy peas at Elder Uncle's back. Another boy hurled a clump of sod.

Hoi Wing stopped and waited for Elder Uncle to explode. *He would teach these little hoodlums a lesson!* But to his astonishment, Elder Uncle only increased his pace. The children followed, keeping just out of reach, spraying Elder Uncle with peas and showering him with handfuls of soil.

Hoi Wing could scarcely believe his eyes. Just past the blind woman's house, a rock toppled the cap from Elder Uncle's head, but he didn't stop to retrieve it. At the livery stable, two grooms nudged each other, enjoying the spectacle. Hoi Wing was incensed. How dare they!

He kept following. The instant Elder Uncle reached the safety of the laundry, Hoi Wing sprang into the midst of the little devils and grabbed the biggest one by his shirt. Taken by surprise, the boy jumped, and his face twisted in sudden panic.

"You little—!" Hoi Wing raised his fist as the lad burst into tears. The others scattered. Suddenly, he couldn't bring himself to strike the child. Instead, Hoi Wing yanked the peashooter from the boy's hand and crushed it under his heel. He kicked the weeping lad in the seat of his pants. The little hooligan fled, calling for his mother.

Shaking with rage, Hoi Wing went back and picked up Elder Uncle's hat. When he entered the laundry, Elder Uncle had already removed his jacket and changed his shirt. He and Second Uncle were conversing by the wringer.

"I found your cap outside," said Hoi Wing.

"Oh?" Elder Uncle's eyes searched Hoi Wing's face, but Hoi Wing kept his features carefully neutral.

"The wind must have blown it off," said the man.

Hoi Wing handed him his cap before retreating downstairs into the basement.

Later that evening, after work was done for the day, Hoi Wing's mind returned to the incident he had witnessed. How could a pack of school-children harass an older and respectable adult in such a manner? Was that the "privilege" of being a British subject?

Hoi Wing sat at his workbench, organizing his thoughts. Elder Uncle was a powerful fighter, but as a grown-up he had retreated from the taunting and harassment of the ragamuffin gang to preserve his dignity.

Having power and wielding it were obviously different things. A responsible adult could not assault a child, although Braddock had felt no compunction about throwing Hoi Wing to the ground last fall. Hoi Wing rubbed his hip absent-mindedly. There was a lesson here if he could make sense of it.

In the end, Hoi Wing set aside this new conundrum to review the notes he had compiled for his essay. He could write all manner of untruths and hypocrisies to placate Professor Marsden, or he could tell him what he really believed and had experienced. And Miss Adele had said the assignment was as much a chance to express himself as it was to demonstrate his ability to think logically.

When Hoi Wing considered everything, the choice was simple. At his workbench, he tore up the draft he had been working on for over a week and a half. Two days remained until the deadline. With his father's dictionary at hand, he started again.

17

Every day was warmer than the previous. As the days grew longer, St. Catharines turned green with leaves, and in the backyard Elder Uncle's peonies thrust from the soil like blood-red spears. The bone-biting chill of the Gold Mountain winter faded from Hoi Wing's mind.

In the month of June, Hoi Wing's voice began to croak at inopportune moments. Hair sprouted on his body where it had not before. His knees and elbows ached with new-forming cartilage. As his energy levels shot to new-found heights, he boasted he could churn laundry around the clock, but each night he crashed into bed, exhausted by his labours, falling asleep the instant his head touched the pillow.

Hoi Wing completed his essay and handed it to Miss Adele at an English for Foreigners class. She glanced at it, and her eyes went wide before she sealed it in a large envelope. "Take out your notebooks," she said. "We still have a great deal to cover before the fall."

∞

The morning came when Elder Uncle sent Hoi Wing to Grandfather Foo's in the Foreign Quarter for the sewing lessons he had spoken of several weeks before. Hoi Wing left after breakfast with a sack of alterations jobs over his shoulder and a bag of apples in hand. Despite his complaints about sewing, he was glad for the change in his everyday routine, and he had wanted to visit Grandfather Foo's laundry since their meeting at the New Year's party.

Soon, Hoi Wing was trudging through St. Catharines' Foreign Quarter. The streets grew ever more narrow, and rows of workmen's homes listed like drunks returning from a night at the taverns. The air was thick with the odour of garlic, paprika, and cabbage simmering in soups. He came across a group of men, seated at a small table outside a house, passing a bottle as they smoked hand-rolled cigarettes and played cards.

Second Uncle had told him the neighbourhood was home to many of the city's foreign labourers and their families. The men had come from warm, distant climes to excavate the canal systems and build its locks. They were scarcely more welcome in St. Catharines than the men of China, but they, at least, had not been denied the comfort of their wives and families.

Hoi Wing continued onward and came to a little bungalow where a smoky-eyed woman stood on a wooden porch watering several plants that had sprouted in large clay pots. She was not overly tall, but she was striking in the red robe she wore. Her hair was dark and bound in a diaphanous scarf. Brass hoops dangled from her wrists. Her perfume wafted to him, and Hoi Wing surprised them both by smiling and touching his cap. When she smiled back, he hurried on, feeling suddenly shy.

Finally, Hoi Wing came to the juncture of two streets at an acute angle. A tiny shop was pincered between a furrier and a bicycle maker's, but he easily recognized the words CHINESE HAND LAUNDRY in bold red paint on the window. He gripped a rickety banister and climbed three worn steps, his boots fitting neatly into the half-moon grooves in the treads. A bell jangled as he opened the laundry's door.

Inside, Grandfather Foo's vestibule was even gloomier than the uncles', but a shrine to Gan Goung the Warrior Guardian sat on the floor by the counter. It was a symbol of loyalty and integrity, promising protection, prosperity, and luck. The little red altar was adorned with candles, and burning joss sticks injected a metallic tang into the air. Hoi Wing bent to examine the miniature figure of the red-faced warrior in silver cuirass, clutching a gleaming halberd.

"Ah, there you are!" Grandfather Foo poked his head through the curtain.

Hoi Wing stood. "Grandfather, thank you for your invitation. The uncles wanted me to bring you these apples."

The old man accepted the gifts and asked Hoi Wing if he had had his rice. Hoi Wing answered affirmatively as Grandfather Foo invited him into the backroom. The small space was crammed with a mangle, a wringer, ironing boards, tubs, troughs, baskets, and all the accoutrements of the laundry, but one wall featured a full apothecary's cabinet, replete with jars and vials of roots, herbs, dried insects, and coarse powders. Stacks of books (in both Chinese and *lofan*) and copies of newspapers cluttered the floor. Shirts hung from wires attached to the ceiling.

Another wall was covered with framed photographs and paintings of horses. Hoi Wing stared at the pictures. "Grandfather, that's not . . . It can't be—"

Grandfather Foo chuckled. "Yes, that is Dr. Sun Yat-sen."

Hoi Wing studied the photo. The Chinese president stood amongst a crowd of well-wishers, his curved moustache unmistakable. But at the very edge of the picture was a slight man in spectacles. "In that corner, isn't that—?"

"That is me." Grandfather Foo beamed. "I travelled to Toronto three years ago when the great man visited on his North American tour. On that night, I stood with a thousand brothers in a packed hall and cheered and cheered until I had no voice. And still we rejoiced because we were men of China, and we had never, even after so many years of absence, forsaken our homeland. After Sun's speech, I waited as he was mobbed by acolytes and fans. Most were turned away by his bodyguards, but I persevered and reached his side."

Hoi Wing nodded. He remembered his own father, Ying the Scholar, bursting through the doors of their little house with the news that the Chinese republic had been declared. Tears flowed from his eyes as he extolled Sun's Three Principles of Governance. "Nationalism, democracy, and the livelihood of the Chinese people!" Ying had cried. "No more will we be called the sick man of Asia! No more will emperors or foreign powers rule us!"

Hoi Wing then recalled his experience in the woods, and he questioned the old man about the secret palisade and the troops he had discovered outside St. Catharines.

"Do you not see?" Grandfather Foo's golden eye tooth glimmered. "That is the revolutionary fervour I mentioned before. Armies are forming as we speak. It's a powder keg! These *lofan* countries are following China's lead, with ordinary people fighting for independence and self-rule!"

Hoi Wing opened his mouth to ask his next question—he had so many—but there was a sudden hammering at the front door. Grandfather Foo went to answer the knocking, but when he opened the door, no one was there.

"Who was it?" asked Hoi Wing.

Grandfather Foo's face turned dark. "It was that little gang of *dead-naughty* rascals who live in this quarter. Sometimes they'll spend an entire afternoon knocking at my door and running away."

Hoi Wing wanted to continue their conversation, but the old man began rummaging through Hoi Wing's bag of alterations. "Enough small talk," he said. "We can discuss the changing world order another day. I promised your Elder Uncle I would teach you the craft of alterations. Let's get to work."

The next day, Miss Martha and Miss Adele surprised the uncles by coming to the laundry in the morning. Hoi Wing was in the backyard, hanging the wash, when Second Uncle told him he had visitors.

"We have wonderful news," Martha said to Hoi Wing at the front counter. "Professor Marsden has passed your essay! It meets the grade eight standard he was seeking."

"I was worried Stephan might take umbrage at what you had written, but it seems I've underestimated him," said Miss Adele. "I think your essay opened his eyes about many things he's always taken for granted—what those who are not subjects of the Empire have experienced, and the negative impact the Empire has had on their lives."

"Hoi Wing, there's not a moment to lose," added Martha. "Professor Marsden has said you must write a comprehensive intelligence test in late July. It'll cover everything—Reading, Arithmetic, History, Spelling, Dictation, Literature, Nature Study, and even Mechanical Operations. If you pass this, he'll have no choice but to enrol you in school!"

"Enrol in school?" Hoi Wing had to grip the counter to remain standing. It was the chance of a lifetime. Everything he had ever hoped for. And as much an opportunity for him as the Imperial Examinations had been for Ying the Scholar. "I need to study—"

"You need to get back to work, Farmboy!" Elder Uncle poked his head through the curtain behind the counter. "I'm not paying you to chit-chat with customers, and those clothes aren't going to dry unless you hang them up. Now get back outside!"

Two days later, Hoi Wing was sent to Grandfather Foo's for more instruction. The old man was overjoyed to learn of Hoi Wing's opportunity to attend school, but not so much that he neglected to continue their training. Today, he taught the art of embroidery, and Hoi Wing spent the day working with needle and thread, trying to fashion a delicate red peony on a white handkerchief.

In the early afternoon, Hoi Wing posed a question that had been on his mind for months. "Grandfather, who is this Rosie I've heard of, and where are her girls?"

The old man almost pricked his finger with his needle. "Who spoke to you of Rosie?"

"Tell me!" Hoi Wing said. "I need to know."

Grandfather Foo looked him in the eye. "You are thirteen now, old enough to understand. There are women like Rosie in every town, village, or city, although she has a different name everywhere you find her. Some condemn her as a *bad girl*, but Rosie's kind have served emperors and kings, as well as fishermen and farmers. Rosie is a *girl of comfort*, shall we say, and her services are for sale. You can find Rosie's establishment by the four broken pots sitting on her front porch. There are other such places in the Foreign Quarter, but the House of the Broken Pots caters to the town's most prominent citizens."

A girl of comfort! Hoi Wing turned back to his embroidery. He thought of the smoky-eyed woman he had smiled at a few days earlier. Was that Rosie? Then he remembered the older boys back home whispering stories about his mother. He had fought them all, regardless of how much bigger they had been, no matter how often his mother had told him to ignore them. Now he wondered if there had been any truth to their tales.

That night, Hoi Wing ran through the darkened streets to the Sanctuary. He had not seen Heather in several days, and he wanted to tell her the good news about his essay. When he arrived at the ravine behind the big house, all was quiet. He slipped quickly into the little root cellar and stumbled down the ladder. Heather was not there, but when he lit a candle, he saw her note: *Harry, I'm at my duties, preparing for the Master's big picnic. See you there.*

Hoi Wing spent the next day picking up laundry in the Golden Li. After Dragon of the Snows was destroyed in his battle with Ratface, he had toyed with the idea of rebuilding it with wheels to allow him to use it through the summer months. Nevertheless, with his increased duties and studies, he had never found the time. Thus, he passed the afternoon performing the Golden Li circuits with the laundry once again slung on a pole across his shoulders.

In the early evening, he returned home and found a letter waiting for him on the dining room table. Once more, he descended to the basement to read in peace.

To Hoi Wing, the son of my heart, if not my womb:

What can I tell you of your father's "great failure" at the provincial capital? How can I explain the "stories" you've heard about your honourable dead mother?

Perhaps the best place to start would be in Teacher Lee's class at the ancestral hall, where your father's education began.

It was during your father's second year in school that he began to distinguish himself. While other boys were forever fumbling in their pockets for crickets or fishing hooks, he discovered he had a gift for mimicry, an ear for Teacher Lee's high-pitched inflection, and, best of all, a loud voice. He learned to shout out verses, stanzas, and Tang Dynasty poems fearlessly in class.

Did he understand even a little of what he recited? Who knows? But as he grew, we called him Ying the Scholar, and soon the name became apt to his own ears. Quickly, he progressed to the Trimetrical Classic, the Thousand Words Classic, and the Incentive to Study. He read the Analects of the Great Sage and the teachings of Mencius. The Five Classics and the Odes, Spring and Autumn.

In adolescence and beyond, he was in constant study. Our family ate a poor man's diet of salt fish paste and tofu one week out of every four to finance his textbooks and extra tutelage from Teacher Lee. How proud we were! Like the new dawn, Ying would rise from our farmer's fields, pass the Imperial Examinations, and accede to the ranks of the Imperial Civil Service. A mandarin's position beckoned!

But how, then, did he fail to win his diploma?

I was awake the night your father came back from the provincial capital, and although most noted only the ignominy of his return, I saw the tall, raven-haired woman (she with the slight lisp) who accompanied him. In the days that followed, many chuckled at your father's failure in the Imperial

Examination Chambers, but rumours also began to circulate about the mysterious beauty he had brought home.

What was her honourable family name? Where was her ancestral village? Some whispered (more tsk-tsking and head shaking again) that Ying the Scholar had rescued her from a brothel. This woman strode boldly. Her legs were long and her shoulders broad. Need I say all eyes (especially those of the menfolk) followed her robust form whenever she shopped in the market stalls?

Whatever the truth, Fong-Fong (that was the only name she gave) worked as hard as any farm girl, threshing rice stalks mercilessly on fieldstones, filleting fish your father netted in the nearby lakes, and tending chickens in her red silken shoes(!). As she laboured, she often sang with a lilting accent, and neighbours paused their busy tasks whenever she lifted her voice. Others suggested she had been a mere two-yuan song-and-dance girl when your father found her, but your parents were blissfully oblivious to such disparagement.

Together, they lived in their tiny home on Beggars' Row, adjacent to the outhouses where the villagers composted human waste, the ashes from their hearths, and anything they couldn't feed to their pigs. On hot summer nights, an easterly breeze would waft the odour of the night soil through the windows of the little house, but Fong-Fong never complained.

Ying put down his pens and took up farming, often planting too soon or too late, composing poetry as he forgot to water his crops beneath the withering sun. Sometimes I would find him standing in his fields, seemingly lost as he scribbled verses on the hilt of his hoe.

Ying the Farmer, the villagers then chuckled, but I and a few others noted that the once bow-shouldered bookworm now seemed taller as he spent his days straining behind a plough, rather than hunched beneath a lamp.

Occasionally, raised voices were heard from their house, and at least one neighbour swore he had been startled by the shattering of a dish, hurled against the wall. How did Ying permit Fong-Fong to treat him thus? Why did he not send her to the rice closet? Nevertheless, after such episodes, there often came a time of intense stillness, during which the village grannies whispered that he was teaching her to read, but others hinted perhaps the couple was engaged in other activities. In another land, it might have been said they subsisted on but love and fresh air, but in Toisan no one said such a thing.

That is all I can tell you, son of my heart. Know that your parents were as happy a couple as I ever knew. Whatever caused your father's great failure, he never regretted his choice. So it should be when you make your own.

Your Eldest Great Auntie

P.S. Remember, never go to bed at night with wet hair. Keep your armpits dry of sweat. Wear my lucky charm! And of course, don't forget to send your next remittance as soon as possible. Perhaps you could send more?

It was Sunday morning, June 21, the day of Jonathan Braddock's annual picnic. Hoi Wing slept in and did not come up from the basement until almost ten o'clock. Then he took the rare opportunity to lounge about the laundry until lunchtime. He ate sparingly, telling the uncles he was saving his appetite for the big picnic.

"Young Man, I would not go if I were you." Second Uncle sipped his tea. "It's not what you think."

"But everyone is invited," said Hoi Wing.

"Farmboy." Elder Uncle waved his chopsticks. "Are you really so foolish as to believe they want you at their party? No one can predict what a gathering of *lofan* will do at any given moment."

"I'm going to go." Hoi Wing folded his arms. "And you're not stopping me."

∞

"It's like a carnival!" Heather's voice was breathless.

"What's a carnival?" Hoi Wing saw a trio of acrobats turn cartwheels across the lawn and watched jugglers toss bowling pins near an enormous red tent. Lanterns shone from the branches of trees. At the bandstand, a brass band struck up a jaunty tune as the crowd swayed to the music. Beneath Montebello Park's trees, the summer air was deliciously cool. It was the perfect Sunday afternoon for Jonathan Braddock's annual summer picnic.

"I've only a half-hour before I'm back at my duties," Heather said.

Hoi Wing and Heather strolled past an open-air kitchen where a side of beef was being roasted on a spit. Ribs, ham and cheese sandwiches, pound cake, digestive biscuits, lemonade, and tea were being served to the hungry picnickers, all courtesy of Mr. Braddock.

Everywhere Hoi Wing looked, people were laughing, talking, and eating. The uncles were wrong. Everyone was welcome. And Heather had been right. Who would notice him if he did not make a spectacle of himself?

"I have good news," he said. "My essay is passed! Professor Marsden says I only have to write a comprehensive exam next month, and I will go to school."

"Will Professor Marsden really let you into school? What's this exam about?"

"Everything," Hoi Wing answered. In the crowd, he noticed a long column of men and women waiting to enter a small green tent. "Why are those people in line?"

"I thought I told you. Master Braddock gives a twenty-five-cent piece to every picnicker. Everyone in town is here. That's a councilman and the man with him is a judge. Over there's the parson. The roly-poly fellow is the chief of police."

At the northern edge of the park were mess tents, picnic tables, and a cluster of booths where picnickers could engage in games of skill and chance. Past the stalls, dozens of men milled about a grey tent. As Hoi Wing watched, several emerged with tankards in hand. Grinning over their drinks, they kept to the trees.

"Braddy's Beer," said Heather. "It's what most have come for, though no one's supposed to know, especially the Temperance League and the Total Abstinence Society."

Hoi Wing nodded. Members of St. Catharines' constabulary were in attendance, but they had turned blind eyes to the grey tent. For the next ten minutes, he and Heather skirted the crowds as they watched a three-legged race and an egg tossing competition for teens. At the pond, they came upon a hotly contested tug-of-war between two teams, one of which was dressed in pinstriped uniforms that had the words *Braddy's Best* printed across the chest.

"That's the inter-county team sponsored by Mr. Braddock's brewery," Heather explained as the baseball squad dragged the losing team into the pond amongst the frogs and lily pads.

At the far end of the park, Hoi Wing approached a booth, confident that he could win a ceramic bulldog for Heather. To his chagrin, he found himself unable to toss any one of three leather ringettes over a glass bottle from what seemed to be a very short distance of only six feet or so. "Try again, young man!" The attendant winked cajolingly. Hoi Wing paid another penny and then another. He had spent fifteen cents—nine more than he could afford—before he let Heather drag him away.

"Speech!" someone shouted in the crowd. "Speech!"

"Mr. Braddock's going to speak!" someone else called.

A sudden fanfare erupted from the brass band. On cue, the mess tents ceased serving. At the beer tent, the flaps were pulled tight, and the barkers fell silent. Although many in the crowd might have preferred to remain at the picnic tables, most of them made their way toward the big red tent.

Soon, the congregation before the stage was ten or more deep. Magnesium powder flashed as photographers took pictures. "Down in the front!" someone cried out. Hoi Wing and Heather craned their necks over the rows of heads. Union Jacks waved, and a banner was strung across the trees: *Johnnie Braddock's Summer Picnic 1914!* The stage was six feet high. A podium and a newfangled electrical microphone had been placed at its centre. When the assembly had stilled, a small man climbed on stage.

"Ladies and gentlemen, boys and girls!" His voice squawked over the loudspeakers. "Thank you all for coming. It is my very great honour and pleasure to introduce our most magnanimous host this afternoon, the esteemed MR. JONATHAN BRADDOCK!"

Cheers and applause broke out when Braddock appeared. Wearing his trademark bowler hat and dark suit, he strode to the podium. "Welcome, welcome, welcome all to our annual picnic!" There was another screech from the loudspeakers.

"Hear! Hear!" shouted someone. Hoi Wing and Heather edged closer. The lanterns cast Braddock in a golden glow, and he twirled his wolf's head cane as if it were a twig. The handkerchief in his breast pocket was vermilion, and his gloves were of white silk.

"Are you all having a good time?" Braddock addressed the crowd.

There was a roar of applause and shouts of "Yes, we are."

"Has everyone had enough to eat?"

Another thunderous roar of approval met this question.

"Enough to drink?"

Now the cheers were deafening, and the men (including some baseballers) who lingered near the grey tent whistled and waved their caps wildly.

"My friends, I am so pleased you have joined us today!"

More polite applause greeted this statement as the assembly settled in for a speech they hoped would not keep them too much longer from the free food and drink.

Braddock removed his hat and slicked back his mane of hair. "Ladies and gentlemen, I have been honoured to serve you as the president of the St. Catharines Businessmen's Association these past few years, and I have worked tirelessly on your behalf."

"Hurrah for Mr. Braddock! Three cheers!" someone cried out.

"Braddy's Beer is best!" another man shouted from the back.

Braddock waited for the applause to die down. "I want to make you a promise." He took a deep breath for emphasis. "I promise to make St. Catharines a better home for us. Prosperity for all is my motto. Business people and the working man, toiling together for the betterment of everyone!"

"That's a hoot!" Heather whispered to Hoi Wing. "He couldn't care less about the working man!"

A man shouted suddenly in a deep, booming voice. "Will you run for mayor, Mr. Braddock?"

There was a hush as Braddock seemed to consider the question. He cupped his hand to his ear. "What did you say, sir?"

"Will you be our mayor, Mr. Braddock?" the question was flung out again. Suddenly, a multitude of voices took up the call. "Braddock for mayor! Braddock for mayor! Braddock for mayor!"

"Why, that's Collins the gardener," said Heather, identifying the man with the low voice. "And there's Willis the coachman too!"

Braddock let the accolade go on. The wave of adulation washed over him. He spread his arms and smiled beatifically. "Friends, thank you so much for your gracious words of encouragement, but please, I've not yet made up my mind to serve you in that capacity."

"Braddock for mayor! Braddock for mayor!" the throng repeated.

"But if I were mayor"—Braddock motioned for silence—"my first priority would be to address the plague of insalubrious and filthy elements that has descended upon our fair city. I would clean up those unsightly businesses run by those degenerate immigrants. They are a blight in our midst!"

"Clean up the town! Clean up the town!"

"That's Collins again," said Heather.

Braddock shook his fist. "You know those I mean. A pestilence of immoral and disease-ridden establishments has infested our streets for too long. If elected mayor, I will shut those establishments down and have our constabulary escort those dirty foreigners right back to their homelands!"

"Foreigners go home! Foreigners go home!" The ovation was deafening now. Wild applause and raucous, foot-stomping enthusiasm greeted Braddock's last words. At the podium, Braddock raised clasped hands. The band began to play. More magnesium powder exploded. A half-dozen men rushed the stage and lifted Braddock onto their shoulders. "Braddock for mayor! Braddock for mayor!"

Bedlam had broken out over the park. People were shouting themselves hoarse. Dogs barked madly as boys in short pants flourished sparklers. Hoi Wing ducked his head and wanted to disappear.

"You should leave," Heather whispered.

For days, Hoi Wing brooded over Braddock's speech. As he worked in the laundry, he remembered how the man had first spoken innocuously of prosperity and then ratcheted up his rhetoric. *Foreigners go home!*

What could he do about it? Hoi Wing was reminded of the garbage strewn in the backyard last fall. Would that happen again? Who could show the townsfolk the folly of Braddock's words?

One evening, Grandfather Foo visited, and the four laundrymen sat at the dining table, drinking Scotch and discussing Braddock's rally.

"I was living in Vancouver seven years ago," said Grandfather Foo, "when a mob of thousands of crazed *lofan*, armed with guns and clubs, tore through our Street of Chinese People. Dozens were injured in the chaos, and our homes and businesses were ransacked and looted. What caused the riot? The *lofan* are filled with fear and hatred for us, and sometimes it takes but a single spark to light an inferno of violence."

Elder Uncle clenched his fist. "What did I tell you about that picnic? And Tiger-mouse is right. We have faced violence before. We must be ready if it comes again."

Hoi Wing stared at the photos on the Wall of Family as he contemplated the possibility of more *lofan* attacks on the laundry. Suddenly, he rose from his chair and pointed at one of the photographs. "Grandfather Foo! That's you in the picture of the Chinese miners, standing with Elder Uncle!"

"*Ayah*," said the old man with a smile. "That was so long ago, I still had my hair."

"Were you hunting gold?" asked Hoi Wing. "Where were you? When was it?"

"So many questions!" Grandfather looked at the uncles. "Have you told him nothing? Although I have a part in the narrative, it's really more One-Arm's tale than mine."

"Tell me the story of the photo." Hoi Wing demanded of Elder Uncle.

"Go ahead, Big Brother." Second Uncle sipped his Scotch. "We could use a good story now."

Elder Uncle raised his glass. "To old friends and valiant comrades."

"May they hunt gold in heaven forever," added Grandfather Foo.

Then Elder Uncle's face darkened, and he began to speak in a low voice. "Nineteen men of China we were, in that cold, distant place, most of us young and unformed from our southern villages. Back then, I had seen only seventeen summers, but I had come to hunt my fortune in the land called America, which we named *Mei Gok*, or the Beautiful Country.

"One of us was a veteran sojourner. Wise, with a keen vision, he was learned in the ways of the *lofan*. He had the oddest name. He called himself the—"

"Tiger-mouse!" Hoi Wing interrupted.

Second Uncle and Grandfather Foo laughed, but Elder Uncle glared Hoi Wing into silence before taking up the thread of his story again.

"All of us had journeyed to that frozen land in search of gold. But the *lofan* would only sell us claims on lands they had already mined. They mocked us as 'yellow monkeys,' believing they had already extracted the last pinpricks of the precious metal from the stakes we had purchased, trading us nothing but a 'Chinaman's chance' for our hard-earned dollars.

"But they knew little of us men of China and what we could do. Together, we hewed the earth, tunnelling, channelling, and diverting the icy streams. We built water wheels, sluices, and screens. Shovel, bend, rinse. Bend again, rinse again, sift again. Every minute, every hour, every day. Sun-up to sun-down.

"Slowly, our pans began to sparkle with golden flecks. Slowly, our sacks filled with gold dust. As the weeks passed and the frost gnawed at our fingertips, the heat of our new-found wealth kept us warm at our campfires.

"Somehow the *lofan* learned we were prospering at claims they believed exhausted. All summer, they harassed us, stealing our pans and battering our sluices at night. The *lofan* were many, and we were few. They had guns and horses while we had none. And of course, the law was theirs to enforce.

"All of us had borne our fill of harassment and nuisance. Those of us who possessed woodcraft dug pits in the forests around our camp, blockaded the trails, and strung tripwires to warn us of incursion.

"One night, after the moon appeared, the *lofan* attacked. Most of our men had already fled the cold, retreating into our tents to fall like dead men in our bedrolls. Some lingered at our fires, listening to our musicians play their instruments.

"Suddenly, one of our sentries emerged from the woods. It was Ming Hat, a man so soft-spoken he could scarcely trouble you to pass the rice bowl at dinner, but so fierce at chess he could don a blindfold and defeat any six of us simultaneously. Blood marred his cheek, and one arm hung limp from his shoulder. He collapsed as he neared.

"Tiger-mouse leapt to Ming's aid as we heard a great keening from the forests. Confused, we stared into the darkness. Then I spied shadows beneath the trees. 'Raiders!' I shouted. 'Wake up! Raiders are come!'

"I rushed from tent to tent, pulling sleeping men from their blankets. Torches illuminated the woods, and there was a pounding of horses' hooves. 'Riders!' I pointed to the trail. 'Beware the *lofan* riders!'

"Whether because of cold or fatigue, our brothers were slow to rouse. But then our preparations bought us a few precious moments. The horsemen fell, tangled in our tripwires and pits. Our countrymen spilled from their tents as flames erupted at the western edge of the camp.

"The *lofan* riflemen loosed a hail of bullets. Tiger-mouse toppled into the campfire. Another man spun away, clutching his shoulder. I pulled Tiger-mouse from the flames as one of our musicians collapsed, snapping the neck of his *er-hu* beneath his body.

"There was a second volley of gunfire, and I felt a blow to my left arm as though I had been kicked by a mule. I fell to the ground, writhing in agony. Then Tiger-mouse lifted me up, throwing my good arm over his shoulder. The two of us broke into a shambling run across the uneven rock. Brothers fled in all directions. As we ducked into the forest, rifle fire cracked and bullets flew like angry wasps, snapping branches and thudding into trees.

"We plunged into the pines, with a single horseman in close pursuit. Breathlessly, I stumbled on, leaning on Tiger-mouse's shoulder. Whether by terror or intention, we fled toward the trails where we had dug gopher holes in the ground. Running and tripping, we led the horseman into our trap. Just when I thought he would ride us down, the horse stumbled and fell. The rider flew through the air and landed almost at our feet.

"In a rage, I shook free of Tiger-mouse and ran back to where the *lofan* horseman lay half-conscious, his lower leg twisted at the knee. I leapt upon his chest and pulled my knife from its sheath. With a mad cry, I lifted my blade.

"'Stop!' shouted Tiger-mouse. 'Hold your weapon!'

"Somehow his voice reached me through the red haze. I looked down. The *lofan* at my mercy was young, perhaps even younger than I was, with smooth skin and an unshaven jaw. Terror filled his eyes. 'Please,' he whimpered. 'Please.'

"I don't know what stayed my hand, but I found I could no longer kill him. I lowered my knife. Then I limped back to Tiger-mouse. Together, we staggered into the woods, where we bound our wounds. We spent the night in hiding.

"Four men of China died in the attack. Of the fifteen who survived, three, including me, were sorely wounded but would recover. I lost my arm. The dead had been shot or trampled, but the next morning we found one man hanging from a tree, his body rotating slowly as we came upon him."

In the laundry, Elder Uncle bowed his head, unable to continue. Second Uncle and Grandfather were silent.

"What happened then?" asked Hoi Wing. "What happened?"

Grandfather took up the tale. "We carried our wounded into a nearby town and had them treated by a kindly *lofan* doctor. Our dead we buried in a cemetery, and they lie there still."

Elder Uncle took a gulp of whisky and looked at Grandfather Foo. "Many times I have thanked Tiger-mouse for saving my life, but in truth, I owe him an even greater debt."

"What debt is that?" asked Hoi Wing.

"He saved me from becoming a killer." Elder Uncle's face was wan. "I need never carry that on my conscience. And for that, I am eternally grateful."

Hoi Wing sat back in his chair, caught up in the account. Once again, he studied the older man's face surreptitiously. If only he could have known the young and courageous Elder Uncle! How could he ever have believed him to be a coward? Hoi Wing wondered if he might ever face such dire circumstances. Would he be as brave as Elder Uncle? He fervently hoped so.

When Hoi Wing next saw Heather in the Sanctuary, he recounted Elder Uncle's story of the mining camp and railed once more against Braddock's vitriol. "Words, words, words!" He brandished the latest vocabulary lists assigned by Miss Adele. "What good they are if I am not using them? How can I answer Braddock?"

Heather's face lit with sudden inspiration. "I know how we can respond to him!"

He stared at her without comprehension.

"You'll write him a letter. I'll help you. We'll send it to every newspaper in town!"

The idea captured Hoi Wing's imagination. He would tell these townspeople what he really thought.

At the next noonday lesson, he arrived early at Miss Martha's and found Professor Marsden seated in the living room. He had come by, bringing sandwiches purchased from a diner and a bouquet of flowers, proclaiming that he was interested in Hoi Wing's scholastic progress.

Adele seemed flustered by his visit and placed the flowers in a vase. Hoi Wing wondered whether Professor Marsden had really come to evaluate his learning or if the man's interests lay elsewhere. The four of them sat down to tea and lunch. Hoi Wing told them of his idea to write a letter to the newspapers.

"A response to Jonathan Braddock?" said Martha. "Is that a good idea? He can be a difficult man."

"John's views are rather extreme," Professor Marsden noted. "I wasn't at that picnic, but I can well imagine what he might have said."

"I think writing a letter to the editor is a terrific idea." Adele put down her sandwich. "It's time someone took on Mr. Braddock. There's even talk of him running for mayor this fall. Show me your letter when it's complete. Any expository writing you do will also aid your preparation for the exam. What do you think, Stephan?"

Professor Marsden sipped his tea. "There are always risks when one expresses an opinion in public, but I've already underestimated Hoi Wing once before. Certainly, he should write his letter. I think it would show some real initiative!"

18

For the next two days, Hoi Wing was so busy at the laundry, he had no time to work on his letter to the editor. Then one night, he pulled out his draft at his workbench in the basement. After much consideration, he decided to reject most of Adele's input. Once again, he wrote what he most wanted to say. The next afternoon, he mailed it at the post office while running an errand for Second Uncle. He sent it to several of the town's papers, hopeful that one of them might print it.

The next night after work, he met Heather and the dogs at Montebello Park. Under the cover of darkness, the two of them strolled over to where Braddock had pitched his tent and made his speech almost a week before. Heather threw a hard rubber ball across the grass, and the dogs raced to retrieve it.

Hoi Wing walked beside her, breathing in the fragrance of the rose gardens and feeling content in her company. His body ached from hours of ironing, and his mind was almost as spent from his studies and letter writing. Neither of them wanted to talk, and it felt good not to think about the exam he would be sitting at the end of the month. And he didn't want to worry about the school he might attend that fall.

As they sauntered over the deserted grounds, the temperature dropped, and the wind began to tug at Heather's hair. The air grew thick with ozone. Lightning flashed, followed by a rumble like a distant cannonade. Droplets began to fall.

"Come!" Heather took his hand. Suddenly, they were running madly across the grass with the dogs barking wildly before them. By the time they reached the edge of the park, the downpour was steady. Tree branches writhed in the wind. The sky released a cold torrent, and they broke into full flight, their skin puckered against the deluge.

It was as if weeks of pent-up rain had burst some celestial dam. In the Golden Li, weather vanes spun and bricks tumbled from neglected chimneys. Eavestroughs filled and overflowed. Drenched, they reached Braddock's grand residence.

"Follow me!" Heather jerked him forward. At the house, they squeezed between the hedge and the backyard fence. Amongst the topiary, they ducked past the pergola and skirted the pond. They came to a carriage house, where Heather opened the door and led the dogs inside. She wiped them down with a rough towel. "Antony and Cleo sleep in here," she said.

The back door to the main house was locked, but Heather produced a key from a loop around her neck. "No one will hear us over the storm."

Hoi Wing hesitated. This was Braddock's sanctum, his great fortress. He wondered what the man would do if he caught Hoi Wing inside. Was this courage or insanity?

Heather drew him in through the mud room, past a second door, and into a dark hallway. As quietly as possible, they put one foot before the other. Despite Hoi Wing's nervousness, his body thrummed with excitement. Where was his jade amulet? Heather had said Braddock kept it in his drawing room. Where was that?

Hoi Wing wiped the rain from his eyes. The rug was plush, and they passed a life-sized oil painting of a man standing by a large globe, gripping a sword. One glance told Hoi Wing it was not Braddock, but enough like him to be some venerable ancestor.

As they passed a pair of ornate glass doors, Hoi Wing peered within and saw a suit of armour in the shadows. The room itself was long and dark, with tall windows at the far end. Could this be Braddock's drawing room?

"Stop gawking and follow me!" Heather whispered.

She led him into successively narrower hallways. Then his feet fell onto worn wooden steps, and they descended to the basement. The smell of the kitchen range came to his nostrils. A single electric bulb hung from the ceiling, but simple candle sconces adorned the walls. He could feel the dampness, and the mould tickled his nose.

She lit a candle on a small table. "Quiet now," she whispered. "Most everyone sleeps upstairs, but I've my quarters down here."

Her room was the last in the hallway. He followed her into a bedchamber scarcely larger than a closet. Bending, she lit a lamp. Her face was pale, and her eyes reflected the kerosene wick. "Welcome to my home."

They could barely turn around. Most of the floorspace was taken up by a cot, a tiny writing desk and chair, and a wooden chest of drawers. A chamber pot sat in a corner. It occurred to him that she had decorated the Sanctuary with more care than she had this room. She handed him a coarse towel from a hook on the wall. "Dry off while I go change." Heather went out the door and disappeared into the hallway.

Left alone, Hoi Wing rubbed his face and hair. The rough cotton was invigorating, and his shivering subsided. His thoughts returned to the room he had seen upstairs. Was that the drawing room where his enemy hatched his plots? Was his amulet inside? For a moment, he vacillated. What did Elder Uncle always say? *Great risk accompanies great gain.*

He lifted the kerosene lamp. Quickly, he retraced their route: past the kitchen, up two short flights of stairs, and then two right turns. In the great house, there was only the sound of wind and rain. Within a minute, he found himself before the glass doors again. This time, he stepped inside.

He studied the suit of armour, with its beaklike helmet, and the long spiked halberd. Hoi Wing lifted the lamp. High upon the walls were the heads of beasts, some horned and antlered, others with gaping, fanged jaws. On another wall was a map of the world. He saw an elephant's foot stool. Crossed spears and an ebony shield. Framed photographs were everywhere: Braddock crouching beside dead tigers, lions, water buffalo, and rhino. Braddock, accompanied by native guides and bearers, pulled in a rickshaw or borne aloft in a wooden sedan chair.

Hoi Wing made his way deeper into the room. He put his palm on a crystal skull set on a small round table. How could he understand this man? Braddock had visited more foreign countries than Hoi Wing could name, yet he despised all immigrants and strangers.

At the far end of the room, Hoi Wing found Braddock's Chinese collection: silken fans, parasols, and a wall of watercolours. There were swords in ceramic hilts, mounted on mahogany stands. A cloisonné vase, blue-green tripod pots, and a miniature tree in a bronze basin, its branches bent as if blown by a blustering breeze. Everything was here, except the jade charm he sought.

By the window was an enormous oaken desk. Beside it was a stack of cardboard placards piled waist high. Hoi Wing lifted the top one: *Johnnie Braddock for Mayor!* Against the wall was a glass cabinet. Inside were miniature figurines, coins of every size and shape, polished stones, pendants, and necklaces hanging from tiny brass hooks. Lightning flashed, lighting up the room. Hoi Wing gasped. There was his own jade amulet!

"Harry!" Heather stood at the doors. "What do you think you're doing?"

Hoi Wing withdrew his hand. "I wanted to—"

"We have to get out of here!"

Heather had changed into a simple grey dress. The audacity she had shown all evening was gone. Something akin to real fear had taken over. She rushed over and dragged him from the drawing room. As quickly as they could, they made their way through the house to the servants' entrance at the rear.

Heather opened the door. The rain had lessened, but the trees still shook in the wind. "That was chancy, going to the master's drawing room. You could have cost me my position!"

Now he realized how stupid he had been. "Sorry, that is not wise. Heather, I did—"

She shushed him with her finger. "Don't talk. Just go. Someone's going to hear us." Suddenly, she leaned forward and planted a kiss on his lips. "Good night." Then she shut the door.

Hoi Wing stood there, feeling the touch of her kiss and remembering the sensation of her hand when she had pulled him through the park. He walked quickly and passed through the gap in the backyard fence. In the ravine behind the house, he reached into his pocket and drew out his jade amulet, recovered from Braddock's trophy room. He had tried to tell her, but she hadn't given him the chance.

19

There it was. His letter to the editor in print. Only thirteen years old, and his words were published in black and white—in the *lofan* tongue, no less! For sure, the letter was tucked in a lower column (of the tiniest font), squeezed at the back of the broadsheet, the *St. Catharines Weekly Post*. And Heather had helped him draft it. But there it was. What would Ying the Scholar have said?

```
Dear Editor,

I am an immigrant and foreigner. Last week, I attended at
the summer picnic of Mr. Jonathan Braddock at Montebello
Park. All was very delightful until Mr. Braddock gave his
speech. Why are you fearing us? We are quiet and hard-work-
ing. Your inspector says we lack diseases or contagion. Our
laundry is clean and without stains. Every customer receives
warm welcomes. We are your neighbours and friends!

Hoi Wing "Harry" Woo, Sam Kee Luk Chinese Hand Laundry
```

Elder Uncle shook his head. "Farmboy, do I have to lock you in the basement when you're not working?"

"You're goading *Blah-dok* to take further action against us!" Second Uncle thumped the paper with his fist.

"But what I said is true." Hoi Wing fingered the amulet around his neck.

It was late evening after another washday at the tubs and troughs. Grandfather Foo had come to visit again, and the four laundrymen were huddled over the newspaper at the dining table. The old man looked at Hoi Wing with a hint of admiration in his eyes. "I must admit the letter is well written, although the wise man never acts without considering the consequences of his actions. Still, events in the world are moving so fast that these words may soon fade from anyone's thoughts."

"What do you mean, Tiger-mouse?" asked Second Uncle.

"Most of the small newspapers have not mentioned this incident, but just last week the heir to the throne of a European empire was assassinated while visiting a vassal state. These *lofan* nations are all interrelated, and this individual act may have great repercussions across the globe."

It was after Hoi Wing had gone to bed that the old man's remarks reverberated in his mind. So much had happened in the past few weeks. Had he really published a letter that chastised Braddock himself? Could one person change the world? A disturbing thought made him sit up. Might his letter affect his chances of getting into school that fall?

The next day, Hoi Wing manned the front counter. All morning, he served customers. No one treated him any differently, and it seemed his foray into newspaper writing had gone unnoticed. When he had a spare moment, he reviewed the "History of Canada" notes from Miss Adele's class, a course of study that detailed the heroics of the *lofan* explorers who had wrested the land from the "savages" who had inhabited it before them. As he read, he couldn't help but wonder what those same "savages" might think of this "history."

"Harry! Is this your doing?" a man said to him.

Hoi Wing looked up. A smiling *lofan* stood before him, a bag of laundry in one hand and a folded newspaper in the other.

"Mr. Inspector!" said Hoi Wing. "How are you?"

"Please call me Mr. Smythe. I'm here as a customer today." He placed his laundry on the counter. "Good letter, every word of it. I'm not surprised the *Post* published it. They've never liked bigwigs like Braddock. And I'm here to get some of those 'warm welcomes' you spoke about. Especially because I cleared this place myself."

"Thank you, Inspector Smythe, sir!" Hoi Wing beamed as he counted out the man's shirts.

Mr. Smythe touched his hat as he went out. "Keep up the good work, lad. Not everyone is happy that Braddy has decided to throw his hat into the election this fall. You've touched a nerve with your little letter, but have a care. He's not a good man to cross."

The second surprise came in the afternoon. Hoi Wing was still on counter duty, wrapping laundry for Pinched-face Lady. The doorbell jangled, and he looked up to see a woman wearing a wide-brimmed hat, decorated with a red ostrich feather. At the sight of her, Pinched-face Lady made a stiff, affronted huff. As quickly as possible, she grabbed her packages and left.

The second woman approached the counter. Her eyes were shadowed and her lips rouged. The neckline of her dress was low; the top buttons of her bodice were undone. A frisson danced up and down Hoi Wing's spine. Suddenly, he remembered. She was the smoky-eyed woman he had seen on a porch in the Foreign Quarter!

She held out a newspaper. "Did you write this?"

Hoi Wing breathed in her scent. The woman's voice was husky, and her bust was high. "Yes, that is my letter," he answered.

"How old are you, kid?"

"I'm thirteen."

"Well, I'm Rosie. And that's a good piece you wrote. I heard what Braddy said about degenerate businesses and such. Sometimes he gets up on his high horse and overdoes it. Then folks get all riled up, and they want to throw out the baby with the bathwater, know what I mean?"

Hoi Wing did not understand, but he sensed her approval of his letter.

"Give 'em hell, kid." Then she left the laundry.

Hoi Wing let out his breath. *So that was Rosie!* He ran to the window. Outside, the woman strolled down the street. There were few pedestrians out, but another woman crossed the road to avoid her.

No one else mentioned Hoi Wing's letter, but aglow from the praise, he thumbtacked his article onto the wall beside Elder Uncle's price list. Why not? The response had been unanimously good; it had even won them one new customer.

In the late afternoon, Elder Uncle took over, and Hoi Wing went into the backrooms to tackle the sorting tables.

He whistled as he worked. In his mind, he was already composing further letters to editors he would publish in bigger and more expansive newspapers. What he could teach these *lofan* if only they could read his words!

"Farmboy, get out here," said Elder Uncle, coming in from the front room.

Hoi Wing hurried to the counter. As he came through the curtain, he saw Heather standing in the vestibule. Her eyes were red from crying, and an old cloth valise lay at her feet.

"Harry, the master's sacked me!"

"What? Why?"

"He's accused me of theft. Stealing a jade—" Her eyes went to Hoi Wing's neck. "Oh, you did take it. How could you!"

Hoi Wing's hand went to his throat. "Yes, I wanted to tell you. And why are they blaming you?"

"I was seen with you at the picnic. They say I stole it for you."

"But it is not your fault!"

"The master's furious. First the amulet, and now your letter to the editor. You've cost me my job! I've nowhere to go."

"See what comes from opening your big mouth?" said Elder Uncle to Hoi Wing. "And she can't stay here! The town would go crazy if they learned a *lofan* girl was living with us!"

"I've no place to sleep tonight." Heather's voice broke. "Where can I go?"

Hoi Wing had no answer. It would be dark in several hours. Somehow he had to make it right. But where could he take her?

"You were sacked for what?" Adele asked.

"What did Hoi Wing do?" Miss Martha leaned forward.

"Hoi—well, Harry—he took back his jade charm," Heather responded.

"But why did Mr. Braddock blame you if Hoi Wing took the charm?" Adele continued.

"Because—" Hoi Wing found himself tongue-tied once again.

He and Heather were seated in Miss Martha's living room. They had left Elder Uncle at the laundry and gone directly to the home of the two *lofan* ladies. When they arrived, Hoi Wing could see the surprise in Adele's eyes. What was he doing here on a Tuesday after dinner? And with a strange girl? It was also clear the women had made plans for the evening; Adele and Miss Martha were dressed in navy-blue uniforms with white sashes. Nevertheless, the teens were invited in.

Now Heather spoke in the living room. The black-and-tan cat arched its back against her leg. "It was Harry's amulet to begin with, ma'am. He lost it in the woods at the fox hunt, but Master Braddock picked it up. Last week, Harry stole it out of the master's drawing room. But they say I did it, and now I've been canned."

"I understand. You've lost your position because Hoi Wing stole back his amulet," said Martha.

"I recognize Hoi Wing's charm from when I first met him on the street," added Adele.

"Now I have no place to go!" Heather put her face in her hands.

"Can you help, please?" Hoi Wing begged. "I make this trouble for Heather. It is all my fault."

"Do you have no family, dear?" asked Martha.

"I've only my brother, Aemon, and he's up in the north."

There was a silence as the two ladies looked at each other. "Well, perhaps Heather could stay with us for the time being. What do you think, Auntie?"

"Yes, certainly. Until she makes permanent arrangements," answered Martha.

"Oh, thank you!" Hoi Wing gave a huge sigh of relief.

"I'll pay for my room and board." Heather spoke before they could change their minds. "I can work. I've always worked."

"My dear, we haven't had a maid for years," said Martha. "There's nothing for you to do, apart from making your own bed each morning and perhaps a few chores."

"She has been studying with me. All year," said Hoi Wing.

"Do you have your letters, dear?" asked Martha.

"I read and write better than Harry does," Heather answered proudly. "And we've been practising arithmetic."

"I am better at arithmetic," Hoi Wing added quickly.

Adele looked at Heather. "Perhaps you might want to attend the Thursday night class with us? Formally?"

"Class for Heather?" Hoi Wing was surprised.

"Why not? We can easily incorporate Heather into the sessions. I'll invite Stephan this week. He's agreed to give Hoi Wing a chance to enter school this fall. Maybe we can do likewise for Heather."

Heather looked disbelievingly at Hoi Wing. "Can you imagine? Me in school again?"

"It might be a little premature to talk about school yet, but we can certainly put you in the spare bedroom tonight," said Martha. "That just leaves the question of what we'll do this evening."

Adele glanced at the clock over the fireplace. "Martha and I are leaders at Girl Guides, and we have a meeting this evening at seven thirty sharp."

"Girl Guides?" said Hoi Wing.

"That's why you're wearing uniforms," said Heather.

"We're the first unit in the country," Martha said. "Do you think you might like to accompany us tonight, Heather?"

"I . . . would they have me, ma'am? I'm a maid!"

Martha's mouth fell open for a moment. "Oh, how silly of me. I forgot. Agatha Braddock is one of our founding patrons."

"Ma'am, I won't be joining any clubs that don't want me. You must have a lot of upper-class girls, members of the Imperial Order of the Daughters of the Empire and such."

"Perhaps it's too early for you to get involved with the troop," said Martha. "Why don't I just stay home tonight? We can get to know each other a little better."

∞

The next day, Hoi Wing threw himself into the drudgery of the wash, spending long hours churning laundry and passing the irons over sheets. The sweltering heat of the July day made the work even more tortuous, but the physical labour was a much needed distraction from the recent events that had so upended his life.

Grandfather made a surprise visit that afternoon. "The great leaders of Europe are posturing like imbeciles! One empire has demanded humiliating reparations for the death of their monarch, but the other powers have seized upon the assassination as an excuse to mobilize their armies!"

In the late evening, Hoi Wing studied, knowing the examination was now only three weeks away. He reflected on what Ying the Scholar might have said about his preparations. Adele had hinted that Professor Marsden would include an essay question as a major part of the test. How could he prepare for that?

That night, he went to bed with his brain feeling as if it might burst. As he lay there, he wondered how Heather was faring at her new home. Her situation had to be an improvement over her previous lot as a scullery maid. But what would Professor Marsden say when Adele presented him with another candidate for school that fall? He had a sobering thought. Would that diminish his own chances of entering the public school system?

Hoi Wing arrived early at the church for the next *lofan* class, still wondering about Heather and worrying about the essay portion of the exam. When he entered the little classroom, it was crowded as never before. Heather was seated at the desk beside his. One look at her alleviated any misgivings he had about his actions in Braddock's study. She was clean, freshly scrubbed, and wearing a new lime-green dress. A notebook and pencils were placed on her desktop. At the front of the classroom, Adele, Miss Martha, and Professor Marsden were seated around the large desk in a heated debate.

"I can't promise anything now," Professor Marsden said to the two women. "We're not even sure Harry will qualify. Everything is contingent on his passing the examination."

"Most assuredly he will," said Martha.

"In any case, we're not asking for promises," added Adele. "Heather has joined our little class, and she's been studying with Harry all along. The two of them could sit the examination together, couldn't they?"

"But I've already moved heaven and high water to find a place for Harry, in the event he qualifies. I haven't made any arrangements for a second student. Has the young lady attended school before in this jurisdiction? It's too late for her now—"

There was a shout from the hallway. The door was flung open. Before anyone could say a word, a police officer barged in. Jonathan Braddock followed on his heels.

Heather gasped. A look of panic blanched Hoi Wing's face.

"That's him!" Braddock pointed at Hoi Wing. "The miscreant who stole the amulet from my collection!"

Hoi Wing's hand went to his throat. "I am not stealing! This is my jade!"

The big policeman grabbed Hoi Wing's shoulder. "Got you, you little thief!"

"What are you doing?" Martha said. "Unhand him at once!"

Mr. Braddock spoke. "This incorrigible street urchin stole that necklace from my collection right out of my house. And that is his accomplice. She needs to be placed under arrest as well."

"This is my amulet!" Hoi Wing twisted as the policeman's fingers bit into the muscles of his arm.

"I've done nothing wrong!" Heather protested.

The policeman jerked Hoi Wing to his feet. "You're coming with me, boy."

"Wait, officer!" Adele grabbed Hoi Wing's hand. "That is Hoi Wing's necklace. I can swear I saw him wearing it around his neck—back in November, I believe."

"Nonsense!" said Mr. Braddock. "The amulet has been in my collection for years! It's even been evaluated by the Royal Museum!"

The policeman hesitated. He glanced at Braddock and then at Adele. "Are you certain, miss?"

Professor Marsden stepped forward for a closer look. "I say, John. I remember you pulling that jade piece out of a campfire when we were riding last fall."

"What's that, professor?" said the policeman. "You've seen this too?"

Marsden nodded. "And I believe Mark Smythe, our Master of Hounds, saw it too. We can fetch him to see if he recollects the incident as I do."

There was a silence as Mr. Braddock looked from Adele to Professor Marsden and back to Martha. The man cleared his throat. "This is most unusual. An amulet has been stolen right out of my collection. A very valuable piece. Surely you're not suggesting that I . . . that this is not . . . I'm sure this is—"

"No one's suggesting anything, John," said Martha. "Except perhaps you are mistaken about this young man's necklace. Are you sure it is the same item that's missing from your collection? We have two independent witnesses who say it can't be the piece you've had for years. Hoi Wing, will you let Mr. Braddock have a look at it?"

Hoi Wing freed himself from the constable's grip. With great reluctance, he undid the clasp to his amulet. He passed the jade charm to Braddock.

The man held it to the light and scrutinized both sides. "You may be right, Martha." He grimaced. "Now that I have a better chance to examine it, this may not be from my collection. Mine was a much more valuable piece, finer and of a more delicate hue, a much higher quality jade as well. This is but a cheap imitation."

"You're sure of that, Mr. Braddock?" said the policeman. "It's not your stolen property?"

Mr. Braddock handed the charm grudgingly to Hoi Wing. Then he glared at Professor Marsden. "It may be stolen, but it is not my piece."

"It's not yours, and it never was!" Adele said triumphantly.

"Perhaps an apology is in order," Martha added.

There was another silence. Finally, Mr. Braddock spoke. "I apologize for intruding on your little class tonight. My pardon, ladies."

"I don't need your apology, Mr. Braddock," Adele answered. "It's Hoi Wing and Heather whom you maligned with your false accusations."

Braddock's face grew red. "These two will be getting no apology from me!" With that, he left the class. The policeman tipped his hat and followed.

Adele shut the door. The room let out a collective breath. Hoi Wing refastened his jade amulet around his neck. He thanked both Adele and Professor Marsden for their help in rebutting Braddock's accusations.

Professor Marsden shook his head. "We've proven the good luck charm is yours, but I'm afraid we embarrassed Jonathan badly tonight. We made him eat his words, in front of the constable, no less. His hate has no bounds, and if I know him at all, he won't rest until he has his vengeance upon you."

"Harry's not afraid, are you?" said Heather.

Hoi Wing shook his head, although he felt his gesture was little more than bravado.

"Perhaps we can return to the discussion we were having before that rude interruption," Martha suggested.

"Yes." Adele went to the front of the room. "I think we were discussing whether Stephan could find a way to test Heather as well."

Professor Marsden sighed. "Well, I concede these youngsters are facing a great deal of adversity. How about this? Why don't I hold a little contest for our two candidates? The one who scores higher, as long as it passes the academic standard, enters school this fall."

"But we want both of them in school!" said Martha.

Adele placed her hands on her hips. "Or perhaps they will make you eat your words."

"Nothing would make me happier"—Professor Marsden smiled wryly—"but I fear this test will be quite a stretch for them. Perhaps if we push them in this manner, one of them might just squeak through."

Martha rolled her eyes at this statement.

On Friday, Elder Uncle assigned Hoi Wing a new task: chopping wood in the backyard. The wood was used to augment their coal fires in the braziers, water heaters, and hearths. Hoi Wing spent the day at the woodpile, lifting and swinging the heavy axe as he split logs into small chunks. When he came in for supper that night, he saw he had received another letter from Eldest Great Auntie.

To Hoi Wing, the son of my heart, if not my womb:

One story remains to be told. And this account answers as many questions about me as it does about your honourable dead mother. Ayah! I'm dying! How to speak of the wonderful/terrible night your sister was born?

It was noon, the day before the New Year, and the whole village was primed for a celebration that was to commence with fireworks at midnight. For months, I had tended your mother's troubled pregnancy, feeding her a daily infusion of sweet ginger-chicken broth and prescribing complete bedrest in the last trimester. I dreaded the delivery that was to come.

That morning, I was again at the mah-jong tables when you summoned me. I knew the feared hour had arrived. For the rest of the day and well into the night, I succoured your mother at her labour, making her walk and crawl, massaging her belly, and trying to turn your sister from within. As the long hours passed, I knelt between your mother's knees, and my back stiffened to an iron post. I prayed to the Ancestors and even the lofan Jesus-ghost.

Finally, the awful moment came. Your mother was exhausted, and all my skill had come to naught. The dire choice lay before us. "Save my baby!" your mother whispered. "Save my baby!"

I reached for my scalpel. When the hideous deed was done, I lifted your baby sister in the lamplight. At that instant, the sky erupted with a barrage of fireworks, and I gasped: your sister had been born at the precise stroke of the New Year! No birth was more fortuitous; yet your mother had passed from life at the very same instant. No portent was more ill-favoured!

My mind reeled with contradiction. How to reconcile the omens? But as I comforted Little Mei-Mei, I felt a surprise heat bloom in my old woman's breasts and between my legs. My fate was suddenly clear. The gods had waited (so long they had waited!), but now, they had given me not one but two children to raise. No more would I be known as the midwife who brought forth many but none of her own. I would be mother to you and your sister, and grace you both with all the love, hope, and good teachings I had nurtured in sixty-three lonely years.

Weak-kneed with epiphany, I whispered a promise into your dead mother's ear: "My home will be their home. My hearth will be their hearth. My rice will be their rice."

Now you know the full story of your sister's wonderful/terrible birth. Now you know how I came to be known as your "Second Mother." Now you know that caring for you two has been the greatest and happiest accomplishment of my life.

Your Eldest Great Auntie

P.S. Your last remittance was late. Please do not make this a habit. And a little more would be much appreciated.

As the weeks counted down to the examination, Martha and Adele increased the number of study sessions at their home. One evening, Hoi Wing arrived to find Professor Marsden waiting on the front porch. He and Adele were going to see a play at the Grand Opera House.

That night, Martha assumed command of the tutoring. "There are eleven children in the Christmas pageant and twice that number in the nativity play. There are twenty-six boys and half as many girls in the church youth group. If each child participates in only one activity, how many children are there in total in the Christmas pageant, nativity play, and youth group?"

At one noonday session, Adele surprised everyone by serving a lunch of stir-fried chicken with rice. It was a recipe that Martha remembered from her days in Honan. The two teens sat down before their bowls as Adele traced a series of geometric figures, composed of triangles, half-circles, and rectangles, on the slate board. "When you've finished your lunch," she said to Hoi Wing and Heather, "I want you to calculate the areas of these shapes."

Another time, Hoi Wing entered Martha's dining room and found Professor Marsden again in attendance. The man took no part in the instruction, but he stood in the corner, nodding encouragingly as Adele assigned excerpts from newspapers. "Write three paragraphs on the topic I have printed on the slate board. Is the author's argument well-founded? Support your opinion with reasons." She grimaced as she peered over Hoi Wing's shoulder. "Capitalize names, proper nouns, and places!"

Hoi Wing had never been so busy. During the day, he worked harder than ever under Elder Uncle's watchful eye—the man was adamant that Hoi Wing complete every iota of work assigned to him. But every evening not at Martha's was spent in the basement, where Hoi Wing rubbed his tired eyes as he tried to make sense of the scribbles in his notebooks.

Sometimes he wondered about his father's preparations for the examination that led to his great downfall. He had written to his father again, telling him of the possibility of entering school, but Hoi Wing had heard nothing back. Eldest Great Auntie's letter had been deeply touching, but it only added to the mystery. How had Ying the Scholar failed so spectacularly at his great chance? If he could not make the grade, how would Hoi Wing possibly succeed?

When his mind wandered, he thought of Heather. It was paradoxical, but now that she had been freed from her duties as a scullion, they met only when they crammed in the dining room at Martha's, and they were always chaperoned by one or both of the *lofan* ladies.

Heather had become little more than a study partner and, worse (if he took Professor Marsden at his word), a competitor for his very spot in school that fall. Without a doubt, she was his superior in English and social studies. How ironic that, after everything, she might enter the eighth grade and he might not. He felt guilty hoping she might do poorly on the examination, but there was no other way to guarantee his own placement.

Hoi Wing wanted to spend time with Heather away from their books, but he knew little of what young people in town did with their spare time. One afternoon, while drying laundry, he turned to Second Uncle for advice.

"Young Man, the secret to pleasing women is to discover what they want and to place yourself on that path."

In bed that night, Hoi Wing pondered those words. What might he do with Heather? He thought back on her stories of the Old Country and how she had roamed the streets searching the gutters for lost coins or glass bottles. He remembered her speaking of ice cream. *Ice cream.* But where, in town, would they get that?

20

It was noon on Wednesday, the week before examination. Hoi Wing studied the windows of McGregor's Department Store. Not only was it the largest retailer in the region, it housed St. Catharines' most popular ice cream counter. At Christmas, the big window had displayed the mannequin of the old man on a sledge, but today it showcased a miniature train that *chug-chugged* around a Lilliputian countryside populated by tiny cows, horses, and sheep.

Hoi Wing retreated from the window. He had invited Heather to join him for ice cream at lunch, but she was uncharacteristically late. Could he meet her inside? With a last glance at the train set, Hoi Wing stepped through the revolving glass doors.

Inside, McGregor's was a vast space of soaring ceilings, wooden pillars, and marbled floors. Wide aisles displayed islands of merchandise. Hoi Wing's head swivelled left and right. Scores of hats were arrayed on rows of wooden heads. Enough shoes to fit every man, woman, and child in the city. A perfumery that stung his eyes. In housewares, he saw chairs upholstered in jungle flowers, with straight or curved backrests, thick or thin cushions, and long or short legs. An entire wall devoted to fireplace utensils.

He came to a moving staircase and placed his foot onto a wooden step, which folded, accordion-like, into the one above it. On the second floor, he found himself amongst walls of coloured rugs and plush carpets. Linens were displayed on beds wide enough for whole families. Dish sets, glassware, and china in an eye-tingling smorgasbord of patterns. Mesmerized by the glut of consumer goods, he allowed his feet to draw him from one department to another.

It was then Hoi Wing noticed the surveillance. At this hour, the store was quiet, but salesmen eyed his every move. He reached to touch a silk scarf and drew his hand away before he made contact. Three burly men traced his steps at a discreet distance. Hoi Wing turned one way and then another; his back began to itch as though it were swarming with ants.

At the far end of the store, he came to the soda fountain. The floor was honeycombed in black-and-white hexagons, with padded stools set before a marble counter. A large wall clock told him Heather was now twenty minutes late. He climbed onto a stool.

Behind the counter, a door swung open at the far wall. The soda fountain attendant emerged. He wore a peaked cap, matching white smock, and a black bow tie. Embroidered in cursive script over his breast pocket was a name: *Buddy.*

Buddy moved with a bouncy step, but he halted at the sight of Hoi Wing. His gaze hardened, and he drew a rag from under the counter. With great diligence, he began to polish a pyramid of glasses by the sink.

For a time, Hoi Wing watched the young man. A folded copy of the *St. Catharines Herald* was tucked between the menu and a chrome napkin holder. The front-page article leapt to his attention:

PROMINENT ST. CATHARINES BUSINESSMAN THROWS HAT INTO RING

Jonathan Braddock, well-known brewmaster and entrepreneur, announced his candidacy in this fall's mayoralty race before dozens of well-wishers at a meeting of the St. Catharines Businessmen's Association on Tuesday.

The popular businessman vowed he would beautify the city's downtown areas and address ratepayers' complaints about the immigrant problem.

"I'm going to rid us of those infernal Chinese laundries!" Braddock declared to wild applause. "The Chinamen will no longer lower our property values. Brothers, this is a white man's country. Spurn his leprous laundries! Ladies, resist his temptations! Banish him before he corrupts us with his opiates, gambling, and depravity."

Mr. Braddock also responded to questions about the continued proliferation of backyard pigsties and a proposed reduction in the numbers of chicken coops permitted per house within city limits. (continued on page 9)

Hoi Wing read the article three times. With each reading, his belly constricted. Had everyone seen this news? If Braddock became mayor, he would close their laundries. Hoi Wing glanced from the paper, searching the store for Heather. There was still no sign of her.

At the other end of the counter, Buddy continued polishing the glassware. Hoi Wing wondered if he should leave, although Heather had told him to order if she was late. How would he manage that?

"Uh . . . hello. Hello!" Hoi Wing beckoned to Buddy. "Hello." He spoke louder. There was no response. "Hello!"

At that moment, the store employees who had been trailing Hoi Wing converged. They were thick-necked and broad-shouldered. Buddy dropped his rag and waved them in. Hoi Wing rose to his feet. What was going on?

"Here I am!" Someone touched his arm. "Sorry I'm late."

Hoi Wing turned. "Heather, you came!"

"Of course. Have you been waiting long? Why didn't you order?"

"You know this Chinaman?" said Buddy as the store detectives surrounded them.

"What do you mean?" Heather looked from the security men to Hoi Wing.

For a moment, none of the store employees answered. Then the tallest of them flashed a badge from his jacket. "Girl, I'm the chief store detective. This Chinaman isn't with you, is he?"

"What if he is?"

"He can't sit here," said Buddy.

"Why not?"

"Because he's a Chinaman!"

Heather's face reddened. She straightened her shoulders. "He's here with me. And I can sit here, can't I?"

The security men looked uncertain, but the senior detective crossed his arms. "Of course you may. But he's got to go."

"All the way back to China!" Buddy added.

"Heather," Hoi Wing whispered. "I go. You stay for ice cream."

"Don't be daft!" She gripped his arm. "We're both having ice cream."

Buddy snickered. "No way in hell he's eatin' here!"

A few shoppers had noted the commotion. Two young boys grimaced at Hoi Wing.

The store official spoke to Heather as he dropped his hand on Hoi Wing's shoulder. "You'll both have to leave if you insist on accompanying him."

Heather's lower lip trembled, and her eyes flashed. She gripped the napkin holder as if she might throw it in the detective's face.

"Please, no." Hoi Wing grabbed her arm. "Come on. We go."

Heather let herself be tugged away. "Fine. We'll leave now."

"Dumb Irish bitch," Buddy muttered, wiping the counter where Hoi Wing had rested his elbows.

Flanked by store security, Hoi Wing and Heather were marched from the soda fountain. McGregor's had become busy with shoppers, and Heather glared at anyone who met her eyes. Within the cordon, she gripped Hoi Wing's hand tightly.

The security men led them to the front entrance. A small crowd had gathered. When Hoi Wing was ten feet from the revolving doors, he jerked his hand from Heather's and sprinted for the exit. Someone screamed.

"Hey, you!" the store detective shouted.

"Harry, come back!" Heather cried.

Hoi Wing hurled himself through the doors. The glass panels spun and he fell onto the sidewalk outside. He was up on his feet and running immediately. Behind him, Heather shook her fist. "We're never coming back! Ever!"

21

Dear Miss Manners:

Our lovely excursion to your city's finest department store
was ruined last week when a local Chinaman invaded the ice
cream parlour. Before our very eyes, he elbowed his way to
the soda fountain and demanded service! What an affront!
When store staff intervened, he steadfastly refused to
leave. The display of Chinaman distemper was exacerbated
when he rampaged through the aisles, toppling displays and
shoppers alike. And with some wayward girl accompanying him!
Needless to say, this molestation tainted our visit and left
us shocked beyond words. It will be a long time before we
return to your "Garden City."

—Mr. and Mrs. C.E. Millgood of Grimsby
St. Catharines Herald, July 28, 1914

Miss Martha tossed the newspaper onto the table. "And you didn't even get your ice cream."

"They refused to serve us," said Heather.

Hoi Wing shook his head. "It was because of me."

It was the evening before the big examination. Hoi Wing had come to the home of Martha and Adele for a final session, but the incident at McGregor's and its repercussions in the town newspapers had superseded studying.

"This is outrageous!" said Adele. "And this silly letter is just icing on the cake."

"More like salt on the wound," Martha noted.

"Well, I'm going to do something about this," Adele said. "My book circle is meeting this week. I'll organize a boycott! Hoi Wing has every right to sit at that ice cream counter."

Martha spoke again. "Will your book circle add this latest affront to its list of charitable causes? Between getting the vote for our sisters, bottled milk and blankets for unmarried mothers, and hot water in the Foreign Quarter, will the circle now adopt a motion to procure ice cream for our Chinese laundrymen?"

"Martha, how can you be so cold-blooded about this? I am incensed!"

"So am I, but let's stop crying over spilled milk." Martha motioned to the slate board where she had printed out her *Five Rules for Writing Examinations*. "Instead, let's get back to what we planned and show these two how they will tackle that exam tomorrow. Come now. Rule number one . . ."

Two hours later, Hoi Wing sat alone on the wooden bench on Martha's front porch. The session had ended early to give the teens a good night's sleep. Darkness had fallen, and bats flitted in the moonlight. Hoi Wing breathed deeply, anticipating the great challenge of the morrow.

Once again, he mused on the strange parallels between his life and his father's. Like Ying the Scholar, he faced an examination with life-altering consequences. But what had caused Ying's failure? Back home, some whispered that Ying had been cast out of the examination room for cheating. Was that possible?

"I was looking for you." Heather came out, bearing a plate of biscuits. She sat beside him. "Have one. Adele is teaching me to bake."

"Thank you." Hoi Wing was glad to take his mind in a different direction. For a time, the teens ate their cookies and drank in the cool air. Through the front window, they could hear the murmur of conversation between Martha and Adele.

Heather shifted a little closer. Her eyes were bright, and her face was flushed. "Aren't you excited for tomorrow?"

Hoi Wing nodded.

"The ladies have been wonderful with their teaching. We'll ace that exam. I can feel it in my bones!"

Hoi Wing didn't want to dampen her exuberance, but he felt he had to point out the obvious. "But Professor Marsden says he has only place for one student. Not two. Will be me or you?"

Heather touched his hand. "I haven't forgotten. We just have to do our very best. That's all we control."

"But what if only one goes to school?"

"That may happen—but even if only one of us enters school, the other can still share that happiness. We'll still study together. Perhaps the other might start school next year. Don't you see that?"

Hoi Wing nodded, although he was not as convinced he could be happy if he was the one who did not qualify. She was so magnanimous. Was he just too selfish?

"Think of it. A bare month ago, I was just a scullery maid. Now I've been given a chance I never had."

He looked across the street at a raccoon climbing the trunk of a tree. There was no way for him to construe it otherwise: it would be a bitter disappointment to be denied entry into grade eight this fall. If only he could be as happy for her as she would be for him.

Hoi Wing turned to face Heather. She had sidled up beside him, and their bodies were separated by a fraction of an inch. For the rest of his life, he would never forget how it felt to have a girl move as close as humanly possible without touching. Heather's lips were parted. Her eyes were inviting. Almost unconsciously, he leaned forward. She met him halfway.

Her mouth tasted of sourdough cookie and sugar. Her lips were moist and soft. *He was kissing her!*

For a long moment, they held their kiss. He pressed his lips gently and then with more insistence. He kissed her again. And again. His head spun, and his heart raced. His tongue tickled her lip. It was delicious! Exhilarating! Magical!

"Ahem." Martha cleared her throat. "Ah, excuse me."

The two teens leapt apart. Hoi Wing stood, and Heather smoothed her hair. "Miss Martha!"

Was Martha upset? She did not seem overly surprised, although Hoi Wing sensed some disappointment.

"It's getting late," Martha observed. "Perhaps it might be time to say good night and get some well-deserved rest for tomorrow?"

"Yes, of course!" Heather said a hasty good night and hurried inside.

Anxious to escape, Hoi Wing mumbled a goodbye and turned to leave.

"Don't go just yet," said Martha. "I need to have a word with you."

Hoi Wing groaned inside. Was she going to scold him for kissing

Heather? It had happened so spontaneously. What was she going to say?

Martha looked back into the house before shutting the door behind her. She nudged Hoi Wing into the shadows. "You and Heather remind me of the time I had in China with my friend, Han. It was a wonderful part of my life. Unfortunately, it ended tragically."

"What happened?" asked Hoi Wing, relieved that she was not talking about his kiss with Heather.

"It was toward the end of my years in China, after the Boxers began to strike at our missions. British soldiers were sent to protect us, and a curfew was declared in the village. No one, Chinese or non-Chinese, was supposed to be out after six o'clock in the evening. Anybody out of the compound would be considered an enemy.

"Han insisted on coming to see me. I should have refused, but he wouldn't take no for an answer. He got word to me that I was to meet him at the village well.

"That night, there was a full moon. I got to the well before him and waited in the shadows. Finally, he arrived. As he stepped out from the trees, there was a shout from some soldiers on patrol. I don't know if Han heard or misunderstood. He should have halted in his tracks. He should have knelt in the grass with his hands over his head. Instead, he turned and ran.

"There was a volley of rifle fire, and Han fell. I screamed, but it was too late. When I got to Han, he was still alive, but breathing hard. There was blood, so much blood. He whispered my name as I held him in my arms."

"I am sorry," Hoi Wing said.

For a moment, Martha said nothing. Then she shook herself. "My experience ended tragically, but I want yours to be successful." Her voice dropped to a whisper. "I want to give you something to help you at the examination tomorrow."

"At the examination?"

"Shh! Don't talk." She reached into her apron and handed him an envelope with the words *Hoi Wing, For Your Eyes Only* printed across its face.

"What is this?" He lifted the flap on the envelope. Inside was a single sheet of folded paper.

Martha spoke even more softly. "Don't open it now. Have a look at it before you go to bed. It's just for you."

"But what about—?"

"Hush! This envelope is for you. Do you understand? I haven't given a copy to Heather."

"But—"

"Listen to me." She placed her hand on his shoulder. "I'm very glad that Heather has been given this opportunity, but you were offered it first. She has an advantage. She's a native speaker of English. You are not. You've worked so hard these past months. As hard as any student I've ever known. As hard as my old friend, Han. What I've written on this paper will even out the odds. And you mustn't tell anyone about this. Now, shush. Someone will hear us."

In the shadows, Martha's eyes were earnest. Hoi Wing understood he was not to share this secret, but it didn't feel right. What was on that paper? "I will take envelope home."

"There's a good lad. Now hurry home and have a good rest. I'll see you at the church tomorrow at seven."

Still uneasy, Hoi Wing tucked the envelope into his pants and stumbled off the porch. In the darkness, he headed down the road. The moon had ducked behind clouds, and the temperature had dropped. Even the crickets were silenced. He turned to look back, but Martha had extinguished the porch light. On the second floor, Heather's bedroom window was dark. The envelope burned in his pocket all the way home.

∞

What was Martha's secret message? Unable to sleep, Hoi Wing sprawled on his basement cot. The envelope lay untouched on his night table. It would be so easy to take out the sheet of paper and read it. Perhaps it was the topic of the essay question Professor Marsden had concocted.

Martha was right: he had been chosen to write the exam long before Heather entered into the equation. Martha had offered this information freely of her own accord. And it would even out the natural advantage Heather held over him.

But it was still cheating, wasn't it? All the stories he had heard of Ying's great failure flooded his mind. Would this be a repudiation of everything he had been taught? He remembered Ying the Scholar lecturing him on his first day of school: "Better to fail honourably than to cheat at anything!"

Hoi Wing thought of the taste of Heather's lips. How her eyes had shut when he closed the distance between their faces. He would do anything to kiss her again. Could he betray her in this manner? What if he shared Martha's secret with her? They could both have foreknowledge of the contents of the examination.

For another half-hour, Hoi Wing's thoughts churned as he vacillated from one choice to another. Finally, fatigue and sleep overtook him.

22

The next day, Elder Uncle had Hoi Wing chop wood again. All morning and into the afternoon, he worked feverishly in the backyard under the hot summer sun, raising the heavy axe and bringing it down, over and over and over. He welcomed the mindless labour, not wanting to think of anything else.

After much consideration, he had resolved to return Martha's envelope without reading its contents. Regardless of whatever disadvantage he might face at the examination, he would sit the test honourably or not at all. Moreover, he was also a little insulted that Martha believed he could not succeed without her help. It was a decision he felt would have pleased Ying the Scholar.

At five thirty in the evening, Elder Uncle called him to an early supper. "Your work is done for the day." The man beckoned him to the table on which he had set a tureen of soup, a plate of steamed fish, and bowls of rice.

Second Uncle was already seated. "You have won the right to sit that examination, and you need to fortify yourself first. No one thinks well on an empty stomach."

Hoi Wing was surprised. "Elder Uncle, Second Uncle, thank you so much for all—"

"Farmboy, just sit and eat!"

Hoi Wing wolfed down his dinner. Then he grabbed his satchel and his best pens and pencils, and left the two men at the table. On the street, Hoi Wing's spirit soared. This was the chance he had been waiting for all year, or perhaps his whole life. Although he was physically tired, his belly was full, and his mind was at peace. Whatever challenge Professor Marsden had set, he would do the best he could.

He walked briskly toward Martha's, where he would first return the envelope to eliminate any hint of impropriety. The evening was fresh; he saw families walking with children and pedestrians out for an after-dinner stroll. No one gave him a second glance.

As he neared the ballpark, he saw dozens of spectators seated in the wooden stands, watching that game where the players tried to strike a ball with a wooden baton. He remembered Heather telling him Braddock's Breweries sponsored a team that challenged others from nearby towns. As he strode by, there was a crack of the bat and a raucous cheer from the crowd.

"Where is Miss Martha?" Hoi Wing asked when Adele opened the door.

"Shouldn't you be at the church?" answered Adele, who had another Girl Guides meeting and would not be at the examination.

"First, I must talk to Martha."

"Have a seat, I'll find her. It won't be long."

Hoi Wing sat down in the dining room where so much of their preparation had taken place. Everything was still there: the slate board, the chalk, the pencils, textbooks, and the notes piled on the buffet. He took

Martha's message out of his pocket and placed it on the dining table as Heather entered the room.

Her face lit up. "I'm so glad you're here! It's just about time. We can walk to the church together."

Hoi Wing froze, his hand still outstretched. "I thought you had already gone."

"Adele said you were here. What's that letter? Is it a note for me?" She smiled.

"But where is Martha? I need to speak to her first."

"Martha's already gone to the church." Heather stared at the envelope. "Hoi Wing: For Your Eyes Only," she read aloud. "In Martha's hand. What's in that?"

"Oh, something she wants me to read . . ." He racked his brain for a better, more plausible response, knowing Heather would intuit if he lied. "Something for me to look at, but I did not read it. I am giving it back to her."

Heather looked at him strangely. "Why didn't you read it if Martha wanted you to? What's the note about?"

"It's . . . it's for the . . ." His mouth went dry, and he couldn't find any words.

"Does it have to do with the exam?" Heather's breath caught.

"No. Well . . . yes. Kind of. She gave it to me."

"Only to you? Martha gave you a note about the exam and didn't give it to me?"

"I didn't read it!" His face was burning, and he felt guilty even though there was no reason for it. "I didn't even open the envelope!"

Heather blinked sudden tears. "Oh, how horridly unfair! I thought we were studying together so we could both pass!"

"No, I didn't read the note!"

"You should have told me you had this!" Her face twisted as she fled the room.

"Heather!" Hoi Wing called out.

Adele entered the dining room as Heather brushed by. "What's wrong, dear? What's all this yelling about? You two need to be heading to the church."

Hoi Wing sat at his desk in the church basement. His exam paper—all six sheets of it—lay face down on the desk before him. Martha sat at the front of the room, along with Professor Marsden and Mr. Smythe, who was acting as an impartial invigilator.

The desk beside Hoi Wing was empty. Heather's test paper was there, face down as well, but Heather was not. Hoi Wing glanced at the wall clock—it was 6:58, two minutes to the beginning of the examination. He looked at Martha. There had been no time for them to talk when he arrived at the classroom. Nevertheless, the same question was written all over her face: Where was Heather?

Hoi Wing knew Heather had been upset, but he had assumed she had merely rushed from Martha's home and come directly to the church without him.

He raised his hand. "Please, professor, can I go find Heather?"

Professor Marsden studied his pocket watch, synchronizing it with the wall clock. "Harry, I'm sorry, but the examination is scheduled to start in less than one minute. I commend your loyalty and sense of fairness to your friend, but I have to take all circumstances into consideration. If you leave now, you will forfeit your chance to write the exam."

"But what of Heather—?"

Professor Marsden shook his head. "Heather has not said a word to any of us to explain her absence. I don't know why she is not here. Perhaps she did not value the opportunity that was offered to her. Perhaps she feared it would be too great a challenge."

"But I can't write the exam without her!" Hoi Wing said.

Professor Marsden looked at him. "Don't be foolish. You are here, and she is not. This is your chance to gain something you have worked very hard for. I have gone to great lengths to make this happen."

"But surely we can give the girl a few minutes of grace," said Martha.

"I'm truly sorry, but if a student cannot even manage to attend at the appointed hour for a test, then she cannot greatly value this opportunity. Her actions speak louder than words."

Professor Marsden looked at his watch and lifted his finger in the air. He brought it down with a flourish. "You may turn over your papers and begin. You have three hours to complete the examination."

The clock ticked on. As the minutes passed, Hoi Wing left his examination untouched and his pencil in its pre-cut groove at the edge of his desk. Martha motioned frantically at him to start, but he ignored her pantomime. He would not begin until Heather arrived.

Three hours later, Professor Marsden checked his pocket watch for the final time. The clock struck ten. "The examination is over. Please put your pencil down and place your papers face down on the right-hand corner of your desk."

The last direction was unnecessary. Hoi Wing's exam was still face down as it had been from the first moment he entered the room.

Professor Marsden looked troubled, but he collected the test papers. Was he disappointed that neither Hoi Wing nor Heather had attempted the test? The man slipped the blank papers into a large envelope.

"Oh, Hoi Wing!" Martha said in a stricken voice. "Why didn't you write the exam! Why didn't you even try?"

"Heather is not here," he whispered.

"But that was her choice, not yours. You need not have sacrificed your own chance because of her folly."

"I know why she is not here." Hoi Wing looked down at his hands. "She thinks I cheated."

Martha sucked in her breath. "How . . . how did she find out?"

"I told her you gave me a secret paper, but I did not even look at it. I did not even open the envelope."

Martha's mouth fell open. "Why didn't you—? Perhaps I should never have given you that envelope, but you should have written the exam. Especially if you didn't look at it. Let me speak with Stephan and make amends."

At the front of the room, Professor Marsden slid the examination papers into his briefcase. He snapped the latch shut with an audible click. The Master of the Hounds, who had sat quietly and almost dozing throughout the evening, looked curiously at Hoi Wing and Martha.

"Whatever happened to the young lass?" he asked.

23

"Heather has left us!" Adele handed a note to Hoi Wing.

"It's all my fault," said Martha. "We've already checked with the conductor at the train station. She left yesterday evening. She blames me for trying to help you with the examination."

It was the day after the exam. Hoi Wing stood at the laundry's front counter. Adele and Martha had come in that morning with a note they had found in Heather's bedroom. *I can't live here anymore. How could you have done this? I'm leaving to stay with my brother up north.*

"What can we do?" Hoi Wing asked. "Can we make her come back?"

"I'm afraid we can't make her do anything," said Adele. "She was always free to come and go as she pleased."

Martha looked as though she might cry. "I've made a mess of everything. Why did I even think of giving you that message?"

"What's done is done," said Adele. "Maybe we can all write to Heather and apologize. She left her brother's address. She's hurt now, and rightly so, but perhaps she'll come to her senses in a few days. There's still time if I can talk Stephan into rescheduling that exam."

Elder Uncle stepped through the curtain. "Farmboy, I know you think this laundry is your personal meeting room, but I've still got a business to run. Now finish up your chit-chat with these two and get back inside! There are three tubs of dirty shirts waiting for your attention."

Hoi Wing went back to his tubs. Not only was he despondent that Heather had left town, but he also wondered if he had just sacrificed the greatest opportunity of his young life. When he told the uncles what had happened at the examination room, Elder Uncle asserted that he was a fool for squandering his great chance. Even Second Uncle, who commiserated with Hoi Wing, felt he should have written the examination under the circumstances. After all, he had not even peeked at Martha's message.

For the rest of the day, the laundry was quiet, and few customers came to the front counter. There had been a noticeable drop-off in walk-in traffic, and Elder Uncle wondered aloud about the recent downturn in their fortunes.

"I don't know who to blame more—*Blah-dok*, with his incendiary comments in the newspapers, or Farmboy here, who can't keep out of department stores with his little *lofan* friend!"

The next day was Saturday, and the laundry was no busier than the day before. In the afternoon, Elder Uncle took advantage of the lack of customer traffic to send Hoi Wing out for groceries. "Try to keep out of trouble, Farmboy!"

With the heat of the August day, Hoi Wing's back was slick with sweat by the time he arrived at the city's outdoor market. Horses and wagons were clustered along the perimeter, with farmers setting out their produce on long wooden tables inside the square. Shoppers moved in and amongst the displays, lifting a bag of green peppers or string beans, or discreetly sampling a basket of strawberries.

As Hoi Wing wandered through the crowd, he stopped before a table of corn and green beans. Some in the crowd began to eye him suspiciously. He heard his name, whispered along with Heather's name.

Hoi Wing dropped the corn back onto the table and walked on. Stares followed in his wake, and children began to trace his path. *There he is*, he heard. *The Chinaman who rampaged through McGregor's!* His heart beat faster. Keeping his gaze down, he left the market, heading straight home.

He was almost running when he reached the laundry. Shutting the door behind him, he threw his weight against it. He peered into the street. No one had followed him. Could he have imagined it all?

Elder Uncle came to the counter. "Where are those groceries I sent you for?"

On Sunday, the laundry was closed, but none of the men could relax. Hoi Wing continued to berate himself for his missed opportunity and spent the morning writing a letter to Heather in which he implored her to return to St. Catharines. In the afternoon, the doorbell jangled. Hoi Wing came out of the backrooms and peered through the curtain into the vestibule.

"How you holdin' up, kid?"

"Rosie!" Hoi Wing stepped to the counter with alacrity, feeling the familiar frisson dance over his spine. Today, the woman was wearing another wide-brimmed hat, but this one was decorated with a golden ostrich feather. Her dress was the colour of cream and had a delicate floral décolletage. She held a parasol in one hand, and her cheeks were flushed with heat. As always, her eyes were darkened with kohl.

"I know you're closed today, but I brought you some work." Rosie held up a bag of wash.

Hoi Wing took the bag and spilled the contents onto the counter. She was perhaps the one customer who could rescue him from his mood.

"Listen, Harry." The woman leaned close. "My girls have told me something's up."

Hoi Wing breathed in her perfume, not comprehending her words.

"I mean something's goin' to happen tonight. Something bad. My girls say a few of their gentlemen callers have been boasting."

"What's going to happen?"

Rosie reached out and pressed Hoi Wing's hand. "I don't know 'xactly, but our Mr. Braddock has got folks all incensed about you and your little girlfriend. How you rampaged through McGregor's. Now the gossips say the girl's left town. You know what people think when a girl leaves home for no reason. They blame you."

When she left, Hoi Wing rubbed his hand where she had touched him. Then he turned his attention to the clothes she had brought in: old blouses, threadbare sheets, and worn pillowcases. None of the laced and frilly unmentionables he expected. Hoi Wing glanced at the packages of customers' clothes on the counter. Then he eyed the shelves of abandoned laundry. Rosie's warning rang in his ears. What did she suspect would happen that night?

∞

The rest of the afternoon passed quickly as Hoi Wing and the uncles prepared the laundry in response to Rosie's warning. By the early evening, they felt they had done everything possible, and Hoi Wing stood at the counter, watching the street. Outside, all seemed calm. There was little vehicular traffic, and most folks were home for dinner. Feeling like a prisoner himself, Hoi Wing decided to go out.

The day was still hot, and the street was warm underfoot. Without thinking, he wandered into the Golden Li, where another ball game was being played at the park. He wandered into the ravine behind Braddock's house and went to the Sanctuary.

Within the root cellar, he lit a candle. Nothing had been moved. The blanket was still folded neatly on the ground. He sat for a time, remembering the many occasions he and Heather had huddled in the little space, discussing the minutiae of their days or sharing the books they so enjoyed. This time, he tucked a message under the blanket: *Heather, please come home!*

When he climbed out, the sky had darkened. A breeze cooled the sweat of his forehead, and a red glow lit the horizon. He shut the lid over the Sanctuary and headed home. As he passed the ballpark, a game had just ended. The crowd mingled with players in pinstriped uniforms and others in blue and white. A few spectators brandished baseball bats and some carried placards. At a picnic table, servers handed out tankards of ale under a sign for Braddock's Breweries.

Hoi Wing saw a tall figure climb atop the stands. The man waved his hands over his head. Spectators began to cluster before him, elbowing to get near. At that moment, someone handed the man a cane. *It was Braddock!*

Hoi Wing felt a rush of blood. Braddock's hair was slicked back, and his beard seemed thicker than ever. The lines on his face were etched deeply. A torch was lifted, and a warm light reflected over his face. Men and women cheered. "Speech!" they cried. "Speech!"

Braddock lifted his hand as if blessing the throng. Then he began to talk. At first, Hoi Wing could not make out the words, but the rhythm of the oration was alternatively mellifluous and brusque, cajoling and exhorting.

"You all know why we're here tonight!" Braddock's voice carried like a shout across a lake. "You all know why you came!"

"Yes, we do!" someone called back.

Braddock pointed into the gathering. "Men, do you know your duty?"

"Yes!" The answer was louder this time.

"Why are we here tonight?" Braddock shouted.

"Because of the Chinamen!" someone in the crowd cried out on cue.

"That's right!" Braddock called back. "Who's polluted our city with their degenerate laundries?"

"The Chinamen!" the crowd answered.

"Who's polluted our city with sickness and disease?"

"The Chinamen!"

"Opium and depravity?"

"The Chinamen!" the crowd roared.

"Men!" shouted Braddock. "We have to clean up our city!"

"Clean up our city!" they shouted back.

"Who is with me?" cried Braddock.

"We are!"

"Come with me now!" Braddock descended the stands. The crowd surged forward as men threw their hats in the air. Others brandished their signs. They began to chant: "Clean up the city! Clean up the city!"

Hoi Wing felt a chill. With Braddock in the lead, the throng began to snake toward him, chanting as it advanced. Hoi Wing turned and fled.

Behind him, their voices grew louder. As the mob marched, it assimilated the curious and the eager. The cry rose: "Clean up the city! Clean up the city!"

When Hoi Wing reached the laundry, he slammed the door shut and shot the deadbolt. The street was still empty, but they would soon be there. He grabbed a broomstick and held it against his chest. What good would it do against ten, twenty, a hundred crazed men?

"What is happening?" Second Uncle came out of the kitchen.

"What's wrong?" Elder Uncle asked.

The laundrymen heard the mob before they saw it. Faint at first the shouting intensified as the crowd neared. Soon the cries were deafening. "Chinamen go home!" they chanted. "Chinamen go home!" Before Hoi Wing's eyes they filled the sidewalk. More than he could count: tens, dozens, perhaps hundreds of angry townspeople.

From the window, he scanned the dark, seething mass. Many were strangers—had they come with the visiting baseballers?—but others looked familiar. Some raised fists and placards; others shook torches and bats. Hoi Wing saw Braddock. "Chinamen go home!" the man shouted. "Chinamen go home!" roared the crowd.

Boys appeared at the edges of the assembly. One bent and picked up a stone. Another searched the ground. In an instant, many lifted rocks in their hands.

Just then, a woman rushed into the street. "Stop it! Stop it!" she shouted.

Hoi Wing gasped. It was Martha! Her hair, normally piled over her head, fell loose over her shoulders. Her face was pale, and her eyes were wide. She shoved through the horde and stood before the laundry window.

"Go home! All of you, go home!" Her voice was shrill and on the edge of panic.

The crowd paused. Those in the forefront hesitated, rocks in hand.

"Go home!" The timbre of Martha's voice became stronger and more sure. Her arms were outstretched and high. "Don't do this! Friends, go back to your homes!"

Uncertainty fell over the mob. Their rage seemed to lessen. Then someone pushed through the mass of people.

"Martha!" Braddock brandished his wolf's head cane. "Get out of the way. We need to clean up this city!"

Martha's response was steady. "Go home, John! The Chinese are not your enemy!"

A ripple of doubt coursed through the crowd. Hesitation and sober second thought caused some to pause, but Braddock's voice came again, fiercer than ever. "The Chinamen have to go! Step aside, Martha. Move out of the way."

"No! You'll have to go right through me."

Braddock grimaced. "Don't be a fool! You'll only make things worse." He lifted his hand to signal the charge.

At that moment, Elder Uncle rushed forward. "Come on! We're not going to hide behind that woman's skirt!" He threw open the door and stepped into the evening light. Second Uncle followed. "Stop!" Elder Uncle bellowed. "Stop now!"

Martha turned. "Go inside! Get inside!"

A roar rose up from the mob. "There's the Chinaman now!" A rock sailed out and ricocheted against the doorway over Elder Uncle's head. Martha screamed.

"Get him!" Braddock yelled. A barrage of stones flew through the air. The big window exploded into shards of glass. Martha screamed again as another woman ran to her side. It was Adele!

A man raced out to help the women. Even in the dim light, Hoi Wing recognized Stephan Marsden.

"Get them!" Braddock exhorted. Like water breaking a dam, the rioters surged forward. Rocks flew and placards were thrown.

Elder Uncle and Second Uncle ducked back inside. Hoi Wing slammed the door and dived over the counter. As the mob roared like a beast, another fusillade of rocks flew through the window into the vestibule. Stones thudded over the floor and against the walls. Bits of glass and pebbles sprayed Hoi Wing's head and hair.

"Get them! Get them!" Three men clambered through the window, oblivious to the shards of glass projecting from the sill. The laundrymen crawled into the drying room as others forced the door. "There they are!" someone shouted. "There they are!"

Hoi Wing regained his feet. He saw Elder Uncle knock a man down as the mob crashed through the curtain. Second Uncle threw a punch at a rioter swinging a club. Hoi Wing stumbled over the mangle and rose again, desperate to keep ahead. Behind him, chairs were hurled against the walls and racks of clothes were thrown to the floor. In the distance, he heard the wild barking of dogs.

The three laundrymen ran through the kitchen and out the back door. Outside, the moon had just appeared, but the twilight was grey and brown. Behind them, the mob ransacked the laundry. Hoi Wing felt tears running down his cheeks. Someday he would get even, but first they had to save themselves.

He and the uncles staggered through the backyard, ducking the rocks and raw vegetables thrown at them. Glancing behind, they slipped through the gate and into the alley. The men fled into the shadows, heading for the laneways that would lead them to the Foreign Quarter and Grandfather Foo's. As they ran, Hoi Wing heard the shrill note of a police whistle, blowing again and again. Too late, he thought. Much too late.

24

"It's a wreck," said Hoi Wing.

"The window is destroyed," added Grandfather Foo.

Second Uncle picked a shirt up off the ground. "What a mess!"

It was Monday morning. Hoi Wing, the uncles, and Grandfather Foo stood outside the Sam Kee Luk Chinese Hand Laundry. They had spent the night at the old man's laundry, waiting with knives and broomsticks, but there had been no further attacks.

Now Elder Uncle nudged a discarded placard with his foot. Clothes were strewn over the sidewalk. "At least they did not set fire to our premises."

They stepped through the broken door. Inside, the front vestibule was filled with shattered glass and rocks. The mangle was upended, and the big vats were rolled onto their sides. Chairs had been broken, and the dining table was overturned. In the kitchen, the cupboards were empty, and shards of dishware littered the floor.

Hoi Wing descended into the basement and sighed in relief. The rioters had not come downstairs. After receiving Rosie's warning, he and the uncles had hidden all their customers' laundry downstair, and replaced it with packages from the shelves of unclaimed wash. None of their customers' clothes had been despoiled. Further, they had safeguarded the laundry's cash box behind a stone in the foundation's corner, and it was untouched.

When Hoi Wing went back upstairs with the good news, Elder Uncle clasped hands with Second Uncle. "Your savings are safe!" said Grandfather Foo. "You can rebuild!"

Galvanized, Elder Uncle righted one of the big vats. "Those bastards must pay for these damages! But first, let's have some tea and refreshment. Then we can account for what has been lost, what needs repair, and what must be replaced. We can formulate a plan of action and reconstruction. I want to be back to full operation within a few days. Let's not waste a single minute!"

For the rest of the day, the men rolled up their sleeves and worked. Hoi Wing was tasked with closing up the front window with lumber from the woodpile. A glazier would be hired to replace the glass later. As Hoi Wing worked, he wondered how Martha and Adele had fared. Had they been injured in the riot? He remembered Professor Marsden racing before the crowd, his hands outstretched and his hair wild and uncombed. Hoi Wing would have to go see them as soon as he found some time.

The cleanup and repairs continued into the next day. Elder Uncle straightened the rollers on the wringer, and Second Uncle fixed the lock on the front door. Grandfather Foo swept and mopped. When Hoi Wing hammered the last plank into the windowsill, the laundry grew dark and shaded, but at least it was secure from wind and weather.

The big policeman arrived around noontime and engaged Elder Uncle in a long, tedious conversation about the events that had occurred two nights earlier.

"Who did you see during the riot?" the policeman asked over and over.

"*Blah-dok! Blah-dok!*" answered Elder Uncle.

"Apart from Mr. Braddock, was there anyone else?"

"Yes, many, but I not knowing their names!" Elder Uncle gesticulated wildly.

Later in the afternoon, as Hoi Wing was mending a set of crushed baskets, Adele, Martha, and Professor Marsden arrived. Martha carried a covered dish in which she had prepared another Chinese lunch of rice and chicken.

Hoi Wing hugged both women, overjoyed to see they had not been injured, although Marsden had a bandage wrapped over his forehead. The uncles thanked them for the food and their help during the riot.

"Well, Harry," said Professor Marsden, studying the boarded-up window. "It was bedlam here a few nights ago, but it looks as if you're getting this place back into shape."

"Thank you." Hoi Wing shook the man's hand. "We will open again tomorrow."

Professor Marsden smiled. "You know what they say—it's hard to keep a good man down."

Hoi Wing noticed again how attentive Professor Marsden was to Adele. When the three of them left the laundry, Adele and the professor walked side by side, their hands almost touching.

The laundrymen worked steadily until the late afternoon, when Elder Uncle called a break. They sat down at the just-repaired dinner table to enjoy of the food Martha had brought them. As Hoi Wing lifted a drumstick to his lips, a man began shouting outside. There was a sudden hue of answering cries. A drum pounded, and a woman screamed. As the din of voices rose, there was a roar of explosions like gunfire.

The four laundrymen looked at each other uneasily. Grandfather peered through the boards covering the window. "The street is filling with people!"

"They're coming to attack us again!" Hoi Wing gasped.

"Not this time!" Elder Uncle raced into the kitchen. In a moment, he was back with a knife and two meat cleavers. He handed one to Second Uncle and the other to Grandfather Foo. "We'll not let the *dead-bastard* demons destroy our business again!"

Elder Uncle flung the front door open, with Second Uncle and Grandfather on his heels. It seemed as if the entire population of St. Catharines was outside. Men shouted and threw their hats in the air. Boys lit firecrackers.

Hoi Wing stared as an automobile drove by, blaring its horn. Had everyone gone mad? In the crowd, he thought he recognized some of the rioters from two nights ago, but today's ruckus seemed celebratory rather than hostile. Across the street, a man kissed a woman before the gates of the livery stable. People were singing "God Save the King."

"What's happened?" Hoi Wing asked a man who waved a Union Jack.

"Don't you know?" he answered. "The King has declared war on Germany! We are at war! Finally, we are at war!"

The euphoria was unabated the next day. A palpable sense of excitement hung in the air, and spontaneous dance parties broke out on the street. "We are going to war!" In no time, two enlistment offices opened—one on Ontario Street in the west end and the other on St. Paul. Within minutes, both had lineups of men and boys that stretched the length of a downtown block. Everyone agreed the Hun had grown too big for his britches. They would put the Kaiser back in his place. Fritz would be taught a lesson.

In the meantime, Elder Uncle reopened the laundry. A few regulars began to drop by, peeking through the boards that had replaced the glass window. How had the laundry fared? Had anyone been injured in the unfortunate "event" that occurred a few days before? Some were genuinely shocked by the actions of their compatriots, although Hoi Wing couldn't help but wonder where they had been when the laundrymen made their stand against a mob of five hundred.

Others, such as Thick-Moustache Man, were simply ecstatic to learn their clothes had not been destroyed. His shirts were awaiting pickup on a plank Elder Uncle set up beside the cracked counter.

Word soon got around that customers of the Sam Kee Luk Chinese Hand Laundry could retrieve their wash. In the afternoon, Rosie visited to pick up her clothes (bringing a lift to Hoi Wing's spirits), and later the Master of the Hounds brought in a bag of laundry he needed as a rush job.

"Our first customer after that insanity!" Elder Uncle spilled the man's garments onto the counter after he had departed. "This is a good omen."

For most, the riot was soon forgotten. Were the townsfolk shamed by the actions of their neighbours, or had the war caused a sudden, collective amnesia? In the aftermath, no mention was made in regard to reparations for the Chinese businessmen.

When the police conducted their investigation, no one could identify the rioters with certainty. An intrepid few mentioned Braddock's speech, but it was unclear what had been said or how it might have been taken out of context by a few unruly and hard-drinking visitors. Little more was said about Braddock's involvement in the riot.

Hoi Wing leaned his elbows on the makeshift counter. The same people who had attacked their home were going about their business as though nothing had happened. In fact, what had happened? The window had been shattered and the mangle badly damaged. The counter was splintered, but the vats, tubs, and water heaters were intact. The brushes, washboards, and braziers were still operable. Even Elder Uncle's spirit seemed as indefatigable as ever.

Outside, the war celebrations continued. Every so often, a boy would light a firecracker, and the sudden crack like gunfire never failed to make Hoi Wing's heart skip a beat. He felt empty. He had not passed the examination. He would not go to school in September. He would be stuck in Elder Uncle's laundry for eternity.

The doorbell jangled. Adele, Martha, and Heather stepped through the door.

"Heather!" Hoi Wing cried. "It's you! You're back!" He rushed forward and threw his arms around her. "But why did you go? What happened?"

"I went to see my brother at the farm. After Martha gave you that note, I couldn't stay here. I couldn't write that exam."

"I've apologized to Heather for my actions," said Martha. "She has chosen to forgive me."

"Harry," said Adele. "That's not all the good news. Professor Marsden has agreed to allow you both to sit the test again. He says it's the least he can do, after what happened to the laundry. You'll write it in two days!"

At that moment, Elder Uncle came in from the backrooms, and Martha greeted him with a few words in Chinese. Hoi Wing and Heather took advantage of the excitement to slip into the backyard for a few precious moments alone.

"I did not read Martha's note," Hoi Wing repeated when they stood outside. It was important that she know he had not cheated.

Heather nodded. "I believe you. I couldn't stay at Aemon's farm. He told me to come back here. He said I had an opportunity that was too good to miss."

Hoi Wing didn't know what else to say. Things felt awkward between them, and he longed for their easy rapport of the past. Would their friendship find its way back to where it had been? Something told him that relationships never went backwards. Everything in life moved forward, transforming into the new, the untested, and the unforeseen.

He looked into her eyes, wanting very much to kiss her again. The way he had kissed her on Adele's front porch.

"Farmboy!" Elder Uncle poked his head through the doorway. "Get in here! I need you at the counter."

Hoi Wing groaned, but Heather only laughed. "In a minute!" he shouted. As the two teens headed inside, he saw the naked stalks of Elder Uncle's peonies. The blossoms had withered weeks before. Hoi Wing reached into his back pocket and drew out a neatly folded square of cotton. It was the handkerchief on which he had spent so many hours embroidering a bright-red peony. "Here," he said to Heather. "This is for you."

The next day, Hoi Wing scrubbed shirts on a washboard. Business was still slow, but picking up. The excitement of the past few days had faded, and his anxiety about Professor Marsden's examination returned. How would he do tomorrow? He worried about his father's legacy. Would he pass, or would he repeat Ying the Scholar's great failure?

In the afternoon, Second Uncle returned from the post office. Today, there was a thick envelope for Hoi Wing, and he instantly recognized his father's calligraphy. The men took a break to digest their letters from home, and Hoi Wing went into the basement to read Ying the Scholar's words.

To my son, Hoi Wing the Scholar:

How to tell you the truth? I have held the secret so long that, even today, my pen shakes and ink smears this page. Now I will answer your questions about what really happened when I wrote the Imperial Examinations.

I arrived at the provincial capital after five days' travel by bullock cart, weak-kneed and nauseated, stumbling past the stinking canals of that coastal city. Tall ships moored at the harbour, and lofan sailors frolicked in the brothels along the wharves. As I wandered the streets, a covered palanquin of mahogany appeared, borne aloft by four slaves.

"Out of the way, Countryboy!" A bearded swordsman in black robes thrust me to the ground. As I sprawled in the dirt, the palanquin passed by, but a beautiful maid peered out through the silken curtains.

"You were wise to say nothing, Stranger." A man reached out his hand to help me. "That was the daughter of the concubine of the Warlord. His guardsmen have beheaded men for merely gazing upon the girl's face." I thanked the man for his wisdom and continued my search for lodgings. Later I learned my purse was gone.

The next morning, I attended at the Hall of Imperial Examinations. Guardsmen handed me a chamber pot, a pitcher of water, and a small chit, stamped with the Emperor's insignia. The invigilators locked me within a tiny chamber. The examination commenced.

For the next three days and two nights, I read, pondered, analyzed, composed, and wrote. In that windowless chamber, time lost all meaning. My mind grappled with question after question, and my hand grew weary and cramped.

Finally, the examination ended. I left the compound. My plan had been to spend a month at the capital, waiting for the examination results, but with no money, I wandered the streets in a daze.

I came upon a handbill. A wealthy household sought a private tutor. The wages were low but sufficient for room and board on the wharf.

The next day, I went to the House. A servant ushered me into a hall of white marble. At the far wall was an immense five-panelled screen of painted silk.

Adjacent to the screen was a long table. On it were sheets of paper, ink, and brushes. A guardsman in black robes approached. "What is your name, Scholar?"

I gasped inwardly. Although he had no memory of me, it was the swords-man who had thrown me to the ground days before. "I am Ying."

The guardsman led me to the table. He motioned at a red line across the floor. "Never may you pass this line, if you wish to keep your head." His hand reached toward the longsword at his side.

I nodded. "But where is my pupil?"

"Here I am, Young Scholar," came a voice from behind the screens.

I stared at the wall of painted silk. Silhouetted behind was the delicate form of a young woman. My task was to teach her to read and write, but never could my foot cross the red line. Nor was I permitted to see more than her shadow.

So began my time in the House of the wily Warlord. Each day, I attended the marbled chamber, always in the company of the bodyguard. As the days passed, I was struck by the acuity of the young woman's mind. Words and con-cepts came easily to her. Poetry and odes followed. Then whispered laughter and chuckles. One day, the configuration of the silk panels was shifted slightly, and sure enough, it was the beautiful girl I had seen in the palanquin!

Holding a finger to her lips, she reached out her hand and caressed my own. I froze. Not twenty paces behind me was the warrior, leaning against the door. His eyelids were shut and his breathing slow. He was asleep!

I began to count the hours to each day's lesson. Often we passed our time in whispered amusement. A day came when she asked me where I lodged in the capital.

Late that night, there came a knock at my door. When I opened it, a small man stood in my doorway. "Scholar Ying!" he spoke. Suddenly, I laughed in recognition, and the Warlord's daughter leapt into my arms. She had come in disguise!

Each night thereafter, she came. All her life, she had sported disguises to escape her father's compound. Fearless and brave, who better than a warlord's daughter to navigate the cutthroat alleys along the wharves?

Finally, the morning came when I returned to the Examination Hall for my results. My heart almost burst through my chest. I had passed the examination! I collected my Golden Diploma and departed.

But that afternoon, the servant at the Warlord's house spat at my feet and told me the lessons had been discontinued. I turned away in confusion.

That night, I lay in bed, fingering my pens and inkstones. What should I do? How could I communicate with the Warlord's daughter? There came a knock at my door. I yanked it open, and the young woman fell into my arms.

"You must escape! My father's guardsmen hunt you even now!"

"But how can I leave you? Look, I have won my diploma! Come with me and we will seek our fortunes together."

At that moment, the black-robed guardsman burst through the door, his sword drawn. For long, cruel minutes, he toyed with me, thrusting, pivoting, and riposting, as I gripped my best pen like a dagger.

Finally, he lunged forward, and I fell backwards over a chair. He raised his blade for the coup de grâce.

In that instant, the Warlord's daughter leapt upon his back. The warrior toppled over me. My arm swung forward, and I plunged my pen into his left eye.

The bodyguard shook. Blood spurted from his punctured eye socket. Then he sagged to the floor. He was dead! My pen had sunk into his brain.

"Your father will hunt me to the ends of the Middle Kingdom," I said. *"You must return to the compound and forget me."*

The Warlord's daughter weighed the possibilities. "For years, I have sought to escape my father. Perhaps we may yet transform calamity into opportunity."

"But they will find us wherever we go."

"Look," she said. *"You and the swordsman are of a size! What if you were to exchange garments?"*

Slowly, I understood. "I will wear his clothes. We will flee on his horse. Witnesses will attest that they saw the guardsman spirit you away after killing me." But then I paused. *"What of the body?" I asked. "They will recognize his face."*

A mixture of grit and determination came to her eyes. She lifted the broadsword. "Will you do it, or shall I?"

Thirty minutes later, I stole outside beneath the moon, gripping a sack that held a grisly trophy. I tossed the bag into the canals. The fish and crabs would accomplish all else we desired.

In the morning, I drew on the swordsman's clothes. Then I clothed the headless man in my scholar's robes. I spilled my inks and papers to the floor.

I studied the tiny chamber. "Your father is a renowned trickster. Is there anything else we can do to fortify our subterfuge?"

The Warlord's daughter looked at me. "There is one more ruse we may make, my love. But I do not ask it of you. You must decide yourself."

For an instant, I didn't understand. Then I saw her wisdom. Slowly, I unfurled the Golden Diploma, bearing my name. I tucked it within the dead man's shirt. No scholar in the Middle Kingdom would abandon such a document.

As the sun rose, we mounted the guardsman's horse and rode through the streets for all to see. All day we rode, until we had left the provincial capital far behind. Then we freed the horse. I divested myself of the guardsman's robes. The Warlord's daughter assumed her young man's guise. Patrols passed, but never did they stop. They sought a mounted warrior and a woman.

In this manner, we walked for weeks. Sometimes we shared a farmer's wagon with chickens or ducks. There was little to eat, but each night, we huddled in the forests, warm in the heat of our embrace. So it was that I returned to Drink the Waters Deeply with your mother.

Now you know why I returned without my diploma. You need no longer wonder if I cheated or failed at the exam. Perhaps you ask yourself if I regret the sacrifice I made? No. Never. I would do it over and over, exactly the same way.

Now go, my son, and write your own tale.

Your father,
Ying the Scholar

On Friday evening, Hoi Wing was at his desk in the church basement. As always, the air was dank and a little chilly. On the desktop before him was his examination paper—all six sheets—face down. He had his sharpened pencils—Martha had suggested he bring five—a soft eraser, and Second Uncle's best pen and ink at hand.

At the front of the room, Professor Marsden commanded the big desk. Seated beside him was Martha, and beside her, folded newspaper on his lap, was the Master of the Hounds, once more acting as chief invigilator. Everything was as it had been one week earlier, except tonight Heather was also at her desk, a scant five feet away.

"Students." Professor Marsden clapped his hands. "You have three hours to complete this exam. The time is 6:59. You may begin the exam in five, four, three, two, one—now! Turn over your examinations and begin the test."

Out of the corner of Hoi Wing's eye, he saw Heather flip over her exam and lift her pencil. She began to write furiously and without pause.

Hoi Wing breathed deeply. He imagined the oxygen invigorating his body for the great task at hand. The long months of preparation—all he had done in Adele and Martha's lessons, in the laundry's basement, and even back home in his father's study—were over. Everything that had happened since his arrival in the New World boiled down to this moment.

He shut his eyes and the room seemed less stifling. His desk and chair were a good fit. What did he have to fear? He was the son of Ying the Scholar, was he not? And now he knew the truth of what really happened to his father. Hoi Wing imagined himself back in Drink the Waters Deeply, reviewing the day's lessons with the man. In the background, he could almost hear his mother's humming.

The basement classroom thrummed with possibility. Hoi Wing opened his eyes. Beneath his fingertips, the exam paper was crisp and luminescent. He rubbed his hands briskly and lifted his pencil. He touched its tip to his tongue. Then he turned over his examination paper.

25

From a distance, Hoi Wing could hear the strains of pipes and the beating of drums. A ripple of anticipation coursed through the crowd. "The parade is coming, Mama!" a little boy breathed. "They're coming!"

It was two weeks after Hoi Wing and Heather had written Professor Marsden's exam. The late August sun was hot, and the two teens stood in a crowd of spectators, six and seven deep, that lined St. Paul Street along the length of the commercial core. Streamers, red-and-blue banners, and Union Jacks adorned the storefronts behind them.

Hoi Wing gave Heather's hand a quick squeeze as the first musicians rounded into view. The crowd gave a sudden rousing cheer. "I see the bagpipers!" Heather's voice was high-pitched with excitement. She craned her neck to see over the shoulders of those in front.

Hoi Wing gripped her palm. It was rare that he got the chance to hold her hand in public, but in the dense mass of spectators, no one would notice. As the keening notes of the bagpipes grew louder, many in the crowd began to shout and wave flags. Fathers lifted sons onto their shoulders. One man climbed a lamppost for a better view.

"I see them, Mama!" the boy cried out.

"God save the King!" shouted a man.

Now Hoi Wing could see the cavalry riding in tight formation behind the rows of drummers. As they neared, he marked the rhythmic *clip-clop* and sudden sparking of the horses' hooves over the rough cobblestones. He studied the mounted men, resplendent in their dress uniforms, polished epaulettes, and white gloves.

His gaze fell on a tall, bearded rider at the very rear of the column, riding in a simple khaki uniform with little decoration or piping. "Look!" Hoi Wing pointed.

"I see our Mr. Braddock," said Heather, pursing her lips.

So the rumours were true, Hoi Wing thought. Jonathan Braddock had enlisted in the cavalry. The man had declared he would rather kill Germans than be mayor, although some in town suggested his actions at the riot had led him to withdraw his name from the race. In any case, there had not been a moment to lose. Everyone knew the war would likely be over by Christmas.

"He'll soon be too busy in Europe to trouble us here," Heather mused.

Hoi Wing nodded grimly. Grandfather had warned that the coming Armageddon would be far more murderous than the wars of the past. And Elder Uncle said anyone who enlisted was a fool or a madman.

As the cavalry paraded by, the first foot soldiers marched into view. Here the cheering rose to a crescendo as most of the recruits from St. Catharines—who were the sons, brothers, fathers, and uncles of the spectators on the sidelines—had enrolled as simple infantrymen. Hoi Wing admired the long ranks of men in their regimental colours, arms and legs swinging synchronously, rifles ready at the shoulder. How much had changed! Again, he could not help but compare this sight with his memory of the amateur soldiers and their comical antics of the previous fall.

Heather squeezed his hand tightly. "Look in that row behind the flag-bearers!"

Now it was Hoi Wing's turn to be surprised. At the far side of the street was another familiar face. Marching in unison with the other soldiers was Ratface.

"You won't have to worry about him anymore," said Heather. "He'll be fighting for his life in Europe very soon."

Hoi Wing watched with mixed feelings as the young recruit strode past. The battle in the laneway seemed to have exorcised much of the hatred he had borne over the past months. Punching Ratface and being punched had been a catharsis of sorts, although he remembered how the boy had levelled his rifle at him in the woods. Nevertheless, Hoi Wing found it difficult to wish Ratface ill fortune overseas.

When Ratface's battalion vanished around a corner, Hoi Wing felt he had had enough of the parade. Heather shared his feelings. The two of them began to make their way through the crowd. At the edge of the gathering, they almost stumbled into Adele and Professor Marsden. The man's bandage had been removed, and only a faint bruise lingered on his forehead.

"We were hoping we might find you here!" Adele nudged Professor Marsden forward. "Stephan has news for both of you."

Professor Marsden cleared his throat. "I've had the opportunity to grade your examinations, and I must confess, you both surprised me greatly. Not that I am disappointed, of course. That is, I'm happily surprised."

Adele gripped his arm. "What does all your science say to you now?"

Professor Marsden laid his hand over Adele's. "I know what all the literature says, and as a scientist I recognize that science is never perfect. Your examinations represent only two points of data, but a hypothesis can always be corrected or amended or updated."

"What are you saying, professor?" asked Hoi Wing.

"I'm saying that I owe you two an apology. That at the very least, you have injected serious doubts into my mind as to the validity of the science of intelligence at this time. You've made me wonder if there might be errors in the experiments, or problems with sampling, or biases on the part of the experimenters themselves. What's needed, of course, is more testing of Asiatic students and girls. If I could just expand the sample size and find a good control group, I might even consider—"

"Stephan, will you just tell them their results?"

"Oh, of course! You both passed with flying colours. You've both qualified to enter the eighth grade next month."

Hoi Wing leapt into the air, and Heather screamed with joy. It was almost too good to be true. When he and Heather calmed down, Adele invited them for ice cream, but the teens declined the invitation. The day was already perfect.

26

The school bell rang. The clock struck 3:15. It was Friday afternoon. Hoi Wing leaned back in his chair. The boy at the desk beside him began to shove his books into his school bag. Hoi Wing's grade eight teacher, Miss Wright, was an Englishwoman who had recently migrated to the "colonies." She spoke with a crisp, nasal accent and punctuated everything she said with a thrust of the yardstick that was always in her hand.

"Students, have I dismissed you?" Miss Wright thumped the slate board with her yardstick. Two boys who had already risen from their seats froze. The rest of the class paused all movement. "Your homework assignments must be on my desk"—tapping her desktop—"first thing Monday morning. Late assignments"—waving her yardstick ominously—"will not be accepted!"

Hoi Wing groaned inside. He had survived his first week in grade eight, but just barely. Every morning, he had come to school, primed to listen, learn, and, above all, pay attention. After five days, his ear was finally growing accustomed to Miss Wright's accent, although many of the idioms she used were unfamiliar. Only once had he made the mistake of asking her to repeat herself.

"Class is dismissed!" Miss Wright waved her yardstick. A tentative cheer rose from a few of her charges, and several intrepid boys rushed for the doorway.

Hoi Wing slid his notebooks into his satchel and glanced across the room. Heather caught his gaze and smiled back. They had been ecstatic to be assigned to the same classroom, and Hoi Wing knew he would not have made it through his first week without her.

"Harry," Miss Wright called out as he was at the door. "Remember what I said. People judge us by how we speak. Elocution is everything."

"Yes, ma'am."

In the hallway outside, Heather touched Hoi Wing's elbow. "What did I tell you? Miss Wright does like you."

"No, she hates me," he answered. "But she likes you."

"Nonsense. She wouldn't be encouraging you about your pronunciation if she didn't care. I think she's just being fair. I like everything about her. Her posture when she stands. How she brandishes the yardstick. Even her penmanship is superb."

Heather was in bliss; grade eight was all she had expected. But Hoi Wing just rubbed the amulet at his neck. Everything Miss Wright had taught during the first week was a blur. The woman had warned of the pitfalls of falling behind, unannounced quizzes, and a comprehensive unit test each month. How was Hoi Wing to keep up? He still had to perform all his duties at the laundry.

He and Heather passed the principal's office, where portraits of bearded *lofan* with colourless eyes hung on the wall. They crossed the corridor and exited through a side door. Outside, the afternoon sun was bright, but the breeze was cool and foreshadowed the autumn soon to

come. Hoi Wing had a sudden premonition of finger-numbing tempera-
tures and long, sunless months of snow and ice. A whole year had gone
by. Had anything changed? Was everything just the same?

The schoolyard was empty except for a cluster of students near a large
oak tree. Something was not right. A group of upper-grade schoolboys
were tossing a smaller lad's hat back and forth. The little boy wept and
chased but could not regain possession of his cap. His school books, pencils, and satchel were strewn over the grass.

"Chase your hat, Hans!" One of the bigger youths tossed it thirty feet
into the air. "Get your school books, Fritzie!" shouted another. A third
boy sent the school bag flip-flopping over the ground with a solid kick.
"Go back to Germany, you lousy little Hun!"

By the time Hoi Wing and Heather reached the younger boy's side,
the bullies had thrown his hat into a tree and were sauntering through
the schoolyard gate. Hoi Wing recognized one of the tormentors: it was
Ratface's younger brother.

Heather helped the blubbering child to his feet. Hoi Wing heaved
himself onto a branch and retrieved the hat. He handed it to the boy,
whose face was smeared with tears and dirt. His skin was very fair, and
his arms and legs seemed no thicker than twigs.

"You all right?" asked Hoi Wing.

Still snivelling, the boy nodded.

"Those nasty bullies!" Heather glared at their backs. "They should
know better!"

Hoi Wing picked up the boy's satchel and brought it back to him.
The handle had been partially torn away and the straps ripped apart. At
the sight of the damage, the little boy wailed and scrunched up his face
once again.

"There, there," said Heather.

Hoi Wing watched the gang walk away, still laughing amongst themselves. They were very much amused. But now he realized he had been wrong. Not everything was the same.

Heather and Hoi Wing parted ways with the lad after he had calmed down. They watched him depart, whimpering and clutching his torn satchel to his chest.

As the two teens began walking home, clouds gathered in the sky, and the wind picked up. There was a distant rumble of thunder. Heather looked upward. "It's going to storm."

For a time, neither said a word. Hoi Wing wanted to talk about the incident they had just witnessed, but the bullying and humiliation were too familiar. Heather sensed his mood and kept quiet. Comfortable in their silence, they came to the park where Braddock had incited the riot. Hoi Wing scanned the diamond. How quiet it seemed now. Half a block later, they neared the intersection where Heather would head off toward Martha's home.

They stopped at the corner. Parting was always difficult. Hoi Wing never knew what to say; he wanted to hug or kiss her, but he had not so much as touched Heather's hand since the day of the parade. As she said goodbye, he reached out and caught her fingers in a clumsy squeeze. Heather blushed. "See you soon," he said as nonchalantly as possible.

Hoi Wing watched her go, feeling envious of her situation. Adele and Martha had decided to hire Heather as a maid, but in fact her duties on any given day amounted to little more than an hour's work. The rest of the time, she was free to come and go as she pleased.

Adele had asked her once more if she might be interested in joining the Girl Guides. The organization appeared to have rethought its entrance requirements, but Heather had not yet decided whether she wanted to join.

On the street, Hoi Wing felt the first raindrops strike his face. Dense clouds scudded overhead, and he turned up his collar. The sudden turn in the weather seemed a fitting end to his first five days of school.

"Speak properly," Miss Wright had repeated a half-dozen times during the week. "We must rid you of that Asiatic accent." She had singled him out for extra lessons in diction, elocution, and public speaking, requiring him to read aloud at the front of the class.

In his satchel were the extra grammar and reading she had assigned him. They were new texts, with crisp pages and unbroken spines. The chapters were dense and without illustration. He had a supplemental homework assignment for next week. And further homework if he wished to succeed. And another assignment if he dared to excel.

When would he find time for all that? Second Uncle had told him he would undo his father's perceived failure with his own academic success, but Elder Uncle insisted that Hoi Wing complete his daily laundry duties before beginning his homework. It was inevitable: he would be sacrificing many of his free Sundays from now on. He had written to his father and Eldest Great Auntie, telling them he had achieved his dream of entering school, but now he realized that staying in school would be far more difficult.

On St. Paul Street, Hoi Wing heard another rumble of thunder, and a gust of wind chased a sheet of newsprint across the sidewalk. The sky had darkened two shades, but Hoi Wing maintained his slow pace. Why rush home when there was nothing to greet him but unwashed sheets and cantankerous Elder Uncle?

At a corner, Hoi Wing let an automobile motor by. Soon he caught a whiff of wet horse from the livery stables. He passed the hackman's quarters and the farrier's. Halfway down the street was the laundry. The big window had not yet been replaced, but Second Uncle had hung a hurricane lantern over the front door, and it shone like a beacon, flickering as the afternoon grew ever darker.

Suddenly, lightning flashed overhead, followed by a deafening clap of thunder. The sky burst open, and a deluge spilled down. Hoi Wing broke into a dash and sprinted the last fifty paces to the laundry.

The doorbell jangled as he flung open the door. "Grandfather!" he called to the old man in the front room.

"Welcome home, Young Scholar!" Grandfather answered. "You have arrived just in time for the celebration! I brought sweet breads and fresh oranges."

Second Uncle emerged from the kitchen. In his right hand was a familiar bottle of golden liquor. Elder Uncle was already seated at the big table with four shot glasses. "Farmboy, put away those books and help us cement our new partnership!"

"Partnership?" Hoi Wing wiped the rain from his face. His clothes had been drenched in the downpour.

Second Uncle poured Scotch. "I wanted to tell you earlier, but you've been so busy. Next month, I will be sojourning back to China to spend a year with my wife and children. It's been almost five years since I last saw them."

Hoi Wing swallowed. "You're going back to China?"

Grandfather grinned. "In the meantime, I'm going to close my laundry. One-Arm and I will join forces here."

"He'll bunk up in the attic with me," Elder Uncle said. "With you in school, and the laundry still in disrepair, I figured we could use another hand. Between the two of us, we have enough clientele to propel us through this lean period. Let's drink to the profits we'll be making!"

Hoi Wing blinked the rain from his eyes. "Just let me change out of these wet clothes first. I'll be right up."

"Don't be overlong." Elder Uncle quaffed his drink. "There's only so much whisky."

Hoi Wing went downstairs. In the basement, he checked his satchel to ensure that his texts were dry. He placed his notebooks on the workbench, where his Chinese-English–English-Chinese dictionary awaited. Then he removed his shirt and towelled his body. The faint laughter of the men filtered through the floorboards overhead.

Hoi Wing would miss Second Uncle dearly, but he couldn't begrudge the man a chance to see his family again. And he would be away for only a year. In the interim, Grandfather Foo would join their little enterprise. His presence would surely mitigate the effect of Elder Uncle's dour personality in the laundry.

Rain drummed against the small window, and there was another flash of lightning. An eardrum-splitting clap of thunder followed. Hoi Wing heard the men laughing again, and then a series of notes from Second Uncle's *er-hu*. Elder Uncle began to sing. Astonishingly, it was another melody he remembered his beloved mother singing years before.

Buttoning on a clean shirt, Hoi Wing hurried to join the party. Fresh oranges, cake, and Scotch whisky beckoned. He would play Second Uncle's *er-hu*. Chess, cards, mah-jong, and games of chance would follow. Perhaps a story hitherto unheard. And songs.

Hoi Wing raced up the stairs.

ACKNOWLEDGEMENTS

Over the years, many people helped me during the course of this journey and I am glad to have the opportunity now to thank them for their kindness, encouragement, and wisdom.

In no particular order, thank you to Katherine Govier, Catherine Bush, William Kowalski, Kenda Gee, the late Steven Heighten, Daphne Marlatt, Shyam Selvadurai, Larissa Lai, Nino Ricci, Cordelia Strube, the late Wayson Choy, and Judy Fong Bates.

I am also grateful to Daniel Side, Kim Murray, Scott Mathison, Randal Heide, Rob Brunet, Brian Jantz, Danny Dowhal, Rob Crabtree, James Papoutsis, and Rekha Lakra, who all read early drafts of this novel and gave me their comments and critique.

Thanks to my editor, Janice Zawerbny, who was invested in this book at an early stage, and the entire team at HarperCollins, including Canaan Chu and John Sweet.

Thanks to Marilyn Biderman, who helped me through the negotiations.

Thanks to the Banff Centre and Diaspora Dialogues.

I'm also very grateful to the many friends and family members who sat with me and shared their life experiences. Many thanks to the late James Wing, David Wong, Bill Wong, Jean Ann Wong, Warren Wong, Claire Wong, Roy Lee, and my dad, the late Donald Lee, as well as my mom, Mary Wong.

And of course, thanks to Jinah and Erica, who believed in me from the very beginning.